THE PEOPLE NEXT DOOR

CHRISTOPHER RANSOM

sphere

SPHERE

First published in Great Britain in 2011 by Sphere

A CIP catalogue record for this book
is available from the British Library.

ISBN 978-0-7515-4380-3

Typeset in Caslon by M Rules
Printed and bound in Great Britain by
Clays Ltd, St Ives plc

Sphere
An imprint of
Little, Brown Book Group
100 Victoria Embankment
London EC4Y 0DY

An Hachette UK Company
www.hachette.co.uk

www.littlebrown.co.uk

For my big brother Mike
who protected me from the monsters
and fixed up my dirt bike

It is evidently consoling to reflect that
the people next door are headed for hell.

ALEISTER CROWLEY

pop. 786*

Later they called it running away from home, but Keelie Kennerly just plain walked out and no one tried to stop her. She thought the population sign on Walnick's fringe could use an asterisk, because by tomorrow the number would be wrong by at least one. Actually it had been wrong for a while now. People, even whole families, kept leaving the 'Nick. Usually they packed up and left without saying much, and sometimes, especially when it came to the kids Keelie's age, they just up and disappeared. Parents, teachers, the police – no one knew how or where they went, though maybe they understood the impetus.

Keelie adjusted her backpack and walked faster. Inside were socks and underwear, a couple of shirts and one pair of jeans, plus her totems: her brother's pocket knife, her journal, eyeliner, iPod, and the last photo of her dad. She also had her mom's ATM card, and that was another kind of totem right there.

It was plenty warm out, which was good because she was still wearing shorts and just her light cotton military coat over her favorite T-shirt. Favorite because it was

1

bright red and featured a nurse who looked like a total needle-wielding psycho, with that wavy black hair and the white surgical mask in the form of letters that spelled Sonic Youth. And because it was one size too small and Blake Garton said it made her guns look pretty much awesome. No one in the 'Nick knew who or what a Sonic Youth was, not even Heidi Eggers, who thought she was all worldly because she went to see Kid Rock at the fairgrounds in Des Moines last summer. And that was all the proof a girl needed, when you thought about it. Keelie Kennerly was too big for the 'Nick, kind of like how her guns were too big for her Sonic Youth shirt.

All the stores on Antique City Drive were dark and hollow, filled with old things for old people, and the sidewalks were empty, because it was almost midnight and the whole town went to bed at six. The nearest city was Omaha, and in Keelie's estimation that wasn't a real city at all.

She walked under the town's only stoplight, the yellow throbbing dimly like the power supply was running low. Not a single car passed her, and in less than two minutes there were no more lights, only deep fields of dark country.

Keelie thought whoever decided to name a convenience store chain Kum N Go had to be a perv. He had to have known changing the C to a K didn't fool anybody, not with that U in the middle. They even sold Kum N Go shirts so you could take one back to whatever cooler place you lived and have a real laugh. The Walnick Kum

N Go was one of the nicer ones: clean, with the video section and a whole grocery store crammed into two aisles, so it was easier to pretend you were shopping.

She killed half an hour refueling on green tea and a Polish dog with mustard and relish, using the bathroom, and reading a celebrity magazine while she worked up the courage to withdraw four hundred of her mom's dollars from the ATM.

The guy behind the register looked like an army cook, with those faded green tattoos on his hairy arms, the sad red eyes. His scalp was patchy and his nametag said Schluman, and Keelie felt sorry for him if that was his first name. Schluman watched Keelie move around the store, but mostly he was reading his own magazine or making coffee and so far he wasn't bothering her.

Some college types in a big SUV came through and bought a case of energy drinks. The truck was packed. They headed off in the wrong direction anyway.

A few truckers stopped for diesel, but Keelie had already made up a set of rules and one of the rules was *no truckers*, unless the trucker was a woman, but she doubted her luck would be that good.

After one a.m. it got real slow. Schluman began to mop the aisles. He passed her in toiletries, said, 'Still no luck?' Keelie shrugged, wondering if he could tell just by looking at her. Then the Kum N Go went from real slow to dead.

Tuesday, middle of the night, that's why. Unless you were about to emergency run out of gas, you'd press on to Omaha, where there were gobs more choices for motels and real restaurants. In between games of Ms Pac-Man she went outside and smoked on the sidewalk.

She had promised herself she wouldn't get desperate and ask any old creep. She imagined a woman in her twenties, tough and savvy from livin' in the city, a woman who would pity her enough to give her a ride but admire her enough not to give her shit. But in the event of no woman, a man might do. So long as he looked decent. Older would be better, 'cause he would be slower, and if he tried something Keelie could use her cell to call 911 or dive out of the car. Her fingers were memorizing the keypad as she smoked, practicing the quick dial.

Schluman came out and smoked on the sidewalk too. He didn't try to smoke with her, though. He stood at the end, beside the metal cage holding the propane bottles. He looked over at her once or twice, smiling tiredly, and when he went back inside, all he said was, 'Welp, guess I better get back to it.'

A little before three, a newer Ford sedan pulled up. Guy, fifties, graying black hair. Yellow sweater and stiff pleated shorts. The sweater looked safe. He put the gas nozzle back and walked to the front doors. Keelie bounced on her toes, thinking *do it, do it, do it, go on, dummy*. But the script in her head went blank and she was dry-mouthed. The man nodded courteously as he slipped inside.

She looked away, her face tingling hot. She paced, moving around the ice machine, spying him cruising to the restroom. It was quick, probably just a pee. He exited carrying a gallon of milk. That seemed like a good

4

sign too, the milk. He stepped off the curb, his back already to her.

'Excuse me, sir?' She tried to smile but her mouth locked in a grimace.

He paused, turning. 'Yes?'

'Are you by chance going that way? West, I mean?'

'I suppose.'

'Would you maybe mind giving me a ride?'

After a few seconds he said, 'Where is it you want to go?'

'I'm going to see my sister, in Los Angeles? Not that I would expect—'

'Los Angeles?' he blurted.

'She's in the hospital.'

The man looked at the Interstate. 'Afraid I'm just going home. To Omaha.'

It hardly seemed worth hitching it, but then again it was three in the morning and progress was progress.

'Well, maybe I could—' she began, stepping off the sidewalk.

'You should try the bus station. This is no way to go about it, miss.'

And then he was ducking into his car, gone. Probably thought she was a hooker. Keelie refused to cry, but it was tempting. Why hadn't she just waited until tomorrow, in daylight, and made one of her friends drive her to the bus station? She could probably take a bus to Argentina on four hundred dollars. Except that she had already *left home*, and the walk back was at least five miles, and if she asked Julie or Reyna to drive her, they would blab to their parents, and then Keelie's mom would find out and have a shit fit.

Also, Keelie needed every penny. Mom's balance was only eleven-hundred something (before tonight's withdrawal), and the rest might not be accessible once Mom noticed that her card (and daughter) were missing. Keelie was counting on this four hundred (the maximum withdrawal allowed per day), and maybe a couple hundred more tomorrow, to help her get established. The other four kids said they were bringing at least five hundred each, and she had to be ready to contribute her share. She kept thinking of the photos Lee had posted on their Habitat page. The warehouse was rough with only a couple walls, but it was in the artistic part of downtown and they would make it up really nice, have a painting party and then get on with their new lives. A band, a co-op, an online 'zine. Whatever it became, it would be creative, something to call their own and far from here.

Anxiety and the green tea made her have to pee again. When she set off that annoying-as-fuck *bing-bong* door signal for the fifty-thousandth time, Schluman looked up from his *Car & Driver* and did a double-take. When she came out of the bathroom he was standing with his hands on his hips, scowling.

She bought another green tea out of guilt. 'Don't worry. I'm leaving soon.'

'If I find out you're doing drugs in the shitter ...' Schluman said.

Keelie shook her head quickly. 'Promise.'

Right then a silver minivan pulled up at pump six.

Soon as she saw it, Keelie just had a feeling. This one would make or break the whole deal.

A woman got out first, then a man – the driver. A married couple by the looks. They were neither young nor old, and dressed like models in a Sears advertisement. The wife swiped her card and began pumping. He used the squeegee to clean the windshield, raking the rubber blade in perfect rows. When he finished with one side, he did it again from the other, overlapping his patient strokes. People who cleaned their windshields so thoroughly were on a long road trip, weren't they?

The wife racked the nozzle and got back in the minivan. She flipped the visor down and touched up her eye make-up, dabbing with a pinky. The husband set the squeegee in the bucket and turned toward the highway, stretching his arms. He leaned one way then the other, kicking his legs out like he couldn't make the blood go back into them. He walked to the driver's side and got in and shut the door.

'Oh, shit, shit, nooooo!' They were supposed to come in and use the bathroom first! Keelie shoved through the doors and jogged after them, waving frantically.

The van inched forward.

'Hold on, hold on, wait!'

The van almost hit her, then stopped abruptly, rocking. The husband and wife looked at each other, then watched as she approached the driver's side. The window powered down and Keelie saw he was handsome, even with the weird glasses (steel frames, huge lenses). He had nice, shaven tan skin and his smooth blonde hair was

7

parted on one side and the woman had elegant features and lustrous brown hair.

She smiled at Keelie in a skeptical but pleasant way. 'Everything all right?'

When she got to the part about Los Angeles, the man put a hand up.

'Hey, hey, whoa. See, we're headed to Las Vegas.'

'Second honeymoon,' the wife said. 'But my sister lives in Casper so we thought it would be nicer to drive.'

'Oh, that's perfect,' Keelie said. The minivan smelled clean and new. The seats were empty and Keelie couldn't help imagining how nice it would be to stretch out. 'I could take a bus from Vegas. I can pay for gas? It's super important.'

'Oh, but honey,' the wife said. 'Casper is in Wyoming. We're stopping for a few days ... there's a reunion ... '

Keelie clenched the straps of her backpack. 'No, see, that's not a problem. Casper would be—'

'Casper is not the issue, I think.' The husband shot his wife a stern look, his voice deep but gentle. 'We don't actually ... got to be some sort of laws against, I mean. Honey?'

The wife rested her hand on his arm as she leaned over the console. 'Do your parents know about this lil' adventure, dear?'

Lie, girl, but just the right amount. 'Totally. I'll be nineteen in July.' Keelie paused, humbled. 'I have to go. She's my sister. We can call my mom to check in tomorrow. I won't be a bother, I promise.'

8

The woman frowned in sympathy, awaiting her husband's verdict. He was shaking his head slowly, staring at the wheel.

Keelie pressed the wife. 'If I go home now, my mom ... I don't know what she'll do to me.'

The husband searched Keelie's eyes. He looked at his wife and threw up his hands – *what am I supposed to do here?*

'Oh, come on, Dave. We can't leave her out here.'

Dave the husband sighed. 'I guess that means hop in.'

Keelie ran around to where a motorized door was already opening. 'Thank you, thank you, thank you ...'

She took the first bench seat. The third row was empty. The cargo bay was piled up with bags and a couple of pillows that looked very soft. Keelie watched the 'Nick vanish behind them, a lump of manure in the dark, and she had to suppress a whoop of triumph.

She semi-awoke on her side, backpack scraping her cheek, the highway's mellow thrum rising up to rock her gently. An evangelical murmur issued from the radio, the dim green glow of the instrument panel cool against the glossy black windows.

She remembered the introductions in fragments. Dave and Sheila Galloway from Indianapolis, married ten years, still no children but hoping to adopt one day soon. He was like a special kind of architect, a maker of models for city plans and communities. She was a teacher, fifth grade. They had asked about Keelie's parents, but didn't pry too deeply into her imaginary sister's alleged chemotherapy.

She was twitchy, her mind working against the tide of green tea, her legs trying to find the right combination against the arm rest, her neck stiff. She remembered the pillows. Yes, a pillow. Then she could really sleep.

There was a weird smell, so faint she hadn't noticed it at first. It wasn't bad, exactly, just odd. Burned iron, like the metal workshop at school, and maybe a little fishy too. Nebraska. Pig farms. Tilapia farms. God knows what kind of farms. Keelie held her breath for thirty seconds, then sniffed again. The smell had passed.

She sat up and rubbed her eye. Sheila was dozing upright, one of the pillows between her cheek and the passenger window. Dave was quiet, his attention fixed on the road, both hands on the wheel. Should she ask permission? What did it matter? They had offered everything else when she got in – Gatorade, sunflower seeds, teriyaki jerky, pop, ham sandwich. They wouldn't care about a pillow.

She grabbed the backrest and bent to keep from hitting her head on the roof. Bingo – on top of the bags, in the far right corner. White and fluffy.

She reached out and Dave's voice called back. 'What do you need, hon?'

Keelie twitched in surprise. 'I was hoping I could borrow one of the pillows. My neck hurts.'

Dave didn't answer. Keelie waited, hunched over.

'Oh,' he said finally. 'Help yourself. Just watch the bags underneath. I have some important work in there and it's pretty darn fragile.'

'Okay, thanks.' Keelie stifled a yawn. Jeez, did he

think she was going to flop down in the cargo area, smashing one of his models?

While she was reaching, she realized her butt was sticking up, and she was suddenly sure that Mr Galloway was watching her in the rearview mirror. Not because he was a perv, but maybe to make sure she didn't mess with his work stuff. But perv or not, if he was looking, he'd definitely be getting a view of the full Keelie right about now. She reached back and snugged her shirt hem over her locust tattoo, and when she turned back for the pillow it was gone.

Wait . . . *what*? Five seconds ago it had been on top, in the corner. Now there was only the pile of black canvas bags. She hadn't felt the minivan swerve, but . . .

'Everything all right?' Dave said.

'Yeah, one sec . . .' She leaned way over the cargo area, patting the bags, reached for a corner of white . . . and her arm shot back up as if scalded. She hissed, her skin breaking out in ripples of revulsion. The white patch was not a pillow. It was cold and firm and slimy, like a fish. That would explain the weird smell.

'Did you find it?' Dave said.

'Uhm . . .' *They went fishing is all. It's a big bass in a cooler or something gross like that. Stop being such a baby.*

Dave was mumbling to Sheila. Great, they'd woken her up too. Keelie didn't even want the pillow any more, but it would be weird if she came back without it now, and Dave might think she'd messed up his fragile work stuff.

'You can use my pillow, Keelie.' Sheila's voice seemed

11

too loud. Too alert for someone who just woke up. 'I don't need it.'

Keelie plopped down on the third row seat. 'That's okay. I have my pack.'

In the rearview mirror, Dave's eyes were two black dots. They went from the mirror to the road and back like one of those cat clocks.

The van cruised.

A couple miles later, Dave and Sheila had become very still. There was something cold in the air now, a weird vibe. Reminded Keelie of being in the check-out line when her mom was taking for ever to write a check that everyone – like all eight people waiting behind them and the cashier – knew damn well was going to bounce anyway. The vibe coming from Mr and Mrs Galloway was like that, except Keelie was the one behind them. How could you feel people with their backs to you *staring at you*?

Keelie focused on the road. Where were they now? The Interstate was straight and flat, had to be deep into Nebraska. The minivan sluiced the night in ear-drum popping silence. Miles, so many miles to go.

Her eyelids grew heavy. She was about to let them close when she noticed something odd. Up ahead on the highway, the slashes of white lane paint were changing. Hurling toward them in a single blurred line at first, then thickening and thinning, coming slower with breaks in between, until they were just ticking by and the black clarity between each slash was agonizing. Keelie sat up.

The van was edging onto the shoulder.

She gripped the back of the seat. 'You don't have to stop for me.'

They didn't respond.

'I didn't move anything. The pillow just fell over, so I left it.'

The van was inching forward at a crawl, the tires crunching gravel and weeds. It stopped. There were no cars passing in either direction. There was no rest stop. There were no fast food places or Kum N Gos. There was nothing. Only black night outside. They were going to throw her out, leave her here in the middle of nowhere.

Dave was holding the wheel with both hands, staring at the road.

Sheila was sitting up straight, staring at the road.

A minute passed. Why wouldn't they answer her? The smell was horrible now. Like a whole basket of dead fish that had been laying in the sun, and something else that smelled like a cooked battery. Burning metal, tickling her throat.

Keelie heard herself whimper. 'I'm sorry, okay?'

They did not acknowledge her. Another minute of silence, the longest she had ever known. Time stretched, stopped. There was no more time. She was in the car with statues, mannequins posed in a display window. She had never felt so alone in the presence of people.

Keelie screamed. Again, until her throat hurt.

They did not flinch. They did not speak. She might as well have screamed at a family on a billboard. The white stone faces of Mt Rushmore.

Her breathing grew hoarse. Her legs wouldn't move. She reached for her phone in her pocket, her thumb sliding around the buttons. She might have pressed a 9 before the sound of canvas scraping against more canvas startled her. Her hand slipped and the phone thumped onto the floor.

She was about to lean down when Mr Galloway reached into the console and plucked something from the drink holder. It shined briefly, a small flash of silver that disappeared into his mouth. He bit down and there was a single clack.

Together, as if their heads were attached to the same rubber cord, husband and wife turned all the way around in their seats and stared at her.

They weren't the same people that picked her up, and Keelie Kennerly wasn't the same girl ever again.

PART ONE

On the Lake

Death is a friend of ours; and he that is
not ready to entertain him is not at home.

FRANCIS BACON

1

Mick Nash, a man well into the third year of what he had come to think of as a total life-hangover, stood on the boat trailer's fender, attempting to raise forty gallons of rainwater from the canvas cover. He knew damn well using a bucket would simplify the task, but he didn't want to stand here all morning bailing water onto his driveway like a feeble castaway in a punctured rubber raft. He wanted to overpower the laws of physics, heave the weather right back in Mother Nature's face.

Jamie, his youngest server – filling in today for his shift leader, Tanya, who had called in sick because her autistic son, Drew, had a tummy ache and, well, autism – was pelting him with questions from the cell phone pinched between his shoulder and ear, but he would not be lured back in.

The last two hundred days, sure. The next five years, fine.

But not today.

He raised his arms like Moses, knuckles whitening as the canvas fiber mashed the pads of his fingers into his

17

short nails. Perhaps a cupful of water sloshed overboard. He needed a waterfall.

Jamie said, 'Okay but how am I supposed to load the receipt tape—'

'Purple stripe on the left. One sec, Jamie.'

Mick's neck cobra-tented with exertion. The water surged, retreated, rolled forward in a triumphant tide . . .

Until his flip-flop slipped from the fender, the canvas slipped from his fingertips, and the water rushed back as his elbow banged on the steel cleat bolted to the fiber-glass gunwale, shooting tickle pins up to his neck. His arms windmilled, squirting the phone out like a minnow into the small pond now pouring into his boat. He unspooled a string of profanity that equated the boat's design and functionality with certain amounts of excre-ment and which suggested the vessel had a history of performing lewd sexual acts for money.

'What on earth are you screaming at?' his wife said behind him. Amy was still in her pajamas, despite being awake for nearly five hours.

'Stormed last night. The runoff pole thing fell down. My fucking phone just went in the drink.'

'Do you need some help?'

'Can't get one day here. They won't leave me alone.'

'They?'

The sound of a cow urinating on a piece of shale directed their attention to the stern, where the water was now fanning down the driveway, around Mick's feet.

'Unbelievable.'

'Jesus, Mick, if it's going to be like this,' Amy said.

'We're going to the lake. So don't even.'

She stared at him with her you're-being-an-asshole look.

'Come on, Ames,' he said. 'And why don't I hear a lawn mower?'

'He's still in bed.'

Mick looked at his rubber watch: 10:22 a.m. Pathetic. This is how empires fall. He said, 'I asked you to wake him up two hours ago. Supposed to be a lesson here, or have we bagged that too?'

Amy rolled her eyes. 'I've got my hands full with B and I still have to make the sandwiches. You want your son to mow the lawn, you wake him up.'

She walked back into the house. Mick climbed up and pulled his phone from the wet carpeted floor. The screen was blank, a flat pool of water sliding beneath the glass like one of those puzzle toys. He put it in his pocket, then rolled the wet cover over the bow and threw it on the driveway. A cloudless sky, the morning already eighty-some degrees. A Wednesday, so with any luck the lake wouldn't have more than a dozen boats. Their first real day of summer together. Last chance to enjoy the boat before it went up on Craigslist. Hard not to be a little steamed about that part of it, especially with the monstrosity on the next lot watching over him.

That house. The gall of it.

Built deep on the old, six-acre Jenkins property, its three stories, double-balcony windows with ogival arches, and wide mouth of a terrace with its toothy columned parapet, The Eyesore (as the residents around Juhls Drive called it) loomed over the Nash spread like the grinning face of fuck-you money. Amy said it was a modern interpretation of a Venetian palazzo.

Mick thought the estate – set against the backdrop of Boulder's foothills, in their loose and spacious neighborhood of low ranches, A-frames, and log cabin homes – was about as tasteful and subtle as a clown at a daycare center. Construction had begun last fall, with interior work continuing through winter, and the last of the landscapers – men who knew nothing of the owners or move-in date – had drifted away by Easter.

Voila, a palace.

Almost three months later it was still vacant. The three arched mahogany garage doors set under the house's main floor had yet to admit a vehicle (Mick had a bet going with Amy one of them would be a Jaguar), and the wrought-iron gates at the end of the long, brushed travertine drive were secured electronically, cameras mounted every fifty feet along the stucco perimeter wall. Nobody came, nobody went. It just sat there waiting, its peach walls and terracotta tiled roof shooting them a blinding glare of solar stink-eye. Mick imagined the owner would be a short, cherubic pirate of a CEO, with a large waist and florid cheeks, a kind of twenty-first-century Roman general returning to paradise after sacking one final company of lesser men.

God love Boulder. For these wealthy outsiders, Mick's scenic, overpriced, health-obsessed hometown had become shit for flies.

He kicked his son's bedroom door open. 'Get up, Kyle. We're running late.'

The boy appeared to have fallen face-first from a building.

'Up, I said. You don't mow, I'm not pulling you around the lake.'

Kyle groaned into his pillow.

'Work before play, champ. When I was fifteen my old man used to make me mow and trim the lawn, clean the boat, sweep the garage, and clean my room, and we were always on the lake by eight a.m.'

'But do I have to go?'

Okay, what? He'd rather sleep than go waterskiing with his father now?

'You don't want to spend the day with your family, fine. I'm throwing your Xbox in the lake, you ungrateful little shit.' Mick walked away.

Kyle scrambled out of bed. 'Okay, Jesus. I'm up, I'm up.'

2

Amy Nash stood before the mirror behind her bathroom door, studying her new green swimsuit. Full coverage, the catalog said, but she didn't feel covered fully, or look like the laughing woman in the photo. She felt like a hippopotamus sculpted from butter pecan ice cream. The bra support was good, though, padded and secure. Still got my girls. Nevertheless, she pulled on a sweatshirt and yoga pants and wrapped a beach towel the size of New Mexico around her waist.

The door banged open and Briela stood in the hall, fists bunched at her sides, face screwed up. 'My swimsuit hurts!'

Mine too, baby. 'That's because it's on inside out, honey. That tan thing down there? Not a pocket.'

Briela looked down in horror and ran back to her room.

In the kitchen, Amy filled a canvas tote with shoestring potatoes, a Ziploc of carrot and celery sticks none of them would touch, a bag of sunflower seeds Mick would spit all over the lake, two questionable oranges, her large bottle of Pellegrino. Her book club paperback, the one about the dysfunctional family of carnies, a sort of Salinger's *Nine Stories* with flipper hands and hunch-backs.

She ran the opener around two large cans of albacore, the escaped stench somewhat revolting. Threw it into a plastic bowl, stirred in the relish and tabasco, added a shot of parmesan. Smeared the mix in large goops over the seven-grain nut wheat bread, wrapped them in wax paper. The jar of peperoncinis. She really wished for once they could just beach it in front of the concession stands and send the kids up for burgers and fries and floats, but Mick was a fanatic about his boating tradi-tions. What exactly he was trying to instill by making them eat peppers and canned tuna she did not know.

When she finally emerged from the house, the rest of them were loaded into Blue Thunder, the trailer hitched, everyone suddenly waiting on her. Even Kyle, apparently excused from lawn duty. Amy set the cooler and tote in the truck's bed, next to the other cooler loaded with Mick's beer.

'All set?' Mick drummed his fingers. He was wearing his pith helmet again. His Hawaiian shirt. And his 'hilar-ious' mirrored cop sunglasses.

'Oh, shit, forgot the sunscreen.'

'That was a cuss,' Briela said from the king cab as Amy ran back to the house.

She found the SPF 30, the 45, and the Bullfrog for B's nose. Melanoma? Mela-not on my watch. Anything else? She halted at the door. Forgot to feed Thom. She ran back in, poured kibble, topped off his water, hurried back out.

23

The nearest gas station was the old Sinclair on the Diagonal. Mick pulled in, filled Blue Thunder with sixty-eight dollars, then nudged the truck forward, turned it off again, and pumped another eighty-four into the boat. He went inside. The old man who maybe lived there ran the card on a machine screwed to the wall. It took forever. Mick's lips moved. Grandpa shrugged. Amy started to feel sick again.

'Kyle, would you turn up the A/C?'

He did, then leaned his head against the window. What time had he come home? He probably snuck in through the basement again. And what was that smell? Fruit cocktail?

Mick came out of the station, sheepish.

Amy powered her window down. 'What?'

'That old machine can't read the stripe. Need one of your cards.'

Amy tilted her head. He was maxed out again. Mick looked at the kids and back to her – don't start. She thrust a hand into her purse, held out her wallet.

'Thank you,' Mick said, pinching Briela's cheek through the rear window. 'Wanna candy bar, sweetheart?'

'Snickers, please!' the daughter shouted.

Amy gritted her teeth.

3

Kyle was standing in two feet of chilly-ass water, bow line in hand, sandals slipping on the mossy ramp. He forgot to pee before leaving the house and now his bladder was killing him, but he was not quite in deep enough to let it go. His head was a washing machine full of last night's gin and his punishment for leaving his Revos at Shaheen's crib was the sun beating him across the temples with a baseball bat.

His dad barked out the truck window. 'You paying attention back there? Huh!'

'Yes.'

'Let me know when the fenders are below the surface. Two inches below!'

'I know!' Kyle glared at the back of his father's head. Dad thought he was a fucking retard. Mom and B were on the dock right behind him, watching every move, which only made it worse. A line of trucks above, waiting to unload. Soon as the boat started to float off the trailer, Kyle was supposed hand Mom the bow line, climb onto the dock, and walk it all the way to the end, because blocking the entrance was bad etiquette. They'd only done this a hundred and fifty times, but for some reason it was always a fiasco that made his dad blow his stack.

The truck reversed. Kyle stared at the trailer's wheel going under. His mind drifted to Michelle Harper, the way she'd dragged her nails in a slow line up his arm last night when they were standing next to the keg beside Shaheen's pool. Shaheen was awesome, his house was awesome, his weed was awesome, his parents were always in Dubai. Kyle blinked, realizing the fender was six inches underwater.

'Stop! Stop! That's good!'

The truck braked. His dad's face bobbed in the side mirrors.

'You're doing a super job, Kyle,' Briela said behind him, giggling.

'Shut up.'

'You shut up, butthole.'

'Knock it off,' Mom said. 'Don't say that word, Briela. It's ugly.'

'All clear?' Dad shouted.

The boat drifted. Kyle checked the rubber fenders, the amount of play in the bow line, the wind. 'We're good.'

The truck eased up the ramp and the bow line went taut, pulling Kyle off his feet. He fell in the water up to his neck, shocking him awake.

'Stop!' Amy shouted. 'Stop, stop!'

Kyle popped up, rope in hand. Dad braked and jumped out. 'What happened?'

'I'm fine.' Kyle peed into the lake a little.

Dad tromped down the ramp, removed his glasses, rubbed his eyes. A serpent of gray strapping lay in the water, leading up to the trailer's manual winch.

'Jesus Livin' Christ, Kyle. You forgot to unhook the tow strap. I almost dragged the goddamn boat up the concrete ramp.'

Shame climbed into his cheeks. 'If you let me drive it off . . . I'm juggling a hundred things at once down here.'

'Yeah, right. And what happens when you lower the drive onto the ramp and break a four-hundred dollar prop?'

'I'm sorry, okay?'

'Mick, come on,' Mom said. 'You're making it worse.'

Dad sighed and placed a hand on his shoulder. 'All right, all right. Everybody calm down. Did you hurt yourself?'

'I'm fine.' His knee was bleeding but he pulled away, afraid his dad would smell gin fumes oozing from his pores.

Atop the ramp, a tattooed maniac in a huge black Dodge truck with hood flames pounded his horn. 'Let's go, hotshot, let's go!'

'Settle down, asshole! I'm talking to my son here.'

Kyle grinned at that, unhooked the strap's carabiner from the prow, cranked it snug against the spool. 'All clear.'

Dad drove out, leaving twin contrails of lake water across the hot parking lot. They cleated the ropes at bow and stern, lobbed the bumpers to keep the hull from smashing into the dock. Kyle stepped in and turned on the blower, but it didn't make that noise. He set the choke, turned the ignition. It went *click-click-click*.

'What's that mean?' Mom said.

Kyle smirked. 'Battery's dead. Been sitting all winter. He forgot to charge it.'

4

It was a beautiful day until they saw the dentist's boat. That's when Briela knew it was never meant to be.

But for a few hours, it was like old times. The sun was out, the lake was smooth, and no one had gotten dibs on their favorite dock. After the Leather Lady came down from the boathouse to give them a jump, the boat roared to life and Dad made two full passes around the lake. Briela claimed her favorite seat in the bow and let the wind press her red sunglasses to her nose, her magnificent blonde hair flying behind her. Boulder Reservoir seemed huge today, even though she knew it was only a couple miles across. As they cruised, she counted the floating docks to make sure they were all there. Yep, eighteen, just like last summer, with a fresh coat of orange paint, scattered across the lake like little islands.

Once the battery was charged, they slowed, the bow lowering toward the green surface until it seemed it would slosh up and soak her. Briela watched the sun's rays twirl like crystal beams in the depths, spacing out a little. They tied off at their dock.

After Mom coated her face and shoulders with lotion, Briela spread her towel neatly across the boat's sun-bathing deck and lay perfectly still, imagining she was a movie star. Dad turned on the oldies station, which she normally hated but was somehow okay out here on the lake. A man was singing about a woman named G-L-O-R-I-A, which Briela guessed was his girlfriend. Kyle jumped in for a swim 'cause he was hungover, but she wouldn't tell. She didn't want to start an argument now that the parentals had finally calmed down.

'Now this is the life,' Dad said, which is what he always said first thing on the lake. 'Already noon but we made it.'

'It's gorgeous out,' Mom said. Briela wondered when her mom was going to take off her yoga pants.

'Water temp's sixty-eight,' Dad said to Kyle. 'Don't know what you have to complain about, champ.'

'Feels like fifty.' Kyle clawed his way out like he'd seen a shark. 'What's for lunch?'

'Tuna fish,' Mom said.

'Not just tuna fish,' Dad said. 'Mick Nash's World Famous Tuna Fish Sammies.'

'Don't worry, honey,' her mom called to her. 'I didn't put tabasco on yours.'

'M'kay.' But she secretly liked tabasco when they were boating. It was a part of the whole scene and flavor of the day, fitting in with the oldies songs, the tuna fish, and the smell of the lake in her hair.

A huge motor growled near them and Briela sat up, dizzy from the sun. It was bigger than their boat, white with fast lines of sparkling blue and purple, a high metal rack for wake boards and a wall of speakers across the top like a portable rock concert. Steering it was a goofy-looking man with bald red hair and a thick chin beard that was mostly gray. His shirt was off and he was almost orange, like he had been out here for weeks even though summer just started. And he was seriously buff-muscled in that icky way some of the middle-aged men at the rec center were. Briela recognized him, but she couldn't remember from where.

'Hey-O, Nash family, welcome to Boulder Reservoir!' the man said, like he owned the lake, which Briela knew he didn't. It belonged to the community and her family paid six hundred dollars every year so they could own part of it too. 'Let's get this party started!'

She didn't like the woman he was with, either. Reminded Briela of the women on that show, *Witches Lane*, the ones who cast spells on all the other wives' husbands.

'Hi, Roger,' her mom said.

Dr Roger Lertz, that was his name. He was a dentist in town, at least before that thing happened and he was in the newspaper.

'What's shaking, Mickey?' Dr Lertz said. 'You need a vodka bomber?'

'Little early for that, Roger,' Dad said. Though he was drinking his second beer, Briela noticed, and she had seen some of Dad's little Schweppes bottles in the cooler with the limes already inside. My lake grenades, he called them.

'This lovely gal here is Bonnie,' Dr Lertz said. 'She used to work for me.'

Everyone said hi to Bonnie. Bonnie waved. Her boobs were oily and her white bikini was the size of three Band-Aids. Briela vowed she would never be caught dead in something like that.

Dr Lertz looked at Kyle. 'You gonna ski today, big man? Get up on one?'

'Yeah,' Kyle said, squinting. 'If Dad lets me.'

'He was supposed to mow the lawn,' Dad said.

'Uh-oh, sounds like somebody's got a tough guy for a dad,' Dr Lertz said. Briela was sure the larger boat was going to bang into them at any minute, but the dentist seemed to be an expert at sliding it back and forth, grumbling in the same little parking place. She realized he was showing off and maybe this was why her dad didn't like him.

'Thanks for stopping by, Rodge,' Dad said. 'Enjoy your afternoon.'

Dr Lertz looked disappointed. 'We'll buzz you later for a little H2O bazooka battle. You sexy gals make sure you don't get burned.'

He looked at Briela, pointed his fingers like guns and said, 'Smokin'!'

Briela giggled, but her mom was frowning. Dr Lertz's boat raced away, sending a two-foot wave that almost knocked Kyle down and spilled Dad's beer on his shirt.

'What a colossal a-hole,' Dad said.

'I thought he was supposed to be in jail,' Mom said.

'What'd he do?' Kyle was grinning.

Dad looked at Mom. Mom said, 'I don't even know where to begin.'

Recognizing an opportunity to deliver one of his important speeches, Dad stood and adjusted his sunglasses. 'Well, Kyle, it's not a secret. Dr Lertz got caught over-prescribing pharmaceutical cocaine to his patients. He lost his practice, his house, his wife and kids. He was having an affair with one of his assistants, not that Bonnie there, some other woman, the hygienist, real sexy little brunette used to work there, what was her name? Deena? Not important? Right. And she told the police he tried to lure her down to the office after hours because he thought it would be fun to get high on nitrous and use the dentist's chair for—'

'All right,' Mom said. 'That's enough, Mick.'

'I'm not making this shit up,' Dad said. 'He's a dork who doesn't know his limits, Kyle. He wasn't content to have a little fun. He had to have *all* the fun. That's the point.'

'That boat is beast,' Kyle said, watching Roger and Bonnie race around the lake, that Journey song even Briela was sick of blasting surprisingly clear.

'It's not his,' Dad said. 'He's completely broke. That I can promise you.'

That's when she noticed the look in her dad's eyes. The one that was angry and disappointed. Like he really liked Roger's boat too, but would never admit it in front of Kyle. Briela didn't care. Her family's Bayliner was smaller, but it was still clean and nice, and it was *theirs*. It

33

even had a sign on the back that said *Kickin' it in Nashville.*

'I like our boat better, Dad,' Briela said.

'Atta girl,' Dad said. Mom was biting her lip.

Briela knew they wouldn't sell their boat unless they were getting a new one just like it. Though she guessed bigger would be okay, too. With white leather seats and pink sparkles. That would be suh-weet.

5

By three o'clock the water was dead calm. The sun was blazing and Kyle's hangover was mostly gone. Dad nursing an IPA, Mom reading in her lawn chair on the dock, B painting her face with a Snickers.

Kyle wanted to ski in the worst way, but he also didn't want to ski at all, and the duality of this was eating at his nerves. He had gotten really good at two, and knew how to drop one to slalom, but the deep water start was another story. Last summer he had swallowed half the reservoir, Dad giving him pointer after pointer, refusing to let him into the boat until he tried *just one more time*. Getting up on one had become Kyle's Everest.

'Water doesn't get any smoother than this,' Dad said. He was reclining in the boat, chomping those sour Greek peppers just about as fast as he could, belching loud and then laughing when it echoed across the lake.

'Yeah,' Kyle said, dangling his feet off the boat's swim platform.

'Gonna be a busy summer, champ. You should get a hold of it while you can.' Why couldn't he just say it?

They were selling the boat, everyone in the family knew it.

'Maybe I should drop one,' Kyle said.

'Tell you what.' His dad removed the Connelly from the ski locker. It was a beautiful thing, this blade of ceramic and graphite, with the double hi-wrap bindings. A tournament ski, a five-hundred-dollar report-card bribe. 'You're bigger this year. Your arms are stronger, your legs. You let it get in your head. This is a fresh start. You can do it, bud. I know you can.'

Kyle accepted the ski, dunking it to lube the bindings.

'That's the spirit,' Dad said. 'You remember what I told you?'

'Arms straight, knees tucked to my chest, deep breath, head down.'

'And don't let go. That was your problem. It's going to feel like you're going under, but I promise you, if you keep the ski tip right in front of you and count to five, you'll pop right up.'

'Okay.' Right after I take a cold-water enema.

'Do I get to be flag girl again?' Briela shouted.

'Sure, honey,' Dad said. 'I need you in the bow.'

Briela took her position, her yellow life vest riding up around her ears.

Mom climbed in the boat. 'What do you say when he falls?'

'DOWN! MAN DOWN!'

'Except he's not going to fall down,' Dad said. 'Once he gets up, he's going to ski all the way around the lake, aren't you, champ?'

'I guess.' Kyle pushed off the dock and bobbed in the water.

When the boat had drifted a safe distance, Dad lowered the drive and fired the engine. Mom twirled the handle like a lasso, let it fly. He caught it in mid air, suddenly had to pee again. He let it go while the tow line played out. His stomach fluttered, he had to remind himself to breathe. The Bayliner's 4.3 liter Mercruiser burbled blue smoke and spat water as it chugged toward the mountains. Briela raised the flag. Dad looked over his shoulder every three seconds. Mom watched him, murmuring prayers. The rope went taught. His body coiled into itself, hardening as the boat dragged him gently in a perfect line. His arms locked, the ski tip poking above the surface. Breathe, breathe. Don't let go, he told himself, don't let go.

'Ready?' Dad hollered.

Not yet. Not yet. Not yet. Now or never. Okay, now.

'Hit it!' In the split second before his dad rammed the throttle, Kyle lowered his face to the water, waiting for the evil suck. The deep roar filled his ears and the placid green glass before him became a white thundering waterfall. The strain was merciless, packing water into his sinuses like a punch to the forehead. The ski danced wildly, but he used his hip muscles to hold it true.

One one thousand, two one thousand, three one thousand ...

It was an endless avalanche, filling his throat, puffing his eyelids.

Four one thousand ...

The rubber handle was slipping from his palms, as if

some demon were prying at his fingertips with a crowbar. But he realized this was *the* moment, the moment when he always caved in, and he decided no, evil suck, not today.

Kyle tucked his knees to his chin, becoming more ball than man. Felt the ski rotating like a great lever, an invisible hand shoving him up onto a table. Gallons of water fell away and then he simply unbent his knees, blinking into sunshine. The boat reached its cruising speed of thirty-four and Kyle released a cry of victory. His entire family was standing in the boat, fists pounding the sky. He couldn't remember making them so proud.

Actual skiing had never been difficult for him, and he had gotten good at crossing the wake, managing the tension in the rope, rotating from edge to edge to make his turns. But he had never been up on the Connelly. This wasn't like the clunky O'Brien family skis. This dense black stiletto was part of his body, reading his every intention without the slightest hesitation. He merely *thought* about exiting the wake, and the ski led him out in a gliding arc, hissing as he rotated to his inside edge, leveraging the boat's horsepower to fire him back across the wake like a bullet.

He expected a huge jolt, but the slalom cut the wake with only the briefest *bump-bump*, and then he was hooking once again, free, riding the water like a porpoise, a god. The Connelly threw a twenty-foot rooster tail and he looked back to see a handful of rainbows falling in the glittering wall. Kyle had never had sex, but he was pretty sure this was better. He *owned*.

The swim beach raced by and he wondered if any of his friends from school were watching him now. He made six seamless cuts, side to side, falling into an effortless snaking rhythm. *Bump-bump-hiiissssss, bump-bump-hiiisssss.* To the inside, the orange docks flickered, the occasional fishing boat, and then they were coming up on the dam, a long wall of rocks to his outside right.

Boom, slide, boom, slide ... Another six cuts.

Easing back into the wake with thighs burning, Kyle crooked the rubber handle inside his elbows. He shook out his cramped hands, exhausted but nowhere near ready to give up. He would make a full loop if it killed him.

6

In the bow, flag snapping against her hip, Briela lost her brother in the sun's white glare. She blinked and twisted her head side to side. She saw the dam flashing by, and something odd on the path atop it. There was a family standing together, watching her. They were very still, like a photograph, and there were four of them. Mother, father, daughter, and son. Holding hands, dressed in clean white clothes like people at a tennis match. Their faces were creamy smears, their eyes specks of dark fixed on her, and then she was blinded again. She put a hand over her eyes, but the top of the dam was empty from end to end.

The other family was ... gone.

She felt sick in her tummy, everything inside of her suddenly hot. Oh no, she thought. It's happening again. The flag fell to the floor. Luckily her parents didn't notice, and she scooped it up just in time.

7

A slight breeze had picked up, studding the lake with diamonds for him to crush. Kyle leaned away from the boat, drawing almost parallel to the stern, looking at his family sideways now. The dentist's boat was floating a hundred yards up ahead, but there was plenty of clearance. Dad was obsessed with safety; he would never drive them within two hundred feet of another boat.

Kyle's arms were cooked spaghetti. His mouth was dry, lungs heaving. He decided to take one more pair of turns and then drop the line.

Briela mouthed something at him, then ducked.

Kyle edged in briefly before swerving right. He glanced at the dentist's boat – he was passing it now, less than fifty feet away – and saw long streaks of dark red across the white hull. A woman's hand was hanging over the side, slapping against the fiberglass before withdrawing in a jerk, leaving a red handprint, the fingertips dripping in thick rows. He caught all of this in perhaps two seconds, looking back as he was towed away.

Blood, holy shit, that was blood –

A wild ripple of adrenaline coursed through him,

sliding the ski, and the hardtop of the lake turned to mush. The rope went slack and he flailed, yanking the handle up to his chin. His dad was still holding the throttle at cruising speed and Kyle knew he should let go, but his arms wouldn't disobey the order so recently mastered. The Connelly's tip snagged as the rope leapt out of the water, locked taut, and ripped him from the bindings.

It was as if God flipped the lake with a spatula, the water rushing over his head as he somersaulted. His hands actually grazed the surface twice before he made a third revolution and his legs knifed in and he slammed to a halt chest-first in the water. It felt like running into a tree. The wind was knocked out of him and his brain seemed to vibrate in its casing. Something sting-grazed the top of his head and the Connelly javelined low across the surface, landing and skiing by itself for another sixty feet or so before tipping drunkenly on its side. Little ripples of water lapped at his throat. He closed his eyes and shivered as he bobbed.

The evil suck had gotten him after all.

8

'Down! Down! Kyle fell down!' Briela raised the orange flag.

Mick looked up from the depth finder – he had been hypnotized by the small school of digital fish beeping across the gray screen – and saw too much concern on his daughter's face. He looked over his shoulder. The rubber handle was skipping across the empty wake, his son nowhere in sight, and only then did he remember to pull back on the throttle. The Bayliner came off plane as he made a laborious U-turn.

Amy pivoted in her seat, a bottle of sunscreen in one hand. 'Whoa, he's kind of far back. How fast were you going?'

'Not very.' Mick frowned at Briela. 'I'm sure he's okay.'

But when he saw the Connelly floating so far away, he wasn't sure Kyle would be okay – it had to have been a fantastic wipeout. Mick pulled into neutral and the boat coasted in a circle. Kyle's head was back, his eyes aimed at the sky.

'Jesus, Mick, he's bleeding,' Amy said, scurrying to the back of the boat.

'I'm okay.' Kyle sounded dazed.

'B, honey, wind the rope, would you?' Mick said. She crawled onto the swim deck and began hauling the rope in. Kyle was paddling feebly toward them as Amy unlatched the ladder. 'What happened, bud?'

'Something's wrong,' Kyle said, blowing water from his nose, eyes scrunched in pain. Mick frowned, killing the engine. Kyle pointed toward Roger's boat some two hundred feet behind them. 'Someone's hurt . . . blood . . . all over the place.'

'His head is cut,' Amy said. 'Oh my God.'

Kyle ran a hand over his wet hair. 'I think the ski's fin nicked me.'

They helped him in, easing him onto the back seat. Amy made him sit still while she inspected his scalp.

'It's deep. He's going to need stitches. Where's the first-aid kit?'

Mick searched under dash, found the orange plastic box. Band-Aids, a roll of gauze, a tube of ointment, a packet of Advil. A boo-boo kit, not a holy-shit-emergency kit. But this wasn't too bad, right? His son looked okay. Amy fumbled the contents onto the seat. Her hands were shaking, Kyle's blood on her fingers.

'This is useless,' Amy said. The Band-Aids didn't stick to wet hair.

'I'm sorry, champ,' Mick said, knowing this was all his fault.

'Guys, I'm fine.' Kyle pushed his mother away. 'There's something wrong on their boat. I saw someone struggling. You didn't see the blood?'

'Blood,' Amy said. 'On Roger's boat?'

Mick said, 'Jesus, I guess we better go have a look.'

Amy grabbed his arm. 'We're not going near that sicko. Kyle needs medical attention.'

'I said I'm fine!'

'He says he's fine,' Mick said, smirking with pride.

Amy fumed at him. 'Take us in now.'

'Okay, okay. Let's get the ski, then I'll radio the lake patrol on the way in. Swim ladder up?'

Briela latched the ladder in place. Amy wrapped a towel around Kyle's head and pressed. If the boy was in pain, he wasn't letting them see it.

Mick started the motor. 'Tough stuff, Kyle. Damned if you didn't do it. I'm so proud of you, son.'

Kyle grinned.

Mick found the handheld CB radio in the glove compartment. He set the channel to 16, pressed the buttons, but the light didn't come on. 'Brand-new radio,' he said.

'Did you put batteries in it?' Amy said.

Mick opened the case. Nope. 'I have my cell,' he said, removing it from his pocket. The screen was still full of water. He jammed the buttons. 'Hunk of shit.'

'*Mick*,' Amy said.

'I know,' he snapped. He opened the throttle and circled back to fetch the ski. 'B, sweetie, do you think you can lean over and grab it?'

'It's too heavy for her,' Kyle said.

Amy tromped into the bow. Briela scampered out of her way and bumped her knee on the corner of the opened windshield frame. 'Owie!' She burst into tears.

Mick inspected her knee. A little curl of cut gray skin, no blood. 'You're okay, B.'

'*Slow down*,' Amy said, leaning over the bow.

Mick popped the shifter into neutral and held his breath. Amy grunted, snatched it up. She raised the ski and the bindings emptied cold water onto her head. She growled with contained fury. Mick slid the ski into the locker, made another steep turn, and raced for shore, everyone shooting each other unpleasant looks. He dropped them at the end of the dock.

'Find Coach Wisneski in the boat house,' Mick said. 'Tell him to send out a lake patrol unit. Get the kids in the truck, pull the trailer around, and wait for me at the top of the ramp. Be right back.'

'Hurry,' Amy said.

'Daddy?' Briela said.

'What, sweetie?'

'Be careful.' His daughter appeared seasick, in some form of shock.

'I will. Go on now with your mother.'

He chugged impatiently through the No Wake Zone, then aimed for the northwest corner and opened it wide.

9

A hundred feet from the SS *Laughing Gas*, Mick dropped the throttle and stood at the helm to inspect the situation. He saw no one on board, but Roger's ridiculously outfitted Glastron was a cuddy, not a bow rider, so it was possible the couple were below decks. He completed a slow circle, checking for signs of blood, but the exterior was clean. He turned off the motor and floated to port.

'Roger? Hey, Roger, you in there?' No one answered. 'Yo, Dr Lertz! It's Mick Nash. You on board or what?'

The boat was drifting, unanchored. There were no watercraft within a quarter of a mile. The dam was at a swimmable distance, but it was just a slanting, three-meter rock wall with a lot of empty grassland behind it. If Roger wanted to sneak off and screw his new girlfriend on dry land, there were plenty of trees and sand inlets with privacy on the west side.

So, where'd they go? Were they under right now, lungs filling with water? Mick peered into the depth finder, as if a tiny gray version of Roger might appear on screen, floating sideways with X's in his eyes. Nothing moved. Depth: 36.7 feet. He could dive in, but too much time had passed and the reservoir's visibility was maybe six or eight feet. Come on, boss, what are we doing here? The family is waiting. No time to play Jacques Cousteau. He would make a brief inspection, then bug out.

'Roger, I'm boarding you now,' Mick called, feeling like an idiot. 'So if you're down there fooling around with Bonnie, now would be the time to stop and let me know you're okay.' His voice echoed across the lake. The sun twinkled off the Glastron's high white walls and chrome detailing.

Mick threw both port fenders over, and used a gaff to inch the boats parallel. He cleated a twelve-foot section of pink nautical rope to Roger's stern. Slipped into his deck shoes and climbed from swim platform to swim platform. The craft bobbed gently under his weight. The white leatherette seats were clean, as was the wood floor. A few bottles of Beck's in the cup-holders. A wet towel and Bonnie's bikini top draped over one chair. Well, that explained it. They got drunk and Roger took her into the cabin for a check-up. He should get out of here and leave well enough alone.

Except that his son said there was a struggle. Blood. And while he had caught the ski across the top of his head, Kyle wasn't loopy or prone to exaggeration. He was lucid and if he had a concussion, it was minor. And something here just plain felt wrong. The lake was too calm, the boat too recently abandoned. It didn't feel abandoned at all.

Go on. One peek inside the cabin. You won't be able to sleep tonight unless you know. Something awful happens to Bonnie, how's that going to sit on your conscience?

Mick high-stepped over the bench seat and made the cabin in three long strides. For a moment he stood outside, one hand on the chrome handle, feeling sick to his stomach. *What are you afraid of, champ? A little blood?*

He opened the door. At first he could see nothing. There were too many shadows and the angle was wrong. He stepped back and leaned down, removing his sunglasses. He stared for perhaps three seconds, sorting through shapes and forms set deep in the dark berth. Something was moving in there ... maybe ... no. Like a holographic photo that has been tilted, the illusion escaped him before he was even aware that there had been one.

He frowned, concentrating, and a single white flash strobed his eyes, obliterating the bulkhead, the boat, the lake. Mick recoiled, the light spreading white wings that flapped inside his skull, and it was now, with his eyes scrunched shut and temples throbbing, that they became visible.

Bonnie and Roger were sprawled on the floor and seat cushions, and hanging over the table, limbs severed, skin slashed in dozens of places, the cabin transformed into a slaughterhouse. The floor was drenched, pooled with black and deep maroon that leaked from open wounds, their ears and eyes. Their eyes were black, their faces without expression, as if they had died peacefully a moment before being butchered.

Mick screamed and staggered back, blinking against

49

the sun glare. A wave of cold air funneled out, enveloping him, his head pounding as a rotten stench like dead raccoons on the side of a summer highway broke over him in a thick cottony wave. He covered his mouth and gagged and then he was turning with tears in his eyes, careening to the back of the boat. He could almost feel their hands reaching for him, pulling at his shirt, their fingertips dragging down the back of his legs. His knee slammed into one of the seats and he halted as though he had been slapped.

He gasped, rubbing his eyes as the lightning storm in his brain abated. The air was clean, the day bright. When he forced himself to look back, the cabin was empty. The bodies were gone. The room was clean, free of blood. There were no passengers on or inside the boat. Just the padded bench seats and the small table.

Jesus Christ, *what was that?* What the hell is the matter with you? Okay, you're just suffering a panic attack of some kind. You let your imagination run away. Focus on your family. Tamp it down. Forget about Roger and Bonnie. They're not here . . .

And you have to go home.

He climbed back onto his boat. His hand was on the ignition key when he remembered he had tied off at Roger's stern. He turned back to cast off and climbed over the seats one more time. He kneeled on the Bayliner's platform, reached for the loop of nautical line, and the Glastron's cabin door slammed open. He jerked up, a scream trapped in his throat.

But it was only the breeze. The wooden door was

swaying with a creaking patience. No one was coming for him.

Nerves. The stress. *Enough.*

Mick tossed the line into the Bayliner. He turned and set his right foot on the wet seat back and the siped rubber sole of his boat shoe held for a split second, then shot from under him. He fell forward and his forehead bounced off a corner of fiberglass. He saw stars like static electricity and flopped to his chest and rolled left, groping for a hold on something as he spun backside down. The water caught him like a net, cupped high around him, and filled his startled eyes and open mouth. His head pounded once terribly and the bright blue sky retreated, darkening, funneling into a cone, blue turning to green, green turning to brown, darkening until it was all black, and then he was slack and sinking all the way to the bottom.

10

In the darkness, which was cold and infinite and absolute, he was no longer aware of himself. There was no Mick, no Amy, no children. His house, his business, his problems and all of the memories that had been weaved into the tapestry of his life, disintegrated. He was without thought, without conscience. He was outside of time.

But he was not alone.

'I found you,' a quiet but very deep voice said. 'Don't worry now. You're safe with me. No one's going to hurt you. I promise.'

It was the voice one hears through the wall of a motel room at four in the morning. It sounded like death.

'I only want to help you. We can help each other. There are possibilities, all kinds of possibilities.'

He did not understand and could not answer. A small bulb of emotion throbbed deep within him. He did not want to stay here forever, alone in the black void. The other presence cradled him, raised him up, whispering promises, pledging life.

'I've waited so long for this day. We're going to do beautiful things together.'

Slowly the darkness ebbed.

11

Mick regained consciousness on a dirt road. Weeds brushed his elbows and hot sunlight turned his eyelids into veined paisley curtains. His body was sodden and his mouth was dry.

Amy was above him, wedging a towel under his neck, smoothing his wet hair. He realized had been somewhere else, she had been waiting for him. He tried to recall where he had gone off to, but when his mind probed back in time, it ran into a black wall. He was tired but not in pain. His lips felt sealed. Something bad had happened.

Behind Amy, holding a towel to the top of his head, was Kyle. His son appeared at peace, not at all worried, and there was comfort in this. They had been in an accident together, but it was going to be all right now.

'Did you see that?' Briela was standing further back, chucking rocks into a body of water, and for a moment Mick was sure they were on an island somewhere, on a beach beside the sea. 'Mom, he moved his eyes.'

'I know, honey. I told you he was going to be fine.'

What happened? His memory skipped to this

morning – which seemed to be some other morning, a long time ago – when he had been unrolling the cover from the boat, throwing it onto his driveway. Between then and now there was no yawning chasm, not even a crack in the sidewalk. The splice in time was seamless.

'Welcome back,' Amy said, taking his cold hand. Her face was drawn, angry. 'Don't you dare do that again. You scared the shit out of me, Mick.'

'I don't remember,' he said.

'Nothing?'

'I'm sorry.'

His wife smiled thinly, glancing at the kids. 'You had an accident on the boat. Coach Wisneski rescued you.'

It took a moment for Mick to remember that his former wrestling coach from Boulder High had become, in his retirement, the head administrator of Boulder Reservoir's on-site maintenance staff, a life-guard and a certified member of the lake patrol. Memories of the growling old bastard came back, the way he always lumbered around the beaches and boat house in his orange shorts, the metal whistle carried over from his wrestling days dangling on a cord in front of his bald, baby-smooth chest, his legs and torso the color of fudge. Wisneski was six-four, lean, with vain Tom Petty hair, and he had been forced into early retirement ostensibly for breaking a clipboard over the forehead of one of his athletes, a hardass who couldn't evolve with the times.

'Rescued me,' he said, the words coming out in a papery whistle. 'From what?'

Amy shook her head, unable to say it.

'Dad, you drowned,' Briela said, chipper even in her awe of him. 'You held your breath for the longest time. How did you do that?'

'I don't know, sweetie. But I'm happy to see you.' Mick forced himself to sit up. 'Where's Coach?'

'There was some confusion,' Amy said, meeting his eyes as if trying to impart something she could not explain in front of the children. 'One of his eardrums burst when he was diving for you. When I got here you were conscious and he was in shock. I told the first ambulance to take him. He's older and you were coherent before you blacked out again. Do you want to wait for the second ambulance?'

'No. No, I'm good.' The thought of an ambulance ride, the hospital with its sick and dying, its probing doctors, revolted him. It wasn't just the lapse in health insurance. He did not trust *them*. 'Help me up.'

'But honey—' she started.

'But nothing. We're going home.'

'But what if—'

'I said I'm fine, goddamn it.'

Amy looked away, shaking her head.

As they headed to the truck, his children hugged him and talked over each other in their relief. Mick smiled and put on a brave face, ruffling their hair and telling them he was really okay, but inside he was still recoiling from something, repressing tremors.

He did not understand why, but something about his family did not seem real. He felt duped, tricked by some

56

dark hand of fate. For a moment, as they touched him and kissed his cheeks, he was certain that these people, while bearing every hallmark of his pairing and making, were not his real family at all, but others hiding beneath clever masks of artificial skin.

12

After stopping at the pharmacy to buy a better first-aid kit and patching up Kyle's scalp in the truck (the bleeding had stopped and the cut was much shallower than it had seemed during their panic on the boat), they stopped for take-out subs at Deli Zone. Most of the staff had coffee-break bong smoke wafting from their beards and the order took so long and they were all so hungry, they decided to eat dinner in one of the small booths, chewing in happy silence.

After, Briela was dying to watch a movie she couldn't wait for their Netflix queue to deliver, so they wasted another forty minutes in Blockbuster, loading up on candy and popcorn. Kyle milked his head injury for three action-packed Blu Rays and Amy bought two pints of ice cream. The rules had been suspended. Tonight they could have whatever they wanted.

They got home a little before nine and the kids ran inside. It was difficult to lift himself out of the truck and, after his first attempt, Mick sank back into the seat with a sigh. Amy had driven them home in Blue Thunder. She told him the Lake Patrol had already towed the boat in and would dock it until Mick felt like retrieving it.

Amy opened her door but paused. 'I don't feel good about this.'

'I'm sorry I gave you a scare. If anything changes, I promise I'll ... '

'Go to the doctor?'

He forced a smile. 'It's possible.'

'Don't lie to me, Mick.'

'What do you want me to say? You know our situation.'

Amy leaned her head against the steering wheel. 'Nothing ever changes.'

'It will.'

'When?'

'Soon.'

'That's what you always say, but it just gets worse.'

'I need you to trust me, Amy.'

She stared at him. 'Myra Blaylock. Should I trust you about her too?'

This was out of the blue. 'What's she got to do with anything?'

'You said her name while you were ... half-comatose or unconscious or whatever it is you were doing lying there on the dam, swooning.'

'I have no idea why,' he said, feeling neither guilt nor alarm. 'What else did I say?'

'"I've been looking for you." You said, "I've been looking for you for a long time." And then, "We're going to do beautiful things together" ... several times.'

Mick shook his head. 'I doubt it means anything.'

'You haven't seen her?'

'All that was a long time ago, Amy. You know that.'

Amy nodded, but he knew she was not convinced.

'She has breast cancer,' he added, surprised by his own words. 'Doesn't she?'

'I have no idea. Where did you hear that?'

'I don't remember.'

'Uh-huh. But she didn't tell you herself.'

'No, I swear. I would remember that.'

Amy stared at him as if he had just given her a box of ammunition but taken away the gun.

'Maybe I'm confused,' Mick said. 'Don't worry about it.'

'I think you should walk yourself inside.' She ejected herself from the truck and slammed the door.

Mick exited the Silverado and stood in the night air for a moment, waiting for his equilibrium to falter, but it didn't. He felt sound on the ground. He headed for the back doors off the living room and breakfast area, but paused on the patio. He looked out over his back acreage, to the palazzo looming behind them. He didn't see any cars, but new rows of lights were jutting from the mulch berms to illuminate the driveway like a landing strip. Inside the house, at the back west corner of the first floor, several windows glowed warmly.

They're here.

Higher, up on the terrace, a solitary figure in dark clothes stood watching over him. The figure did not move, but its stance was that of a lookout, a kind of sentinel. Mick knew it was absurd, but he had the strangest

60

feeling that the figure had been there all evening, waiting for him to come home.

It was alone, its size hard to estimate. The lower half was obscured by the parapet, and it was too far away for him to guess at its gender, but he assumed it was a man, the man of the house. Mick watched for a cigarette ember, a task, anything that would suggest a purpose to what appeared to be blatant lurking, but there was nothing of the sort. He was prepared to accept that it was a statue, maybe a gargoyle or knight, but when he started toward his own back door, the figure moved with him. Mick took six or seven steps and the figure moved sideways along the terrace an equal number, though its own steps were not discernible as such, but rather a smooth sliding motion, a shadow pacing in a mirror placed half a football field away.

Mick halted. The figure on the terrace halted.

Mick waved and the figure waved. Not back, but at the same time.

With the same right arm.

'Sonofa . . .' The man was taunting him. He had half a mind to go over there and rattle the gates, introduce himself to this paranoid asshole. He headed back toward his truck and, sure enough, after only two paces the man – had to be a man, some macho peacock strutting his feathers – was matching Mick's every stride.

He stopped. His neighbor stopped.

'Hey, bite me!'

The sentinel did not respond.

'You want something from me?' Mick called out. 'Why

don't you fuck off back into your ugly house!' The sound of his own voice made him giggle.

'Mick?'

He turned. Amy was standing at the open sliding glass door.

'Are you coming in?'

'Be right there.'

'Who were you talking to?'

'This asshole thinks he can ... ' Mick pointed, but the terrace was vacant from end to end. And the house was dark, not a single window was glowing, even though just seconds ago the entire back half of the house seemed to be filled with light. He lowered his arm.

'What is it?'

'Forget it. I'm just tired.'

But he suspected already that this was not true.

13

He watched half a movie with Kyle before nodding off. Amy tugged his ear gently and he rose from the couch. She carried his boat shoes in one hand as they went down the hall, her fingers under the tongues like hooks in fish gills, and he wished she would throw them away. She set them on the carpet, just inside the master's walk-in closet and he suppressed the urge to walk over and shut the door.

Those are the shoes I almost drowned in. I don't ever want to see them again.

He sat on the bed, feeling stoned.

'I did some research online,' Amy said. She had some papers in hand. She was always probing around on WebMD, reading about symptoms and treatments on various internet forums frequented by people who loved playing their own doctor. 'When someone suffocates in a body of warm water,' she told him, glancing at the print-outs, 'damage at the cellular level is swift. The most common danger is hypoxemia, lack of oxygen in the blood, which deprives the brain.'

'My brain is fine,' Mick said.

Amy squished the papers at her side. 'You were out there all alone for at least ten and possibly as long as eighteen minutes, Mick. You could have serious problems we aren't even aware of.'

'You're overreacting. I hit my head, is all.' He pointed to his forehead, which was not bleeding or bruised, only swollen. 'Does this look serious?'

Amy read from her papers again. 'Dizziness, auditory hallucinations, physical tremors, lapses in memory, fatigue, mania, lethargy, foreign smells, loss of motor control, clumsy limbs, rage, depression, mood swings, PTSD, seeing things out of the corner of your eye. This goes on and on. Do not lie to me, Mick.'

'Is that all? I've had most of those symptoms for years.'

'That's supposed to be funny?'

Mick shrugged. The fight went out of them both. His thoughts then leapt to something so alarming, he could not believe Amy hadn't said something earlier.

'What happened to Roger?' He noticed how she stiffened. 'Him and the woman. Something happened to them, didn't it?'

Amy tugged at her sleeves, avoiding his eyes. 'You're remembering this now or it's just a ...' She made a whirling motion with her fingers.

'It's more than a feeling and less than a memory.'

Amy cleared her throat. 'We saw them, earlier in the day. We were tied off at the dock when he stopped by. Typical Roger, in party-guy mode. He was with Bonnie Abrahams, one of his hygienists. No one knows where they went.'

'Was he there on the boat when I went to check on them?'

Amy hesitated before saying, 'No.'

Something was wrong with that. 'You're not sure,' Mick said. 'Because I don't remember. And Wisneski didn't see them when he saw me fall in. Jesus, Amy, do you think I did something to them?'

'Of course not.' But she sounded like she was considering just that.

'Right. Did someone call the police?'

Amy nodded. 'Coach was talking to Terry Fielding before the ambulance took him away. Terry will be by to see you in the next day or two, to get a formal statement.'

Sergeant Terrance Fielding of the Boulder Police Department was a former friend and classmate of Mick's from their CU days. They had circled some of the same parties together as undergrads, and Terry used to stop by the Straw for a beer every couple of weeks before he quit drinking. Mick hadn't seen the small but intense cop in a year or so, and he didn't want to see him now.

'He wants to question me,' Mick said. 'There's going to be an investigation.'

'And you're not going to be a suspect in it,' Amy said. 'Don't start down this road and get yourself all worked up. It won't help, so just don't.'

'Two people are missing and I'm the last person who saw them. Kyle said there was a struggle and I drowned and Roger and Bonnie are probably having their eyeballs eaten out of their heads at the bottom of Boulder

65

Reservoir right now, but I'm not a suspect. That's a relief.'

'*Stop it.*' Amy's voice was shrill, not quite a scream. 'It was an accident.'

'But you don't know that.'

'Why would you want to hurt Roger?' she said.

'Maybe he was doing something to Bonnie. Maybe I saw something I wasn't supposed to see.' He was suddenly very tired of talking to her.

'No one found any blood,' Amy said. 'His boat was clean. Kyle probably saw them fucking and got excited. He plays too many video games and watches those awful movies.' She returned to her post at the doorway, folding her hands together. 'I'm sure Roger will turn up and, when he does, this will all seem ridiculous.'

'You're not sleeping in here,' he surmised.

'I'll be in the guest room. I have a big day tomorrow and you'll sleep better without me tossing and turning beside you.'

He guessed that Myra Blaylock escaping from his lips had something to do with it, but not all of it. Amy was disturbed by the entire episode. He had scared her and was still scaring her, in a number of ways.

'I'll be back at work tomorrow,' he said with more hope than promise.

'Don't worry about it. Just call me if you need anything.'

He eased back on top of the sheets, still dressed in his sweats, and admitted to himself that he was afraid to close his eyes. The thought of *going under* again, in any

66

way, made his stomach queasy, as if he were standing on line to ride the roller coaster at a shoddy amusement park.

Eleven to eighteen minutes, he kept thinking. I might have been clinically dead, gone, out of this world for eleven to eighteen minutes. He didn't know what to make of that, there was no context for it. It was just a new fact, a piece of trivia that had been inserted into his life without his permission, like learning he had a felonious third cousin somewhere in Indiana. He wasn't worried, but he wasn't about to invite it over for a reunion, either.

He watched the enormous window they had cut into the bedroom's south-facing wall, a six-by-four-foot postcard view of the Foothills, half of his backyard and, in the far left corner, somewhere behind the lamp's glare, the mansion that had been constructed.

He thought about the shadowy figure he had seen on the terrace. The house had looked empty yesterday and this morning, before the accident. Why hadn't he asked Amy when they had moved in? Told her about the man he had seen on the terrace? It seemed important in the moment, but he felt foolish, like maybe he was imagining seeing the guy up there.

You're worried there's something wrong with you, that's why. But you're fine. Walking, talking, thinking clearly. Why wouldn't you be fine? You hit your head, fell in the lake, took on too much water. Your hard drive crashed and rebooted, but everything is back online now, running smooth. Leave it at that.

Or maybe there are no new neighbors.

Maybe whatever you saw, it wasn't real. Maybe he's not even a real man.

But that was silly, wasn't it? What else could he be?

There are possibilities. All kinds of possibilities.

Well, there was one very simple way to resolve this non-mystery. Tomorrow morning he would take a short stroll around his backyard and see what he could see. And maybe, if he was feeling up to it – and why shouldn't he feel up to it, he was in fine health – he might just walk up the driveway and knock on the door. Hello, I'm Mick Nash, that's my house right there, my family lives here. I thought it was time we had ourselves a nice neighborly greeting. Stop by for a beer sometime, bring the wife and kids, but in the meantime stop fucking standing there watching my house like a creep, all right? That would be that, and then he would know.

Unless of course no one answered the door, no one had moved in, and the house was empty. How about that, Mickey? What would that mean? It would mean you are seeing things. It would mean you need to tell Amy we have a problem with the machinery, time to explore some unpleasant medical possibilities. Right? Right.

I've been looking for you for a long time.

The sound of the voice echoing in his head lowered his core temperature so abruptly he felt as though he had just stepped out of the shower on a January morning between furnace cycles. For the first time since waking up, the gravity of what had happened – and what had almost happened, the lake pinning him to the wrestling mat of eternity – hit him full force. The very end of Mick Nash was no longer an idea, a distant event. It was right outside his window, stretching itself around his neighborhood, and it wanted to come in, cozy up with him, reach its fingers in and close his eyes for good. He could feel it out there, beckoning. There was no logic to it, but it had something to do with that obstruction sitting in the dark, and the man who had been watching him.

Mick turned away from the window and crawled back onto the bed. He pulled the covers up, balling them in his fists. He closed his eyes and experienced an echo of the unnatural feeling when his family had hugged him, kissed his cheeks. None of it felt real. Today did not feel real. His life did not feel real. He wondered what had really happened out there during the missing eleven to eighteen minutes. He wondered where he had gone and what he had seen.

He wondered what he might have brought back.

14

Mick sat up some hours later, in middle-of-the-night darkness, tangled in the bedding, feeling trapped. He hadn't heard a door creak or window breaking. He simply surfaced from a shallow pool of near-sleep and with primitive certainty *knew*.

Someone was in his cave.

He surveyed the bedroom, catching the scent of stale water and something muddied, like silt at the bottom of a lake. He turned to shake Amy, but her side of the bed was empty; right, she was in the guest room. Outside the big window, the five largest Flatirons stood risen from the earth like stone tents crooked with time.

He got out of bed and found the three-foot scrap of stainless-steel pipe he kept behind the walk-in closet door. The gummy handle wrapped in electrical tape was comforting. Nice heft. You want it, you got it, fuck-o.

He took a few steps toward the open bedroom door and cocked his ear. He imagined the sound of drawers opening and closing, the telltale creak of a floorboard, but nothing came. The scent of fetid water was less potent now, as if it had originated in the bedroom and since moved on.

He stepped into the hall. The carpet was wet in places near the door. He went further, feeling around with his bare toes, spots of it squishing under his feet. He looked up, to the end of the hall where it opened into the foyer and front living room. A large whitish form was standing there, squared off as if blocking the exit, waiting for him. It was a man. Mick's soft insides seemed to swell and shudder, his head began to throb. The man did not move but there was a steady *pat pat pat* on the carpet where water yet dripped from his arms and sodden shorts. Mick couldn't see the face, but something about the man's posture – the set of his shoulders, the slight bend in the left knee, blocky head – was disturbingly familiar.

'Come on, Mickey,' the pale figure said, and though he was still twenty feet away, the dentist's voice carried as if he were whispering in Mick's ear. 'We have to go now.'

The steel pipe slipped from Mick's fist, thudding on the floor. Roger Lertz wasn't supposed to be here. Not in the middle of the night, not in his wet swimsuit.

'What do you want?' Mick said in a dull croak.

'This is your fault. You owe me. If you don't come with me now, it's all going to be very bad for you. For Amy and the kids.'

The bald fact of Roger's presence here at this hour carried Mick forward. Whatever the hell Roger wanted, he did not need to be here, inside the house. Mick had to get him out before Amy woke up and this turned into some kind of scene. He approached slowly on unsteady legs.

Up close, Roger's hair was matted to his skull. The lake smell was on him, and something sweetly decaying with it. His skin was so pallid in the darkness it seemed cold blue. Gaping wounds in the flesh appeared like plaster impressions taken from sharks. Three of his ribs were exposed and his throat was slit, ragged near the ears. His mustache and chin hair were a deep amber, sodden over his plump lips, and the eyes were filmed over with a cotton glazing that reminded Mick of old dogs, searching, caressing Mick with a gentle desperation.

What happened to you? Mick said or thought. He could not hear his own voice beneath the ringing panic in his ears.

The dentist leaned closer. 'My demons caught up with me. Soon yours will too.'

Mick did not know what that meant but he knew Roger was dead, which meant this could not be happening, which meant it was a nightmare and he would wake up any second now. He thought about waking up, willed it to happen, but Roger only stared at him with his filmy eyes and nothing changed.

'You're not supposed to ...' Mick couldn't finish. It was too awful to speak of.

'You're in a lot of trouble,' Roger said and, without waiting for a reply, turned and walked away. Mick followed him across the first floor, out into the backyard.

The air was warm. They moved past the pool and the guest house, toward the row of pine trees at Mick's property border, then down the old Jenkins driveway that had been repaved for the new house. The ground seemed to move under them, the borders of his property retreating in great gaps and strides, and the land beneath his feet changed – fresh asphalt to cracked dry dirt, then grass again, then back to dirt and the rocky prairie of Boulder's open space. Seconds turned to minutes and Mick began to think in terms of acres, a country mile, with no sense of direction.

This is exactly how location and distance get warped in dreams.

The thought was not comforting, but it was enough to allow him to continue.

No owls hooted, no dogs barked. If they crossed near prairie dog holes and darting foxes and bull snakes nestling beneath rotting timber, the fauna called no attention to itself. The land felt barren, cooling as night progressed. There were fields and the occasional tree far off in the distance, but no other houses, and Mick found this to be further proof he was dreaming.

Roger continued with purpose, a man in a wet swimsuit out for a brisk hike, off to some newer, better beach. 'That's it. This is how we do it, Mickey, you see? You know the way.'

Soon they were crossing a dirt lane, moving into a field dotted with thistle and small cacti and rocks, but Mick felt nothing under his feet. The clouds moved overhead, letting moonlight glow at Roger's back. Though they had been outdoors for what seemed like half an hour, the dentist's bathing trunks – pink and chocolate in a flower motif – were still dripping, the water running off the hems in rivulets that coursed down his legs, pasting the hair to his hamstrings in dark whorls.

Mick felt a sadness and pity for the man. All at once he felt guilty for severing the friendship in a cowardly way, by cool temper and years of neglected invitations to parties, blatant shunning in public places. By all accounts, the man had spiraled into addiction and familial despair, and all through it Mick had shed not one ounce of empathy for him. A real friend would have told Roger to his face that he was out of control, behaving like an asshole, and that he needed to get his shit together for his own health and for the sake of his family.

'I'm sorry, Roger,' Mick said. They should have reached Boulder Municipal Airport by now, but he saw no gliders or the fence or the runway. Apparently there were entire pockets of land back here that Mick had driven by a thousand times growing up but never explored. He felt like crying. 'I'm so sorry.'

'Sorry?' Roger said without slowing or looking back. 'What for?'

'I should have been there. I could have done something for you.'

'There's nothing you could have done for me,' the dentist said. 'What do you think you could have done?'

'I should have been kinder to you on the lake, and the other times.'

'Maybe,' Roger said. 'But in your own way, you did save me. I'm free of all my addictions. Now it's my turn to help you.'

Mick was frightened beyond his adult understanding of fear. Something terrible was out here. Roger was leading him to some awful intersection of knowledge and possibility, a place where the ground opened up and showed you the eventual, final future, a place where worms fed on dead prairie dogs and dried-up birds and gray-muzzled raccoons who died without anyone to comment on their departing souls, where there were no pretty flowers or fond memories, only the absorption of the decaying carcass into soil.

'Where are we? Roger?'

The dentist did not respond. Mick hurried, head down for a while, and when he looked up again Roger was standing against a white wall that extended hundreds of feet in either direction. It was his new neighbor's security wall, and the house stood lightless on the other side. What should have been a walk of only three or four minutes and covered less than an eighth of a mile had taken an hour or more. The house seemed to tilt toward him, leaning like a parallelogram, a shadow of itself.

My demons caught up with me. Soon yours will too.

'Who are they?' Mick said.

'I don't know,' Roger said, and in the dark his eyes were soft, almost childlike. 'But they are very interested in you and your family. They have been searching for a long time and now they are here. They want to be your friends, but they aren't anybody's friends. They will do anything to get what they want. They use other people, make them do horrible things.'

'They did this to you,' Mick said.

'What happened to me has already happened,' Roger said, his tone suggesting that he did not like to be reminded of his condition. 'It is no longer important. This is about you.'

'I don't understand. None of this makes any sense.'

'True, but it's happening. They found you, Mick. If you're smart, you'll get away, move, take your family some place far from here and hope they lose interest.'

'I can't leave,' Mick said. 'This is our home. The restaurant . . .'

The dentist took what was supposed to be a deep breath, his face creasing with sadness. 'Then there's only one other option for you.'

'What?' But he did not really want the answer.

'Kill them. Kill them in their beds, destroy them, before they come for you.'

'This isn't real,' Mick said. 'I can't accept it.'

Roger shook his head slowly. 'It's survival, Mick. If you don't put an end to them, they will infiltrate your lives and break you down and your family will spend the rest of your days in a living hell. I promise.'

Roger turned and trailed his fingers along the rough stucco. Mick watched him shamble along the length of it and turn the corner, disappearing on the south side.

'Roger?'

The dentist did not answer. Mick walked to the

corner and peered around, but the field was empty. Roger was gone.

Mick stood alone in the darkness, a hundred questions in his mind. What was he supposed to do now? He turned in a circle and saw only deep black rolling land in all directions – except for this white wall. He couldn't see his own house, which was supposed to be just a couple of acres behind him. He made his best guess and started walking in that direction, feet cold, everything cold, shivering.

When he had gone only half a dozen paces, a sound brought him to a halt. Low voices. Urgent mumbling, and then whining. A girl was whimpering, on the edge of hysteria, and someone older was talking to her, whispering, telling her to stay quiet.

Mick turned and stared at the wall, the large house looming behind it. The noises were coming from the other side of the fence. The girl was hiccupping with grief, keening softly. *Briela*.

His daughter was over there, on the other side.

'Daddy?' she said. 'I'm scared. I got lost and I can't find my way back home. Please, I just want to come back. I promise I will be good—'

Briela gasped and was silenced.

Mick ran toward the wall and jumped, reaching over the top and pulling himself up as his feet paddled against the rough surface. He was halfway up when his feet slipped and his knees slammed into the stucco grain, scraping skin there and on his elbows as he dragged himself upward. He got his hips over the flat top, and rolled, twisting as he fell down into the yard. He landed on his feet and staggered to one side, catching himself with one hand, his skinned knees burning with rash.

'Briela? Daddy's here, sweetie—'

But she wasn't near the fence, not in either direction, and the rest of the yard was one great field of grass that seemed to be expanding as he surveyed it. He searched the house's many windows for his daughter, or whoever had her, but they were all dark. The house grew taller, enlarged, rearing back as if tilting on high stilts. The sight of it sent a spasm of vertigo through him and he groped for something to hold onto. Beneath him the ground shifted and for a moment he seemed to totter on the edge of the world.

Where there should have been a yard of grass, a patio, or even a foundation, now there was nothing but a giant gaping hole, a drop-off that went on for hundreds of feet, a thousand, became bottomless. Mick swayed above it, feeling like a man on a balance beam. It seemed infinite, containing nothing, but the longer he stared, the more he could see. It wasn't bottomless. The bottom was liquid, a mirror disc of silver and black reflecting the night sky.

Laid out on this cold surface as if floating were three white figures, one larger than the other two. From this distance they looked like piano keys, flat white bars with thinner bars of silver-black in between. But they were shifting, moving, changing in some way, and soon he realized they were rising, coming up to meet him.

The floor of the well rose like an elevator in a stone shaft and a cold draft blew up into his face, his hair. An awful butterfly sensation wound through his stomach and he couldn't breathe. The surface wasn't rising, he understood at last. He was falling. The cold wind sailed around him, and the squirming figures beneath him enlarged, magnified, resolved.

They were his family members, white as Roger's back had been, naked and dead. Their eyes were fleshed over and their mouths were open in the manner of infants mewling in the newborn wing of a hospital. But if that soft warmth was their beginning, this was their end. He knew they were dead, even as they writhed in agony, their bodies animated by unholy energies whose purpose was pure pain and endless chaos and the sucking of human souls.

Amy. Kyle. Briela.

They were suffering in a purgatory of lifelessness outside of time and he fell to meet them, knowing it was too late, he had been tricked, and they had fallen for his mistakes. His failures, his weakness, his sins. It was too late to save them, or himself. Mick screamed in everlasting despair as he slammed into the blackness.

15

Mick dozed in and out of the morning light, too comfortable to get up for another hour, until his lower back was stiff and throbbing. He forced himself to rise and made his way to the shower.

Stepping under the rain spout's hot spray, he felt strangely rested and upbeat, ready to move on from the disaster that was yesterday. He knew he was supposed to take it easy and avoid stress, Dr Amy's orders, but he thought he would whittle away the morning until she left for school, then sneak by the restaurant for an hour or so, just to make sure everything was functioning smoothly.

The hot water beat against his forehead, the steam opening his sinuses, loosening his shoulders. He was in less than a minute when his knees began to sting and spots around his elbows began to burn. He reached for the lever to adjust the temperature and froze. His mouth fell open in sigh of stunned remembrance. He rotated his left arm so that he could see his elbow.

The scrape was the diameter of a baseball, with a comet streak of red up his tricep. His knees were also raw, one of them bleeding a pink trail down his shin, across the pebbled shower floor.

Sleepwalking, it had to be, and yet Mick had never been a sleepwalker, not even as a child. He exited the shower and wrapped a towel around his waist, then walked the length of the hall, flicking on the lights to inspect the carpet.

A single wet footprint waited for him outside his bedroom door. The blot of it had faded but was still visible in the low wool blend. He touched it with his hand. The dark spot was moist, if not wet. He stood and held his naked size ten over it, heel and toes hovering less than two inches above the gray outline. His foot was at least two sizes too small. This print belonged to a man with a size twelve, maybe a thirteen. Someone heavy, solid, maybe six-two or six-three.

Kill them. Kill them in their beds, destroy them, before they come for you.

Of course the water might have soaked in and spread, making the print appear larger than the foot that had made it. There were no other prints in the bedroom or hall. If Roger had actually been here, there would be more of them, a trail. Mick might very well have made this print less than a minute ago, when he was inspecting the hall.

But then again, summers in Colorado were known to be very dry. Nights when Mick came home from work feeling hot and filmy, he often showered before bed, and then again in the morning, and the same towel would be nearly dry after hanging on the rack for only eight or nine hours. So it was impossible to say when this print had been made, and a person could go crazy thinking about such unprovable details. The worst nightmare you've ever had doesn't make it more than a nightmare. The real world does not allow for things like he had experienced last night. Whatever had happened to the dentist, Roger and his warnings were the product of Mick's traumatized subconscious, his mind's way of working through the stress of his drowning accident.

Such were the reassurances Mick supplied for himself as he dressed for work, pulling his jeans over his bandaged knees.

PART TWO

Close Encounters of the Neighborly Kind

An empty belly hears nobody.

ENGLISH PROVERB

16

Amy was crossing town on the Foothills Parkway in her Passat wagon when she saw the white hood in her side mirror and realized Jason Wells and Eric Pritchard were following her home from school. Half a mile ahead, the stoplight at Valmont turned red. The Honda gained as she let off the gas. If she coasted a while, maybe the light would change and she could speed up again without having to stop and look at them. What more did they want? Hadn't they done enough? She tried to pretend it was a coincidence, then flushed with shame, then felt like crying, but refused to give them the satisfaction. And how far were they going to take this? Were they going to follow her all the way home? If so, then what?

The light turned green. She pushed the Passat up to sixty and zoomed through the intersection. The Honda fell off a bit, but within half a mile had returned, racing up on her ass and swerving into the left lane. She tried to get a look at them as the car looped around her, but the windows were not so much tinted as opaqued. She dropped the Passat down to fifty and the Honda took the lead. This Civic had the same giant gray louver fin. It was them, no question. She gripped the wheel and slowed to forty as the Honda left her far behind.

They aren't really dangerous, she told herself. Get a hold of yourself. We've got too much to do to spend the rest of the day in a funk. She listened to her voicemail – Lowry, the coordinator from This Takes the Cake, about the design Amy had submitted. Deep Sea Wonderland in blue chocolate with white fudge frosting, preliminary bid: $320. It would be ready in time for the party, but Lowry had a few questions about the creatures and logistics. Did she want sea lions or walruses? In plastic figurines or sculpted frosting? I dunno, Lowry. I just don't know.

She merged with the Diagonal Highway tiredly, the long summer afternoon as oppressive as her To-Do list. She had yet to decide about the balloons, go to the party store for cups and napkins, follow up on the email chain of questions flowing back from the e-card reminders she had blasted out, and hit Grand Rabbits for more plush take-homes. Plus the groceries, but it was too early for that, the big day still ten days away.

Cancel the party, a voice inside her warned. It was getting out of control before Mick's accident. Now you have to worry about him too. It's not too late.

But it *was* too late. Things had been set in motion. The RSVPs were trickling in and if they scaled down now, it would only worry Briela about her father and the strength of the family in general.

She reached Jay Road, turned right, and half a mile later her mailbox came into view. She turned into the long driveway and parked in front of the garage on the house's east side. She sat motionless as the A/C bled out and the heat baked in.

Go on, look again. Confront it, deal with it.

She looked in the rearview mirror and the vicious graffiti on the wagon's rear window jangled back at her in reverse, horror-movie-style red letters.

STIT GOHTRAW

She had left the high school annex today in the same mood as she had left the first three sessions: in a hurry, feeling dirty, wishing she had taken a part-time job as a cashier at Best Buy, anything but this. She had not looked at any of the students milling around in the parking lot-cum-smoking area. She could not understand why they lingered when they resented having to be there for summer school in the first place, and she couldn't bear another glimpse into their bitter, listless, pimply faces. She had kept her eyes on the ground until the Passat's Mojave metallic rear end entered her field of vision, looked up, and it hit her like a thrown cup of urine.

WARTHOG TITS

She knew immediately that Eric Pritchard and Jason Wells were the culprits. The skinny, smoke-reeking boys had been acting up the entire three hours of the morning session. When she finally snapped at them, after fifteen or so polite reminders to *please pay attention*, they had scowled at her from the back of the classroom and whispered conspiratorially.

People's evidence number two: when she twirled, scanning the parking lot to see if anyone had noticed it yet – her first instinct was to avoid embarrassment, not ascertain the perpetrator – they were already laughing. Standing just six spaces away, leaning against Eric's hopped-up Honda (with its giant gray louver fin), smoldering Marlboros in hand, feasting on her reaction. Identified, they covered their mouths and fell into each other, guffawing, 'Aw, damn!' and 'Ouch!' But they did not run away or deny what they had done.

They hovered at a safe distance as she scrubbed the glass furiously, but the wad of purse Kleenex failed to do so much as smudge the letters. They had used permanent markers, and there lay the smoking gun. She'd seen them in the halls last week, tagging lockers with their artless signs and calling cards. By then it was unbearable. Going back inside to track down Dick Humphries, the custodian, was out of the question. She'd be here another hour, and Dick'd probably enjoy the dirty insult almost as much as Eric and Jason were enjoying it now.

As their laughter reached its crescendo and began to fade into a morbid curiosity about what she was going to do next, Amy wanted to march over and remove the cigarettes from their mouths and plant the coals in their eyeballs. Instead she gasped like the schoolmarm she was becoming, chirped the power locks, and sped away.

The saddest part was that she knew she wouldn't do anything about it. She could sit them for detention, but she wasn't getting paid enough to spend her summer afternoons making them read *Great Expectations*, and she doubted they could read. She had only the next four weeks to get through, eight more sessions, and then Eric Pritchard and Jason Wells would be free to make their disgusting jack-off faces at their teachers at Boulder High or September School, or at the guards at the Boulder County Jail – the eventual if not next stop on their descent.

But it would only get worse as the weeks wore on. She had no experience with average high-school students, let alone the kind of metal shop 'n' meth miscreants that were her charges this summer. She had taught grades three, four, and five, and taught them well, for eleven years. But it had been a bad (couple of) year(s) for the restaurant.

To pick up some of the slack, Amy had used her background in human resources to wrangle her way into teaching Workplace Economics, the vocational technical program created to reward high-school kids who were also holding down jobs of at least twenty hours per week, and who were – due to their financial demands, sloppy grades, difficult home environment, or lack of discipline – at risk of not graduating. Successful completion of WorkEcon earned the kids fifteen credits, the equivalent of three regular semester classes; for Amy, an extra fifty-five hundred before taxes and health insurance. Her net take-home would be less than one mortgage payment. But it was something at a time when every little bit helped.

WorkEcon was supposed to be a snooze, for her and the kids. And for the first week, it was. But that was before Ronny Haskovitz got expelled for smoking pot in the back row, before Lisa Klein punched Angela Valdez in the possibly pregnant belly, and before Amy herself became

WARTHOG TITS

She was a coward, she knew. She would pass Eric and Jason right on out of WorkEcon with a C-, just so she didn't have to face the bureaucratic wrath of Jeff Wheatley, the program's supervisor and most ardent champion, whose criteria for WE success was summed up in the motto, 'Twelve summer days earns a triple A.' So long as the students attended and didn't kill anybody, she was expected to pass them. After all, some of these kids were supporting their families.

But breadwinners or not, Eric Pritchard and Jason Wells frightened her. They were tall. They stank. They looked at her with rapist's eyes. She feared that if she turned them in for this bit of graffiti, next week it would be her tires slashed, a broken windshield, a blouse-ripping assault, her face pressed to the chalkboard.

She hated herself for allowing their juvenile insult to gain traction in the ruts of her self-esteem. But she couldn't ignore the fact that this was, in essence, what she was to them. The randy, jack-booted, ADD-afflicted teen boys – *men*, when you accepted the reality of their facial hair – in her class did not see her as a milf or slut or hotbox or some other insulting but at least suggestively attractive being. To them she was porcine. A tusked pig. A beast with eight hairy gray teats.

Whatever happened to the harmless nicknames of yore? It seemed like only yesterday her wily fifth-grader Tyler Sampson had admiringly referred to her as Muggle Nips. She'd sent him to the principal's office, of course (and vowed to start wearing thicker bras), but she'd at least been able to laugh at that one over a glass of wine. No matter how you looked at it, there was no silver lining in warthog tits.

Of course it wasn't just the awful insult. Or the vandalism of her car. It was the decision to take on a class she was not prepared for. It was her vivid nightmares of becoming an Obese American. It was the pressure of this job, how frighteningly important the extra income had become. In short, Eric and Jason's real crime was not defacing her window with the red tip of their inhalants. It was that they had successfully boiled down everything that was wrong in her life to two words.

'Warthog tits! Warthog tits!' a voice squealed behind her, giggling with delight.

Amy looked up to find Briela standing behind the car with Ingrid, their family assistant, pointing at the obscenity.

'Briela, noooo,' Ingrid said, pushing B toward the house. They must have just gotten off the 205, at the bus stop across Jay Road. 'Don't say that. Go inside while I talk to your mom, please.'

Briela ran by as Amy powered down the window, dabbing her eyes.

'Amy? You okay?' Ingrid said.

'Fine, I'm fine.'

'What happened to your car?'

The rags and turpentine would have to wait. 'Just another fun day at Vo-Tech. How are you? You two have a good afternoon?'

'We're all right. Now. Do you have a minute?'

Amy cringed, preparing for more bad news.

17

Trouble follows this family around like Pigpen's dirt cloud, Ingrid Gustafson thought. Thank effing God I'm outta here in August.

Ingrid had graduated from Colorado State University two years ago, her red-and-black cowboy boots a proud remnant of her aggie heritage. Her parents were good old-fashioned non-organic farmers, but the rest of their daughter, above the boots, was all Boulder. She favored hippie skirts and her straight black hair fell to her waist, swishing around the armory of bracelets and rings adorning her thin limbs.

She had been the Nash family assistant – which let's face it really meant glorified maid and abused babysitter – for two years and had somehow given them the impression she would do just about anything for eleven bucks an hour: make lunch, fold laundry, schlepp B to the zoo, and make that ridiculous salad every day to save Amy the headache that was chopping vegetables. Funny how most of that salad was still sitting in the fridge the next morning. The Nash compost heap was a regular arugula and balsamic Bugs Bunny all-you-can-eat buffet.

If she had one trump card up her sleeve at all times, it was that she was great with Briela. Amy would be lost without her and both of them knew it. Briela's teachers had been hinting at something serious near the end of the last term – space cadet answers on her assignments, eye-bulging David Banner tantrums, shoelaces tied in compulsive knots – and summer break had not diffused the situation. She'd had another blowout two weeks ago, when Amy refused to let her stay up till midnight to watch the rest of the *Witches Lane* marathon on AMC. And then the movie theater incident last week, when B got ejected from the multiplex for licorice-whipping tykes in the next row, the new Miley feature making their prodigal go Keds-stomping *cuh-ray-zay*. Ingrid had almost thrown in the towel then, but here she was.

Amy was rinsing her commuter mug in the kitchen sink. She stared out the window and a look of bemused charm erased the folds of her forehead.

'Oh, look, Ing! Did you see this? The new people are settling in.'

Ingrid looked over Amy's shoulder and saw the two Range Rovers, one black, the other olive green, parked in the Eyesore's roundabout. 'Those were delivered this morning. Like, seriously? People are still buying Range Rovers? It's like take-out destruction.'

Amy whirled on her. 'Have you seen them? The people?'

'Nope.'

'We're all dying of curiosity. That house must have cost three, four million dollars. And Melanie, you remember my friend, the runner?' Ingrid nodded. 'She knows Brian over at Kingdom Realty and he said no one can dig up a thing on them. No brokers, no titles, no deeds, no paperwork whatsoever. And the permits, in this town? They cut into open space, which requires some kind of serious leverage with the city council, but no one's talking. It's like something out of East Hampton.'

'Right.' Ingrid blew air up at her bangs. 'Briela had a little problem at the ice-cream shop today.'

Amy turned from the window and mustered concern. 'Right, yes, go ahead.'

'And before I forget, do you think it would be okay if I got a paycheck?'

Amy mustered more concern, with a side order of alarm. 'How long has it been?'

'Five weeks.'

'*Five*? I thought Mick was paying you.'

Ingrid shrugged. 'He told me to ask you.'

Amy blushed. 'I'm so sorry.'

'It's no big deal.'

'It is, though. And where is Mick, anyway? I didn't see his truck.'

Ingrid braced herself. 'I'm not supposed to say.'

Amy's eyes widened. 'He did not go to work.'

'He sort of snuck out the back.'

Briela came running in as if a stagehand had shoved her through a door. 'I didn't do anything! It's not my fault!'

'You be *quiet*,' Amy said, and Briela shut her mouth,

then ducked out of the kitchen. Amy looked back to Ingrid. 'All right, so?'

'We were getting ice cream at Glacier. She said there was a boy making faces at her through the window, and then she sort of lost it. I don't think anyone was hurt, but. To tell you the truth, the whole thing scared me. I think she's very angry about something. All that stuff last spring, it kind of feels like it's starting up again.'

'I was sleeping!' Briela reappeared. 'I fell asleep and he scared me!'

'Enough! You take a time-out, now.' Amy pointed. Briela ran down the hall.

'That's the other thing,' Ingrid said. 'She said the same thing that time in the movie theater, but it's not sleep. It's more like she just spaces out, you know?'

'It used to be called daydreaming. Now it's ADD-HD-LMNOP – who can even keep track of these acronyms? Are you okay? This must be wearing you out.'

Gee, ya think? 'I'm fine but, Amy, the thing is, there wasn't any boy. I looked, and there weren't any boys within a hundred feet of that shop. I asked her to describe him. She didn't sound like she was making it up, but the details didn't really make sense. She said he was pale, with fuzzy hair, and he had a long face, like a wolf-boy. With huge teeth.'

After a disquieting gap, Amy said, 'A wolf-boy. That's, uhm, disturbing. I guess I better make an appointment with her pediatrician.'

Ingrid accepted her check. 'That might be a good idea.'

She'd suggested this very thing three or four times, but they never listened to her. It wasn't her place to push, but at a certain point neglect becomes a form of child abuse. They must be in worse financial trouble than she ever suspected.

18

The late afternoon sun beamed in low on the boy's face, leaving him pliable and slightly high on the park bench. He was pretending he was blind, cataloguing sounds: high heels clopping along worn bricks like an anxious pony; the shaggy messiah dude with the bone necklace hunched over his hammered dulcimer, lost in a sonic desert without structure or destination; a group of chattering ladies, their shopping bags paper-rattling against each other. Nearer, in an almost symphonic spurt, an avalanche of flavored popcorn tinkled into a tin barrel, a Labrador panted, and the waxy rubber buzz of skateboard wheels swerved and faded away. The air smelled of waffle cones and incense and Kyle Nash's childhood.

It was here on the Pearl Street Mall, at age nine, he saw his first live topless woman, a pagan sprite in a circle of other brown, barefooted creatures in tie-dye skirts and rope bracelets, dancing an ancient footbag to one another. Beaded blonde braids clicked off her darkened shoulders and wet thickets of black hair gleamed under her arms. The breasts were round and smallish, the nipples changing shape while she laughed. She was something from the myths, and no one seemed to care.

Maybe that's why they kept coming back, he and his friends. You never knew what you would see, what fun you might chance into.

'Is he sleeping?' a bored voice called. 'Hey, nut-chugger, wake up.'

Kyle raised his head and blinked, realizing Lucas and Will were talking to him. They were slouched on the animal sculptures like overgrown toddlers; Lucas on the white rabbit, Will leaning against the brassy frog. They were staring at Kyle as if he had done something wrong again.

'What?'

'Do you need a nap?' Lucas was lean, his muscles tight under his pale skin, and his red hair was cut low for the summer. He had three earrings and was always fondling himself, rubbing his pecs or diving a hand under his shorts.

Kyle shrugged. 'Where'd Ben go?'

'He's in 'Bo's,' the taller boy said. Will was six-three but stooped, a sapling in need of cables to keep him upright. His eyes were dark and his pajama bottoms hung loose around his hips as if he'd just gotten out of the hospital.

'We just ate,' Kyle said, still full of the tacos they had scarfed at Juanita's.

'Yeah, well, maybe he's still hungry,' Lucas sneered.

'Hungry for cock,' Will said. They each shot Kyle a look and laughed.

Kyle pretended to laugh, but this was becoming more difficult as summer wore on. Everything that came out of Ben, Will and Lucas's mouths these days was about one of four things: cock, vadge, weed, and dooty. Who had the biggest, who was gonna put his finger in some tonight, where they could score more, and who had taken the grossest one that day (or, even better, where the all-time greatest place to take one would be; Taylor Rutledge's pool was this week's consensus). Kyle tried to contribute, but it always sounded false and their suspicion of him seemed to be growing. Like they were trying to decide how much longer they could hang with a kid who wasn't convinced the world revolved around these four elements.

'I'm hungry for some of *that*,' Lucas said.

Kyle and Will turned to see a girl of perhaps thirteen walking with her mother. They were high-end prep, Boulder Country Club tennis kittens in plimsolls and pink skirts, the girl a near clone of her mother.

'Dude, you are fucking warped,' Will said.

'She's gonna be a stone-cold fox.' The conviction in Lucas's voice made Kyle feel sick. 'In, like, a year.'

And Kyle thought, Now Will will say something evil about the mom.

'Hell with the girl,' Will said. 'I'd hit the mamma-san.'

'Both. At the same time,' Lucas said. 'That would be the trifecta.'

'Trifecta means three of something,' Kyle said, but Lucas ignored it.

'I like mine mature,' Will said. 'Are you kiddin' me? Moms know how to tug it.'

100

'You guys are fuckin' idiots,' Kyle said. Any mention of moms made him think of his mom, and he didn't understand how anyone could think about sex in such terms.

The fourth member of their entourage strutted out of Abo's like he had just gotten laid and purchased a really kind bag of grass, though he had done neither. He was dressed like a middle-class panhandler from the Bay Area: perforated surf shirt, skate shorts, neck bandana and old school Dunk lows, the ensemble as carefully coordinated as a prom dress. He was holding a slice of cheese pizza above his head, letting the point drip hot oil onto his tongue. He craned his neck and leapt, teasing himself with his own treat, and bumped into a woman walking with her boyfriend or husband.

The couple gave him a look, but Ben didn't even acknowledge them. The slice scalded him and he made a yowling noise as he spit the gob of mozzarella onto the mall. It was classic Ben and of course Will and Lucas found it hilarious.

'That's disgusting,' the woman said. She was pretty in a plain way, Kyle thought, with a kind of long face and frail, pointy frame.

'Watch your step, dickhead,' the guy added. He was sorta buff, but it was going soft, like he had stopped working out once he hit his twenties.

Ben halted, snapping to attention. 'Sorry! Did you want a bite of my pizza pie, baby girl?'

The woman scoffed and kept walking up the mall.

'Hey!' The man stopped and turned. There was

101

something sad and defeated in his eyes, in the puffy face, as if he expected to step in dogshit every time he went out the front door. 'Knock it off, all right?'

'Sorry, man,' Ben said. 'Accident. It's cool. We're cool.'

The guy shot the others a look, then turned and rejoined his girlfriend.

Kyle thought, Jesus, that was close. Fucking Ben.

Ben waited until their backs were turned before he threw the slice. It folded through the air like a sheet of paper and slapped against the bare skin between her shoulder blades. Held for a moment. Then unglued and left a trail of sauce as it slid to the promenade. The woman tensed and began to hiss.

Will and Lucas burst into raucous laughter. Kyle bolted up from the park bench and the boyfriend whirled and charged at Ben in five big strides, face purpling.

'Gonna knock your fucking head off!'

They scattered, the guy's hand missing the collar of Ben's shirt by about two inches. The mall became a tunneled blur as Kyle passed the Russian Tea Room, the Art Mart, Mountain Sun Brewery, and weaved through the bus-stop shelter at the mall's east end, watching the backs of his friends as they zigzagged madly, hurdling planters and fleeing around the corner.

Behind them the woman was yelling. 'Doug, no, stop! Doug! You're on parole! Pleeeeease!'

The word 'parole' made Kyle's hair stand up. He could hear 'Doug' closing behind him, a man's breathing, labored and heavy as a bull's, and Kyle thought, Oh, holy

102

fuck, if he catches one of us, he isn't gonna chew us out or call our parents. He's really going to beat the ever-loving shit out of all of us. He's praying for the chance, can fucking taste the beating he's going to throw down and –

'Dead, ya fucking dead,' the guy chanted. 'DEAD!'

Flying past the First Presbyterian Church, doubling back toward the post office, it finally dawned on Kyle: they weren't kids any more. The world was no longer their playground. It had become an angry place, full of pleasant-faced people waiting to explode. He'd seen them on the news, in school, in his dad's bar. But he'd never been the target, until now. Sneakers slapping the sidewalk, Kyle understood at a fundamental level that the next Mercedes they pelted with a few green apples would not dislodge a finger-wagging old coot who'd say, 'Why, you little rapscallions, shame on you!' They had crossed a barrier. From now on, all the drivers and life-guards and mailbox owners would just as likely brandish a tire iron, a baseball bat, a gun.

Kyle cut across Canyon Boulevard's four lanes of traffic. Up ahead, the guys were jogging into Central Park, already slowing to a confident trot. He chanced a look back. Doug had been no match for kids who had spent most of the school year and every day this summer pushing skateboards five or six miles across town, walking another three or four miles to some party or another at night. They were greyhounds, high on energy drinks and candy and the fumes of their own adolescence. They dispersed into downtown Boulder's alleyways and tree-lined bike paths like terrorists retreating into the mountains of Afghanistan.

Kyle was shocked to realize it had all lasted less than a minute, and now they were free again. Lucas cut through the grass at Canyon Park, the others coming upon the bandshell, hooting and slapping each other on the backs. From a distance they looked older, bigger. Unlike Ben's sad little goatee, Will had a real beard going, and with his height you could see how he might be mistaken for eighteen or twenty instead of fifteen. Kyle didn't feel the way his friends looked, and he had the feeling maybe the others wouldn't have minded if he got caught while they escaped.

'Close one, huh, Nash?' Lucas said, wiggling his eyebrows.

Kyle only shook his head in disgust.

'I could have taken him,' Ben said, but Kyle could see he was rattled. His eyes were still jittery, a fresh layer of sweat over his pimples.

'Yeah, right,' Kyle said. 'That guy would have caved your head in, Ben. He was out of his mind. Why you gotta do shit like that, man?'

Ben scowled. 'Because I feel like it, faggot.'

'What time is that thing at Shaheen's house tomorrow night?' Lucas asked, bending to retie his shoes.

'"Because I feel like it, faggot,"' Kyle echoed. 'That's brilliant, Ben. You're an asshole, you know that?'

Ben shoved Kyle and Will walked between them. 'Cut the shit, guys.'

'Do you think he's gonna have any booze?' Lucas

continued. 'I want like six Captain and Cokes. I'm gonna get red-assed. That's what my dad calls it. What do you think about that, Nash? You ready to get red-assed?'

Kyle shrugged, hoping to appear coolly detached. Ever since spring break, when he'd drunk eleven shots of peach Schnapps and vomited all over Ben's dad's walk-in closet, alcohol made his mouth water for the wrong reasons. Maybe he was allergic to the stuff. When he woke up after that little swing dance with the sauce, he had black magic marker drawings all over his face. One of them – he never found out which – had drawn a big veined penis aimed at the corner of his mouth and a set of hairy balls on his chin. The drawing made him feel worse than the hangover, and suddenly going to Shaheen's party seemed like more trouble than it could possibly be worth.

'Who's gonna be there?' Kyle said.

This caused Will to perk up. 'Why, you finally gonna try for some wool, Nash?'

'He likes Michelle Harper,' Lucas said. 'Talk about wool. That girl's got a patch like Bigfoot.'

'Yeah, like you know,' Kyle said. Though now that he thought about it, Michelle *did* have dark hair, and her arms *were* a bit fuzzier than the other girls'. Kyle had never gotten further than frenching Rachel Simms last summer (and that was for all of about twenty seconds, because dumbass Lucas was spying on them and Rachel got spooked), so he was in no position to be picky. But the thought of Lucas being with Michelle Harper, in any way, ruined something.

105

'Strong stable,' Lucas said. 'My girls be willin' and able.'

'Let's hit the Cornucopia,' Will said. 'If that Daryl guy's working, he'll sell me some forties.'

The others fell into a heated discussion about beer-purchasing strategies, but Kyle tuned them out. Standing about twenty yards down the bike path, at the edge of the tree line on the north bank of Boulder Creek, was a girl, maybe *the* girl, the most beautiful he had ever seen.

19

She was maybe a year or two older than him, sixteen or seventeen, but in another way newly born, as if fallen from the sky fully formed. Her long brown hair was plainly styled or not styled at all, but radiant against her creamy skin. Dressed in white sneakers, a simple denim mini-skirt, and a red T-shirt, she was standing in profile, facing the creek. She wasn't flashy or vamping, she just seemed the very model of unblemished, wholesome girl.

He felt guilty for staring, but it didn't seem to bother her. She studied him a moment and turned, letting him look. She wore a red T-shirt featuring a strange silk screen, a kind of negative space of a woman with dark flowing hair, white nurse's cap and surgical mask. The mask spelled something in distorted letters, but Kyle couldn't read the message. Her lips moved as if she were whispering, and then she stepped out of her white sneakers one at a time. She set her bare feet down as if she had never walked on grass, savoring the texture of moist blades and cool soil. She was still smiling as she picked up her shoes and walked down the bank into Boulder Creek.

'Nash, you coming?' Ben said.

He imagined touching her leg, just the back of her calf, oh so delicately, and maybe that perfect milk chocolate hair . . .

'Nash! Yo, assface!'

Kyle turned, blinking. 'What?'

'I need five bucks for a High Life,' Ben said.

'You just bought a slice of pizza.' *And your parents have more money than mine.* 'What's the matter with you?'

'Nah, I stole that shit. I'm tapped. Come on, help a brother out.'

Kyle looked back toward the creek. The girl wasn't in the small section of burbling water that he could see, or on the banks, or the bike path. What the hell? She couldn't have gone far. Boulder Creek was only a few feet deep here, not really any kind of swimming hole. This was cruel, her sudden disappearance from his life.

He walked up to the moist bank. The soil at the water's edge was matted with dead grass raked smooth by the current. The water was clear, the stream bed pebbles golden in patches of sunlight filtering through the trees. A downed branch of green leaves fluttered in the small rapids. A thick stick, rubbed smooth of its bark, was trapped in the eddy beneath the branch, along with a stray soda can bleached pink.

But there was no girl.

All at once he was standing in a pocket of cold, almost frigid air. The sun glinted off the water and his insides turned liquid. Kyle's teeth clacked and he stepped back, heart tripping as a kind of déjà vu of the body told him he had been here before and something bad had happened. He stepped back on weak legs, slipped and almost fell on the moist grass.

He reset his feet, turned – and almost walked into the pudgy guy who had crept up behind him. Kyle jolted and tried to step back, but the guy reached out with the speed of a boxer and balled Kyle's T-shirt in his fist.

'I didn't do any—' Kyle started, and Doug's hamsteak of a right hook slammed into his mouth.

'Think that's funny? Hurling your lunch at my gal?' Doug shook Kyle back and forth inside his shirt, eyes murderous. 'Fucking little cocksucker, show you funny.'

On the second punch Kyle's feet went out from under him and he slapped down into the mud, face numb, the copper taste of blood threading back over his tongue. His teeth seemed to be floating and involuntary tears spilled freely. Doug waded in for another blow.

'I'm sorry,' Kyle cried, raising one arm in defense as he dragged himself closer to the water's edge. 'Jesus, don't!'

Doug hesitated, fist cocked. 'Where'd your weenie dick friends run off to?'

'I don't know,' Kyle blubbered. 'It wasn't me, I swear.'

Perhaps Doug realized it hadn't been Kyle who'd thrown the pizza, or that if he pushed this any further he could very easily tumble head-first into Boulder Creek or, if there were any witnesses, into Boulder County Jail. Whatever the reason, he took pity and dropped his fighter's pose. He sniffed, his thick face draining of color.

'Find yourself some new friends, shit for brains.'

When he was certain Doug wasn't coming back to

kick him in the gut, Kyle crawled up the bank and got to his feet. He wiped blood from his lips and spat. The entire lower half of his face felt puffy but his teeth weren't loose, so that was something. He glanced around, wondering if the girl had seen him get KO'd, but no one in the park was watching him and the girl was still missing, or vanished, whatever she had done, and that was another small relief. Once he was on the bike path, his friends emerged from a thicket of bushes, their eyes wide with a kind of awe they had never applied to him.

'Dude!' Will yelled up to him. 'You all right?'

Ben and Lucas stared slack-jawed. Kyle nodded and wiped his face with his muddy shirt.

'That was fucking awesome!' Lucas said. 'Strong stable, Nash. Tough little fuck, aren't you?'

Ben smirked, and Kyle knew he was somehow jealous.

'You dicks are buying the beer tonight,' Kyle said, because it sounded like the right thing to say after you'd been in a fight, though he couldn't fool himself that was what it had been. 'Especially you, *Benjamin*. I took one for you, you asshole.'

Ben nodded miserably as Will and Lucas seized upon his weakness. 'Your fail, bro,' Will said, batting Ben across the noggin. 'Yeah, Ben, way to go, fuckin' pussy,' Lucas added, kicking him in the ass.

Kyle walked after them, smiling despite it all. His friends were already moving down the path, jumping on and off each other like they were running on some

110

electrical current he had not learned how to plug into yet. Though this thing here today, maybe it was some kind of a start.

He glanced back at the creek once more, wondering if she was real or something conjured in his waking dreams, and either way when he might see her again.

20

The proprietor plunged beer glasses into scalding basins of sterilizing water, hopping them onto motorized brushes until his fingertips were raw and numb. He'd only been here since one, but already Mick's forty-four-year-old body felt like a sack of hot hammered coins. Steam clung to his face like a fever. Glasses clinked, people laughed, silverware crashed in a tub. He zoned in and out of the dining room's warbling early bird din. He went through decades-learned motions until the last of the twenty-two ounce pins porpoised out and landed trophy upright on the rubber-webbed beach to dry. An hour after entering the restaurant, he wanted to dig a hole in the ground and bury himself. For a moment he imagined refilling the sinks and climbing atop the bar's worn cherry veneer to soak his feet in the sink, but there were health codes to observe.

Even here, in The Last Straw, his dying sports bar.

He fountained seltzer into a highball glass, swirled the fizz and swallowed it warm. He glanced at his rubber watch, wiping a little sperm of soap foam pooled in the cup of the digital face – 6:22. *Shit.* Amy was going to be irate. He had to get the hell out of here, pronto, and yet something was nagging him, urging him to stay. Something was in the air. *Something's going to happen in here tonight. Something the others can't handle. What, or who, is it?*

He surveyed the dining room. Reggie was off-loading a plate of wings to the young couple in the corner at table 6. Reggie was a nice guy, always well groomed. He dressed loud, a white kid from Greeley who drove a heap of a Cadillac he called The Lac and fancied himself a playa. He seemed to be on top of his game, his patrons content with their food.

Jamie had been circling a businessman hiding behind a wall of newspaper, the untouched mountain of nachos at table 9, slick blond hair, the guy's sleeve appearing like a puppet every few minutes to hoist another free refill on his Arnold Palmer. Good kid, Jamie – earnest, motivated. Never needed a push, her pixie hair and peasant thighs and that firm little runner's butt in perpetual motion, and she always earned a decent tip. If there was trouble here, it wasn't with her tables.

A head of wavy blond hair high up on a golden brown neck bobbed by and Mick did a double-take. Oh, you gotta be shittin' me. Brett was supposed to have been cut over an hour ago, but there he goes with another pitcher of Buff Gold, nowhere better to be. Yukking it up with the rugby studs at 14, the ones getting loud in their grass-stained elbow pads. Brett was a semi-pro sand volleyball player with a volleyball for a head and a penchant for milking the time-clock. In an industry where even

113

strong profit margins were eight to twelve per cent, mismanaging payroll was the lethal serpent in the garden.

'You're long overdue, Brett.' Mick snapped his fingers. 'Time to clock out.'

Brett didn't hear him. Goddamn Alt Rock satellite channel cranked, Chris Cornell caterwauling off the window panes another brain-numbing and unnecessary expense.

Expenses, payroll, money, accountant – where was Eugene Sapphire, anyway? Boom, that was it. Maybe that was why Mick's gut was full of acid. Wasn't their monthly meeting today? Mick retrieved the new Droid Amy had bought him, poked, scrolled, scoped his calendar: nothing about the accountant, but then maybe the new phone hadn't synced his calendar. Maybe the meeting was next week. Good. Next week was always better than this week. Mick didn't want to hear about money.

He holstered the device. 'You're bleeding me dry, Brett!'

'You need something, Mick?' Jamie dipped behind the bar with a round corked tray piled with glasses and a half-eaten burger the size of a car tire, it's center flesh bleeding over a wasteland of fries. Pig portions, fat customers, more wasted overhead. Time to design a new menu, start interviewing chefs.

'The hell's Brett still doing here?' The edge in his voice sent Jamie back a step, so he softened the follow-up. 'I told you to cut him loose at five. We're dead.'

Jamie paled. 'I thought maybe ... Amy wanted to make sure we were covered.'

'I know, I know. You didn't know I was going to be here.' Mick smiled, realizing he had slung his wrath in the wrong direction. He shot more club soda, slugged it back, stifled a burp. 'Thanks, Jamie. You're the one holding the entire trapeze show together these days. Another Arnold for the newspaper man?'

'The news – oh, no, he's fine.' Jamie was blushing, pulling her lip. The customer had gotten under her skin in some way.

'Everything all right?' Mick said.

Jamie glanced toward the hovering *Daily Camera*. 'He's a little strange.'

'He hit on you? You want me to take care of him?'

'Oh, no, not like that. Though he is kind of handsome. He just looks sorta not there? He keeps smiling but his eyes ... They're, like, dry.'

Mick panned the room, got distracted by the rugby team. They seemed to have multiplied, their scrum erupting. Two combatants lining up plastic cups, the teams swinging pitchers like steins in a mead hall. A ping-pong ball *thwocked* wetly on the table and the jeers of six college boys scraped the rafters. 'Drink, motherfucker, drink!'

Tuesday happy hour beer pong special: Brett's idea. The goal was to prop up their slowest night of the week. The result was ogre clientele, bad news for the carpets, absolute zero net increase in the nightly take.

'Was it the nachos?' Mick bent to straighten the foul

rubber mat between them. 'Swear to God I'm going to fire Carlos. I mean, it's *nachos*, right? I'm no longer asking him to do *au poivre*—'

'He didn't eat the nachos,' Jamie said. 'I offered, like you said, always push the apps. And he said okay, but he's just been sitting there. Every time I check in, he like just stares at me.'

Mick thought the girl was controlling some kind of weird shiver. 'That's it?'

Jamie frowned. 'And I don't think he blinked. At all. He just—'

'I'll handle Brett,' Mick said. 'Let me know if the guy keels over. I gotta get out of here anyway. Can you handle the closing tonight?'

Jamie tensed again, but nodded. 'I'm getting used to it.'

'You sure?'

'Yeah, no problem.'

'Okay. I owe you one.'

Jamie scurried off to the kitchen. Mick turned and pulled his daily wage from the bar register. He hadn't cut himself a paycheck in fourteen months and the two hundo he removed tonight just about cleaned out the till. As he was pocketing the wad, he caught movement in the bar mirror: Eugene Sapphire entering, black wind-breaker trailing like a cape, thwarting Mick's escape. Sapphire's eyes were bloodshot, his mouth set in a crooked snarl, and Mick thought, So this is what the grim reaper looks like. A fucking accountant dressed in a K-Mart suit.

21

'So that's it,' he said. A small miner with a pickax seemed to be standing behind Mick's forehead, digging for gold. 'Thirty days. Fourth of July weekend plus, what, a week?'

The accountant's neck turtled up from the shell of his starched collar. 'Forty-five or sixty if you can renegotiate some of the invoices with your suppliers—'

'I won't stiff my partners,' Mick said, upending his whiskey sour. 'They've already gone above and beyond.'

'—and run a skeleton crew, pull double shifts, and go into a liquidation mode with half a menu, maybe ninety, but—'

'I was already pulling double shifts and I'm not keeping it a secret until the last day. Not happening, Gene.'

Eugene Sapphire had been the Straw's numbers man since the doors opened. He had roomed with Mick's father, Bernard Nash, in college, and remained bright-eyed, sharp in his calculations and sage in his advice, with a nice head of gray hair Mick associated with members of the Senior PGA Tour. He hadn't apologized for being late and Mick guessed that Sapphire now regarded Nash Jr as a lost cause.

'If it comes to *that*,' Mick said, 'we're going to maintain our dignity, go out with a bang. I'll throw a party for one of the local charities, put a full-page ad in the *Camera*, a sort of farewell to the community that's been so good to us, some bullshit like that. But I'm conceding nothing at this point. Let's be clear.'

'All well and noble, Mick,' Sapphire said. 'But my job is to give you your options. Realistically. Have you heard from your strong man in Denver lately? The police apprehend your Bonnie and Clyde?'

'The police are useless and Jim Butler is no one's strong man. He's the new breed. Cyber crime, corporate espionage, ID theft. Says he's working on a last-known address, but I think he views this whole mess as a waste of his time. And maybe it is. I mean, what's the point, Gene. Principle? Pride?' He laughed.

The accountant did not laugh. 'One hundred and eighty-two thousand of your hard-earned dollars. That's your principle.'

Mick finished his drink. 'You know what kills me? These fucks, Greg and that dingbat Leslie, they weren't kids or addicts. It's not like I hired some ex-con for a bartender and his dime-store grifter girlfriend for a hostess. They're fifty years old, for Christ's sake. Leslie has two kids in Wyoming. Greg used to own a car wash. Here, in my town, right down on Valmont. Known Amy since she was in braces. They knew what this would do to me. I thought I was doing a good thing giving regular people some responsibility, a living wage. But these leeches ...'

Mick held his hands out over the table like ram's horns, his face reddening.

'I saw them now, I'd choke the fucking life out of both of them myself. I'm serious, Gene. My father would be proud. *Proud*. It'd be worth this place going down the tubes if I could wrap my hands around their fucking throats, just for a minute. That's all it would take. One minute.'

Something in his neck fluttered and he wished Jamie would bring him another double. His device purred against his tired dick, setting off Pavlovian dread. It was after nine and he had a new text. From Amy.

Are you insane? Do you want to have a stroke? Get your ass home now.

'Right,' Mick said to his phone. When he looked up, the newspaper man was exiting his booth, two tables behind Sapphire. Mick had forgotten the guy was still here, and now all he caught was a head of slick blond hair above a plain black suit. Had he been listening in? Was he some kind of bill collector, maybe an agent from the IRS? It seemed uncanny the guy had sat in the Straw for almost three hours without Mick ever getting a good look at him. He caught one final glimpse of the shoulders pushing through the doors, and without knowing why, Mick was up out of his booth, giving chase. His forehead felt like molten iron as he burst through the front doors.

119

But when he scanned the sidewalks, the patio seating area, and the parking lot beyond, there was no sign of the stranger. The dozen or so cars in the Straw's corner of the lot were empty. The man had vanished into the night.

Someone grabbed his arm and Mick jumped, cocking a fist.

Sapphire reared back. 'Easy, easy. Jesus, Mick.'

Mick deflated. 'Sorry, I thought you were ... you see that guy sitting behind us? Blond hair, the suit?'

'No, I did not.' Sapphire looked at his watch. My God, the man wanted to go home.

Mick's eyes darted around the lot. 'It's like he's been waiting for me. I know him from somewhere. He wants something ...'

'Mick, listen to me.' Sapphire wagged a finger. 'You've got to stop this. This anger. You're wrong for it, and you need time to get back on your feet. You're a parent, a man in the community. This stuff happens. Even the best businessmen don't always see it coming. You want to do your father proud? Go home. Talk to your family.'

'About what? How do you do that?'

'Focus on what comes next. You need an idea. I can help you form a new plan around something. But you need to start looking at this as a blank slate.'

Only now did Mick grasp that tonight was *the* talk, the moment the surgeon comes out of the theater and informs you he has done everything in his power. The Straw was no longer on life support. It had been pronounced.

The reality staggered him. 'I could pull some money out of the house ...'

Sapphire tsked behind his long graying teeth. 'You go to the bank with a personal guarantee, they attach you to the note, and everything the note's attached to is now attached to the rest of your life. Your residence, all of your personal assets as well as Amy's, would no longer be exempt. Keep your home out of it. At all costs, Mick. Pay your mortgage first, keep a roof overhead. Everything else is secondary.'

'Goddamn it. This wouldn't have happened to them. Dad might have missed the signs, but Mom would've sniffed it out. I killed it, Gene. I killed my parents' restaurant.'

'Sometimes a thing has to die before it can be reborn.'

'What the fuck does that mean?'

'We're living in a different world. They had their battles, believe me.'

'Yeah, but they won. My dick's in the dirt here.'

The accountant nodded. 'Boulder is brutal on restaurants. There's money here, but it's fickle. Pete Pomfrey couldn't make it in this town and he pulled two of the best seafood capers I've ever dined in. Restaurants don't last, champ.'

Champ. Sapphire knew Mick's father had called him that.

'What does, old man?' Mick said. 'Tell me. I really need to know.'

'If I knew that, young man, I wouldn't be an accountant.' Eugene Sapphire clapped him on the shoulder and –

Flashes of orange strobed behind Mick's forehead and he was free falling, plunging into the water. The sun was blinding and the scent of mildewed astro-turf wafted over from the dock and the lake cupped around his eyes and he went down into the darkness. There, in the cooler depths, where the green-blue surface gave way to deep brown and then black, and the temperature dropped ten degrees, and the silent murmur of the lake tightened in his ears, he saw –

Hands. An old man's hands. Liver spotted, arthritically gnarled, with thick green veins. A black trench coat, the hands unbuttoning this garment from the throat down. The coat draped over a chair, the water pattering to the wood floor. In a room both familiar and secretive, a large wooden desk with a green leather top and all the implements and tools that bespoke the workspace of an important man, a trusted man, a banker or lawyer or councilor of some kind.

The old man sat in a large leather chair with cracking seams and brass wheels, rolling himself tight against the desk. He opened a ledger and made a few notations in fine black ink, numbers with a series of initials, then withdrew a check from his breast pocket, inserted this into the ledger, and wheeled himself backward with expert control and bent to open a low cabinet door.

Inside the cabinet, a safe.

A black numbered dial, the small door gunmetal gray. The old fingers with yellowing, almost feminine nails, ran the dial back and forth too fast for him to read the combination. The safe door opened and there were shelves, and he heard the old man grunt with the effort of bending to insert his ledger. Inside, on the bottom shelf, were stacks of tightly banded new bills, hundreds, tens of thousands in Benjamin Franklin paper all bricked up, two of the stacks plastic-wrapped. On the top shelf sat a piggish gun, short and black, as well as three inches of Wells Fargo statements bundled with a thick blue rubber band.

The safe door closed, the dial spun, the cabinet door closed, and then he was looking over the old man's shoulder as he turned at his desk and looked up, to the door. The office door opened and a woman in a blue flannel bathrobe entered with a tray set for tea: a steaming silver pot, two small china cups on their saucers, a short jar of honey with a wooden swizzle with a beehive tip. The woman's gray hair was thick, middle-parted, falling to her shoulders. Sad, Jane Goodall eyes that were still lovely. Her lips were moving but the sound was muffled, as if they too were underwater. Each rose from their chairs and walked out, the old man's arm around her waist, the office door closing.

Mick churned beneath the water, lungs tight, blood surging as he kicked to the surface, toward the light of a new day.

My father's best friend.

The one man with the inside line to my entire operation.

I trusted him and the filthy old bastard bled us dry.

He broke through, gasping, and found himself standing in the Last Straw's parking lot. For a moment he was shocked to find himself dry, standing on wobbly legs, out of breath. His arms felt loose. He blinked, searching the parking lot for Sapphire and his powder blue Lexus, but the accountant was gone.

He had left right after patting Mick's shoulder. Is that when it had happened? Had the old man's touch set off some kind of vision? Did I come to this realization on my own, or did the insight come from something else?

123

What the hell was happening to him?

He didn't know. What he did know was that his headache was gone. In its absence there was dull anger and tired depression. Years this man had worked for his parents. He tried to imagine his mother, who kept track of everything in her leather-bound pencil ledgers, missing this parasite's tricks. He couldn't fathom it. He had thought it a lapse of inventory control, then theft at the hands of Greg and Leslie, his former head bartender and his waitress-girlfriend. He'd caught them comping drinks to friends, pocketing cash, hiking a case of champagne and a prime rib out the back door one New Year's Eve. It seemed to fit, though he'd never uncovered a real trail of evidence. But of course now that seemed stupid, too piecemeal. An accountant, though, a man you trusted, that was a man who could do some real damage, and disguise it cleverly.

This was why he had felt the need to stay tonight. His accident on the lake had shaken something loose, if only his complacency. Maybe that was it. Or maybe he had a new edge going on here, something altogether more powerful. If so, what else could he do with it? The questions left his hands shaking with the possibility of life-changing payback.

22

This is not my daughter. It's an alien life form. A minion of Satan.

'Where's Daddy? Where's Daddy! I want my *Daaaaaaaaa-ddeeeEEE!*'

If it was her daughter, she would know how to make it stop screaming.

'Lemme go! Lemme go! Daddy, you have to bring Daddy home now!'

Amy's body was being used as an ultimate fighting ring for B, who was shaking, slapping, kicking and burning hot with the fire of her shrieking. For the past ten minutes, she had been using her Soothing Mommy voice, but if this went on much longer she thought she might be justified in breaking out her Thermonuclear Mommy voice, and quite possibly the soft end of the pink leather belt laced through her daughter's Gap Kids skinny jeans. But the mere thought of hitting Briela made Amy feel sick, so goddamn her husband for putting her in this position.

'Daddy's on his way home, sweetie. Listen, *listen* to Mommy, Briela stop, stop it, *would you please stop*. He'll be here soon.'

'No-no-nunh-nunh-nunh,' Briela said, the argument grinding out from her belly. Her stringy blonde hair whirling, blue eyes rolling, spittle flying. 'He's not, he's not coming home! You have to make him, makedaddy-comehomenow!'

'I'm trying!'

Briela's patent leather Mary-Janes – the ones with heels like sharpened hockey pucks – began chorus-line popping up at Amy's chin, so close she could see the surprisingly thick sweep of blonde hairs on the fleshy caps. A heel stamped down on Amy's shin, the plastic edge biting into the bevel of tibia and muscle before scraping out and continuing down with a knife-like swipe.

She howled and lost control, jerking away. She meant only to release her daughter as she hopped to her feet, but wound up knocking Briela back. The girl snagged a heel on the thick carpet and slumped into a wailing pile of defeat.

'Goddamn it, B, you hurt Mommy *bad*. Jesus Christ, what is wrong with you!'

Amy barely recognized her own voice, and this scared her. She limped a few paces and rolled Briela over, checking her for welts or scrapes just in case, but there were none. Briela jerked away, downshifting into a quieter series of sobs and soon would be empty chuffing herself into sleep.

Enough. Enough for now. She had to deal with her leg. She couldn't talk any more, even if she thought talking might help. But after fits of this magnitude, Briela never remembered much of what had triggered them, let alone the softer cooings that brought the proceedings to a close. Amy hobbled to the door and looked back.

'I don't give a shit how upset you are. Daddy working late is no excuse for this behavior. It's not okay to lash out at Mommy. Never, ever ...' At which point she hated the petulant, playground inflection in her voice and left.

In the kids' bathroom, she dragged the small first-aid kit from under the sink and sat on the toilet, resting the leg along the edge of the tub. She rolled up her pant cuff and gritted her teeth. The gash was less than an inch from end to end, but deep, not so much a cut as a disturbing dent that had probably bruised the bone. She rubbed it weakly, bandaged it.

First she imagines a wolf-boy and throws a fit at the ice-cream shop. Now she's in a state because her father – who almost drowned yesterday – is working late. That had to be it. Briela was processing her father's accident, and his old work habits were no longer acceptable. Well, that makes two of us who are fed up with it.

She stood over the sink and dumped three ibuprofen into her palm, but did not swallow them. She was numb, she realized, and she almost wished she could feel the pain. She dropped the pills in the trash and stared at herself in the mirror. Her mascara had run, her face was pale, blotchy and bloated, and Pillsbury orange cinnamon roll frosting – tonight they had tried baking together, but when the rolls were finished Briela spat hers out and said it tasted like toothpaste – was smeared into her hair like highlights from the Special Moms Only salon.

She limped into the hall and poked her head in Briela's bedroom. The girl had fallen into a deep sleep. Amy scooped her daughter up and set her on the bed, blanketing her to the shoulders.

Back in the kitchen, she searched for the magnum of pinot she was sure she had stashed in the Sub Zero, but it was not on the bottom shelf. Or on any of the shelves. The crisper. The door.

'Damn it!' Amy slammed the fridge. She thought of running to the liquor store in Gunbarrel, which was only five minutes away, but she looked like hell and it was late. She grabbed her car keys, halted, set them back on the counter.

She looked at the tray of cinnamon rolls on top of the Wolf range. She moved to them. Inserted her pointer finger into the center of the spiral. Still warm. She really shouldn't. But before she realized what she was doing, the finger was in her mouth, the orange-flavored sugar crackling on her tongue. She closed her eyes and swayed. Pushed her tongue against the roof of her mouth, smearing the glaze around, biting into another piece of the stiff-edged dough. Oh. *Oooooh.*

Mick, she decided, was going to pay for this night in a novel way. He was putting his health in danger and by extension putting them all in danger. What would be his excuse? The usual. *Had to cover a shift, babe. It's a restaurant. What do you think my job is, anyway? I fill the holes.*

Question was, why were there so many holes? He'd

spent half his life in the Straw and still didn't know how to be a manager, let alone hire one. He was too nice, too soft on his staff. And, though it gave her no pleasure to think so, her husband was a shitty businessman. He had no sense of numbers, spreadsheets, budgets. Worse, he seemed to know this and yet he never changed, never sought to improve his skill set. He was still the carefree boy who had been born into a flourishing family business. But, once his parents gave him the keys, was he content to stick to what had worked for twenty-seven years? No, he had to remake the Straw in his lost jock-stud image. Out with the family buffet, in with the raucous sports bar. Obscene portions, wall-to-wall hi-def displays, the trend of the new millennium.

Well, the millennium was a little too excited for its own good. After all this time, he still didn't grasp that owning a restaurant was Darwinian bloodsport, not a place to park your ass in a corner booth with the sports pages and a bottle of scotch as you regaled college students with tales of your glorious youth.

True, after his father died in '04, he'd finally knocked off the two a.m. benders, folding the Straw's softball team and other sponsorships in favor of college savings accounts for the kids. But how much had he really changed? Amy knew his friends too well, the other Rogers in town, fortysomethings twice divorced and still hustling ass fresh out of grad school. Boulder was a utopia, a place you went to college or retired to. A fantasy playground of ski bums, trustafarian students, and cashed-out tech wealth. Mick bitched about working late, but he didn't want to let go of the bar life. As long as he was in it, he was still Mickey Mouse, Fun Mickey, Mick the Swinging Dick.

Her husband, her oldest son.

She took another bite of the cinnamon roll. God, the orange frosting *was* a little like toothpaste, but the artificial flavoring only made it better, like some kind of new chemical substance, a Pillsbury anxiety pill: now available in chewable, lickable, nom-nom-nom-able.

She stared at the window over the sink, across the long lawn of the backyard, considering the guest house on the other side of the pool. It was a ramshackle shed of a cabana they used mostly for garden storage, but it had possibilities. Two rooms plus a loft, the suggestion of an apartment.

Apart. Ment.

Apart.

The thought came to her like an unexpected kiss. *Once he gets better, Mick could move in there.* She stared at the guest house, imaging the first step to something new. Not freedom. She wasn't that naive and wouldn't give up her children. She would always need Mick ... in some capacity. But something new was out there. Starting with that pool-guest-house-apartment.

Amy turned away from the window. She stared at the baking sheet, pressing the back of her hand to her smeared lips. There was only one roll left. A few minutes ago there had been eight of them. A quiet moan of disgust escaped her. No, no way. She remembered chewing one of them, savoring every crumb. She had not gone hog wild, devouring them like one of those Japanese kids in the hot-dog-eating contests. She couldn't believe that, refused to believe that. And yet: Briela was sleeping, Kyle was out for the night to stay with his friends, so who else could it have been?

Her tummy made a swamp sound, a little BP spill down in there in the Gulf of Amy. She felt high, her head spinning from the sugar.

I'm a beast, I need help . . .

She took a glass of water out onto the patio, tottering along the flagstones. She found a ceramic pot and removed her secret pack of Capris, then used the burner on Mick's six-thousand-dollar Alfresco grill to light one. The gleaming silver cathedral to meat seemed to hiss at her, mocking her in some way, and she resented him for spending their money on crap like this, even if he had gotten it at a restaurant auction for half-price. Tomorrow she would put this monstrosity on Craigslist, and maybe Blue Thunder too, right next to the boat. Sell the truck right out from under him. He had no business owning a forty thousand dollar truck in times like these. They needed to hunker down, start squirreling away some nuts.

She settled into one of the padded loungers beside the limestone-ringed firepit. It was a summer darkness, palpable and solicitous. She smoked greedily, as if the nicotine would curb her appetite for the next month and erase the little hit job she'd just put on that tray of cinnamon rolls. A hundred feet east stood the palazzo's perimeter wall, its white flank soft in the open field. Her

131

eyes wandered to the pool house, tracing the border between the two properties.

A shadow peeled away from the pool house and moved across the yard, stirring like a small tree coming to life. It went ten or twelve paces in an animal crouch and stopped at the property line, between two blue spruce pines as if hiding.

Hiding, or just waiting for her.

23

Myra Blaylock came into the Straw a few minutes after eleven. She wasn't there when Mick ducked around the corner to drain off the last three whiskey sours in the bathroom, but when he returned, she was perched on the barstool, brown hair roped into its single thick braid around her neck, her S-curving posture and the crossed legs, one sparkly sandal flapping anxiously from her little tan foot. He stood three or four tables behind her, concocting the nicest possible way to say what needed to be said, what had already been said, what would likely be said again in the future, none of it doing a lick of good.

Myra waved to him in the bar mirror, better than eyes in the back of her head. Something disturbing about that, like she was in the walls. Well, it was all disturbing. It was like she knew where he was at all times, not just here, but all around town. She had a funny way of showing up in grocery lines, in the next lane at the bank's drive-thru window. That one hair-raising episode at Briela's daycare center.

He took a stool to her left, leaving one between them. 'You looking to buy a bar, Myra?'

She aimed all of herself his way, her big brown eyes horned with mascara and glossy with yesterday's tears. 'Oh, it can't be that bad.'

'Worse,' he said. She sipped at her usual Bombay martini and Mick could almost taste the cigarette they would share after. 'Come back tomorrow about this time, the lights might not be on.'

'Poor Mick. You should have sold out years ago and moved to Florida.' She thumbed a pearl dangling at the center of a silver spiral earring.

'Yep.' Mick looked at his phone, feigning distraction. 'How's Henry?'

Myra batted her lashes theatrically.

'Right,' Mick said. 'And the kids?'

She swallowed more of the clouded booze and he wondered who had poured it for her. The rest of the staff had been cut loose for the night. Business was dead and once again he was the last man working, so maybe Myra just helped herself these days.

'That good, huh?' Mick said. 'Glad to hear it.'

'Do you really want to know or are you just being polite?'

And there it was, the first thrust with the guilt knife.

'I asked, didn't I?'

'Geoffrey's with his grandmother in Dallas this week. Caroline's with the dance company in Chicago for another ten days.' In other words, *I'm free*. But it was never free. One ride on the Myra-Go-Round cost you a dozen pleading phone calls and one teary-eyed blowout in the office. Ten, even five years ago, it had been worth it. But he was too tired for such nonsense.

'I'm sure you'll find something to keep you entertained,' Mick said. 'You want a menu? Carlos makes a mean plate of chili nachos.'

'Fuck you.' Myra swiveled, opting for the bar mirror again.

'Hey.' Mick took the opportunity to walk around the bar. He needed some distance from her scent, the combination of that rainwater perfume and whatever else was just there on its own. No woman had ever smelled like that, or tasted that way. 'My accountant just cut off my balls and I'm running exceptionally late, so you picked a bad night to pretend we're old friends who keep tabs.'

Myra tilted the rest of her martini back. She set the empty glass on the edge of the bar as if offering him the olive. But not the branch. Myra never offered the branch. She looked down at her purse for a moment, then up at him with a forced smile.

'I didn't mean to bother you,' she said, gentler now. 'I'm sorry you're having a bad night. I worry about you. I'd miss this place. Lotta memories here, you know. Not all about you, either.'

Mick's throat filled with remorse. 'You're not bothering me, sweetie. You never did that. It's just, you know ...' He almost told her he had drowned, but realized that would only force him to tell the story, which would earn her sympathy, and two drinks later they would be necking in her car.

135

'No, I don't know,' Myra said. 'But I'm willing to listen.'

'We both know where this leads,' he said, feeling how much of a canned line it was. 'And it's never good, for either of us.'

'It was good for one of us not so long ago.' Myra stood. She rooted around in her purse, slapped a twenty on the bar. 'And I didn't say I came here to fuck. But it's nice to know you think I ascribe such importance to your dick.'

Yowza. Strike two, guilt fastball. 'Come on, you know what I mean. Let me buy you dinner.'

'Not hungry, thanks.'

'Myra.'

But she was already walking out, and that was for the best. When the door closed behind her, he took her twenty and stuffed it in his pocket. Something glimmered beside her glass. She'd left her pearl earring for him. Cute, but not cunning enough for Myra. Might have been a genuine loss, fallen out while she was playing with it. He picked it up and searched around for a shot glass. He'd leave it beside the register as a reminder of things not to do, until the next time she appeared, then hand it over like the thoughtful guy he was.

But he couldn't find a shot glass and when he looked up again she was standing out on the sidewalk, smoking, pacing, and he realized she was working up the courage to come back. No, no, that's not necessary. Let's just wrap this up.

He went out, cupping the earring in his left hand. She seemed very small there in her jeans and the pink blouse. Everything in her still firm, a kind of hardness inside her that bounced him back and pulled him in, often through six or seven of her own greedy little orgasms. Was like she didn't even need him there, until he had gone.

'Hey, you forgot something.'

She startled at the sight of him and he held his palm out, a peace offering. Myra Blaylock looked at the pearl. She dropped her cigarette, took two steps and held his face in both of her hands. She kissed him once on the lips, firmly, and released him, pushing him away with surprising force.

'The doctor found a lump in my left breast,' she said. 'But that's not why I dropped by. It's my birthday. I was hoping you would be the first one to remember.'

For a moment he was speechless, the memory of telling Amy that Myra had breast cancer coming back to slap him across the face. But here, tonight, this was news. How had he known? His head was swirling.

'What was I thinking,' she said, not really a question.

'Aw, shit, Myra.' He reached for her but she spun away.

'Good luck with the restaurant, Mickey.'

'Myra, wait.'

'Tried that.'

Her thin sandals flapped off into the night. He watched her get into her latte-bronze Buick Enclave and drive off jerkily, the aspirational, I'm-not-a-mini-van, sultry crossover depressing in its melodramatic exit.

The worst part of it occurred to him then. She hadn't

137

said she had breast cancer. She said the doctor found a lump. She was scared, and Mick felt certain she had every reason to be. She was dying. They would do the biopsy and it would come back malignant. He knew it the way he had seen Sapphire's dirty hands all over his money. Myra was going to lose her hair from chemo, but it wouldn't be enough to save her.

'What in God's name is happening to me?' he said to the empty parking lot, in a voice that sounded scared shitless.

24

Amy sat forward in her lawn chair but did not stand; she was afraid of drawing attention to herself. Who, or what, the hell was this? Had it been watching her the whole time? It looked like an emaciated deer on its hind legs, with thin limbs, an odd shaped head that narrowed. But it had walked upright, like a person. It had to be a person, the shape merely distorted in the darkness.

It was standing there against the pine tree at the edge of her lawn, and she could feel its eyes watching her. It was as if it knew when she was looking, and would only move again once she looked away.

It wants something from me.

She placed her cigarette on the flagstone and stepped on it, and when she looked up the figure was gone. She refocused, seeking along the tree line. There. Standing a few trees down. It seemed to have shifted position without actually walking. Now it lowered itself to the ground while she stared at it, hunching in a crouch, then rose up again, and as it reached its full height there was a new kind of mass to it. Difficult to know from this distance and in this light, but the longer she studied it, the more convinced she became that it was human, a woman. She needed it to be a woman.

Amy was only twenty feet from the house. She had time to run, but curiosity (and gnawing fear) rooted her to the chair. It was probably some girl who had come sniffing around for Kyle. He had been caught sneaking out past his curfew eleven or twelve times this spring and summer. Maybe she could scare the girl away. Because I'm really not in the mood for games, Amy thought, and stood.

'Might as well come out,' she called across the yard. 'I see you standing there.'

The figure retreated deeper into the trees, then pivoted and came walking directly at her. The motion-detector was activated, casting a funnel of blue-white light over the patio and lawn, drawing in the figure slowly.

'I hope I didn't startle you,' it said, resolving into a thin woman approximately Amy's age. Her shiny black hair was streaked with red highlights and she wore black designer jeans and a plain black blouse, buttoned crookedly. Her feet were bare, pale and dirty. Her eyes were shiny black, her expression languid. 'I was just out for a walk.'

'Okay.' Amy was relieved that it was only a woman, but she was mildly shaken by the shifting shape she had seen, and this flat voice and vacant expression. I will never eat seven orange cinnamon rolls again, she vowed. 'Something I can do for you?'

'Were you smoking?'

Amy sniffed. 'Uhm, yes, I was.'

140

'My husband says I'm not supposed to.'

Amy softened, heard herself say, 'Sounds familiar. Is there some reason you're sneaking around my backyard, or . . . ?'

'I'm sorry. I think I'm lost.'

This was like having a conversation with a car crash victim.

'Where's your husband? Is there a problem?'

The woman glanced back toward the palazzo. 'Oh, there it is.'

'That's your house?'

'I was supposed to bring this over.' She clumsily proffered a bottle of white wine. Amy couldn't read the painted label, but the green glass was moist with condensation from its chilling.

'Wow,' Amy said. 'You read my mind.'

This brought the first sign of a smile, albeit a thin one. 'I'm Cassandra Render. That's our name. The Renders.'

Amy nodded politely, thinking, What pills are you on, Cassandra Render?

'I'm Amy Nash. My husband is Mick. Your house is lovely.'

Cassandra Render looked back at the house. 'That's where we live now,' she said. 'In our new house.'

'You just moved in this week?'

'Is your husband home?' Cassandra smiled, her teeth large and white in the artificial light.

'He's working late. We own a restaurant, so he's always working late.'

'My husband works late too. He's always working. You

141

can call me Cass. My husband is Vince.' Cassandra eyed the lounge chairs with a fearful longing. The woman seemed fragile and Amy found this endearing. Minutes ago she hadn't been in the mood for company, but a fault line had shifted inside her.

'Well, I think it's nice,' Amy said. 'That house can only increase property values and we could use some fresh blood around here. Welcome to the neighborhood, Cass. Sit down. I'll grab a corkscrew.' Amy jaunted off for the kitchen.

Cass said, 'I love your swimming pool.'

'Thanks,' Amy called over her shoulder. 'Help yourself anytime!'

'You are very kind, Amy Nash.'

When Amy returned, Cass accepted the corkscrew and then stared at it in her open palm. She looked to the bottle and back to the corkscrew, and for a crazy moment, Amy was sure the woman was contemplating using it as a weapon.

Amy said, 'Here, let me,' and manhandled it open. Cass watched as if trying to memorize it for next time. Amy poured and when she looked up, Cass was studying her.

'What?'

'Sorry?'

'Why are you staring at me like that?' Amy said.

'I'm sorry. Just nervous, I guess. I don't have any friends here.'

Amy laughed but stopped herself. 'Aw, why do I suspect that's not true?'

Cass shook her head and stared into her wine.

Amy decided to change the subject. 'Do you want to hear a funny story?'

Cass smiled.

'Okay, I teach on a program out at Vo-Tech, for kids who are at risk. And there's these two rotten little scoundrels, Eric Pritchard and Jason Wells. I mean, they're all troubled, but these two are another breed. Last week they tried to smoke in class and when I told them to put it out, one of them said, "I'm gonna get you for that." I swear, kids these days have no respect for teachers, and really, that comes from the parents ...'

Cass listened intently as Amy unwound her tale, which became a rant of sorts extending a good ten minutes beyond her best intentions. When she finished, Cass reached across, touching her arm. Her fingers were soft, cool.

'And how did that make you feel? When they called you the c-word?'

Amy twitched, but Cass would not let go. A warmth seemed to ooze from her palm, into Amy's skin, until her touch was as pleasant as it had been startling. Amy scoffed, shook her head, and at last decided to be honest.

'It hurt. It made me feel weak. Like a failure and a pathetic excuse for a teacher.'

Cass nodded, her cold blue eyes unblinking. 'And? What else?'

Amy looked at this stranger in the lounge chair beside

143

her. 'It made me mad. Furious. So mad I could kill them. Make them pay for . . . ' She paused, shocked by her own rancor. 'Well, I shouldn't let them get to me.'

Cass traced the rim of her wine glass. 'I understand.'

'You do?'

'The world is full of mean people. I'm so glad we're friends.'

'Me too.'

Cass sat forward and placed her wine on the patio. Amy realized the woman had not taken a single sip. Cass stood.

'I should go,' she said. 'Before it gets too late.'

Amy stood. 'Oh. All right, then. Do you want me to walk you home?'

'No.' Cass turned and stepped awkwardly and something clinked. Amy looked down to see Cass's bare foot standing on the shattered wine glass.

'Oh my God,' Amy said.

Cass slowly lifted her foot and leaned forward to stare at it with clinical detachment. A triangle of glass jutted from the arch, and smaller speckles were embedded in the sole.

'I'm sorry,' Cass said.

'No, no, it's my fault. Here, please, sit down while I get the first-aid kit.'

Cass took another step, and another, crunching more of the embedded glass.

'Oh my God, no, wait!' Amy said. 'Jesus, that looks serious.'

Cass stopped. 'It's no trouble. Vincent will fix it. I

have to go.' And then she was hurrying away, waving a hand that said please do not follow me.

'You shouldn't walk on that. You could get an infection—' But it was no use. The woman was already slipping back into the darkness. Amy looked around, wishing someone was here to tell her if what she had seen was as strange as it seemed. Cass was probably on Valium, some kind of sedative. Lonely housewife addiction disorder.

She went inside and fetched the dustpan and brush. As she was cleaning up the glass, sweeping all around the lawn chairs and between puzzle pieces of flagstone, even with her face so close to the ground her nose was nearly touching the gritty surface, she found not a single drop of blood.

25

A summer breeze was blowing through Briela Nash's hair. She was standing on a wide black road in her pink elephant pajamas, the ground cold on her bare feet. It was nighttime and she didn't remember coming outside. There were only five or six cars up near the big grocery store's darkened windows. The bright blue sign above the store blinked and went dark. She knew it still said Albertson's, but Mommy called it Fat Albertson's. Which meant this was the parking lot and her family's restaurant was right behind her! She turned, ready to run to the Last Straw – and stopped.

A thin man with a red-and-blue baseball cap was staring down at her, quiet as a cat. His eyes were black and lined with red veins and he was trembling with excitement. He smiled, his lips wet as he bent to reach for her. She backed away, but there were others, circling her. Black shapes, their feet sweeping pebbles on the ground as they slinked closer.

She turned and saw her dad walking toward her. He was playing with the Broncos keyring she gave him for Father's Day, head down, tired and sad. She had to warn him. The man in the red-and-blue cap and the others were going to get him, and she tried to speak but her mouth didn't work.

Everything jumped like the TV fast-forwarding and she almost fell over from the shaking. The whole world was shaking, and there was screaming, and so much violence it was like standing next to a car crash, but it was only people. Roaring with animal rage. Daddy was screaming and they fell on him like a pack of wild dogs.

Briela's entire body twitched like it was one electric muscle, yanking her from terrible dreams. She blinked in darkness, waiting to find out where she was. A lone tower in some dark kingdom gradually became her bedpost. The deep black cave her closet door. And then her bookshelf was there, with Pooh in his red shirt. She hadn't slept with him since she was a baby, but she crawled from her tangled sheets and ran and snatched him down. He was heavy and dusty in her arms and she scampered back to bed and fell onto him, rolling with him pressed to her nose, until the two of them were safe under the covers.

She wanted to run down the hall and make sure Daddy was home safe, but she was too afraid to leave her bed. Nothing could hurt her here. As long as she stayed under the covers with Pooh.

Briela had learned the word 'transmissions' from a show about aliens Kyle was watching late one night, and she thought that sounded exactly the way they felt. She began receiving them a little more than eight months ago, right after construction on the new house in the backyard began (though she had not made this connection yet, only thought of the house's appearance as a kind of marker in her life, a change in the landscape that irritated her parents and piqued Briela's curiosity every time she glanced in that direction, as if she were expecting the house to grow out of the hole in the ground). The transmissions came to her in single shots, like the photos Mommy was always uploading to her Picasa, but sometimes they were longer, like the movie clips Kyle looked at on his Egg.

Except, these photos and short movies were of things that had not happened. Or maybe they had happened, but not with Briela's eyes acting as the camera.

She imagined a device inside her, like a tiny cell phone, or maybe a rubber ball that glowed with light at its center. Sometimes – like that day on the lake, right before Kyle crashed and she saw the family on the dam – she could feel it, hard and round, throbbing warm in her belly. Whatever it looked like, it was growing stronger.

Right before she got one, it was like someone was tickling the inside of her tummy with a feather. Sometimes the tickle made her dizzy and she threw up, which she always did her best to hide, or else Mommy would think she was sick.

One time, when she was taking a hot tub on the night it snowed last spring break, she saw Kyle sitting on a park bench on the Pearl Street Mall, daydreaming with his eyes closed. Another time it was their dog Thom, running away from a chipmunk in the backyard, and Briela had been in school. Those were calm ones. But in the past couple months the images had come to seem dangerous.

This summer she started going away for longer periods, maybe as long as fifteen minutes, the images stringing together like a story whose meaning was just out of reach. One time she had been trapped in darkness, with things on four legs crawling around her bed. She had seen ridges of black fur moving sideways, the smell of rotten hamburger everywhere, and their golden eyes shone in her bedroom. She started screaming and when she 'woke up' she realized she wasn't in her bedroom at all, but in the movie theater with Ingrid. The kids in the row ahead of her were crying and the manager was standing in the aisle, asking them to leave.

Even before she got out of school for the summer, the little movies began to have people in them she had never met. They would show up standing next to Mommy or Daddy, talking and laughing in the daytime, in the backyard, or in the kitchen, and once at Their House, which was familiar even though Briela had never been inside it in real life (because it did not fully exist yet). Only once did they speak clearly enough for her to hear them. They said, 'Welcome to our home. Please come in.' And a pretty woman with two-colored hair caressed her cheek and said, 'You are the angel, aren't you? A real angel among us.'

They weren't scary, the people she didn't know. The man looked familiar, with his blond hair and strong blue eyes. They were nice, and had expensive clothes, and their house was filled with the kinds of things Mom called good taste. But she sensed something magical about them, like they weren't afraid of anything, and they could do anything they wanted. She wondered if they were the people she had seen standing on the dam, all dressed in white. Maybe one day soon she would meet them and learn they were from another planet.

The worst part about the bad visions, though, was that she didn't know how to explain them to Mom, or anyone else. She only remembered little pieces of the visions in the in-between time, like when she first woke up or was just drifting off to sleep. But in daylight, whenever she felt a nudge that something had happened and she tried to remember, it was all gone.

She dozed under her bear, her last thoughts heavy and sad, because she knew that when she woke up tomorrow she would not be able to remember what she had seen, or that she had seen anything all. But even if she could remember *them*, whoever *they* were, she wouldn't know if *they* were real. She wouldn't know if the things she saw had happened in the past, were happening in the moment she saw them, or would happen at a later time.

In this moment, on the edge of sleep, with the night pressing against her bedroom window, Briela Nash knew only that she had seen a scary man coming for her daddy, and that her daddy needed to come home from work because he was walking into a nest of monsters that had the power to take him away, forever.

That, and that she was tired. So tired . . .

Island Living

Before I tell you what makes us so different from the rest of the people walking around on this earth, I should tell you that the names here have been changed to protect the innocent. Except, in this case, concerning the events that made us what we are, there are no innocents.

I am writing this because we don't talk about it. My family and I do not discuss what happened to the people who were there. Nor do we discuss the changes in our lives since it happened, the things we have been forced to endure. Decent people do not talk of such things. Not together around the dinner table. Not in private when it is only my wife and I, alone in our bedroom in the middle of another sleepless night, and certainly not one on one with our children, who are struggling to carry on with things in their heads that no children should have to live with. It is all too ghastly and painful to mention. Nevertheless, the account needs a place to reside *other than in my own mind*.

We have done our best to put it behind us, and in many respects I am continually amazed at how we have succeeded. We have not forgotten, but we have buried it,

151

the way victims of incest bury their childhood and sol-
diers bury wartime atrocity. You come home, you take off
your uniform, you have a private drink – and then you
turn it off. Not as a means to forget, but as a means to
survive.

If you doubt that any person could carry on the way
we have, as I am sure you will be tempted to doubt so
much of what follows, I would suggest this: think of the
worst thing you have ever done, or better still, the worst
thing that has ever been done to you. Now ask yourself
how often you allow yourself to think about it. The hor-
rific details, the moment you did it, the moment it was
done to you. The second-by-second chain of thoughts
that ran through you like a poisonous but addictive injection. The smell of the room, the texture of the other
person's skin against yours, the terrifying sense of isola-
tion when you thought, mistakenly, no one has ever
done this before, this is beyond reality as I understood it.
Followed by the equally jarring realization that you are
not alone, oh no, people have always done things like
this to one another, that you have simply been welcomed
into a darker fraternity of damaged souls who have
known for a long time what you have just discovered.
Nothing is beyond the scope of human depravity. There
is nothing unique about the horrors you have suffered or
visited upon another. You are not special.

You're just here, and you can never go back.

So you hide it. You pick up the pieces and move on. If,
in time, you are able to examine it at all, peer again at the
bracing reality of it under the magnifying scope of

honest memory, you will find yourself paralyzed, rendered immobile, emotionally and physically shackled at your desk at work, standing over the kitchen sink while the clock ticks loudly, sitting in the hot car at the end of a long dirt road. You have only two choices at this point. Succumb to the drowning pull of it, say goodbye to your life, and die. Or wrap the memory in a straitjacket and lock it in an impenetrable solitary cell within a prison that allows no visitors, cutting off a piece of yourself as permanently as the amputation of a gangrenous foot, so that the rest of you may carry on, so that you may survive.

The human mind is a fountain of wonders, capable of ingenious acts of self-deception. We are living proof of this.

Yet even here, in this confessional diary or letter or whatever this may become – a document I simultaneously hope no one will ever see and which I believe the world will one day be forced to hunt down and examine very closely – I cannot bring myself to use our real names. I will borrow his voice, pretend it happened to someone else. I need to see it that way in order to see it at all.

So, for now, the 'I' who is narrating this is the father. His family will be referred to only as my wife, my son, my daughter, our children. In the end, I don't think who we are will be all that important. What is important is the others, the ones we encountered on our trip, the things they did, and the things we – my family and I – have done since.

I planned the trip after our friends described the island as an unspoiled, humble, shaggy kind of paradise. It sounded like the perfect place to spend a month with my wife and children. I thought it strange that Isla Nena, Puerto Rico's little sister island, also known as Isla de Vieques, or simply Vieques, had not been commercialized like so much of the Caribbean. She lies just under ten miles east of the big island and stretches only twenty-one miles east to west, three or four miles north to south. To understand what went wrong there, some history may be useful, though I promise to keep it brief, because no one likes a history lesson and soon, perhaps very soon, history will no longer matter.

Puerto Rico ceded to the United States in 1898, after Spain's defeat in the Spanish-American War, and Vieques was part of the package. The sugar industry was consolidating to the big island, and by the time World War Two came around, the US military decided Vieques would be the perfect spot for a new base. They claimed about two-thirds of the island with the idea that it would be a safe haven for the British navy should our friends overseas fall to Nazi Germany. This never happened, obviously, and the base was never constructed.

But after the war, the Navy decided this nice plot of land was convenient for various military exercises, training, and munitions testing. Bombs, missiles, and so forth. Target practice for training pilots.

Over the decades resentment swelled among the local population and environmental activist groups. Scientists have found traces of depleted uranium in the sand, and some of the locals claim to have suffered from unknown biological agents. Lovely term, unknown biological agents. They say the number of residents who develop one form of cancer or another is off the per capita scale, the water isn't safe to drink, birth defects are on the rise. The truth is we don't know exactly what the Navy dropped, only that it was a lot, and that keeping two-thirds of the island off-limits killed tourism and commercial development on Vieques for nearly half a century. Hence the 'undiscovered jewel' of the Spanish Virgin Islands.

Things came to a head in 1999, when a Navy man was killed during one of the exercises and the resentment that had been brewing for decades sparked a wave of protests. The media coverage was sensational, went international, and the Navy caved under pressure. They pulled out and much of the territory they had rights to was converted to a wildlife refuge.

Interestingly, despite claims of how poisoned the place is, to this day Vieques has one of if not the largest bioluminescent bays in the world. The Spanish, being the superstitious people they are, believed the teeming mass of light to be the work of El Diablo, but I can tell you, paddle a kayak out there at night and it's like swimming amongst the stars, splashing around in heaven. So, maybe some things have been poisoned, maybe others are thriving. Thriving in new ways. Who can say why?

We rented a stand-alone villa on the north side of the island, perched on a hill that looked down onto a small beach and our private pool. To the west was a cinder-block residence with a yard full of roosters being trained by a few local men for the cockfights held on Friday nights. The roosters woke us every morning around three-thirty or four, which drove my wife crazy, but I didn't really mind. It only added to the local flavor.

To the other side of our property lay a complex of six villas, attached in pairs, each pair sharing their own courtyard and pool, with volleyball courts and paved grilling areas. We'd been to a couple of the beaches, Navio and Blue. We'd been hiking. We spent a day or two browsing the shops, enjoying the tacos and those little grilled *jamon y queso* sandwiches they love down there. But mostly we stayed around the house, reading, lounging by the pool, drinking a lot of Medalla. I couldn't get enough of those little eleven-ounce cans of Puerto Rican beer. Stuff goes down like water and you have to drink a thousand to get a real hangover. You're up with the sun, cracking the first beer by eleven, pretty much jelly by dusk. We'd make a dinner of fried conch and red snapper the local fisherman hauled in that morning, sit on the second-story balcony and listen to the waves, have a glass of bay rum on ice, and sometimes, though we had our own problems by then, my wife and I would find time to make a little music together once the kids were asleep. Even if I had another fifty years to live without the demons we now carry, I couldn't imagine a better way to spend them.

By my count there were three, maybe four other families in those villas, but we were close enough to observe only the Percys, a portly crew from Madison, Wisconsin. They had rented a minivan held together by yo-yo string and bamboo, and every morning they would pile in with lawn chairs, badminton racquets, coolers, picnic bags, inflatable rafts … a real family circus. And every afternoon around four they would return, spilling out of the van, red and cranky and run down, one of the kids crying more likely than not.

They'd disappear for an hour or two for nap time. Then around five-thirty or so, the father, Bob Percy, who went two-seventy if he went a pound, and his wife, Lynn, this adorable little brown mouse of a gal who could've sat in the palm of his hands, they'd come out of hiding and fire up the grill by the pool, put together a feast of hotdogs or whole chicken. The kids would come out and they'd eat quietly in their lawn chairs, paper plates and sodas. The kids were all smiles. Tanya, who was eight or nine, and Timothy, who was three or four years older than his sister.

One morning while I was walking the grounds with my coffee, I introduced myself. Bob owned a used-car dealership in Mt Horeb, a small town outside of Madison, and it was failing. He was holding up pretty good, but he told me in the way men do so without saying much that this was their last hurrah. He expected to lose the dealership and, if they couldn't pull something together come the new year – this was in October – they'd lose the house too. Bob walked with a hitching gait and along with a hip that needed replacing, he had a host of other health problems. Diabetes, gout, and probably a heart getting ready to blow a valve. He didn't mention his heart, but his breathing was labored and I saw him massaging his chest on several occasions.

I asked which beach they were spending time at. Understand, the beaches on Vieques are small and the best ones require a kind of short safari to reach. A lot of the roads are bumpy, full of mud puddles, and it seems like you're not getting anywhere, only deeper into the jungle. Which isn't really a jungle, but more like a low forest of bushes and small trees, tightly packed. Eventually you arrive at a little shaded area with fewer trees, and plopped right there like an ivory boomerang cupping a crystal blue cove, is your beach.

There are half a dozen commonly known and relatively easy to get to. But there are others, maybe three or four, that don't have names. The locals, even the ex-pats, don't like to give directions, especially to Americans. It's not uncommon for you to spend all day on one of Vieques's better known beaches and not see more than three or four people. But these other beaches, the ones no one likes to talk about, you could have five hundred meters of powdered sugar all to yourself.

This was what Bob Percy was telling me. Claimed he and his brood finally found one unlike any of the others. 'Had to cut through a rusted chain blocking the road and ignore a few old signs the Navy put up,' Bob said. 'Then hike through another quarter mile of brush to get there, but it was worth every flea in my shorts. Makes Navio look like a catshit-infested sandbox. Most beautiful thing you've ever seen.'

I told Bob Percy to bring his wife and family over for

dessert that night after dinner – my wife had found enough ingredients to make a key lime pie – and I'd get him drunk and make him tell me how to find this beach.

'That sounds good, chief,' Bob said. 'You won't get it out of me, but we could use the company and you're welcome to try.'

We agreed on seven o'clock. Bob and his tribe set out again that morning, and we stayed back, doing our usual thing. I was having another Medalla on the balcony around four o'clock, watching the pelicans dive for supper. The weather turned windy and overcast. Rain started, and it was a wet one. Blowing in from the ocean, soaking most of our padded lounge chairs on the balcony. My wife was worried about a hurricane, but it wasn't the season and this was just your average subtropical deluge. By six Bob and his family were running late, and I was imagining them scrambling off the beach, coming home a wet mess.

Half an hour went by, and then an hour, then two, and by now the rain was really dumping all over the island. Wasn't safe to drive and dusk was near, so I was getting worried. I had a feeling they'd run into trouble. My wife told me to quit being an idiot and come inside. I wasn't cold, but I did have to use the bathroom, though; those little beers add up eventually.

So I ran inside and used the head, helped my wife crank one of the bedroom shutters tight. I wasn't inside more than three or four minutes, and when I went back out onto the balcony, the Percy minivan was parked in its

159

usual spot inside the gates to the side of their villa. The van doors were closed. The Percy villa was dark.

I waited, watching for Bob to unload, but he didn't appear. None of them did. Well, it would be silly to unload in this weather. But why weren't their lights on? The power hadn't gone out in our place, but it was possible the other villas were on different lines and maybe one of them had gone down. I popped inside for my windbreaker and told my wife I'd be back in a few minutes.

I went down the stairs and around the gardens on the side of our place. You couldn't get to the other villas by crossing from lawn to lawn. There were tall stucco fences and locked gates. You had to use the access road behind the villas, and I arrived in less than five minutes. I glanced at the entire row of six villas and saw that the lights in all of them were off.

I think that was the moment I knew something had gone wrong for the families. The families who would change everything, including us.

26

On Friday Mick stood on the northeast corner of the dam, watching a handful of boats gather and fold the surface of Boulder Reservoir into silken green bolts. Further along the sloping rock wall, a Latino father and son duo cast their red-and-white bobbers and patiently awaited a response. It was a typical June day, the sky vast and populated by a scattering of cotton balls that tumbled and burned away from the sun. Standing as close to the accident as was possible sans watercraft, he expected to feel something more – fear, anxiety, additional flashes of insight that would point the way back to the mystery that had unfolded here – but so far there was nothing. It was the same lake he had known all his life, not the dormant monster that had almost ended it.

He had come home late last night to find Amy sleeping in the guest room, so he had escaped confrontation until this morning, when she scolded him for working too much. He had not found the words to describe the things he had experienced his first day back at work; telling Amy would only pile more stress on her. And anyway, he couldn't be sure that any of these 'insights' were real, at least not until he confronted his accountant. Instead, he had pretended he was tired, worn out and chastened, promising to lay low today. She seemed to buy it.

He walked the long path, the sun loosening him up, and thought about Roger Lertz and his mistress Bonnie. The real Roger, and the hideous version that had visited him in his dreams two nights ago. That had been an absurd but terrifying nightmare, but what would it mean now if the police came to him and informed him Roger was actually dead?

Before leaving the house that morning, Mick called Sergeant Terry Fielding to schedule an informal statement and got rolled into an anonymous department voicemail box. He supposed his old police buddy would get back to him in his own time, when there was something worth sharing, but the fact that the police had not visited him yet was unsettling.

What had Kyle really seen? Roger attacking Bonnie? And then what had Mick seen on the boat? He couldn't remember anything, but the idea of Roger trying to drown Mick (a possible witness to Bonnie's attack or murder) didn't feel right. Roger had always been a loose ball bearing, a party guy who could not grow up, but Mick couldn't figure the dentist for a murderer or even an attempted murderer.

You're in a lot of trouble, the dentist had said in his dream. *I'm free of all my addictions. Now it's my turn to help you.*

Far more likely, Roger had been drunk or coked up

162

and got into a skirmish with Bonnie, the two of them had seen Mick coming back for them, and somehow slipped away from the most-likely-borrowed vessel. Nobody had been murdered. Roger was too jolly for homicide. Roger. Jolly. It gave Mick a smile and he decided right then to go for a swim.

He hadn't brought a suit, but he doubted anyone would mind if he went *au natural*. He had almost drowned here; he deserved to re-baptize himself at the scene. He peeled off his T-shirt and jeans, wadded his underwear, and kicked his sneakers off into a pile amid the dam's fortification stones. He stepped down into the water. The father and son fishermen gave him a strange look and then ignored him, no doubt recognizing a Boulder progressive wing-nut when they saw one. When the water reached his knees, Mick took the plunge, pulling himself in broad strokes toward the northwest corner.

It was a good swim of perhaps a hundred meters and Mick reached the dock with energy to spare. His body, so leaden this morning, felt nimble and greased, gliding through the lake in a consistent surge, his shoulders thick with reserves of harnessed power. This felt really good. Why didn't he swim more? He spent his entire summer indoors, on his feet, while less than a mile away from home the natural splendor of the lake waited for him. He became a human torpedo, thriving, daring the lake to take him back.

He slowed as the orange wood of the dock bobbed a few meters off. He paused, treading water for a minute, enjoying the sun on his face. The sun reflected across the surface, twinkling, and a silver glare hit him like a flash.

The floor of the world seemed to drop out from under him, and he was falling in the lake as high stone walls rose around him on all sides. The land above disappeared in shadows and the water around him was silver, the mercurial surface shrinking in diameter, the walls closing in. He panicked, thrashing his limbs, and someone was pulling on his legs. He kicked and frothed in the lake (but it wasn't really the lake any more, it was another body of water entirely, a world away) and felt the fingers grasping his ankles, their fingernails scratching his thighs, trying to take him down.

Mick swallowed water and coughed, pure terror animating him now as he imagined them down there, maybe Roger and Bonnie, maybe other people, faceless forms with alabaster skin from lying in the depths, blind with cataracts, groping for him while the sun shrank into a speck and disappeared behind tropical clouds.

He was drowning again, and it struck him with cold certainty that the people drowning with him, pulling him under, were his own family. Amy and Kyle and Briela were already dead, lost down here in this hellish hole in the world, and they did not want to stay here alone.

No. You can't take them. You can't take me. We will live.

He kicked their hands away, slipped free of their cold slippery fingers, scissoring himself to the surface. He reached out and his hands fell upon the dock. Solid wood, the scent of stale Astro-Turf. Something tangible, from the real world. He twisted in the water, balled his legs up, and kicked off the edge of the floating dock. The stone walls around him were gone, the sun was out, and once again it was just a lake, the lake he had always known.

He began to stroke his way back to the dam, going all out, as if unknown forces were surging from the lake bottom, intent on dragging him back down.

27

Briela leapt from the couch and declared it was time to go swimming.

Ingrid agreed to sit and read a magazine while her charge paddled around and ordered her to count how long she could hold her breath underwater. This made Ingrid think of Mick's drowning, but surely the girl was not making the same connection, and neither Mick nor Amy had forbidden B from swimming, so that was no big deal, right? As long as Ingrid kept a close eye on her.

She plastered B in SPF 30 and made her wait at least fifteen minutes, but she could still see the iridescent lotion slicks trailing across the pool's surface. The temperature climbed into the low nineties, and soon Ingrid was thirsty and regretting not bringing her suit. B refused to come inside for lunch, so Ingrid told her to stay in the shallow end while she went in for some iced tea and maybe a snack. Amy always kept a stash of frozen goodies – pound cake or ice-cream sandwiches, bags of Reese's cups – and during the lulls between paychecks, Ingrid considered these treats one of the main perks of the job.

She kept checking the kitchen window overlooking the back yard. B was paddling back and forth in horizontal laps, and she was a good swimmer, but Ingrid was taking no chances. Briela's mood swings or episodes left no time for distraction. As much as Ingrid liked Mick and Amy, and cared deeply about Briela's well-being, she only needed to get through the summer, at which point none of this family's problems would be her problem. She was moving to Portland at the end of August. Justin and Sara, two of her friends from her Ft Collins college days, had relocated there last fall and they said the art and music scene was amazing, not to mention the cheaper and better medicinal weed.

She refilled an ice tray at the sink and looked out the window. B bobbed up and spat a stream of water, her blonde hair a dorsal fin. She began to hop in a circle, taking long, moonwalker strides, babbling in the way of a girl who is used to having an audience at all times.

Ingrid put the ice tray back in the freezer and gathered up her iced tea and a plate of mini Klondike bars. She elbowed the sliding glass door open, but turned back when she realized she had forgotten her sunglasses. She set the plate down, put her glasses on, got the plate under control again, and made her way out onto the patio.

Briela was still in the pool, more or less where Ingrid had last seen her, but she wasn't moving. She was standing with her back to the house, staring off into the distance. Ingrid set the plate and tea on the short table next to her lounge chair.

167

'B, I brought you a Klondike bar. Better get one before they melt.'

The girl did not acknowledge the offer.

Ingrid looked over the property, trying to follow B's gaze. Beyond the pool house, the grass ended in a wide oval that bordered another three acres of mown hay, and the white stucco border fence the new people had built around their house. Ingrid didn't see anything of interest as she scanned from one corner of the lot to the other.

'B? What is it, honey?'

Briela looked back over her shoulder, her expression vacant.

'What?' Ingrid said. 'You see a prairie dog?'

'There was a man,' Briela said.

'A man.'

'He climbed over the fence and was coming up here but now I can't find him.'

The remark sent a jolt through the sitter, snapping her attention back over the lawn. No man in any direction, and it was a clear, bright day. She wondered if Briela was having another one of her hallucinations.

'What did he look like?' she said, moving closer to the pool. The temperature seemed to have climbed another ten degrees. 'Was he maybe one of the workers? Like the people from last spring?'

Briela turned toward the yard again. 'He was handsome, with light blond hair, and he was smiling.'

Smiling. How would she know this from such a distance? How close had this smiling man gotten to them before disappearing?

168

'So ... where did he go?' Stay calm, don't freak her out.

'I don't know. I guess he vanished.'

'Why don't you come inside for a minute so we can eat our ice cream.'

Briela leapt away, plowing a wave of water. 'I don't want ice cream.'

Okay, well, whatever she had seen, or thought she had seen, it clearly hadn't scared her. No reason to be alarmed. Still, the idea of some man climbing a fence, walking over to chat them up for God knows what. No, they should go inside.

'Your skin is starting to prune and you need to eat some lunch,' Ingrid said. 'Come on, just for a few minutes.'

Briela exited the pool and stuck out her tongue. Ingrid brought the plate and her tea in, then locked the sliding glass door behind them. She went to the bathroom to fetch B a towel and locked the front door on her way to the hall, pausing in the living room to check the lawn through the windows. She saw no one outside.

When Ingrid got back to the family room, B was dripping water on the couch while she scrolled through the channel guide. She settled on a movie they had watched seven or eight times already this summer, and Ingrid made her scoot onto the towel. Briela changed her mind about the ice cream and they worked their way through all six of the mini-bars as they melted. Every few minutes Ingrid pretended to busy herself in the kitchen while she checked the backyard, but half an hour later no one had materialized.

B fell into an ice-cream stupor and soon was asleep on the couch. Ingrid turned the movie down and kicked back on the love seat with her magazine. There was an article about The Ten Things He Really Wants You to Do But is Afraid to Ask. Ingrid decided she would do six, but the other four were out of the question. The air conditioning hummed and the house cooled. She was nodding off when Briela mumbled something.

Ingrid twitched and the magazine slid to the floor. 'What'd you say, honey?'

'He came back,' Briela said through a yawn.

Ingrid sat up. B was still lying on her side, her face aimed at the TV. There was no way she could see out back, and Ingrid would have heard her get up. Ingrid's own back was to the windows and she couldn't decide which was worse now – B's creepy, imaginary warnings or the possibility that when she turned around, the man would be there, on the patio, watching her through the window.

'That is so not funny,' Ingrid said, turning around. The windows were clear, the yard empty. Maybe the girl was just talking in her sleep.

The doorbell chimed.

28

When Mick reached the dam, he was spent, his arms shaking. He felt suicidal for attempting such a swim so soon after his trauma. He clung to the rocks a minute, then climbed out slowly, feeling less like a man than some primordial creature forged in mud.

I panicked. Scared myself with a little flashback to that nightmare.

We're fine now. It doesn't mean a thing.

His clothes were not where he had left them.

'Jesus H. Christ,' a man growled. 'That is about the last thing I needed to see today.'

A bundle of denim flew at Mick and he caught most of his clothes before his shoes fell to the ground. Dennis Wisneski was sitting astride a green four-wheeler, scowling from behind his wrap-arounds. A cotton ball was bandaged over one ear but otherwise Coach looked to be in his usual surly element.

Mick pulled his shorts and pants on, his T-shirt, smirking at how similar this scene was to their old locker-room days. 'Sorry, Coach. I looked for you earlier around the boat house. Didn't expect you to be back to work so soon.'

'All these years, you ever known me to be sitting on my ass at home watching *Family Feud* while you have all the fun?'

'I guess not.'

Coach spat into the dirt. 'I see you had yourself another swim. Was it pleasant?'

'Matter of fact it was. At first.'

Wisneski's mustache arched as he rose to full height and dismounted his steed. 'You always did look like a drowned rat, Nash. Never figured you'd go ahead do the job proper, though. What in *the* fuck did you want to go and do that for? And today? What is it? Once wasn't enough for you? You know goddamn well swimming outside of the designated beaches is against my rules and since when do I make allowances for brain damage?'

Mick laughed. He loved the Coach, he realized, always had. Loved him the way you love any tyrannical family member once they were dead and gone.

'Thank you for saving my ass, Coach. That was a damn brave thing you did the other day and if you ever need anything from me—'

'You can stop smokin' that peace pipe right now.' Coach removed and waved his sunglasses angrily. His eyes were horribly red, inflamed and puffy, as if he'd been crying for a week. 'That's what I wanted to tell you, you fortunate bastard, so don't go getting all sentimental on me.'

Mick gave up on his socks and stepped into his tennis shoes, bracing himself for bad news. He felt now like he had on so many occasions when Coach had taken him

172

aside before a match and whispered some nasty secret about his opponent, late reconnaissance about some deadly move the other weasel was bound to put on you.

'I don't understand,' Mick said.

'You wouldn't, would you? The spill you took, you shouldn't oughta be out walking around let alone swimming. But here you are, dumb as God made you. Point is, I didn't save you. That other fella did, and I want to know who he is, because that sonofabitch disappeared on me and he left a good goddamn number of questions I need answered. He a friend of yours or that asshole Roger's?'

'What friend?' A small wave of nausea rolled through his belly.

'Blond guy, about your age or a little younger, thin, goes around in a chambray work shirt?'

'I don't know who you're talking about.'

'You don't remember seeing anyone else?'

'I remember nothing about that day. Just tell me what happened, Coach.'

So, Wisneski took him through it, and it was a pretty neat story with no real surprises until Coach dove into the water. Soon as Mick dropped the family off, Amy put the kids in the truck and told Kyle to watch Briela while she walked over to the boat house. She told Coach there was an assault or some kind of violent struggle on Roger Lertz's boat. At which point Wisneski, who was short-handed – his supervisor, Jimmy Redding, a hotshot lush of a sports management and kinesiology major at CSU who worked summers at the res, had called in that day

173

with a gargantuan hangover – saddled up and drove out alone.

'I was about two hundred yards out when I saw you go ass over head into the drink,' Coach said. 'I fixed your position as I pushed the throttle full-tilt. When I got there I radioed SOS, man in the water. There was no one on either boat, no one on the nearest floating dock some fifty yards due west. I want you to remember that for a moment. We were alone, you understand, and the dam was at least a hundred yards east, also empty.'

Mick nodded.

'I dropped anchor and dove in after you. Visibility was typical, no more than ten, twelve feet on a sunny day, far less below the first ten feet. I dove three times, to depths of ten, twenty, and possibly twenty-five feet. Bottom's about thirty in that neck of the res. Each time I went under, I swam in a half-circle, hoping to cover a total surface area of about a hundred square, but after three free dives I didn't see you and I was tiring. I'm an old fuck, Nash. My left shoulder has a tendon like pair of torn pantyhose and my right knee's full of gravel.

'I was coming up from that third dive, moving through maybe eighteen feet of water, when my lungs heaved once like a hiccup and the change in pressure made something in my left ear pop like a champagne cork. My sense of direction went a little fucky on me. I could see the sunlight, but all the sudden *up* took me right and when I tried to correct to the left I was swimming down.'

Mick said nothing while the Coach paused to cough

twice into his fist, then drew a deep breath and continued, staring off at the highway and shaking his head as if trying to see again what he had seen beneath the water.

'Damnedest thing. Swimming in a circle like that. I felt like one of those goldfish my granddaughter brings home from the pet shop, the ones that've had their genes all whirled up to make pretty colors and come out of the plastic baggie pop-eyed and a tad retarded. Swim bladder all messed up. I'm tellin' myself to stay calm else we'll both wind up in the mud. I needed air, and I figured I had one more dive left in me. Few seconds pass. I get my bearings and pop to the surface. I take five good breaths and one huge one, and then I head back down.

'I'm at a depth of about fifteen feet and diving at a forty-five degree, right under the boats, when I see him. This other crazy shit. At first I thought he was a fish, a fucking huge striped bass or some goddamn thing. He was just a faded white spot in the darkness, rising up. Then I thought it was you, because while it's still dark down there, I can see legs kicking, and it's clearly a man. White face, blond hair bobbing like a jellyfish. Then the blue of his shirt. Fucker's wearing a button-down and khakis, his left arm just pulling water down as hard and fast as a man can.

'You were folded over his right arm like a hundred and seventy pounds sack of potatoes and he's pulling with the other arm easy as dragging a wet towel. I saw your ugly face in less than ten feet of water, and if I am sure of anything, I'm sure you were unconscious. Legs limp, boat shoes still on your feet, and those khaki pants kicking in perfect scissor motion, driving the both of you to salvation. Your eyes were half open and dead as catfish on a platter, your face was blue-white, and your mouth was open. You looked like the textbook definition of a drowned man.

'I kick after him, rising to meet him on the other side of the boats. I looked up and saw the hull of one of them, Roger's or your boat, I can't say – they're both white and I was still disoriented. I had no more than six feet of clearance as I swam through, and by then the two of you were gone.'

'Gone?' Mick didn't know how much longer his legs would hold him up. He realized he hadn't eaten anything today and this story was making him feel faint. 'What do you mean "gone"?'

'I mean you weren't where you had been ten seconds earlier. I waited a bit at the surface, treading water until I realized Blondie should have been up there, gasping for air like me. But he didn't show up and when I looked under, turning in a complete circle, there was no sign of either of you.

'I panicked, and the water seemed to have dropped twenty degrees. For a moment it was like I had gone swimming in December, like we'd gone through a hole in the ice. Maybe I was in shock, but I don't think so. I was breathing ragged and my arms and legs were palsied. Couldn't go back down again. I'd a drowned myself.

'Anyway, the second of my Lake Patrol boats was on its way, Chad Groeninger waving at me. He'd already

176

radioed 9-1-1 and your ambulance was on the way. He asked me if I was all right and I told him there was another man in the drink. Mr Khakis. Chad dives in but don't see dick. So he comes back up, and we're treading water like a couple of goddamned synchronized swimmers, and Chad heads back to the boat. I'm exhausted but I can't bring myself to climb out of the water yet. I can almost feel something warning me to keep my eyes open, and then I turned in a circle and about shit myself.

'There you are, the two of you, crawling out of the water, right up on the dam. That's a hundred feet away, Nash, and last I saw you were D-E-A-D dead, but now the blond guy's crawling out and you're crawling out. On your own. He's not helping you. You're on your feet, climbing over rocks just like I found you today, and then you plopped down on the path, right about where we're standing now, and you just stared across the lake at us. The blond guy, he bends down and whispers something in your ear for a minute. Then he stands, looks over his shoulder at us, and continues over that steep hill, dropping out of sight. By the time I got to you, he was gone. Chad never saw him, but he saw you. Khaki pants wasn't in the field back here, and he didn't circle back to the boat house or loading ramp. He up and fuckin' vanished.

Mick shook his head. 'Wait. Back up. Amy said you rescued me.'

'Then all due respect to your wife, but she doesn't know what she saw. She wasn't there on the lake when you crawled out.'

177

'You told the police about all this,' Mick said. 'Gave them a description and all the rest?'

For the first time, Coach looked depleted, confused, as if someone had just bonked him over the head with a shovel.

'No, I did not. Yet. I was having trouble hearing and some snot-nosed little shit paramedic insisted I be taken in, as if I was the one who drowned. By the time I was asked to give a formal statement, I assumed this blond chap had come forward.'

'Why would you hold back? What's the big deal?'

'Hold your horses, Nash. That's what I'm getting at. I have one possible theory. It's a weird one, but not so weird if you know anything about extreme survival situations.'

'Yeah, what?'

Wisneski crabbed sideways, putting his back to the sun. 'You ever hear of the third man?' Mick shook his head once. 'I know you think I'm a big dumb jock, but I read a lot of books. I liked that Shackleton story was all the rage a few years back. That's where I first read about him. My wife got it into her head nothing would make me happier than another survival story, so for the past few years all I get on my birthday or Christmas is another one of these survival books. Writer by the name of John Geiger wrote a book called *The Third Man Factor*. Very rare phenomenon. Happens on polar expeditions, solo journeys, men lost in the woods or at sea. POWs have experienced it, even a few people involved with September Eleven claim to have met this third man.

'What it boils down to is a survival mechanism inside us that, in moments of deep distress – we're talking right at the brink of losing all hope – that emerges and comes to us almost as an alien presence, an entity separate of our selves. Some men talk about it as a kind of divine intervention, a spiritual or mystical force. You're huddled in a tent near the summit of Everest, freezing your balls off, your toes are already done in, you're loopy, half-starved, in shock, and the regular you is thinking how nice it might be to curl up and go to sleep. Just let go. Die. But then this third man appears, or maybe you don't see him, but you feel him. He is like your new best friend, a buddy looking over your shoulder. He's not afraid and he's calm, in control, and he's got all the strength you wish you had. And in the darkest hour of your longest night, he leans down and he whispers in your ear. *Here's what you need to do*, he says. *We're not giving up. We're going to make it out of here alive. Just follow my instructions and stick with me and everything will turn out right.* He's comforting, the way Jesus might be to some. It's a survival mechanism, but it feels like a stranger, a higher power. The third man.'

Wisneski spread his hands, a lawyer wrapping up his closing argument.

'That's what you think?' Mick said. 'It was you who saved me, but your mind, under extreme duress, projected this other man? You had an out-of-body experience and watched yourself, in the form of this other blond guy in khaki pants, rescue me?'

'I did at first.' Wisneski smiled a gotcha smile. 'But in

the end, when I got my strength back, I decided that was bullshit. Because I wasn't on death's doorstep and I wasn't ready to give up. Hell, I've been through a lot worse than your little episode. I was in Vietnam, Mick. I crawled in those tunnels and saw men cut in half. A good friend of mine in high school, Ted Millhiser, he rolled his dad's Dodge out on Highway 36 and almost burned to death. I was one of the boys who put him out in the grass with a letter jacket. Ruined the jacket, but it was some Fairview kid's, so no loss there. Point is, I've seen some shit and this wasn't that much shit, all right? I know what I saw, Mick, and it was a real man. He saw you go in and he dove in after you. From there, one of two things happened.

'One, somewhere between the water and dry land, God knows how, he revived you. None of this CPR horseshit. He brought you back to life *en route*. Or two, you "woke up" and swam away on your own steam. Either way, he's out there somewhere right now. I don't just believe that. I know it.'

Mick thought that Coach was bluffing. This whole third man business had made him uneasy, all of it had, and Coach was scared. Why else would he make this big speech, only to brush it off, if he wasn't simultaneously trying to come to grips with something unexplainable and maintain his macho self-image? But he wasn't going to argue, either. Arguing with men like Dennis Wisneski got you nowhere.

'If you say so, Coach. What do you want me to do about it?'

'I want you to find him. I want to know who he thinks he is, coming out of nowhere to save your sorry life and then vanishing without a trace like a miracle. But more than that—' Dennis Wisneski adjusted his glasses and coughed wetly into his fist again. 'Goddamned if I'm not still coughing up the taste of that lake. More than that, I want to know what he did with Roger and that gal Bonnie. I doubt there's a hero in all this, but there might very well be a murderer.'

But why would someone kill Roger and Bonnie, only to save me? Mick thought again, but did not ask.

'Okay, Coach. I'll keep my eyes open and let you know if I hear something.'

Wisneski climbed back onto his Kawasaki, his hairless bronzed old man knees almost as shiny as the green plastic faring. 'Yeah, you do that. And in the meantime stay the hell away from my lake. You've gotten your money's worth this season.'

Coach U-turned on the dam path, the knobbies kicking up a cyclone of dust as he rumbled his way back to the boat house.

Some blond guy had saved his life. Mick thought back to the man who had been eavesdropping on his conversation with Sapphire. Could be a coincidence, but nothing in the past few days felt like a coincidence. The question now was, who was he and why was he so interested in Mick Nash?

29

The doorbell rang again.

Ingrid's limbs pebbled with goosebumps and one hand moved involuntarily over her stomach. How had Briela known he was coming? What was going on inside this girl? And what did he want? If it was even him, the blond man she claimed to have seen. It was probably a coincidence, the UPS man or someone collecting donations for another cause. But it didn't feel like a coincidence. The room was charged with bad energy, invisible plus and minus signs buzzing the air while a metallic taste worked its way onto Ingrid's tongue.

'Told you,' Briela said.

'I'm serious, Briela. Are you playing games with me?'

'Nuh-uh.'

The doorbell chimed a third time, and the babysitter flinched.

Briela looked up at her with dull eyes. 'Aren't you going to answer it?'

It's the middle of the day, for the love of God. Stop being such a baby.

'Stay here, all right?'

'M'kay.'

Ingrid pressed her back against the wall furthest from the foyer window and sidled up to the door. She checked the peephole.

He *was* handsome, with neatly parted blond hair and soft, almost equine features. He wore a chambray work shirt so faded it was almost white, the top three buttons open, giving him the look of a man on vacation. But she only caught a glimpse before he turned sideways, his full lips working as if he were speaking to someone she couldn't see.

Fine, fine. She opened the door halfway.

He moved slowly, as if the air were heavy around him. He looked up at her with mild surprise and then smiled, or tried to. The impression was of a man who wasn't used to smiling, because the one he gave her was strained, using only the corner of his mouth. He didn't say anything for a moment, and his eyes, which were low-lidded with irises of cobalt, did not so much land on her as linger around the space she inhabited. He struggled to fix on a point and she wondered briefly if he was blind.

'Is he yours?' His voice was very deep, though gentle.

'Sorry?'

The man snapped his fingers awkwardly but they made no sound. There was a clicking sound on the porch and then Thom, the Nash's Yorkshire terrier, came skittering inside. She jerked back, then was relieved. Okay, this was all about the dog. Thom had free reign of the property, but usually never strayed far. He must have gotten onto the new people's yard, probably to leave a few chocolate welcome presents. Of course that's what the man had been trying to tell them earlier. He had come to let them know the dog was loose, then probably circled back after the dog got away from him again while Ingrid was in the kitchen.

'Oh, right, thank you,' Ingrid stammered. 'I'm sorry. Was he bothering you?'

The man watched the dog dart in and out of the living room. He was either extremely mellow or shy.

He said, 'Is this where he lives?'

Ingrid thought that was clear by now, but whatever. 'Yes, he belongs to the Nashes.'

'The ... Nash-es?'

'Yes.'

'Are you the Nash-es' daughter?'

Ingrid kept the knob in her left hand, bracing the door with her shoulder. 'No, I work for them.'

He frowned, then smiled as if just now remembering. 'We have a daughter too.'

Ingrid wasn't sure if he failed to hear her or simply chose to ignore the clarification.

He said, 'We have already met each member of the Nash-es.'

'Right, well, is there something else or ... '

He smiled wider and before she even saw it leave his side, his hand had closed around her forearm. His touch was delicate and brief, like a kiss that went around her wrist, leaving a cold ring that tingled and spread up her arm. She pulled away, but his hand was already back at his side and he was still smiling. She was so nervous, and he looked so calm, she couldn't be sure now if he had actually done it or if she was only imagining it.

'I'm sorry,' he said. 'But are you happy with your, ah, employment? Do they take good care of you here?'

Was he hitting on her or trying to hire her? 'I guess so. They're good people.'

'Good people,' he said. 'That is true in many ways, I am sure.'

An awkward moment stretched between them.

'So,' she said. 'That's your house in the back, right? It's really nice.'

'Yes, for now. I hope we haven't stirred up any ill will amongst your employers. We're very respectful of the situation. We believe in live and let live.'

This was now officially disturbing. There was something wrong with the man. He looked like one of what Ingrid thought of as the catalog people, a model for the kind of spread that went out to shoppers with beach homes, with those perfect white jeans and the shirt and the matching white leather sneakers. His eyes widened, then lowered again.

'Well, thank you for bringing Thom back.' She inched the door forward.

'Who is Thom?'

'The dog,' she said.

'Right,' he said. 'Oh, is that the other daughter?' His loose gaze drifted past her and his eyes filled with excitement.

Ingrid turned. Briela was standing in the foyer, at the

mouth of the family room. She was smiling at him expectantly, as if something had been confirmed to her liking.

Ingrid decided this was enough for one day. 'I have to go. Goodbye, now.'

She shut the door.

She locked the door.

'Briela, go to your room for a minute.'

'Why?'

'Because I said so. Now, please.'

Briela scowled and stomped off to her bedroom. Ingrid checked the peephole. He was still standing there on the porch, looking around with his dumb expression. She thought of calling Amy or the police, but he hadn't done anything really wrong. And maybe he was just slow, except at the end there he seemed perfectly sharp. And curious. There was no crime in that. He seemed nice. But there was something creepy about the way this whole thing had consumed nearly an hour.

She checked the peephole again. He was still there. She held her eye against the door a moment. What the hell was he doing?

He turned abruptly and smiled, his face looming right up to hers.

'We have a daughter too,' he said, the words thick through the door. He turned and stepped off the porch and went a few steps. He stopped and looked back. 'And a son. We can always use more help!'

Then his long strides carried him around the front lawn and he disappeared down the Jenkins' driveway, back toward his fancy new house.

Ingrid felt faint, her legs rubbery. She moved around the sofa in the family room and sat sideways to the window. Her stomach was fluttery, as if he had kissed her, done something against her will. He hadn't, though, right? He hadn't done anything. For a moment she imagined that he had. His smooth hands, his easy smile. That shirt so soft, washed out like his eyes. Her heart was not racing, but it was doing something here. Thumping in a heavy rhythm, her chest misty with perspiration. She felt a little ache between her legs, not unpleasant. She pinched her thighs together almost on reflex and the pressure magnified the ache, delicately brushed it to life.

No. This was not okay and did not fit. She had been repulsed by him and his creepy tone, and she was repulsed by him now. But warmth became heat. It was as if her body knew something true that her mind wanted to be false.

She sat forward and looked out the window. He wasn't there. *Good.* She should get up and tell Briela it was okay to come out of her room. But she was fatigued from stress and the air conditioning felt good on her bare legs. It was nice just to sit here for a while. She leaned back and thought of his face, wondering how old he was. Not very. Must have really done something with his life to have a house like that. People like that probably had a family assistant just like her, and a maid, and gardeners, all kinds of help. Probably paid well too. More than the Nash-es. She thought of his eyes again. It was almost like he had been offering her something. Not sex.

187

Something deeper, simpler, a door to a new opportunity. She thought about his eyes ...

Then she thought of nothing.

Time passed.

She sat up, as if woken by a loud noise. But the house was quiet. She had been out of it for a good twenty minutes, maybe even half an hour, but that did not seem important. She went down the hall. Briela was sleeping on her floor, a book folded over one arm. She went back to the kitchen and stared out the window. Wonder what the others are like, she thought, and before she had time to consider what she was doing, Ingrid opened the sliding glass door and walked out.

The driveway was long, but she barely noticed it. She didn't wonder why the gates were open, as if waiting for her. She didn't notice much at all, only knocked on the door and waited. A minute passed. Maybe she had been mistaken. Maybe they didn't need her help. The sour taste of rejection rose up in her throat, and then the door opened. No one was there to greet her, but there were voices.

Friendly voices urging her to come inside.

30

'At the end of the letter, in our last paragraph, we want to sign off by thanking the prospect for their time and consideration, but we also need to use this opportunity to *ask for the job*. Or, as they say in sales – and believe me, this is sales, you are selling yourselves – to ask for the sale, to close the deal. May we schedule a time to discuss our mutual interests? The prospect is now confronted with a question he or she must answer. When might be the best time to reach you? In other words, I want the interview. Do you see what I'm saying, people? You've made your case, attached your résumé. Now it's time to go to the prom, or, in your case, the interview. And we all know you can't go to the prom without a date, right?'

In the third row, Rudy Pieshka cupped a hand over his feathery lip and said, 'I thought you couldn't go to the prom unless you were cooked on loco weed.'

Half a dozen of the others snickered, and Amy wanted to bite Rudy's ear off. She looked at the clock. Twelve minutes left. Nothing of substance would come of that. She'd talked too long, hadn't left enough time for writing, and because the weekend would scatter

189

their brain cells like pixie dust, she would have to summarize the components of the cover letter all over again next Wednesday. They were at least a week behind and the interview process was going to be a circus. She'd mentioned, offhandedly, that they should start digging out their best business attire, for the rehearsal sessions, in order to get used to dressing up for the real thing. That had earned her a round of complaints. I gotta go shopping at TJ Maxx now? What if my moms won't let me borrow her heels? I'm applying for a job as a janitor, Mrs Nash, does that mean I should bring my own mop?

'Let's take the last ten minutes to compose our background bios. We can add this paragraph to the rest of the letter next week. Remember, keep it short. No one wants your life story, just the two or three most relevant sentences. Ready? Go.'

Groans and small talk for the most part, a lot of texting. Two of the sixteen students actually whipped open their notebooks and began scribbling.

Amy returned to the chair behind her desk, her eyes landing on the two empty seats at the back of the class. Eric Pritchard and Jason Wells had not shown up today, and neither boy nor his parent or guardian had called in with an excuse. If one of them had been present, she might have been tempted to believe the other was ill, or had a work scheduling issue. But both at the same time meant they were ditching together. She shouldn't be happy about it, but in truth she was relieved. They never listened, never took notes, and spent most of the three-hour sessions interrupting her and generally filling the room with an air of defiance that the others fed on.

Amy opened her grade book and added some notes in the green margin. *Angela making progress, is genuinely concerned about her baby, future finances, etc. Keith Ramsey slipping, mentioned quitting job (his second of summer), expects more than min. wage, address realistic expect. in down economy.*

She shuffled a stack of résumés she needed to take home and mark up for revisions, slipped them into a manila folder, then into her briefcase. She sipped her Diet Coke but it had gone warm. She thought of dropping it in the steel can but it was mostly full and would splash all over. She would leave it here on the desk for Dick Humphries, custodial engineer. Teach him to chuckle at her window graffiti.

Amy caught movement to her left. Without raising her head, she tilted her chin in that direction. Out in the hall, walking very, very slowly past her classroom doorway, was Eric Pritchard. He wore the same dirty jeans, seventies-era clunking brown hiking boots with their woven red laces, and his camo-shirt-jacket thing.

Swinging in his right hand, the one most visible from her position, was a butterfly knife. The lower gold perforated handle dipped down and looped back into his palm and the blade rotated as the upper handle swung down in the same windmill arc. He was looking right at her as he did this and he was not smiling. He wasn't even scowling or sneering; in fact he looked almost bored. The knife pirouetted lazily in and out of his palm, and the casual ease of the display (he might have been tossing a rubber ball to himself) made her want to throw up.

And then he was gone, continuing beyond the door-frame, hiking boots thunking slowly down the hall until the only sound was the rising chorus of her students' voices as they anticipated the bell. Well, there were no bells here, or if there were, they weren't used for summer-school sessions of Workplace Econ. But the kids didn't need a bell, they knew three o'clock the way roosters know sunrise. Amy remained glued to her chair, eyes on her papers, her mind empty as the authoritarian in her reeled away to some deeper corner of her self. The sweeping second hand cruised past the black twelve, and her students erupted from their dirty, scratched desks and filed out – to her relief – as if she weren't even there.

She thought of waiting until they had all gone before checking the halls to make sure *he* wasn't there, waiting for her, but decided it would be safer to move with the herd. She did not see Eric Pritchard on her way out, his white Honda was not in the parking lot, and his co-dependent sidekick Jason Wells was nowhere to be found. They couldn't be bothered to attend class, and yet Eric had dropped by to send her a message. Impossible to pretend now that the graffiti had been a one-time prank. They were coming for her, and they would keep coming until they got her.

She did not cry on the way home this time. She was too numb to cry, and when the numbness wore off, there

192

was only a white-hot brick of anger. She thought, *I hope something bad happens to them. I don't care how hard their lives have been, or that they are only kids, or that they are lacking good role models, I really don't. Because I am all out of sympathy and empathy and politically correct nurturing teacher bullshit. I hope Eric Pritchard and his dangerously dumb cling-on just have themselves a nasty fucking fall and never get up. I hope the skinny little mouth-breather pulls that knife on someone who can teach him how to use it.*

The intensity of her sentiments made it a kind of prayer. The strangest part was that, when she got home, her fear and anger were gone, all gone, the burden lifted. As if someone powerful had been listening.

As if someone had heard her sin, and absorbed it.

31

Ingrid got back to the Nash place with time to spare.

Briela was still sleeping on her bedroom floor, balled up like a little lamb. The sitter stood in the bedroom doorway, watching her mysterious charge, as she had been hired to do. The degree to which her life had changed in the past hour filled her with an ecstatic terror. The money was going to set her up for a long time, she had been handed a kind of security she had never known. But more than that she no longer felt adrift. She had a purpose now, as if the compass needle that had been spinning inside her had found its true magnetic north. She still didn't understand everything they had planned, but she knew enough, and she had to be careful now. Do exactly as she had been told.

Carry on as usual. Observe. Report. Come to us if their routine changes in any way, no matter how minor. Above all else, tell no one we are watching.

We will protect you. Always.

Her legs never got tired and she stayed there, focused and unmoving, until the front door slammed thirty-seven minutes later.

Amy's voice carried down the hall. 'Hellooo? Anyone home?'

'In here,' Ingrid said, barely able to contain herself.

Amy came in behind her. 'There you are – oh.' She lowered her voice to a whisper. 'She's napping. Everything all right?'

Ingrid nodded and they stepped into the hall. 'She went down about ten minutes ago. I was just checking on her again because it's so unlike her.'

'Were there any ... ?' Amy winced in preparation for another report.

'Not at all. We had a swim. She must have worn herself out.'

Amy sighed with relief. 'It's this heat. I might take a nap myself.'

'Tough day at school?' Ingrid said. 'I hope those two boys weren't harassing you again.'

Amy frowned, stopped. 'How did you – did I mention Eric and Jason to you?'

'Your car window,' Ingrid prompted. 'No girl comes up with that.'

Amy nodded, studying her. 'But how'd you know there were two of them? I don't remember telling you about that.'

Ingrid laughed, surprised at her own insight. 'I don't know. Lucky guess? I mean, don't hyenas always travel in packs?'

'I suppose so.' Amy walked into the kitchen and Ingrid trailed. 'Did Mick sneak off to work again?'

'He was here when we went out back for a swim, but

when we came in to watch a movie, he was gone. He must be feeling better, right?'

'As if he would tell me.' Amy went to the fridge and studied the contents.

'I'm sorry,' Ingrid said. 'I totally forgot to make your salad. Want me to run to the store?'

Amy shut the door. 'Don't worry about it. I'm not even hungry. That's my problem, you know? I eat when I'm not even hungry. When I stop and think about it, I realize half the time I'm bored, or pissed off, or who knows what.'

'You look like you've lost some weight,' Ingrid said, not sure if she really meant it. It simply came to her and seemed like the right thing to say right now.

Keep up appearances. Confirm their own self-image to them.

'I do?' Amy looked down at herself. 'I doubt it. Funny you say that, though. I haven't eaten all day and that's so not like me.'

'I wouldn't worry about it. You're beautiful, Amy. I wish I had your skin.'

'Aw, Ingrid.' Amy took down a cup and held it under the faucet, beaming at her. 'That is so nice. See, that's why I love knowing you're in charge of sleeping beauty down the hall. You have the sweetest manners and set such a good example.'

Ingrid shrugged. 'She makes it easy. Same time tomorrow?'

Amy began to blabber about her schedule and plans for the party next week and a bunch of other meaningless crap. Ingrid smiled and nodded and said, 'All right, see you then.' She walked to the bus stop in a much brighter mood than when she had arrived this morning. She wouldn't be taking the bus much longer.

She had so many fun things to do before she left for Portland. And yet, the more she thought about the possibilities, the more she realized maybe Portland wasn't the thing any more. Maybe the thing, the real thing, was right here with the Render family.

32

Saturday night. Kyle was at the fourth party at Shaheen's house, in the development behind Boulder Country Club, when he saw her again. He was standing by the pool, unsure of his purpose here. Ben and Will were hovering around a table with two steel tubs full of ice and the last few cans of beer. Tiki torches bordered the golf course, and kids were walking around barefoot, pulling tubes and trying to grill frozen pizzas. Lucas was out on the fairway, swinging Shaheen's dad's Ping 5-iron. The sixth or seventh time a ball banged off someone's roof, Shaheen came out and told Lucas to cut the shit, did he want someone to call the cops?

Lucas laughed and handed over the club. Kyle knew most of the guys were afraid of Shaheen, and some of the girls too. He was mellow, but he had scary serious eyes, and he was body-builder yoked at age fifteen, his skin so dark in places it was like smoke-streaked stone. Everyone found it chic being buddies with a Persian dude, but that didn't stop them from staring at him in weird ways. He was only five-five, with flecks of gold highlights in his thick black hair and he always wore dark sunglasses, even at night. Kyle sort of wished he was Shaheen. The hair, the build, the skin, the cool knives and little motorized bong he carried in his leather satchel – all in all Shaheen was kind of sci-fi, a graphic novel dude come to life.

There were maybe forty people, they were down to five beers, and the party was far from over. Michelle Harper was standing on the other side of the pool, next to the portable fireplace, where Samantha Turner and Steph Jameson were smoking and sipping wine spritzers. But ever since he saw that girl in the park, Kyle barely thought about Michelle Harper. She had touched his arm at the last party, and he'd spent the rest of the night following her around like an idiot, not knowing what to say, her friends giggling at him before moving on to a more interesting corner of the party.

Tonight Michelle seemed to be sagging in some new way, and in a rare moment of insight Kyle realized when she was old she was going to be one of those hunched women. Her hair was sort of just hanging there. Twice she gave him a little wave and her thin smile. C'mere, that smile seemed to say. I won't laugh this time.

Kyle smirked and looked away, nervous about what was coming. He had waited in the car earlier – Will had stolen his mom's Corolla while she sat in her condo watching the *Witches Lane* marathon – feeling sick while Ben, Will, and Lucas went into the Gunbarrel King Soopers to get some beer. He knew they were boogying the beer. Ever since Will's fake ID got grabbed that day at Cornucopia, they had no connections. They were in the store for ten minutes or so, and when they came back out, they weren't even running. Will was just walking calmly, a suitcase of Bud pulling his skinny frame to one side. Lucas and Ben were carrying bags of snacks.

'So easy,' Will said when Kyle asked how they did it. 'You go get all the food first, your chips, some brats and buns, a six pack of Coke, whatever the fuck. You pay for that shit, get the receipt, smile at the checkout bitches. Then you circle back to the cooler and grab whatchoo need.'

'That's it?' Kyle said.

'But you gotta be smooth,' Ben said.

'Yeah,' Will said. 'The thing is, you got to let them see you. You just stroll, and if some manager asshole face at the photo booth sees you, you just smile and keep walking. He sees the bags, Lucas here holding the receipt, he figures, well, no way those kids are crazy enough to walk right under my nose with a case of beer. It's all about confidence.'

'What if he stops you?'

'Lucas swings the bag of groceries at his head, we drop the beer and run like a motherfucker. But they never stop you.'

'You gotta go at rush hour,' Lucas said. 'Like when people are stopping by on their way home from work. Look around, Nash. See how full this parking lot is? There's like fifty people going in and out of that huge front door every thirty seconds. They have no clue.'

'It's not even really a boogie,' Ben said. 'It's, like, the mellow boogie.'

Since school got out, Will had done seven beer boogies: four at King Soopers and two more at the Safeway off of Iris. Lucas had done at least five, and Ben was constantly stuffing forties of Busch into his sweatshirt. They had become heroes at every party, charging the other kids full price to boogie for them, pocketing the cash. Lucas was all like, damn, maybe boogying is my part-time job this summer.

Kyle hadn't boogied yet, but they were losing their patience with him. He had offered to pay for the few beers he drank, but that wasn't the point.

'Nash, hey, Nash,' Ben said from behind the table. 'Get your ass over here.'

Kyle went to them. They pointed into the tub, where two cans of Bud floated.

'Guess who's up,' Will said.

'Oh, man, come on,' Kyle said. 'My dad will kill me.'

'You're not gonna get caught. Why would you get caught?' Ben said.

Kyle glanced around nervously, as if they were already in the store. Another group had come in, four guys and two girls. Kyle recognized them as Fairview kids, maybe one from Boulder High. The girls were kinda goth, but in that expensive way, one of them six feet tall, a basketball player Kyle had seen at Baseline games, scaring the other girls with her black sprocket of hair. They filed around the island, fist-bumping Shaheen, the host with the most. Even Shaheen was counting on him to step up.

'I don't know,' Kyle said.

Will shrugged, pulling his pajama bottoms up off his hips. 'Just get it over with. Lucas will be your wingman.'

Kyle imagined his father staring at him with that look of beaten disappointment. His dad had been a party guy in his youth, Kyle knew. He would look the other way over a beer here and there, a C on the report card. But he was a business owner. When he talked about his employees stealing, his face turned purple. Stealing was a line you didn't cross.

'Guys, look, I just can't ...' Kyle was ready to say no and take the consequences, even if his tribe cast him out for the remainder of his high-school tenure.

But then he saw her. Not Michelle Harper. *Her.* The perfect girl. The one from the park. The one who had looked at him and mouthed some secret words. She was right here, in the kitchen behind the others, standing next to the cordless phone on Shaheen's wall, tucking a lock of her Pantene commercial hair behind her ear – shy or above it all, he couldn't tell. She didn't seem attached to anyone. It was as shocking and terrifying as seeing a ghost.

'Whoa, daddy, who is that stone cold Steve Austin?' Will said, and Kyle felt his heart sink. They were onto her already. She was a gazelle thrown in with lions. They would devour her before he got her name.

'Oh my God,' Ben said. 'Oh, sweet Dairy Queen. Who is that girl?'

'No idea,' Will said. 'But she's clean.'

'She doesn't go to Fairview, that's for sure,' Ben said. 'I know because I've jacked off to every page of the yearbook.'

'Bogie in pursuit,' Will said. 'Twelve o'clock and closing.'

She was headed right toward them, shifting beneath a thin, tight-fitting black thermal shirt and a pleated skirt of black and yellow plaid. Black canvas sneakers. In between, the cream white of her thighs. All of the guys and half of the girls were staring at her. She was fifteen feet away, ten, slipping out onto the patio, pausing, glancing around to scope it out. She stared at the pool, hypnotized by the wands of light roving around from someone's dive.

Kyle wondered when he had last showered. This morning? Last night? All at once he felt exactly like the sweaty, slightly pimpled, lanky and foppish-haired fifteen-year-old spaz he was. He looked down to see if there were any stains on his shirt. He was wearing his red Billabong button-down, brown skate shorts, black Vans chukkas. Everything was about as decent as it could be. He thumbed the corners of his mouth.

'Two beers left,' Ben called over Kyle's shoulder. 'Ladies first. Any takers?'

She turned, looking at the three of them behind the beer tub.

'Hey, darlin',' Ben said. 'I saved you one.'

Kyle wanted to ram the beer can into Ben's eye socket, tell them he had seen her first, lay off. But of course it didn't work that way either.

'Okay,' she said, and walked toward them as if approaching a carnival attraction. She would play this game for a minute, but flee at the first sign of anything hinky.

Kyle's eyes darted to her and away and back every 1/32 of a second. He laughed abruptly for no reason, stopped.

Ben handed her a can of Bud. 'And I guess the last one's mine. Cheers.' He raised his can but she didn't raise hers to meet him.

'I'm Will,' Will said. 'This is Ben.'

What about me, assholes? I'm invisible? Ben actually kicked his shoe under the table, trying to nudge him out of the picture.

'Hi,' she said to both of them. She hadn't opened the beer. She was just holding it against her hip.

'What's your story?' Ben said. 'And does it have a happy ending?'

'I doubt it.' She looked over their heads, her smile barely tolerant.

'Bummer,' Will said. 'So, what's your name?'

She opened her mouth to answer, halted, pivoted, and looked right into Kyle's eyes. She aimed the can of beer at him, her slender pointer finger extending past the rim. Her nail was painted bright lemon yellow.

'I've seen you. Who are you?' Her tone was accusatory. For a moment Kyle couldn't speak, and then his throat clicked loose.

'In the park,' he said. 'You were standing next to Boulder Creek.'

'No.' That was it. Her voice dull but firm; he was lying.

But he wasn't lying. He was sure. 'You were wearing a Sonic Youth shirt.' Where was this confidence coming from? He didn't know, but he plowed on. 'The red one with the nurse, from the *Rather Ripped* tour.'

After what seemed a long time, she smiled, her glossy lips revealing perfect white teeth and virgin gums the color of bubble gum.

'That *was* you. You know Sonic Youth?'

He hadn't until that Thursday night, when he spent four hours searching megasites that sold rock T-shirts, using the keywords 'red' and 'nurse', spotted it, then checked out the band's website and downloaded the album. He'd sort of fallen in love with the band, but he couldn't tell if that was because he really liked their sound or because he imagined she did.

'It's one of their catchier albums,' he said, hoping he sounded calmer than he felt. 'And "Turquoise Boy" is pretty epic, some of Kim Gordon's best vocals. But I like *Dirty* better. That record is just plain ... ' What's the word? That word for the Seattle sound his dad used to talk about? Grun—

'Dirty,' she finished for him, beaming. 'Dirty guitars and fuzz and distortion. The sound is the record. Exactly.' Her voice, Kyle decided right then, was the sound of peach-colored popsicles melting in the sun.

'I'm June.' She offered her hand.

'I'm Kyle.' He took her hand, heard his mother say *like a gentleman*, and held it so, raising and lowering it gently. Her palm was hot silk, her nails grazing his fingers as she withdrew. 'Nice to meet you for the sort of second time.'

'The sort of second time,' she repeated with a sly smile. 'That sounds like the title of song, Kyle.'

Will let out a breath as if he had been punched.

Ben stomped off, muttering obscenities.

So far it was a miracle. This girl was easily sixteen, maybe seventeen, two inches taller than him, and perfect in every way. Her eyes were the lightest blue Kyle had ever seen, almost silver in the dark, and her nose and cheeks were dusted with tiny dark freckles. She smelled like warm bread and honey and … girl.

'So, what's the deal?' She gestured at the tub. 'Is this the end of it?'

'Kyle was just on his way to get some more,' Will said, dangling the keys in front of him. Kyle clasped them in his fist before he knew what he was doing.

'You have a car?' she said.

'It's mine, but he's a big boy,' Will said. Lucas and Ben would never back him up like this, but maybe Will understood something was happening here. Maybe Will figured Kyle deserved a shot. 'Aren't you, Kyle?'

'Sure.'

June said, 'I'm starving actually. Mind if I tag along?'

'Cool.'

He could feel her moving behind him as he floated into the house, pushing the warm summer air at his back. Shaheen gave him a thumbs up. By the refrigerator, Michelle Harper froze, a jug of cranberry juice in her hand. Her mouth was set in an unflattering pucker.

Swaying with newfound grandeur as he walked out the front door, Kyle Nash tallied it like this: *I'm fifteen. I have no driver's license. I have seven dollars to my name. And I'm on my way to steal a case of beer with the hottest girl in the State of Colorado. This is either going to be the most humiliating night of my life, or the greatest.*

But once they were in the car and she was smiling at him, her eyes shining almost as if they were filling with tears, her hands trembling just enough to let him know she was nervous too, he realized it didn't matter. Whether he succeeded or failed epically, this was already the greatest night of his life.

33

'Look who's back on his feet. How you feelin', Aqua-man?'

Mick emerged from the Straw's kitchen, where he had been berating Carlos about the size of the side salads they were wasting on entrees, as well as fuming over a lapse in paper goods inventory that had left the restaurant with no take-out containers, plastic forks, and paper cups until next Friday when Sysco delivered (if they delivered at all, his account being 127 days past due), and turned to find a short bald policeman built like a rubber foosball player sitting at the bar.

At last, Sergeant Terrance Fielding of the Boulder PD. Terry was smiling, out of uniform, and Mick had done nothing wrong, but this did not prevent a cold blade of paranoia from slipping itself into him like a shiv.

'Dry,' Mick said. 'Like it never happened. Get you a beer or some club soda?' This was a sort of amateur code for, Are you here to interrogate me on official business or is this just a friendly visit because you're so concerned about my health?

'Just finished an iced tea, thanks. Was hoping to get

with you on a couple things before you clocked out, though I figured you'd be laying low for a few weeks.'

Mick shot himself a tumbler of club soda. 'What am I gonna do at home, Terry? This place is going down the shitter. I want to enjoy my last few weeks as a business-man.'

Fielding nodded without much sympathy. 'How are the kids?'

'Briela's a brilliant but emotional mess. Kyle hasn't landed in the back of your cruiser yet, so there's hope for him.'

'That cut on his head healing up all right?'

'Hasn't slowed him down a bit.'

'Tough kid.'

Mick nodded.

Fielding removed a cardboard Samuel Adams Light coaster from a neat stack Mick had set on the bar. He always stocked them in piles of a dozen, a little OCD habit that sustained the illusion of order amid the greater chaos. Like a Vegas dealer with house chips, Mick could count the stack on sight. Fielding held it between his first two fingers, fanned it like a playing card, and whizzed it sideways along the bar. Mick watched it twirl and slide up to the condiment tray, braking in a patch of maraschino cherry juice.

Fielding said, 'You have any problems around the restaurant lately? Anything weird after hours? Threats, bad customers, creeps lurking in the parking lot?'

'No, unless by bad customers you mean not enough good ones. Why?'

'Oh, could be nothing, could be something. You know Raul down at Casa Miguel's?'

Mick knew the Mexican restaurant off 30th. 'Nice place. Amy likes their *carnitas*. But I don't know Raul or the family. He the owner?'

'Night manager, owner's brother,' Fielding said. 'He got the hot tamales beat the shit right out of him 'bout three, four weeks ago. Closing time.'

'Jesus,' Mick said. 'I think I read something about that in the paper.'

'Yeah. Concussion, broken ribs, punctured lung. He's going to be fine, but it was scary there for a while. Doctors thought maybe brain damage, but he's coming around.'

'You catch the guy?'

'Guys. Three of them, we think. Just boys, really. Same kind of thing happened back in March, one of the bartenders down at Pasta Jay's. Witness accounts weren't worth a shit. You know how it is that time of night downtown. Everyone hammered off their balls. But two college girls leaving the West End said they saw three hot-shot assholes watching the back door about that time. Same routine as Raul had over there at Casa. Assault, then they go for keys or the safe. Robbery to fund drug habits, maybe a small-time ring or sizable one-time buy. Easier than robbing a convenience store at gunpoint, where you got the cameras. We think they hit Chez Thuy in April, but Mr Ngyuen's not talking, so, yeah, looks like a pattern, possibly moving north.'

'I'm next. That's what you're worried about.'

'Maybe, but it's just as likely they moved on. Boulder's small. Stuff like this tends to stand out. They'd have to be pretty stupid to hit the same area more than a couple times. But you should keep an eye out, just to be safe. Alert your staff. Always have two people at closing. Maybe put a light up behind your building.'

'I'll do that, Terry. I appreciate the warning.'

Fielding nodded and they studied each other a moment.

'What the hell happened to Roger?' Mick said. 'He and Bonnie just up and vanished out there that day? I find that hard to believe.'

The cop said nothing for a moment. Was he trying to make Mick squirm? He sighed. 'I got Wisneski's statement. Anything else shaken loose for you?'

'No,' Mick said, not sure if this was a lie.

'Can you think of anything else strange on the boat? Kyle remember any other telling details?'

Mick frowned, the memory of the darkened cabin coming back for the first time. He saw himself standing there, one hand on the chrome door handle, then the shadowed space, and then the white flash hitting him like a strobe. Then nothing, but something had been there in between. What the hell was it?

A bloodbath, bodies slumped and sliced open, like a Manson Family Polaroid. Red lines trickling from their eyes and ears. Bonnie's mouth like a clown's, joker red, with clots in her hair, twisting her neck until her dilated black pupil regarded him with acute recognition and wild-horse fear.

211

'You think of something?' Terry prompted.

Mick blinked, trying to focus. 'No, not really. Just seemed weird that no one was on board. If Kyle saw what he saw, it couldn't have been more than five minutes that passed before I came back. No one else saw anything?'

Fielding shook his head. 'Spoke with Roger's ex-wife Gina, though. She says she hadn't seen him since May of last year. He came back on Mother's Day to get some things out of the garage. They had a blowout, he split. She thinks he's got a fuckpad up in the mountains somewheres, but she wouldn't elaborate.'

Mick experienced some relief that Roger wasn't confirmed dead. 'So what does that make it? A missing persons thing?'

'Gina's not calling it that, but he could be dead for all we know.'

'Are you considering that?' Mick turned his back on the cop to stow a bottle of sweet-and-sour mix. He opened one of the refrigeration unit's steel morgue doors and slid the bottle in by the neck. 'That he might be dead?'

Behind him, Fielding chuckled in a disturbing manner. 'We're considering everything, Mick. Every. Little. Thing.'

Including me, Mick thought, while the sound of the policeman's laughter chilled him to the bone. Mick remembered the baseball bat he kept under the bar. If it was where he had left it, it would be behind him and about three feet to his left.

'Let me know how else I can help,' Mick said, pretending to sort through the bottles of champagne. *Don't even think about it. Fielding's carrying a gun and you're being paranoid.*

'Oh yeah,' Fielding said, pulling a Columbo. 'There is just one other thing I don't understand . . . '

Mick stood but paused, unable to turn around. 'Yeah?'

'Why didn't you take that second ambulance in? A scare like you had, I'd've made sure I got checked out by a doctor. You're lucky to be alive, Mick.'

'I felt okay,' Mick said softly. 'We just wanted to go home.'

He waited for Fielding's reply, frozen in a pocket of guilt. He hadn't done anything wrong and yet he knew he was a suspect now. He closed his eyes and saw the lake, the blinding sun. For a moment he was not here, he was outside, in the heat, running down a beach, his bare feet flicking white sand. He was in a blind panic, running into the trees. He was lost without his family in a nightmare jungle . . .

Mick blinked again, and it took him another minute to remember where he was. Okay, the Straw, behind the bar. Fielding still had not responded. The bar had gone completely silent. There were no customers. No dishes clinked from the kitchen and the dishwasher was silent. The music had been turned off. The air was pregnant with cold tension and for a moment Mick was sure that the policeman had slipped behind the bar and was standing right behind him, breathing on the back of his neck.

213

Mick raised his head slowly. He looked into the wide saloon mirror set above the three tiers of spirits, his eyes darting side to side. The reflection belonging to Sergeant Terry Fielding of the Boulder Police Department was not there.

Mick turned, his throat tight. The policeman was not on any of the fifteen stools. He was not in the dining room, the entryway, or outside on the walk.

He checked the restrooms. The kitchen. The stockroom.

The policeman was not in the restaurant. His entire staff had gone home. The place was empty and Mick was alone.

He went to the bar to pour himself a drink. He held the spigot over a tumbler and froze with his thumb on the button. On the bar, in front of the seat Terry had occupied, the Samuel Adams coasters sat in a neat pile. The one the cop had flung like a playing card was not stuck beside the condiment tray. Mick eyeballed the stack.

House chips, an even dozen.

34

Once they were in the store, she took the lead. He walked half a step behind, like her personal assistant, while she moved down the bulk-foods aisle, running her hand over the bins of yogurt-covered raisins, dried cranberries, banana chips, pausing to slip a fireball into her mouth. Only then did she ask him the big question.

'You have ID or are we knocking?'

'Knocking?'

'Knocking off, snaking the beer, robbing the store.'

'Oh, yeah, right,' Kyle said. 'Unless you're not cool with that.'

She stopped, filling a plastic bag with some kind of nut he didn't recognize, twirled the bag around her fingers.

'I'll pay for this,' she said. 'You go to the cooler. When you get to the front, you'll see me standing at register three. If it's clear, I'll give you the sign. Okay?'

'Sure.' Kyle swallowed. How could she be so calm? How many times had she done this? 'Wait, what's the sign?'

'You'll know it.' She pushed his hip, turning him away

215

with an electrical current that made his heart dance. 'Go on.'

Kyle hurried off, realized he was walking like an asshole, slowed. He walked across the back of the store until he reached the cooler on the far side. The store was so empty it frightened him, reminded him this was not rush hour. With no crowd to blend into, they would stand out like the thieves they were. He began to fidget, wiping his face with the hem of his shirt.

A wall of beer. So many flavors, colors, brands, boxes of every size under bright white lights. The cold braced him. It was a cave filled with treasure, a technicolor display of desire, potions with the power to change the entire mood of the night, the summer, a life. They all wanted *this*. *This* made everything else possible. Until you had a good supply of *this*, everyone was hiding their real face. *This* opened the door, allowed you to get over yourself, made you funnier, more confident, louder, bigger, the you you wanted to be. The guy who arrived back at the party with *this* became the star, reaped the adoration of everyone else who was too afraid to make it happen.

His knees felt like rubber bands. No way. He just couldn't do it.

But Kim Gordon of Sonic Youth, with her husky, oh so sensual croon, began singing in his head, and for a moment he was the Turquoise Boy and Kim Gordon was June whatever her last name was, and they were lying next to each other in Shaheen's parents' bed, heads on the same long pillow, cool cotton and warm breath, not

216

kissing, but staring into each other's eyes, and June was smiling at him. That's all he wanted, to make her smile again. And then it was as simple as $2 + 2 = 4$. He would be a man and take *this*, June would see him as the savior of the party, and some night in the near future, maybe not tonight, but some night this summer, he would lay his head on a pillow next to hers, and they would gaze into each other's eyes while Kim Gordon sang to them and Thurston Moore used his guitar to express the longings emblazoned like golden notes across the sheet music of Kyle's poor wanting heart.

He stepped forward, lifted a cardboard box containing twenty-four cans of Budweiser in his right hand, paused, walked a little further, and took a four-pack of Mandalay raspberry wine coolers in his left, and strolled away.

Someone's mother (and possibly grandmother) in the bakery section looked up from her cart and adjusted the strap of her purse, staring right at him. Kyle smiled and kept walking toward her. She looked back to her list, registering nothing. His confidence sprouted wings. He turned, crossing the back of the store again.

'The spice aisle,' Will had said earlier. 'The spice aisle is the key. No one's ever in it, and it leads you right out the fucking door.'

Kyle watched the signs hanging from the ceiling. Toilet paper, pet food, bottled water. Baking goods. Spices. There it was, two rows ahead. He turned right, catching a whiff of nutmeg. He passed tubs of Crisco, not too fast, not too slow, shoulders loose, grip firm. Don't let go. Defeat the evil suck. The aisle was a mile long. He glanced over his shoulder, peeped Aunt Jemima smiling back at him.

The aisle shortened. In fifteen paces he would be at the front. Register three. She said she would be at register three.

Ten paces. Five.

One.

He was in full view, the tobacco and customer service desk off to his left. The manager usually hovered here, changing out drawers for the cashiers, processing returns. But no one was on duty. He looked to the right.

The creamy thigh, her little black sneaker. June standing sideways in an express lane. Reading a tabloid, bag of nuts dangling from her left hand. She wasn't looking up. What was she doing? She flipped a page. What the hell? Was this the sign? He slowed, ordering her to look up. Shit, shit, shit. She was less than ten feet away and had given no sign. This had to mean bad news.

He stopped, the bright lights glaring off the linoleum, the suitcase suddenly an elephant. He had to put them back. This was insane. He was never going to make it. He was paralyzed. Going back now would be like recrossing a desert. He would die of a heart attack and they would find him face down next to the canned tomatoes.

She turned, eyes wide. Surprised? Why would she be surprised! This was the plan! Had he heard her wrong? Jesus! June! I'm dying here!

She set her magazine back on the rack. The cashier cleared the plastic partition from the rubber conveyer belt and looked up.

'Next?'

'Oh my God!' June buckled at the knee, sprawling, bag of nuts scattering on the floor. 'Ow, ow, oh God, it hurts . . . '

Kyle actually began lowering the beer on his way to help her. She was wounded, his perfect girl was hurt, he had to help her – he froze.

This was the sign! Of course, you dumbass. Go, go, go now!

'Oh, honey,' the cashier was saying. 'Oh no, are you okay?'

A tall man with a hand basket of oranges and Vanilla Wafers stepped in, blocking June from view.

'Hold on, kiddo,' he said. 'Easy, easy now. Just lie still.'

'It's my leg,' June cried. 'I was in a car accident. I just had surgery – no, don't touch it! The floor is wet, I slipped . . . oh, ow, it hurts!'

She's fucking brilliant.

Kyle's feet danced over squares of checkered linoleum, silent as a ninja. His heart was a synthesizer and the entire front of the store took on a hazy white glow, blurring as if he were in a car speeding through a neon city. This was another new drug, like her smile, the rush of the beer boogie. His pupils spiraled open. His veins throbbed, swishing blood in a hundred tiny tides. The registers were behind him, the photo booth a yellow fuzzy spot, gone. The huge rectangle that was the front door opening before him like a steel mouth. The store's air conditioning blasted him from ceiling and floor and it felt like threading the needle, motherfuckin' Luke

219

Skywalker cannon shot out of the Death Star, yahoo, all clear, kid, out into the warm summer night.

I made it! I made it! He forced himself not to run. *Be cool, you're so cool. This was a cakewalk, and I'm not even going to wait to kiss her, I'll do it in the car and she'll let me. We did it!*

'HEY YOU, I SAW THAT! STOP RIGHT THERE, YOU LITTLE SHIT!'

Kyle broke into a run. Footsteps pounded behind him. The parking lot quaking, the world upended, adrenaline splashing his tongue, his bowels turning to water. He ran, fuck it, no going back, he would run all the way back to the party, using the neighborhood and golf course to weave and duck and hide. His breath came in heaving gulps. A car honked as he dashed in front of it.

'I'M A COP! PUT THAT BEER DOWN RIGHT NOW UNLESS YOU WANT TO GET SHOT IN THE FUCKING HEAD!!!'

Kyle stopped instantly – or tried to. His Vans skidded on loose gravel. He went up and then down, hard on his ass. The suitcase smacked the ground and the cardboard flaps broke loose, spewing cans that spit and hissed and rolled everywhere. The wine coolers shattered and slooshed up in a fountain, wetting his lap like he'd pissed himself. He could hear the belt of tools jingling – keys, cuffs, nightstick, radio, mace, gun. A meaty hand slapped his shoulder.

Rasping, 'Guess who's fucked.'

Kyle looked up. The 'cop' was a three-hundred-pound security guard with a stained white shirt, bushy black goatee, and open fly. He was so out of breath his nose was sweating, and the gun was a Nextel walkie-talkie.

Kyle saw stars of red and purple, dots of black. He couldn't see, only imagined her stepping out of the store, witnessing his failure. He waited to be yanked to his feet and hauled off to jail, the humiliation beyond description. He felt trapped in a cell already, the enormity of what he had done wrong thudding into him. He rocked back and forth, moaning, wishing he could disappear . . .

A tremendous forced lifted him up and he was screaming, and the security guard was yelling, grunting, and Kyle thought only of escape. He thrashed, blind with panic. He felt something release him and he was free, running disoriented, and then he was lost. He stopped.

He was standing by the corner of the building. Behind him was the parking lot, with a few cars but no people. To his left was the front corner of the store, a train of shopping carts. In front of him, on the north side, blanketed in darkness where the store's front lights could not reach, was June.

She was looking down at the security guard, the fat man sprawled before her.

Kyle felt as if he were lifting out of his body as he walked toward her. The man on the ground was rubbing his throat and a white line of spittle leaked from the corner of his puffy lips. His eyes were scrunched tight inside a bloated red face, but he made no sounds. His right leg kicked itself stiff and the toe of his shoe bent toward his knee and stayed that way.

'What happened?' Kyle looked back, certain more employees were coming for them, but they were alone.

June did not answer. Her arms hung limp at her sides.

'How did he get all the way over here? June?'

She looked up at him with eyes as large and dark as eight balls. Her cheeks were greenish white. Her mouth moved but no words came.

Kyle took her by the shoulders and she flinched. 'It's okay,' he said, releasing her, showing her his palms. 'I'm not going to hurt you ... My God, what did he do?'

She swallowed, the first tears coming freely. 'He started to hurt you. You were screaming and he ... I tried to stop him and he grabbed me when I tried to run away. He started to shake me and I pushed him away and I, you ... didn't mean to ... this wasn't part of the plan ...'

'Didn't mean what? What did you do?'

'I think I hit him.' Her eyes were black slicks sunken deep into her pale doll face. 'I hit him in the throat.'

Kyle looked down at the man between them. The chest was no longer rising or falling.

'I can't stay here,' June said, near tears. 'My family can't have this. You can't be here. No extra attention of any kind, it's not allowed, I have to leave ...'

She was backing away, shaking her head, and then she was running, and Kyle was running after her.

35

Mick couldn't sleep. Every time he closed his eyes, he kept imagining himself sinking to the bottom of the lake, some stranger diving down into the murk to haul him out. Amy had been waiting for him when he came home from work, sitting in front of the TV with the volume low, watching a reality show featuring a precocious child chef whose apprentices were divorced parents learning how to make a proper school lunch.

'How was your day at the office, honey?' she'd said dreamily, not looking up at him. The wine bottle was on the coffee table, nearly empty.

'What's wrong with you?' he said.

She scoffed with ugly laughter.

'Look, I can't sit around here doing nothing,' he said. 'And in case you still care, I think I figured something out about why our revenues have been so low these past few years. I need to decide out how to handle it, but things are going to turn around in a matter of days.'

'That's good. I'm happy for you.' She wasn't even listening.

'Where are the kids?' he said.

'B's in bed. Kyle's out with his friends.'

'Just out? Do you know whose house? Are there parents involved?'

'Who can say? He's like his father that way. You can ask, but how do you know he's telling the truth?'

'All right, Amy. I get the message. Jesus.'

She clicked off the TV and dropped the remote on the floor. 'Don't "Jesus" me. You're the one who's running around scaring your family half to death, Mick. But then, that's nothing new. I just want you to know, next time you do something stupid and drown, I'm not going to fall apart trying to save you.'

He stared out the patio windows, noting the lights on in the new house. 'Listen,' he said. *Man on the terrace, man in the water.* 'I know things have been a little strange since I fell in. I don't know how to say this ... I think someone's been following me.'

Amy stood and took her wine glass to the kitchen. She dumped the remains into the sink and took the bottle of Advil from the cupboard. She paused, pills in hand, staring at him.

'Following you,' she said.

Mick nodded at the back window. 'Have you met them yet?'

'Who?'

'The new neighbors. They've moved in, haven't they?'

Amy cleared her throat. 'I met the wife. Cassandra.'

'You what? Why? Why would you do that?'

'They're our neighbors, Mick. What am I supposed to do?'

224

'Fucking hell. When was this? What's she like?'

'She's shy, quiet. I don't know when they got here. It was a few nights ago. Why are you looking at me like that?'

'What else do you know about them? What do they do? Where did they come from?'

'I don't know, Mick. I haven't had time to run a credit report and background check. What's this got to do with someone following you?'

'I think we should stay away from them,' he said.

'What?'

'For a little while. I don't want you near them.'

She came at him a few steps. 'What are you talking about? What's wrong?'

'I don't think they're normal,' he said.

'Normal? Who's normal?'

'I don't think they're ... like us.'

Amy scowled. 'What do you think they're like?'

'They want something from us.'

'And what would that be?'

'Think about it,' he said. 'They just appeared the night we got back from the lake. That house was empty for months. I remember looking at it that morning, when I was dealing with the boat cover. There was no one there. Then we got home and you went inside and there was a guy on the terrace, spying on me.'

'Spying,' she said. 'I see. And now you think our new neighbors are following you, is that right?'

'No, yes, there's more, though,' he said. 'I talked to Coach today and he said, he was sure he did not save me. He said someone else, this blond guy, saved me and I

225

crawled out on my own. Did you see anyone else with me on the dam?'

Amy was staring at him as if he were speaking in tongues.

'Why did you say Coach saved me?'

Amy did not answer.

'You don't know what happened,' Mick said. 'You don't remember what you saw from the boat ramp or anything else that happened before you got to me, do you?'

Amy opened her mouth and closed it. She looked frightened, but was quick to dismiss whatever crossed her mind. 'I'm not talking about this with you,' she said. 'You're being paranoid and I am not going to indulge whatever this is. I can't get into this. I can't handle it.'

'We may not have a choice.'

'Fine,' she said. 'What do you think is going to happen? What am I supposed to do?'

'I don't know yet. But I don't want *anybody* in our business or privy to our home life until all this stuff with Roger and Bonnie is sorted out. Someone's been snooping around the restaurant, listening in on my meeting with Gene, and shit is going down that you don't want to be a part of.'

'Well, now I think you have to tell me. You're not being fair.'

Mick stared at her. 'I don't want to upset you any more than I have to.'

'It's about the restaurant,' she said. 'We're going to lose it, aren't we?'

'No. No. I know who the embezzler is and I can get it all back.'

'Who?'

'Sapphire.'

Amy began to simmer.

'I'm working on it,' he said.

'What are you waiting for? Go get him!'

'I have to be sure, Amy. And this isn't about Sapphire. Someone else is watching us. I'm just telling you, who-ever those people are, do not go getting all involved with them until we know we can trust them.'

Amy laughed. 'Get involved? Trust them? They're our neighbors. You think they're going to ask us to join a cult?'

'I have a bad feeling. Something's not right back there, I can feel it.'

'You have a feeling? What feeling? Where are all these feelings coming from?'

'Jesus, why do you have to bust my ass every time I ask for one little favor? Why can't you for once just say, "Okay, honey, sure, if it will make you feel better, I'll avoid that for a few days because I realize it upsets you?" Why is that so goddamned hard?'

Amy crossed her arms and mocked him with her calm. 'Okay, honey. If it makes you feel better, etcetera. But you're being really shitty right now and I'm entitled to make new friends. You have no idea how lonely I am.'

'Yes, I do.'

Amy threw up her hands. 'And yet, as I keep telling you, nothing changes.'

They fumed at each other a moment. He sensed that if he pushed back any more tonight, nothing good would come of it. He nodded. 'I'm just asking for a little space here, so please, don't encourage them. Not right now.'

'What are you going to do about the accountant?'

'I'll handle it,' he said.

'You better,' Amy said, as if there would be consequences if he did not act soon. 'I'm going to bed. You should do the same.'

And so he had, but now he couldn't sleep. Maybe he was being paranoid, but maybe there was a good reason for that. He sat up, mashing the heels of his hands into his eye sockets. The bedside lamp was off and the large picture window was black with clear flecks of rain catching on the glass too gently to be heard.

Footsteps shuffled quietly in the hallway. Mick recognized the cautious gait.

'Kyle?'

His son cleared his throat, did not enter the bedroom. 'Yeah?'

'Everything all right?'

'Yeah.'

'You sure?'

'Yeah, Dad. Are you doing okay?'

'Go to bed.'

'I am.'

'And stop running around town like a goddamned hustler.'

'I'm not.'

'You're scaring your mother.'

228

'Okay, sorry.'

He waited for Amy to pop out of her room and berate the kid, but Kyle shut his bedroom door before she was roused. Mick pulled on a pair of jeans and made his way to the bathroom in the master suite and urinated against the side porcelain, careful to avoid thundering the lagoon.

In the kitchen he thought about making himself a sandwich, but wasn't hungry. He had no appetite any more, nothing tasted good. He drank half a bottle of acai berry juice Amy had seen advertised on the Home Shopping Network. It was supposed to help you crap with A-list regularity and it tasted like it would succeed in fulfilling its advertised promise. The bitter fluid tumbled inside him and his mouth watered and he just made it to the sink in time. He vomited in silence and felt better immediately. He wiped his mouth and splashed warm water over his face. He felt cold again, chilled inside and out. Felt like he was catching something. Probably just anxiety. There was only one thing that would allow him to get back to sleep and he figured he might as well get on with it.

The rain was warm and delicate on his face and bare feet. He kept close to the house to avoid triggering the spotlight as he dropped over the deck railing, onto the grass. A long white car slid down Jay Road, its single red taillight fading like a wetted flame.

He walked the other way, hewing to the tree line, up the cracked asphalt of the old Jenkins driveway until the palazzo was in full view. He stopped outside the front gates, mindful of the cameras. They weren't moving, but he didn't trust them. There weren't any cars in the turn-around. Every window was dark. Even from outside, the house felt empty. And yet he knew it wasn't.

He went across the rear of his own property, toward the patch of city-owned open space. Seen from the sky, Boulder's greenbelt formed a loose, dark band around the town, sealing off development and preventing Boulder from becoming an extension of the continuous sprawl that stretched from Louisville to Denver. The green belt kept the environmentalists from going rabid, leaving token habitats for the prairie dogs and bike-path fanatics. Infringing upon this preserved space was one corner of the long white stucco wall the owners had con-structed, with a Spanish-tiled riser every dozen feet or so. Mick saw no additional cameras. He moved closer, the wall's flat top a few inches above his head, providing privacy for the compound and shielding him from view. As he drew around the rear of the house, he realized he was looking for a place to jump over.

And then what? What exactly are you looking for, champ? Even if you get over without setting off the alarms, what do you think you're going to find?

And: *Didn't we have a sort of nightmare about this same little adventure? How did that one turn out? Not well, as I recall.*

But it didn't matter. There wasn't a doorway to hell on the other side, no obsidian pool with pale corpses set in the ground. It was just a house, and he was drawn to it. Something was waiting for him in there, and he did not believe it was some random family or innocent smoker out on the terrace. Maybe a man, that third man, or maybe something other than a man.

He planted his hands and levered himself up (no limb abrasions this time) until he sat astride the barrier. On the southern side, the house's rear three-story facade seemed even taller. But it did not tilt or change shape. The yard was empty, the newly laid sod showing its seams. There was one long patio at ground level, made of pale stone, set against a wall of windows that extended at least twenty feet to each side – enough exposure to light a solarium, kitchen, and great room. But it was impossible to know what lay behind them; the windows were solid black at this hour.

A shallow set of stairs curved down to a swimming pool. It was covered with a black tarp almost indistinguishable from the grass. Emboldened, he walked the top of the wall, stepping over the risers and making a left turn, bringing him to the southeast corner. The tarp was stretched taut like a trampoline, and Mick imagined jumping, wondering if it would swallow him into the water or launch him out across the lawn.

He began to walk quickly atop the fence, back toward his house. The fence top was flat, perhaps twelve inches wide, and he grew overconfident. Eight or nine paces along, his right foot slipped and he flailed and dropped into the yard. He landed on his right side, his knees absorbing the brunt of the impact, and rolled across the soft sod, then lay still. He waited for motion-detector lights to flash on, the howl of an alarm, but nothing changed. The house was still quiet, dark, uncaring.

Smooth, real smooth, champ. Isn't this about the point where the ground opened up and showed you your family writhing on a liquid autopsy table?

Shut it. It was just a bad dream.

But now that he was on the other side, why not take a peek? If someone was awake, they would have confronted him by now. The south-facing windows loomed above him, eight unusually large black rectangles. They were set in tracks, with thin steel cables, and Mick assumed this whole wall was convertible to open air. He was also sure that if he were to press his face to one, he would be able to see inside.

He told himself not to do it, but his legs were already carrying him across the lawn, onto the terrace. His heels thudded along the stone and he shielded the sides of his face.

The first thing he noticed was the cold. The glass was so bracing, he was surprised it was not frosted. Some kind of serious air conditioning was being pumped into this room, against the glass, which felt like a refrigerator shelf and made him think of the Straw's meat locker, aging steaks ripening with blood.

The second thing he noticed was ... nothing. He could not see beyond the violet-tinted shade screen built into the glass. He squinted, pressing closer, but it was too dark. He craned his neck, peering in at a severe angle.

Something *was* there. You just had to view it almost sideways.

He pressed his face closer until his right eye was almost touching the glass, and gradually the room began

232

to reveal shapes, the outlines of objects: a closed wooden door of wide planks set into the far wall. Two couches facing each other over a coffee table. In one corner, under a mantle of stone, was the deep black suggestion of a fireplace. The rest was open and empty, with a high ceiling and the stone floor spanning at least thirty feet in either direction. It wasn't a great room; it was a court, a veranda that could host one hundred guests who need never rub elbows.

Mick backed away, sidled left a few paces, and reapplied himself to another window. As before, it took a moment to get the angle right, and then he seemed to have gone too far, to the end, where only the blank floor and a wall of empty shelves rose above his sight line. Then he tilted his head to the right and saw a dining room table made up with four dishes, four cups, four bundles of silverware, and then the chairs with the people sitting in them. The people were sitting perfectly still, upright in the dark, and Mick almost shouted in surprise.

Mother, father, daughter, and son. Sitting less than ten feet away, facing one another across the table, heads bowed as if in prayer. Dressed in loose dark clothing, they had looked like a pioneer family at supper, cabin dwellers sitting in the dark as if caught in a storm, all out of candles, waiting for judgment and daylight to return. Except that the plates were empty. The cups were empty. Their hands were under the table. And their faces, what little of them he had been able to make out, were plain and without expression. Their shoulders did not rise or shift, their chests did not expand, their mouths did not open or close. They had looked frozen in time, paused like a video.

They're not real. They're models, dummies, props on a stage.

He backed away slowly, too disturbed to linger. He backed up until he was standing on grass. No, no. He must have been mistaken. What family sits like that in the middle of the night? He couldn't just leave now. He needed to know. He needed a better look at the man, to see if it was the same blond man who had been in the restaurant. He needed some clue as to who, or even what, they were.

Be quick about it, then.

He glanced around as if he had lost something of value, then walked back to the window with his head down and came at it head tilted at the now familiar angle. The dark, purple-hued glass came into view and his cheek pressed against the cold window. He squinted, stood on his toes.

The table was there, the plates and glasses ... but the chairs were empty. The people were gone. Nothing had been disturbed, but they had vanished.

Like ghosts.

His entire body went cold, the arctic chill from the glass seeping into his cheek and spreading. He stared in disbelief, willing them to reappear so that he was not left to question his eyes and sanity, but his calves began to cramp and they did not come back. He turned away from the window and started across the patio, watching the white stone under his bare feet, careful to avoid tripping over a planter or garden hose. The patio was clean, smooth as gymnasium floor. He looked up to the fence and stopped in his tracks.

'Aw, shit,' he said, the words hissing from him like air from a slashed tire.

All four of them were standing on the lawn, in a close-knit line, watching him. The father was on the left, mother at far right, teen daughter and younger son in the middle. Another six or seven paces and he would have walked right into the wall of them. Too dark to see their faces, their eyes. They were motionless shadows. They said nothing.

Mick stood immobile for a moment, waiting for himself or any of them to break the stand-off. Various greetings presented themselves in his mind, but all seemed impossibly naive now, the distance between them stagnant with his guilt. He was caught and he almost wanted them to scold him, accuse him of something.

But still they did not move.

It was like standing before a pack of wild dogs. He sensed that to run now would only provoke them into pursuing him. Chasing him down and then . . .

A purring, gurgling sound issued from one of them, and it was the sound of hunger, an empty belly.

'Now?' the girl said in a soft voice. 'Is it going to happen now?'

The boy's mouth fell open, a hot panting eagerness stirring him to life. He took one step forward, raising his arm, and the rest of his family broke into stride.

235

Mick turned and ran. The grass wet his feet and he nearly slipped before springing up to the wall, scraping his toes and elbows again as he flung himself over, landed in dirt, and scooped himself up from the field of open space to sprint the rest of the way home. He imagined their footsteps scraping and bumping across the field behind him, flashes of their widening white eyes as they pursued him. He nearly screamed when the motion detector tripped and he was exposed him in a prison yard's glare. He stumbled up the patio and banged his way into the kitchen.

He locked the door and leaned over, hands on knees. He backed into the dining room, watching the windows, expecting them to press their white hands and featureless faces to the dark surfaces at any moment. The doorknob would start shaking, they would pound on the glass until it broke. But a minute or two passed and they didn't come.

What in the hell was that all about? What kind of people were they? What were they doing awake at this hour, sneaking up on him in the yard? And what was he supposed to do now that they had seen him? They had to know where he lived now. This was dumb, all of it a very dumb idea.

His feet were wet, dirty with grass clippings. He walked into the laundry room between the kitchen and mud room and found a towel above the dryer. He wiped his feet and rubbed the other side of the towel over his face, threw it in the hamper.

He went back to the kitchen and peered over the

sink. The glare from the track lighting made it impossible to see outside, so he shut the lights off and returned to the sliding glass door. The patio was clear, they weren't on the lawn. He unlatched the sliding door, opening it a few inches. He stepped out and surveyed the yard.

The entrance gate to the new place was still closed. For a few minutes there was nothing, and then he saw a figure walking up the old Jenkins driveway. One body, not four. It was just a black shape, ambling along as if out for a stroll, but Mick felt certain it was him, the sentinel, his rescuer, the man of the house. Mick lost him in the trees, and the seconds stretched on into a minute, then two. He was beginning to think he was seeing things again when the dark shape moved through the tree line again and came to a stop just short of Mick's lawn.

Mick hesitated a moment, considered calling the police or waking Amy, but in the end decided he should handle this on his own. He hurried down the hall to the master bedroom and retrieved the metal pipe from the walk-in closet for the second time this week.

36

The rain had ceased and the night was warm and damp, silent but for the faint swish of tires on the Diagonal Highway a mile away. Mick walked out onto the lawn, swinging the pipe at his side, squeezing the taped grip. He had lost the man's position, but he doubted the bastard had decided to drop his inquiry for the night. They were onto each other now. Whatever it was, it was coming out tonight.

He turned, eyes tracing the sharp edges of the blue spruce and the taller cottonwood columns. The border seemed to zoom in and out, and then he was there, a silhouette no more than twenty feet away, the face a pale oval above a faded blue shirt and flat khaki pants. The hair was light, but he didn't look like one of the shadow people who had been standing in the yard. He looked like a younger, more handsome version of the average suburban dad. About Mick's size, maybe an inch taller and leaning forward with the poised inertia of a prisoner whose cell is about to be opened. Under the moon his eyes were silver demonic coins.

In that moment, Mick knew this was the man, if a

man was all he was, who had saved his life. He fit Wisneski's description and Mick could feel the connection in his bones. He felt exposed again, his thoughts an open book to this stranger.

'I guess it's about time we met properly,' the man said, stepping onto the lawn. His voice carried the same deep resonance that had been echoing in Mick's head since the accident. 'Vincent Render. I've been looking forward to this moment for a long time, Mick.'

Mick laid the pipe across his forearm. Vincent Render glanced at it but his expression remained neutral.

'I realize this all must seem rather strange.'

'Which part?' Mick said. 'The part about you following me or the part where I find you and your family sitting up in the middle of the night like wax dummies?'

'Wax dummies,' Render said. 'That's what it looked like? I guess that makes sense. From your perspective. I've been thinking about that a lot lately. Whatever you saw through the window, I guess we must look like monsters to you. But I promise, my family and I only want to help you.'

'Oh? With what?'

'Everything. I know how hard things are right now. The living hell that you've been through the past three years. I'm a businessman too, retired now, but I see what's happening. Your restaurant, the problems with your accountant—'

'My business is none of your business.'

Render bent and plucked a pine cone from the lawn. He gazed into it, then dropped it. 'I'm afraid it is.'

'And why would that be?'

'Because we are bound by the same tragic circumstances. And neither of us is living the lives we are meant to live. We're both in a lot of trouble. There is a lot of bad ... business in the air these days. But if we work together, we can turn bad business into a very prosperous business, and so much more.'

'Not interested,' Mick said. 'If you know what's good for you, you'll stop following me and leave us alone. I am justified in harming you right now, for being on my property, and don't think I don't want to.'

'Understandable. But first let me ask you: What do you think of that house?' Render angled and pointed one slender finger at the behemoth in Mick's backyard. 'Honestly. It's just a spec home, but with the right input on all the finishing touches, it could really be something. What do you think?'

Mick snorted. 'I think it's an assault on good taste and common decency. If I had it my way, I'd burn it to the ground.'

'That's a shame,' Render said. 'Because I built it for you, Mick. For you and your family.'

Surprise, for about half a second. Then Mick realized the man was being a smart-ass, taunting him. He waded forward and raised the pipe.

'The others are dead,' Render said, not flinching.

Against his better judgment, Mick hesitated. 'What others?'

'The families.'

'What—'

'You know what families,' Render said. 'You know everything.'

'No, I really don't.'

They want to be your friends, but they aren't anybody's friends, the dead Roger had said. *They will do anything to get what they want. They use other people, make them do horrible things.*

'Three years ago,' Render said. 'Up until three years ago, everything was normal. It was let the good times roll. But then it happened. And now there is a price. That's what I'm saying, Mick. There was a price for all of them and they refused to pay it and now those other families are dead. You *know*.'

'I know you're insane,' Mick said.

Render took another step closer. 'No, I am wealthy. Obscenely wealthy. You're right about one thing, though. I have been following you. I'm in your dreams and in your life, because you have something I want. Something I want very badly, Mick. It's really that simple. My family and I would like to be your friends, the best kind of friends. They have already begun to form their own bonds. Our wives and the kids. There is a foundation there I hope you and I can build upon. But if that is not possible, at a fundamental level, I'm talking about a business transaction. A life-changing transaction that will hurt neither of us and benefit both of us. What could be easier than that?'

'Killing people.'

Render bobbed his head. 'Oooo-kay. What does that mean?'

'That's what you're into,' Mick said. 'Roger and Bonnie on the lake. You're either trying to implicate me in something or do something worse, and you think you can buy my silence. What are you, mob? Russian hitman? Hedge-fund owner?'

'No, Mick, but what if I was?' Render smiled and ran a hand over his sleeve, watching his pale hand in the moonlight. 'What are you going to do? Call the police?'

'If this doesn't stop, absolutely. I have friends in the department.'

'Terry Fielding,' Render said. 'Yes, how is that fellow holding up these days? Have you seen him? I wonder, why hasn't he been by to visit you lately?'

'As a matter of fact—'

'He's dead too,' Render said. 'You're running out of friends, Mick, so if you plan to call another one, you'd better do it soon.'

'What did you do to Terry?'

'Me? Little ol' me?' Render pretended to be insulted. His playful game of suggestion and innuendo was beginning to remind Mick of Max Cady in *Cape Fear*. 'What in the world would I want to go and hurt a police officer for?'

'To stall the investigation,' Mick said.

'And what investigation would that be?' Render cupped his ear to the night. 'Do you hear the hoofbeat of cavalry approaching? All I can hear is a dull ringing silence. We have each other, Mick. You are all I need. What reason would you have for calling upon outside forces? We've barely gotten to know each other. Don't you think we should find out how we can help each other before we turn each other in?'

Mick opened his mouth to speak, but the words died on his dry tongue. For the first time it struck him this man really had something on him.

Render seized on his silence. 'It is a vicious world and we live in vicious times. I know why things are the way they are. I know why the others come, preying on you. They are out there right now. They have a nose for weakness, and they will keep coming for you and things will only get messier unless you allow me to help you.'

'I don't want your help,' Mick said.

'You will never have to work again. Money will no longer matter. Your family will be taken care of, for life. That house you despise because you're too fucking weak to stand up and take it from me, will be your house, in title and deed, and there will never be another mortgage payment. All of your worries, your wife's worries, her weight, her threatening students, Briela's tantrums, Kyle's running afoul of the law to find the proper social niche – all that will be taken care of. Save your restaurant, open a new one, or turn it into an ashram. But no matter what, the past three years? The years you have spent watching your life circle the drain? If you work with me, Mick, they never happened.'

Mick stared at his neighbor for a long time. He felt lost, more alone than he had ever been, a man dropped off on an alien planet, staring up at the sky, trying to understand how his fellow man could leave him here, how the world could go on without him. And this stranger was threatening what was left of his existence.

'Last warning,' Mick said, shaking with bottled rage. 'Stay away from my family or I will kill you.'

'Oh, but that's what you don't understand, Mick,' Render said. 'I'm already a dead man. My family lives ... or dies ... with you.'

Before Mick could respond, his neighbor turned and disappeared into the trees.

37

Kyle was zoned out but not sleeping when his Egg hummed against his leg. Lying in his darkened bedroom, he removed the smooth black device from his cargo shorts pocket. It was almost three in the morning. His SMS icon was glowing, sender unknown. He scrolled over the glyph and thumbed the roller. It said,

Are U OK?

He'd texted Will earlier and told him to come get his car at King Soopers, the excuse being that a cop had been watching them and he had to walk June home. But Will and the rest of his friends were in his address book and their names would have been displayed. He sent:

Who this?

The response arrived a long half-minute later.

Your partner in crime

Kyle woke all the way up. Nearly sick with excitement, he typed:

June?
that's me
howd u get my number?
i have my ways
I guess u do. Are u ok?
Yeah just scared. like really scared.
Me too but it wasn't our fault. he had a heart attack. it was an accident.
wish i could believe that
it's true. what else could it have been? he was three times your size. no way you did that.
i know but i feel so guilty for leaving him there

When it was clear the fat security guard was not going to wake up, they had run from the Gunbarrel plaza, across 63rd, out behind Celestial Seasonings headquarters, then walked the two miles toward Kyle's home, through fields behind the houses on Jay Road. But they hadn't spoken much. June seemed to be in shock, so eventually he stopped asking questions and just walked behind her, his shyness compounding within him, and when he looked up again she was nowhere to be found. He was sure he would never see her again, that she blamed him for what had happened, but here she was.

He typed:

it's going to be ok. he was an asshole with
authority complex. I won't let you take the blame.
**u r too sweet. i shouldn't have encouraged
you to steal.**
I was gonna do it anyway. glad you were there.
**You were amazing. almost made it! too bad
we didn't get to hang more.**

This struck him with such force that for several minutes his thumbs locked up and he could only stare at the
screen in a state of amused idiocy. So, whatever had
hurried her away, it wasn't about him.

Where did you go after? U disappeared. was
worried.
**Sorry. it was better for me to go alone, safer
for you.**

He didn't know what to say to that. She added:

Did I wake u?
No, its cool
why up so late?
Just can't sleep
tonight or always?

Now that he thought about it, he realized he hadn't
been sleeping well for a long time. He sent:

guess I am a night owl or insomniac or something.

are you super stressed? i mean before tonight?

my parents are fighting. dad losing job, mom hates dad, sister fucking crazy, etc. but other than that fine, lol. why are you still up? did you get in trouble?

i'm sorry, Kyle. parents suck.

yours too?

they're not my real parents. monsters.

that bad?

worse

like how?

you know

no. tell me

we have same problems as you, but different and worse

different how?

do bad things on purpose = evil

no, seriously

i am serious. you should get away while you can.

run away with me?

i would. seriously. you have no idea what's coming.

Tell me.

later

why not now?

You'll probably h8 me.

No way.

very very disturbed gurl.

Kyle swallowed, pulling another confidence rabbit out of this new hat.

I think u r perfect.
☺

A stupid yellow smiley icon, a dumb sign, and yet it scorched the retinas. For a long time he sat against his pillows, breathing through his mouth. He wanted to know everything about this girl. He typed:

Where do you live anyway?
OMG you don't know yet?
?
your mom didn't say anything?
About what? you lost me
we're neighbors, silly.
Whuuuuuut? u r messing with my head.
so not
You moved to our hood? On Jay?
NEXT DOOR
Why u wanna tease me like that?
come out and see for yourself. keep me company. house behind yours. my room = corner window 1st floor.

He sat up violently and lost the Egg in his tangled sheets. Found it, clutched it to his stomach. *She was practically waiting for him in his backyard.* He could climb out his bedroom window and ... and it seemed like she wanted him to. This was insane. No, his dad was still awake. Kyle had just heard him banging around a few minutes ago and he hadn't come back down the hall yet. If he tried to sneak out again his parents would kill him. But June ... oh, this girl. He sat on the edge of his bed. It was too much, overwhelming how much he wanted her. It scared him, the power she had already. She broke the paralysis.

where did you go?
Sorry, was just trippin. seems unbelievable.
but true.
2 good to B, but ok.
oh, one sec.

She wrote nothing more for a very long time, or five minutes. He began to feel acute loss, the comedown of not being attached to her in the ether. He became certain she had fallen asleep or forgotten about him. He stared at the tiny red screen, waiting, waiting, waiting, waiting. Finally she came back.

sorry. have 2 go out.
now?
i'll explain later. my dad's on a mission.
Aw, well.
but I'll see u at the bbq, right?
What bbq?
a week from Saturday. my mom invited your family over. 2 o'clock.

i'll be there. but wish i didn't have to wait so
long.
**it's going to be . . . uncomfortable. maybe you
shouldn't come.**
no way am I missing chance to see u
**i'm serious, kyle. we're dangerous. i wish I
could stop it. my fam is bad news. you should
get away while you can.**
no . . . really?
they're coming for me now. please be caref

But the rest of that text never arrived. Somebody
caught her texting him? Her dad came in the room? He
didn't know, but after two hours of waiting for the Egg to
wiggle in his palm, the sun began to rise and he couldn't
help but fade into what passed for sleep these days. He
dozed with his eyes half open and dreamed of her,
moving into it seamlessly.

They were in an empty, unfurnished house far away
from here, near a sea, a party house with no guests,
stranded together as on an island. The rooms tropically
hot and gray with light from thick clouds. She was on a
wooden chair, dressed in a sheer white blouse tight
around her stomach, lacy at the shoulders, and a long
skirt, billowing white. Her face was as smooth and pure
as a mask of cold cream, her eyes dark wet spots. Her
tiny nostrils flexing with breath, the air from her lungs
warm on his neck. Extending from beneath the skirt was
her white flesh, too soft to touch, as if she might turn to
wisps and slide through his hands, the sheer lace holding

her entire body together as a vase holds a bouquet, as a room holds smoke, and his hands were delicately pushing the skirt up, each inch higher a day he died and was reborn. Her fingers in his hair, pulling him, her soft belly warm against his lips, the curl of brown hairs around her navel, and the herbal-sweat taste of her skin . . .

And then it all released from him with agonizing force and he was relieved, falling into a dreamless sleep-state that spanned most of a day.

38

Late the following Tuesday night, Eric Pritchard's white Honda Civic left the pavement and began to crawl and swerve over crenelated ruts gouged into the trailhead like a Matchbox car under the thumb of a not bright playground bully. The balding tires slipped against tree roots, and rocks the size of Thanksgiving turkeys stabbed the undercarriage. Eric fought the wheel jerking and spinning in his palms while keeping one eye on Jason, who was clutching the dash as a twenty-four-ounce Red Bull sloshed onto his Dickies work pants. This final stretch of 'road' into the unnamed and unofficial campground (their friends called it Flintstone Park for the vitamin-shaped boulders that marked the site), located seven or eight miles up Sunshine Canyon, had been washed out a thousand times and was known for stalling Jeep Wranglers, but they were too lazy to walk the last half-mile.

Also, if they left the Honda at the turnoff, a ranger would know some kids were up here in the gully fucking around again, starting fires and throwing beer cans into the woods. Eric figured if he could just clear the last couple hairy dips without blowing a tire, they'd be able to get their fucking boom on without any hassles.

'Jesus Christ, dude, slow down.' Jason's face had turned green and looked vaguely plant-like. 'Gonna chuck my pizza.'

'I got this.' Eric's stomach roiled at the reminder of all that cheese tumbling around inside them like a load of wet socks, which made him think of *loads*, which made him think of Justin Timberlake suckin' off five guys, which made Eric want to puke. Not to mention the little morsels they'd sprinkled on the hot mess of Xtra-Large Blackjack pie before devouring it at Chautauqua Park, which were now shooting darts of poison into his organ lining. 'You feeling anything yet?'

'Maybe,' Jason said. 'But I don't think so. You sure Billy didn't rip us off? That shit was mostly dust.'

'Some of that dust was fucking purple, bro. It's only been twenty minutes. Trust me, in half an hour we're gonna be out of our tits.'

Eric saw a smooth slope and steered high and right, the fucking rice burner canting until Jason was sitting above him like a ventriloquist dummy on his shoulder, holding the handle above the window and slopping Red Bull down the side of his face. Bitch just about went up on two before the Honda came down too fast and a smashed-beer-can-sound exploded beneath the trunk.

Jason groaned as they leveled out. 'Fuuuuck, man, wazzat a tire?'

Eric laughed, and it was the laugh of a hungry crow. 'No, but I think the muffler just got ass-raped.'

A few minutes later they coasted into the clearing, the deep pines sloping around them in four directions. A couple of small plateaus for camping, though no one really camped here any more, just loitered. The old rock circle around the fire pit had been kicked apart, but that was okay. It was warm tonight. They wouldn't need a fire.

'You really want to sleep here?' Jason said as Eric shut the motor off. 'We don't even have a tent.'

'I'm not driving once this shit kicks in.' Eric shoved his door open. He plugged his iPod into the Blaupunkt's jack, dished up some club mix that made his heart run like it was playing its own video game. 'Grab the sleeping bags.'

They unloaded their supplies from the trunk. Two thin bags leaking poly-fil, two pillows, a tarp with no straps or stakes, a flashlight, a bag of Glo-Sticks for twirling, a six pack of Mickey's Big Mouths, the bottle of Wild Turkey they never drank but pretended to sip at, and the stale remains of a five-pound bag of animal crackers.

'Do you still have my lighter?' Eric said.

'Yep.'

They hiked the gear another thirty paces to the spot, dropping it around a long log. Jason straddled the timber, lit a cigarette, and sucked like it was an oxygen tank.

'Did you bring the little ax?' Jason said. 'We need fire-wood.'

'Should be in the trunk, but maybe say fuck the fire tonight.'

Jason rubbed his arms. They were thin and nearly bald, though he had a dome of black hair. 'Is this Tuesday? I don't think the rangers care on weekdays.'

'Yeah but why risk it?'

They opened the beers and slouched around in a tired circle, kicking pine cones, smoking. Eric had left the headlights on and the beams cut over the blackened ground before hitting the steep slope where dirt became grass became forest. The pine trees behind them went way the hell up, like narrow jagged ladders to the sky, and the mountainside was a black-thorned maze of them. The car speakers went *uhn-tiss-uhn-tiss-uhn-tiss* with a monotony that should have been soothing but for some reason tonight only made Eric angry. He looked at the plastic bag of Glo-Sticks, the nylon cords to string them, and didn't have the energy to break them out.

It occurred to him for the first time that there was something pathetic about this. Two guys sitting in the woods pretending to set off their own little rave. He wasn't sure why it had seemed so important to come here tonight, only that he was fucking sick of Boulder, sick of the fucking losers they usually hung out with, fucking Sarah and Hannah and Ally, Tyler and Brad, with his fucking skanky Mexican hoodie and ragweed, all six of them sitting around Ally's shithole apartment off of Baseline, the carpets wet, the bedroom with Ally's stupid fucking unicorn tapestries and that black light, the whole place reeking of gerbil piss. It occurred to Eric, not for the first time, maybe he hated all his friends.

'Fuck.' Jason was sitting on the log, clutching his belly. 'This stuff always makes me have to shit.'

'Go in the woods.'

'Did you bring any toilet paper?'

Eric laughed. Jason squirmed. He stood up suddenly, alarmed.

Eric smoked, the nicotine calming his stomach. 'What?'

'If today's Tuesday, we have Workplace Econ in like eight hours.'

'Dude, who gives a fuck?'

'Just sayin'.'

Eric dropped half his Mickey's down his throat. 'Do you think anyone gives two shits if you go to that bitch's class?'

'If I don't graduate my moms will kill me.'

'Your moms is too busy trying to please Mark. Your new fuckin' dad, Mark. Mark the fucking lawn shark.'

Jason actually looked hurt by this. 'Mrs Nash said I might still be able to take some classes at Front Range. I can't deliver pizzas for the rest of my life.'

Something flew sideways in the woods, a glint of white streaking past the corner of Eric's eye.

'What?' Jason said. 'You see somethin'?'

Eric shook his head. 'Probably an owl.'

Jason glanced around. 'All we have to do is show up.'

'You're seventeen. You have years to figure it out.' Eric had to nip this shit in the bud, right now. If Jason didn't stop whining about his future before the fungus kicked in, Eric'd spend half the night trying to talk him out of a tree, like, fuckin' literally. 'You don't need a fucking degree to make big dollars. Do you know how many of these shitheads are going to go off to college like good little fascists and build up a fuckload of debt only to realize there are no jobs? My uncle Burt didn't go to college, started his business with ten grand from a grass buy. He owns three car washes now, plus a Taco John's. He's fucking loaded.'

'Yeah, but—'

'But shut up, is what. You're fucking up my shit. Jesus. You wanna go to school tomorrow, no one's stopping you. But fucking can it for tonight. I'm trying to relax.'

Jason looked away. He's still a kid, Eric thought. Look at him there in his fucking baggy shirt and droopy fucking pants, skate shoes two sizes too big. His moms bought them that way so they'd last a whole year, except the joke was J's feet stopped growing in tenth grade. He looked like a scarecrow who'd slid down the pole, his head too big for his scrawny neck. I could break that neck, Eric thought. Be like snapping a Glo-Stick. You just take it with both hands and push with your thumbs and there'd be a little *click*. But instead of turning bright green or blue and lighting up from end to end, J'd just turn no color at all and lay there.

'Jesus,' Eric said. 'I think it's kicking in. I'm thinking some sick fucking shit.'

'I don't feel anything.' Jason sipped his beer and looked down at his shoes. 'I think Billy fucked us.'

'Billy wouldn't do that. 'Cause if he did, he knows I'd beat his ass.'

Jason stood and walked a little ways into the dark, out of the headlights.

'Where you goin'?' Eric said.

'Take a piss.'

'Aw, don't say that. Every time I'm trippin' all I have to do is think about pissing and then I have to go, and once I start going, it's every twenty minutes for the rest of the night. Where does all this piss come from? You ever wonder that?'

Jason didn't answer. The air cooled. In between songs a tree branch snapped somewhere above and behind them. Eric thought of deer. If a deer walked by now ...

'What are you babbling about?' Jason said, zipping up on the way back.

Eric stared at him. Did Jason even listen any more? Why didn't anyone listen any more? Sometimes Eric felt like he was shrinking out of the world, his voice getting quieter and quieter until one day he would be standing in a corner of an empty room, a gray room with no furniture, just huge gray walls that went on forever, everyone else two thousand miles away, and no matter how much he shouted, they would never hear him.

'Nothing,' Eric said. 'Are you rollin'?'

'Maybe a little.'

Something thumped to the ground, heavy like a boulder rolling into some bushes.

'What was that?' Jason said.

Eric scanned the trees. He saw no movement.

'Hell if I know. A deer?'

'But you heard it too.'

'I hear lots of things,' Eric said.

Jason sat on the log and pulled out a Glo-Stick. He broke it, tilting it from side to side. The stick turned a sad shade of pink. Jason began to twirl it between his fingers, the way his brother Rickie used to twirl quarters over his rings. Rickie went to Afghanistan two years ago. They'd brought him home in that box last fall and even though Jason was at the funeral, he said Rickie was still over there in the mountains, blasting dune coons. Eric thought that was fucked up but never said anything to Jason about it. The Glo-Stick fell in the dirt. Jason stared at it for a while, then dripped a long string of saliva down to it. When the string touched the pink, he cut it off with his teeth and let it fall. He smeared the stick with his foot, burying it in the cold fire ash.

Eric took off his shirt. He was skinny all the way up and down, with the face of a falcon. He liked the bony hardness of his frame. He had no chest muscles. His breastplate was like armor, his belly button a puckered coin standing out. He was wearing his shark-tooth necklace and his goatee reached almost to his throat, soft as silk. In his earlobes were two spikes as long as golf tees, made of tempered steel. Purportedly Maori designs had been tattooed around his left arm; from the blade of his left shoulder, a purple panther that seemed to be clawing its way out of his skin.

'I hate this part,' Jason said.

Eric picked up a long stick and began swiping at the air. 'What part?'

'Waiting.'

'Shit's getting fuzzy. Those trees are starting to woo-woo.'

'You sure you're not just drunk?'

'I don't get drunk,' Eric said, opening another Mickey's.

Jason leaned back on the log, staring up at the night sky, a faint band of the Milky Way streaking over them. The iPod shuffled into Kanye's 'Monster' and Eric's blood roared in approval.

'You know what we should do,' Eric said.

'What?'

'Take this to class.'

Jason sat up and looked at the gun, his eyes darting to Eric's cargo pants pockets like *What else you got stashed in there?* Eric smiled, rotating the weapon before his eyes. It was heavy. You could feel the fucking death heavy in it.

'Where the fuck did you get that?' Jason said.

'Tol' you I was gonna get one.'

'What is it? A .22?'

'It's a .38, dumbass. My uncle gave it to me.'

'It's not loaded, right? Seriously, E. That thing better not be—'

Eric fired a shot into the sky. The buck sent a nice twang through his wrist bones. Jason jumped to his feet as the echo rolled away.

'Cut the shit! What the fuck did you do that for, man?'

Eric snickered. 'I ain't playin'.'

'Fuckin' ranger's gonna come.'

'Let him.'

'Yeah, right.' Jason jammed his hands in his pockets. 'Don't even joke about that, you sick bastard.'

Eric flew the gun in the air, a boy imagining his model airplane's first flight. 'Here, piggy piggy piggy. I forgot to bring my time sheet in, Mrs Nash.' He laughed. 'I hate that fat bitch. You see the way she looks at me, J? I can't decide if she wants to slap me or suck my dick.'

Jason looked away, shaking his head. They spaced out, grooving on their private thoughts. Five minutes passed, though it could have been half an hour. Eric wasn't sure when he realized the Civic's headlights had been doused, but they were now.

Monsta, monsta, I'm a muthufuck— The music stopped. One second it was on, the next the mountain air was bugs and silence, every scrape of their feet on the pine needles too loud.

'Do you have a license for that?' a man with a deep voice said behind them.

Eric spun, thrusting the gun against the darkness. 'Who the fuck?'

The man was standing behind the open door, hardly more than a shadow on the driver's side, one arm resting on the roof. Eric lowered the gun as if he could still hide it behind his leg. He tried to think of something fearsome to say but his brain was crowded with orange balloons, adrenaline making him blink over and over. His mouth was very dry. Yeah, definitely booming now, kid.

The guy just stood there a minute, solid, unmoving. His face was a faint white smudge. Everything else was black.

'Hey, how about you get the fuck away from my car,' Eric said.

'Eric, no . . . ' Jason said. Fucker better not run.

Slowly the man walked around the door and stopped in front of the hood, arms hanging at his sides. Eric couldn't tell if he was wearing a ranger shirt, the belt with the tools. He didn't think so. The shoulders were too smooth . . . and was that their little ax hanging from his left hand? How did he get in the trunk? No, impossible.

'You want to shoot something,' the man said, sounding bored. 'Take a shot at me.'

'We're not bothering anybody,' Eric said. 'We have a right to be here.'

'As do we all.' The man took another step. 'But there's a right, and then there's what's right. Go on. Aim it and pull the trigger.'

Jason twitched, heels digging backward in the dirt. *'Oh shit man, give it up, E.'*

Shut the fuck up! Eric wanted to scream, but he had to play this cool.

'Your friend is smart,' the man said. 'Or, smarter.'

'You're not a cop,' Eric said.

'That's true.' He took another step. 'Do you want to guess what I am?'

Eric was scared, afraid right down into his leg bones. He asked himself, for the first time, what kind of man wanders into the woods like this. They would have heard a car or truck. Dude had come out of nowhere.

'No? Maybe you'd rather guess what I want.' Damn,

his voice was deep, deep and cold as something at the bottom of a well. And yeah, that was the ax.

Eric's voice cracked. 'What you want . . .'

The man seemed to be widening, and floating toward him like a shadow on silent wheels. He said, 'I'm an angel. Sent to change the world.'

Eric held the gun out between them, aiming a little higher, at where he imagined the heart was. 'Don't.' And that was all he had left to say. His tongue was swollen, his throat locked.

'Or maybe I'm just a father out doing his best to provide for his family. Maybe the sound of my children's bellies growling is keeping me awake at night.'

The man stopped about twelve feet away. Eric could not make out the color of his hair under the black cap, but the glassy eyes seemed solid black and wet. His hands were also black and Eric guessed those were black gloves.

'You shouldn't be nasty to other people, Eric.' Wagging the ax. 'You shouldn't write ugly things on people's cars, Eric. You shouldn't take firearms to school, Eric.'

The gun felt like it belonged to someone else now. Like he had already lost it.

Behind them, a trickle of dirt funneled down the mountain.

Jason's voice came to him. 'There's more. Eric . . . they're everywhere.'

Eric turned, casting his saucer eyes around the basin. Behind Jason, at the edge of the trees and standing in a loose line up the hill, were three or four others. There was a small boy, androgynous, thin and dressed in black. And a girl of indeterminate age, featureless and stepping delicately as if avoiding land mines, and then another, a woman with black hair, who seemed to bleed in and out of the trees, closing the gaps between each other like a search party who had found their quarry.

Jason backed up against a pine tree, snapping branches. He bent, clutching his jeans pockets, out of breath.

Eric's belly was on fire with the poison, his face hot. The hills were waves, and every time one of the people in black stepped down, a wave seemed to raise another one up. The woman with black hair, or perhaps another, different woman, was on the ground, crawling on her belly, sliding down the hill like a snake, head raised, the face expressionless. Something gray and thin ran through the dip in the trail behind the car, disappearing up the other side of the gully. Another tree branch broke.

Eric's entire body went slack.

'Think of it this way,' the man said, coming close enough for Eric to touch him. He raised the chrome ax blade between them and it looked like liquid. 'All those children. And that sweet teacher. Are going to live because of you. They're all going to be safe, thanks to the sacrifice you've made tonight. There's beauty in that.'

A ring of them had surrounded Jason, the boy holding J's leg. They encircled him with their arms as he sobbed, hiding his face. Everything was happening too slow, hypnotically, and Eric decided if he didn't act now, his only friend in the world was going down. He stole one glance at the man, who was smiling at the others, then turned and fired twice at the circle.

It had to have been the drugs, because right when he raised the gun and the shots rang out, the people separated like bowling pins – spreading away from J, but not falling down – and both bullets took Jason, one in the chest, the other in his neck.

Eric shrieked and Jason fell to his knees, his neck blown open like a giant red mouth full of white bone teeth, and J's blood pumped into the dirt.

The others crouched over him and watched him die and then began to play with his blood.

Eric's sobs rippled up through him. The man stood over him and Eric was falling, looking up. The man's eyes were silver with clouds and the whole sky seemed to be in there. The man raised his arm high and swung the ax into Eric's back. The pain was explosive, all-consuming, and soon after that Eric Pritchard discovered his destiny. It wasn't a gray room with high walls. It was black, just a world gone forever black, where even his own voice carried no sound.

39

Amy Nash screamed so loudly, only two random factors prevented the rest of her family from wondering if she was being murdered in her bed. The first was that she was sleeping alone in the guest room and the rest of the family were either dead asleep (Kyle and Mick) or out (Briela, who was shopping with Ingrid). The second was that her face was pressed into a pillow and she had inadvertently covered her head with a second pillow to block out the sunrise streaming through the blinds just an hour or so before the nightmare provoked such a siren wail.

It was a nightmare so awful, so convincingly real, snapping herself awake to realize it was 'only a dream' was of no comfort. The poisonous black cloud of death that hung over her, along with the cascading visuals of bloodshed that refused to fade from behind her eyes, could not be shrugged off merely because she was conscious of the fact that the sun was shining and she was in her own home, physically unharmed. Her entire body quaked. Runnels of mascara were streaked across the pillows like Satanic symbols. Her head felt slammed between a car and its door. Her stomach was so hollow and distorted with knife-stabbing pains, she felt disemboweled. It would not be an exaggeration to describe what she had just experienced as rape-level fear, for in the aftermath her mind felt invaded, assaulted, and permanently soiled.

She thrashed the covers away as if they were serpents, eels clinging to her limbs, and when she sat up, the room around her felt turned upside down. She hung her head over her drawn-up knees and sobbed, shivering, trying to erase it – but the images kept coming. She looked up at the window, almost directly into the morning sunlight, but she could not un-see what she had seen.

Eric and Jason, those two idiot boys from her classroom, had been in the mountains, drinking and playing with sticks made of fluorescent light. She couldn't hear their conversation but she could read their moods by the moonlight on their almost fawn-like faces. There was so much sadness and misplaced anger in their eyes, such false bravery in their bowed chests and snarling lips. She had never before seen them so naked, so vulnerable, their commonly shitty family stories etched like tattoos across the masks they wore to conceal the pain, depression, and anger they lived with every single day. Even when the gun made its appearance in the dream, she was unable to see them as anything other than damaged, ignorant, chemically disturbed children.

And then the people, if they even were people – and she didn't think they could be as she had ever grasped the term – emerged from the woods. First the man, as cold and emotionless as a Dahmer or Bundy right before they sunk the drill into a lover's temple. She couldn't hear him either, but she understood from the moment he appeared that he was toying with them the way a feral cat bats around a mouse. He was a hunter, a stalker, man as pure predator, a moral nonentity with zero interest in anything other than the suffering of others. The way he moved, his flat expression – this whole episode was mundane to him, an errand, grunt work.

The woman and her children were worse, because no woman or her child should be capable of such appetites, such focused hunger for death. Unlike the man, the woman and children took more than pleasure in their conquest; they took interest, lost themselves in every stage of what turned out to be a wilderness hunt and dressing of the felled carcasses.

Worst of all was that they were a family, a fact evident to Amy from the first moment. She could not read their faces well enough to see a resemblance, but the fact of their blood relation was evident in their movements, their pecking order, the way they worked as a team, intimate and instinctual. They each had a role, and fulfilled it.

The build-up was an act of sadistic suspense, almost as if Amy could sense what was coming. Things escalated quickly when, in a panic, Eric turned and shot Jason, which was bad enough, but what the woman and her offspring did after that was beyond Amy's capacity to believe her own species capable of. They had kneeled as if in a church, and then after a short silence during which Amy thought she could hear Jason's blood trickling onto the mountain's dirt and pine-needled floor, they lathered in him. The boy pressed his face to Jason's throat and the little girl used her fingers, digging into the abdomen, licking them like her mother was baking a cake and she was the lucky one who got to test the batter. They clawed and scratched, and ripped their way into him at leisure and Amy was powerless to look away, until Eric's sobs and then screams filled the canyon.

When the mind-movie cut abruptly in the way of such nightmares, the man was looming above the fallen Eric, swinging the ax again and again, until his face shone with the crimson spatters of his labor. He packed Eric away in the Honda's trunk. The others dragged Jason's remains across the forest floor and wrapped him in a bed sheet that when cinched looked more like a wet bag of sand than any kind of shroud.

The dreaming Amy – as well as the fractured Amy who understood vaguely that she was dreaming even as the dream continued – knew the meaning of the empty seats then. Eric and Jason would never come to class again. The two chairs at the back of the class would be empty during her next session, and during the one after that, and any others to come, because Eric Pritchard and Jason Wells were gone forever. This man and his family had ended them.

This dream was not a dream. This had happened.

After closing the trunk, as the children walked in

something of a daze and got into the car, the man turned and looked at her. Amy knew in the dream that he was looking directly into his wife's eyes (she was no longer on the mind-screen), but it felt as though he were peering into *her* eyes, into her soul, as if he knew every little secret she carried, and was coming for her. His cold black eyes, filmed over with white cotton like an old man's, searched her most private thoughts, invaded her body and soul, and he smiled at what he found there. She knew then that he was not just some figure in a dream. None of them were. They were real, lived in this world, walking among us, a family of monsters disguised as regular folks, the people next door, and Amy had been caught watching them. They were not merely humans capable of murder and wanton slaughter and other indescribable things. They had an unholy power to step from the other realm, where dreams and demons shared the stage, into this world. Her world.

They were coming for her. Her and Mick, Briela and Kyle.

She started screaming then, screaming until she woke herself up. She was still crying now. She hitched her legs and hugged them a few minutes more, and finally forced herself to get out of bed, needing a shower, wishing she could wash out her mind. In the stall the water pounded her and she cried a bit longer, shivering, turning the water as hot as the dial would go, and still she felt cold inside. She closed her eyes and saw his clouded eyes, his blood-speckled face.

Eventually she found the strength to move on, but

the nightmare, if that was all it had been, never really left her. It was there inside her, infecting everything in the days to come, and it went the other way too. Gradually but relentlessly burrowing into the cave of her past, a torch illuminating things no sane person could live with.

Island Living

It was still raining and all of the lights were off in each of the villas as I ran up the path and knocked on the Percys' front door. No one answered for the first few minutes but I knew they were in there, so I knocked again.

Bob answered a long minute or two later. He was excited, in an unsettling way. He was dressed in his Bermuda shorts and a big T-shirt, and his sandals were crusted with wet sand. 'Come in, come in,' he said, dragging me by the arm, and maybe it was from spending all day in the sun, but his hand on my forearm was hot. Beyond fevered. I could swear that if I had not been wearing that jacket, Bob's big mitt would have left a red welt on my forearm.

It was dark in the corridor, the hall leading into the house. It was like talking to a man in an alley at night, and something about it – about the way Bob was so excited and urging me into the house – immediately made me nervous. I could smell something in the wet air, something foul, like spoiling fish.

I asked him if everyone was all right and he said, Yes, fine, never felt better. In the kitchen Bob lit a candle he'd found in one of the drawers. There was only a small glow and the rest of the house around us was dark from the cloud cover and approaching dusk.

'Did you get stuck out in that weather?' I asked him.

'The weather?' Bob said, tilting his head like he hadn't even thought about it until now. He had a silly grin on his face and in the dark beside that candle he looked like a big Halloween pumpkin. 'Never mind that,' he said. 'You're not going to believe what we found.'

'Where are your wife and kids?' I asked.

'Upstairs changing,' Bob said. 'But listen . . .'

They'd been hearing about a special beach from one of the other families, and found it early that morning. After a few hours, Bob's son Timothy wanted to do some exploring in the jungle, see if he could catch an iguana. His parents told him not to go too far, but of course what's too far mean to an eleven-year-old boy?

After half an hour they were worried Tim was lost, so they gathered up their daughter and the three of them trekked back in about a mile or so. They could see their son's footprints in the sand, and pretty soon they heard his voice, calling to them. His voice seemed to be coming out of a bullhorn, or echoing from a canyon. They knew they were close, and after another hundred meters or so they came to the well in the clearing.

Have you ever been to Chichen Itza, the Mayan ruins outside of Cancun? There is a cenote down there, a sacred well, spanning about sixty or seventy meters across. It's a natural geological formation in the limestone, a depression, caved in from water running underneath the stone for hundreds or thousands of years. The well at Chichen Itza is only about a hundred feet deep, forty of water and sixty of stone above that. The Mayans dedicated it to Chac, the god of rain and lightning, whom they appeased with human sacrifices. We know they threw live bodies into the well. Archaeologists have found human bones and skulls down there, as well as masks of copper and gold, and other ornaments – gifts to Chac, on whose generosity with the rain the Mayans thrived or starved.

What Bob Percy from Madison, Wisconsin, was describing to me then sounded a lot like the cenote at Chichen Itza, but I was skeptical such a thing would exist on an island, and such a small island at that.

'It's smaller,' Bob told me, 'maybe forty feet across, and about as deep. Inside, the water is silver, like melted pewter.'

When he and Lynn arrived and looked down, their son Timothy was swimming in it. Hollering like a wild man, having a ball. At first they thought he'd fallen in, but Tim said he wasn't hurt, and while they were asking him what happened and generally panicking about what the hell to do, their daughter, Tanya, was shaking Bob's hand, pointing. 'Look, Daddy, look.'

On the other side of the well, cut into the limestone or whatever type of rock lies under the sandy forest of Vieques, was a stairway. It looked like a carved rock version of the ladders you see on the side of an oil refinery tank, curving down, only this one was inside the wall. Descending in a spiral until it disappeared into the water. It was narrow but the steps were just wide enough

275

for a small adult or child to walk up or down. According to their son, he stumbled upon the well and decided to see how close he could get to the water. He didn't slip and fall until he was about six steps from the bottom, when he imagined seeing a shape beneath the surface, and an arm reaching up to pull him in.

You might ask now the same thing I asked myself at that moment in Bob's story. If this well was used like the cenote in Chichen Itza, a repository for human sacrifices, what was the purpose of this ladder? The ladder suggested humans had carved it and used it for some purpose, but a gift to the gods is not something you take back. They wouldn't retrieve the bodies. So there would be no need to *go down*. But, you might ask, as I asked myself, what if there was a need to *climb out*?

Of course I was skeptical of Bob's story. None of the maps or guidebooks for Vieques mentioned a well or landmark of any such sort, and I had done my share of research on the place, so I would have remembered that.

'You should have seen the water,' Bob said. 'Even as my son was paddling around in there like some kind of otter, the surface was shifting, reflecting in the shade, rippling with crosscurrents that scaled the small waves the boy was making.' Bob said it reminded him of 'sea monkeys, but instead of pink and brown little organisms, the water in this well is a mosaic of silver and gray … hell, we don't know what it was. Plankton? Algae? Bacteria? Something similar to the bioluminescent bay? Whatever it was, the mercury surface of this water looked like it was alive.'

Despite being frightened when he thought he saw something rising from the depths to pull him in, Timothy did not want to leave the well. He said it felt too good. But his parents were scared. For all they knew, their son was swimming in a toxic puddle (Or amongst the bones and ancient dust and silt of the first Native American peoples who happened upon the island before the Spanish arrived, I thought but did not say to Bob).

Bob and Lynn were screaming at him to get out. Finally Tim agreed, swimming to the base of the stairs, or where the stone steps met the water, and he climbed out reluctantly, pouting. Bob and Lynn were worried he was going to fall, but the kid moved right up and along in a sideways shuffle, never slowing or looking down, as if he had been using these stairs all his young life.

They got him back to the beach and toweled him off, and that's when they noticed that the water – the silver mass he had been splashing around in for at least ten and maybe even thirty minutes – wasn't coming off. It was on his skin and his limbs were running with it in filmy lines that wouldn't dry. It was slick, like oil. They decided to make him rinse off in the ocean. They were worried it was on them now, too, because they'd been hugging Tim and inspecting his body for wounds. Neither Bob nor Lynn found any on themselves or Tanya, but they all hopped in the ocean anyway, scrubbing themselves with sand. They emerged from the sea about ten minutes later looking clean and feeling better. The silver stuff was gone.

Except, of course, it wasn't gone.

I was standing there in the Percys' villa, listening to this rather fabulous tale amidst the candlelight, when I saw it. On Bob's arms, along his neck and, when I held the candle out like a torch to illuminate his legs, it was down there too. On his ankles, up his thighs. I'd never seen anything like it. I don't think now that it was on their skin. I think it was already *inside* them, under or within the epidermis. Have you ever seen one of those new custom cars, with the paint job that changes color depending on the amount of light and the angle from which you view it? It seems black when you stand in front of the hood, but when you move around and stare down the side panel, you see purple and green and silver? Bob's skin was like that. Very faintly luminescent and in no way normal. Even in the darkness, with only candlelight, I could see that it was in him.

Bob wasn't frightened. He felt fine, he said. Better than fine. He was animated by something other than the excitement of discovering a well in the jungle. His eyes were black in the dark villa but wide with a childish delight, and he was grinning. When I expressed my concern and stepped away from him, he laughed at me. I remembered how he had grabbed my arm when he answered the front door, and I was very glad I had been wearing that windbreaker. I wanted to get away from the Percys as soon as possible.

Bob wondered if we were still on for drinks tonight. I made excuses, telling him that the storm had frightened the kids and that my wife wasn't feeling well. I just wanted to make sure you had made it back from the beach in this weather, I told him. Bob watched me curiously and I am sure he knew that I was lying, but he said nothing as he followed me to the door. I was so anxious to be on my way, I forgot to ask him why the lights were off.

I made it home a few minutes later. The wife and kids were eating soup and grilled cheese sandwiches around the glass dining table. Our lights were still on. They asked me if everything was all right. Fine, I assured them, and then I went to have a long hot shower before joining them for dessert.

I don't remember tasting my wife's key lime pie.

I did not sleep well that night. I tossed and turned in half-dreams, the rain pattering on our roof as my mind went round and round with thoughts of the Percy family. Capricious thunderstorms rolled over the island in half-hour intervals, bulbs of lightning flashing inside the belly of cloud cover and illuminating the bedroom like a photo negative every few minutes. Sometime around two or three a.m., I came fully awake to the sound of fading thunder and people screaming.

Ungodly screaming coming from the villas next to ours.

40

The summer days were a blur, and then it was Saturday, her special day.

Briela didn't see the boy for the first two hours of the party, and then he just appeared. He was standing in the corner of the rec room while the other kids played their games, ignoring him. None of the mothers were paying attention to him and she knew he had come alone. He looked different than he had that day at Glacier, when he had stared at her through the window. He was wearing a brown plaid flannel shirt buttoned to the throat, even though it was summer, and dirty brown pants, like he had been playing beside a pond all morning. His face was streaked with chocolate, or more dirt, his lips chapped, with red cracks at the corners of his mouth. His skin was the color of soy milk. He was staring at her, smiling, and there were dark streaks in his teeth. He could have been cute but he needed a bath. He didn't try to play with the others. He was only interested in the birthday girl.

She pretended to lose interest and busy herself at the crafts table, where Tami Larson and some of the other kids were making crowns out of orange and purple construction paper, smearing them with paste and coloring them with markers that smelled like candied fruit. But even as Briela scribbled little jewels at every point, she could feel him watching her. In fact she could almost hear his voice, high and soft, whispering inside her.

Hey, Birthday Girl, look over here. I have to show you something. It's important. Look here, it's about your mommy and daddy ... I know what's going to happen to them, to all of you. You're in a lot of trouble ...

His eyes on the back of her neck were like cold lizard fingers. He wouldn't leave her alone, so she finally looked up, to the corner, and he was still there. Staring at her. His eyes were even wider now. All the other kids retreated and the room seemed to draw her forward, toward him, even though he didn't move, and it was like being on one of those conveyor belts at the airport, only faster. All of the laughter in the room got sucked into a buzzing silence and her ears popped. His eyes were bright green, with long brown lashes, and when she was about to crash into him, a line of blood seeped from the corner of each eye. The top of his head seemed to roll back, becoming taller, and his jaw popped open, until she could see inside, where all his teeth were shining red, his mouth filled with blood. His eyes began to vibrate and his entire body was shaking in a fit.

Briela screamed and thrashed her arms out, trying to fight back, to make him stop, make him stop showing her these terrible things and go away. There was a different scream then, not her own. When she blinked, the room was bright and the boy was gone. She was back at the crafts table and the boy wasn't standing in the corner, or anywhere else in the room, but she didn't even have time to wonder where he had disappeared to, because by then everything was different, flying out of control.

41

Amy didn't see it happen. She was pre-bussing the mess of plates and cups over at the counter where the cake had been destroyed, picking over detritus like a crime-scene technician so as to avoid soiling her outfit. For this very special occasion she had spent half an hour straightening her hair with a hot iron, and wore a new peach blouse with an embroidery motif of flower petals she had ordered from J. Crew. The deep blue denim skirt made her look three sizes smaller while the brown leather gladiator sandals showcased her new lavender-sparkle pedicure. She was brushing a morsel of chocolate cake from her bust (thankfully it did not leave a frosting skid) when the first scream pierced the already loud party in the rec room.

Amy recognized it as one of Briela's screams, shrill and brief, and it was followed by ominous silence. She turned and saw a purple plastic fork jutting from Tami Larson's sweet upturned face, like some kind of a magic trick performed by a sadistic clown. Right in the soft pad of cheek, halfway between eye and mouth. For the first few seconds, even Tami Larson – an obese girl with thick black hair and chocolate freckles almost the same color as the blood dots made by the fork – was too stunned to cry out.

Standing eye-level with Tami was the angelic blonde viper known as Briela, her arm raised. To everyone else it was obvious what had just happened. And yet it took another agonizing moment for Amy to admit what she was seeing. It was like a simple math equation with only one correct answer.

Tami Larson + purple fork + sticking out of her face + Briela's raised hand + everyone in shock = my daughter went fucking psycho.

Everyone in the room – kids, moms, and the one dad, Larry Havas – seemed to be waiting for someone to bark, 'Just kidding! It was a rubber fork, no harm done!' Then Tami started to scream. And the other kids started to scream. But Rita Larson, Tami's mother, didn't scream. She was standing against the stairway railing, conversing with Andrea Grayson's mom, her nose in a goblet of Shiraz. As she absorbed the fact that her daughter had been stabbed in the face with a fork, Rita Larson's face (same freckles, gray streaks in the frizzy hair) went through the kind of sublime transition that wins actresses the Academy Award.

The happy smile crumbled slowly, like a detonated bridge. Then came the paling of her cheeks, followed by a long dawning of anguish (during which the wine leaned over and then toppled from her hand). And finally, just before she lunged in to remove the weapon and cover her daughter as if the basement were about to be filled with a hailstorm of plastic forks and knives and God only knew what else, for this was now the House of the Devil, there came an ugly working of Rita's lips and a hoarse lament that in any other context might have been orgasmic but here was pure maternal anguish and turned Amy's blood to cracking ice.

'Oh, no, Briela, *noooooo* ...' Amy finally played her role, stepping in to yank Briela away. 'What did you do? What on earth happened?' As if it wasn't clear, as if there might be a rational explanation.

By then the other mothers were gathering up their children and leading them away from the monster who had materialized, and away from Amy, the other monster who was responsible for hosting this uncoordinated freak show.

Chaos ensued. The parents filed out, appalled, glaring at Amy as if she had meant for this to happen. Rita Larson ran up the stairs with her daughter in her arms, using words like 'my lawyer' and 'should be ashamed' and 'psychiatric help'. Amy had chased after her, apologizing, offering to call a doctor, only to be repelled by a Godzilla squall of 'Stay the hell away from my daughter, both of you!'

Minutes later the storm had passed. The birthday party was at its ugly end.

Only Melanie Smith, whose daughter was already off to college in Bozeman, Montana, stayed behind to offer sympathy. Melanie had gone to Fairview High with Amy, but dropped out early. Their friendship hadn't rekindled until Kyle reached his terrible fives. Melanie was the non-judgemental mom in the group, a former self-admitted screw-up of various sorts, a recovered addict twice divorced and amazed her own daughter was not by now knocked up or strung out, as Melanie had been at that age. She was the friend the other mothers called upon in their darkest hours, because whatever it was, Melanie had been there. She had come over this afternoon at the last minute to help Amy set everything up in Mick's absence.

'It's the chemicals in the food,' Melanie said. They had retreated to the kitchen after stuffing Briela into her bedroom. Amy was too stunned to cry. 'It could be anything. You're a wonderful mother.'

'I'm an asshole.'

'No. Don't beat yourself up about this, Ames. I've seen kids do worse. Remember the Keenan boy? He gave Jason Turner fifteen stitches with a Lego.'

'It wasn't an accident,' Amy said. 'I know that look. It was, it was . . . *premeditated*.'

'She's at that age, they don't always understand the difference between arguments and physical outbursts. In their minds it's, You hurt me and now I'm going to hurt you back.'

Amy wiped her nose with a dish towel. 'My daughter stabbed that girl in the face. How does she even think of that?'

'Did you get a hold of Mick?'

'He's working. *Again*. The restaurant is failing. What am I supposed to do?' She meant about anything, about her entire life.

'Nothing tonight.' Melanie hugged her. 'Jesus, you're cold, girl. Go take a hot bath. Get some rest and then think very carefully about how you're going to address this with your husband. He needs to hear loud and clear that this is not okay. He needs to start participating in this marriage and be present for these milestones. We'll work through it, hon. Call me tomorrow.'

By the time Melanie left, dusk had given way to night. The house was simultaneously too empty and closing in on her. She was gripped by a need to erase all traces of the crime.

She trotted down with a roll of trash bags, steeling herself in the event she had to scrub blood (and Rita Larson's wine) from the carpet. She did not remember seeing Tami bleeding profusely, but she assumed there would be a hell of a mess. If not here, surely in the Larsons' car on the ride home. Or was it the ride to Boulder Community Hospital? Urgent Care, anyway.

When she got to the bottom of the stairway and turned the corner, she was stricken. She had not grasped the level of destruction fifteen second- and third-graders could leave in their wake. It seemed, in a sickening way, the perfect snapshot of her daughter's chaotic mind.

Twelve hundred square feet of balloons, napkins, cups, plastic silverware, finger paints, kazoos, plastic trinkets, and smashed candy necklaces. Herds of hand-size stuffed animals purchased as takeaways for 'Guests of Briela Nash' (because in this sensitive age, every child went home a winner, one child's birthday was *every* child's birthday) were torn, flung, forgotten, gutted, poised in positions of grave injury and imaginary copulation. There were ribbons, paper hats, streaks of glitter, and blown soap bubble residue. All over the basement. In every corner. Piled knee-high. It was a damp dominion reeking of wet crepe paper, artificial sugar, and bubble-gum farts. It was too much to absorb in one flyover. It was the Hurricane Katrina of birthday parties. She wanted to burn the house down.

No, it couldn't be that bad, she thought, pausing on the stairs. But it was that bad, she realized as she waded in again. Like rioters in a burning cell block, the kids had together succumbed to hysteria and uncorked the unholy.

Grape punch barf streaked the walls. The dish lamp had been toppled. Under the pool table, a cold blackened tofurter was being devoured by the Nash's Yorkshire terrier, Thom, who, unbeknownst to anyone, just twenty-seven minutes ago, having found himself locked inside this amazing new jungle of smells and snacks and debris with no exit to the backyard, had happily and silently urinated into honors math student and chess prodigy Eli Werner's forgotten North Face sherpa vest. The crafts table appeared to be ground zero for a 64-count box of Crayolas that had been chewed, swallowed, and shat out by Ronald McDonald. The couch cushions were a fort, the small flat-panel TV over the wet bar was cracked, and the papery cheese whiz guts of six dozen string poppers was spewed *fucking everywhere*.

Absorbing this aftermath like a state governor

composing her plea for FEMA funds, Amy asked herself the question all parents eventually come around to.

Was it worth it? Did it make my child happy? Will she look back on this day and wipe a tear from her eye as she says the magic words: 'Thank you, Mom. I had the greatest childhood any daughter could ask for. I'll never forget how much you sacrificed so that I could become the woman I am today.'

The answer to that question was a sick joke. If Briela remembered any of this beyond next week, it would be a miracle, or in this case a blessing. Because the truth was she had hated it as much as her mother had hated it. Hadn't she? Ordering the save-the-date cards and envelopes from the printer, the errands and shopping, the decision to allow (force) Briela to design the cake (it would be educational, empowering!), the useless reminders barked at Mick a month ago, cross-referencing all of the snacks with the submitted allergies lists, the racing around town on her lunch hour to get every fucking detail just right, all of it leading up to the main event (Visa total: $1486.73 @ 24.99% APR). Wasn't this excess of excitement and consumption and the disgusting bath of presents and treats and total sensory overload at least half of the reason Briela had gone off the deep end?

In other words, wasn't it all really Amy's fault?

Something was stirring in the corner, beneath a shrub of wrapping paper. Amy froze, drawing it out. A locket of blonde hair emerged, followed by a single blue eye. A heavy chuff of breath.

No.

No way.

'Oh, you better not,' Amy whispered.

The birthday girl was supposed to be in exile, in her room, stewing in guilt and awaiting her sentencing.

'Briela? Briela!'

The daughter prairie-dogged up, party debris sticking to her ruined yellow dress. She was panting hotly, tiny fists bunched at her diaphragm.

'You did this?' But it wasn't really a question now. 'You did *all this*!'

While Amy was talking with Melanie in the kitchen, Briela had staged a prison break and come back down to have herself an absolute Jesus camp blowout.

'Answer me!'

As if in reply, Briela screamed, darting around the sofa as she went hellbent for election across the rec room, whooping in some demented combination of glee and manic terror, daring her mother to give chase.

Amy dared. 'Come back here right now! Briela! Brie—'

A door slammed between them. Briela had locked herself in the guest suite bathroom. But she did not have the foresight to lock the second door, the one on the laundry room side, and Amy barged in. At which point B knew she was in truly deep shit, screamed once and collapsed under the towel rack.

Amy carried her out of the basement, back to her bedroom. She sat Briela on the bed, and counted to twenty, kneeling before her daughter.

'All right. There's no need to holler. Just tell me, honey. Why did you do it?'

Briela was shaking her head. Her eyes were unfocused.

'Why did you hurt Tami?'

'No, no, no ...'

'Yes. Don't lie to me, Briela. Everyone saw what happened.'

'I didn't! The boy was scaring me. It was the people with Daddy! Where's Daddy?'

Amy sat back on her feet. She'd heard this before, and now it was scaring her. The girl really believed someone was hurting her father. 'What people, Briela? Why are you so worried about Daddy?'

Briela stopped crying and looked up, over Amy's head. For the tiniest fraction of a second, the girl's eyes pooled with fear, and then it retreated, sinking deep inside and her expression neutralized, settling into exhaustion.

Amy turned to find Cassandra Render standing in the hallway.

'Amy? Is everything all right?'

Amy stood up too fast and plopped down on B's bed, and barely managed to keep from fainting. She looked up again, just to make sure she was seeing things correctly.

Cassandra Render had straightened her hair with a hot iron. She wore the same new peach blouse with an embroidery motif of flower petals, deep blue denim skirt, and brown leather gladiator sandals which perfectly showcased her new lavender-sparkle pedicure. It was like looking into a funhouse mirror, the kind that makes fat people thin. For a moment, but only a moment, Amy was certain that Cassandra Render was not real, but a reflection, a spirit, some kind of visitor who had attached herself to them and would not let go until she had taken possession of Amy's soul.

'Sorry I'm so late,' Cass said. 'Adolph wasn't feeling well today. I had to stay with him until Ingrid volunteered to watch him for a couple of hours. I saw everyone leaving early and I got worried. Is there anything I can do to help?'

Amy laughed and laughed and soon was crying.

'Ssshhh, shush, now,' Cass said, sitting on the bed, running her hand over Amy's hair. 'Don't you worry about them. They have no right to judge you. You're a wonderful mother. Vince went to help Mick. He'll be home soon and all of this will get better. I promise.'

Almost as an afterthought, Cass said, 'I think we need to have a little talk about the other woman too. Melanie. She's been putting her nose where it doesn't belong and she's only going to cause more trouble for you.'

Amy was too spent to comment. Behind her, lying on her side, Briela was looking up at Cassandra, studying her with great intensity.

42

Mick set the alarm and locked the door. The stencil on the Straw's front window said Monday–Saturday 11–1, Sundays noon–11, but by 8:45 the dining room and bar were empty and there was no point to any of it. He ordered Carlos to turn off the grill and forget about racking the dishes, told Reggie and Jamie to leave the chairs down. The cleaning crew would be in at eight and he would handle the deposit tomorrow. He tipped them out and packed the remaining (thin) leafery of cash into a rubber bank bag and stowed it in the safe. He shooed them out through the kitchen, breaking down cardboard boxes and watching over the back bay until they had all gotten into their vehicles safely. Reggie's Lac bass-thumped off across the lot, revealing someone's topless blue Jeep parked in the corner. Mick didn't recognize it, but it could have belonged to one of the drunks who'd decided not to drive home tonight.

'Night, Mick.' His star waved as she stamped over to her Civic.

'Good night, Jamie.'

One final pass through the restaurant, and then it was

lights out. Confirming that the alarm's 'activated' light was blinking, Mick was stabbed by the realization that – barring a windfall of some two hundred thousand dollars – he would perform this ritual only another nineteen or twenty times. Thirty days, Sapphire had said. And unless Mick struck back at the accountant soon (*Maybe tonight, how about it, champ? Do you feel up for a short drive out to Longmont? What are you waiting for? Let's go put the fear of God into that silver-haired bastard ...*), he would find himself on the other side of Fourth of July weekend without a lifeline, and then he would never again lock up *his own restaurant.*

Someone else's, perhaps, but not the restaurant his parents had built and seen prosper for some thirty years before handing the keys over to their only son. Not the place Mick had played race cars under the tables, falling asleep in booths while Mom ran a pencil in her ledger. Not the place he'd washed enough dishes to buy his first car, the '78 blue Trans Am he never should have sold. Not the place Dad had hosted after-prom parties for Mick and his friends, and helped cater the Buffaloes under Coach McCartney's national championship reign.

Not the very restaurant where, one fateful April lunch hour fifteen years ago, a knock-out grad student had come in to borrow a quarter for the pay phone, broke, in tears, looking to call a wrecker to get her mom's Datsun wagon into the shop before her mom got back from spending the weekend with her jerk boyfriend in Estes Park. Hockey-stick legs growing out her stacked cork wedges, gumball blue eyes under long blonde hair that fell to the middle of her back – it was something closely related to love at first sight. Mick had done his best to get her laughing again while she nursed a hard-luck Michelob on the house, then drove her to the auto-parts store and charged the parts to his dad's account. The bearded heart-attack-on-wheels with greased mitts behind the auto-parts counter giving Mick a raised eyebrow and the pervert grin, Mick nodding back, I know, I know, don't fuck this one up for me, just find that goddamn part. Back at the restaurant, he'd handed her a huge dish of coffee ice cream and changed out the Datsun's solenoid in the Straw's parking lot while she hovered around and spilled her tales of woe and all he asked in return was her phone number. She had a boyfriend, a serious one, but 'the dufus' didn't ask her to move to Arizona with him, so what did Mick think that meant, right? She was supposed to marry Dufus in Tucson that September, but did that deter our hero? Two months later she called Dufus and said she was sending the ring back UPS. Seven months later, after a lot of pulling but not enough praying, Amy was pregnant with Kyle. The wedding had followed quickly, but it was real. He never doubted that their love had been real.

His family was real. His failure was real.

That era of apple pie and mom and dad and Last Straw magic was over. That air of *here, the best days of your lives will happen right here* vitality that perhaps one in a thousand bars manages to capture, was gone. It was his home, his real home, and the sight of it tonight, dark and half-looted, put a mighty hurt in his heart.

He turned away, heading for his truck. The parking lot was as black as a city park until it reached the grocery store and strip mall on the far side. He watched the Albertson's sign flicker and blink out, eleven on the nose. Mick always parked somewhere in the empty middle, leaving nearer spaces for his customers, but that was a useless habit now. Blue Thunder was waiting for him, the tiny red alarm bulb on the dash beckoning, another beacon in the relay of his commute. At home he would disarm a third, in the mud room, at last the captain safely ashore.

He walked head down, the truck fifty paces off.

His conscience fired one last warning across the bow. A bit past the legal limit, boss? How many whiskey sours did we have? Five? Seven? No. Maybe. Sure, but if he called Amy for a ride, she would just browbeat him, and he'd have to ask her for another ride back in the morning, and that would start another day off with a breakfast of cold resentment. And just when, exactly, was the right time to tell your family that the organism which sustained 75 per cent of their existence was dead?

So, no. No phone calls, no rides. He might've been so tired he couldn't hold his head all the way up, but he could drive a couple miles. The Diagonal was empty this time of night. He was a bar man. Alcohol no longer affected him.

His running shoe ground a stray piece of bottle glass.

Six paces from his truck.

Three.

Mick fingered his keyring, dipping into the miniature

Broncos helmet Briela had given him last Father's Day. The helmet squirted from his grip, he juggled the ring spastically, the brass wad fell to the ground. He stared at it.

Is that some sort of a sign, old man?

As he bent, a sharp aluminum *clink* echoed behind him. He recognized it at once, for it was a childhood sound, not easily forgotten. Flinty and cruel, it was the sound an Easton aluminum baseball bat made connecting with the long ball (or falling on warm summer asphalt). Mick's had been a thirty-one-incher with a brushed blue finish and a sticky rubber sleeve, his father's benediction for Pony League.

He scooped his keys and turned to face them. There were three, spread in a narrowing net. Hardly more than high-school kids, but wired for high voltage. Black combat boots, warm-up jackets zipped to the chin, cold eyes in expressionless masks. They requested nothing, offered him no bargain. Mick was not a large man, but he was a former state champion wrestler, fit from working on his feet, and he could still carry a half-barrel on one shoulder.

I wasn't imagining it. It was a vision, another episode like the one about Sapphire, and the other one about Myra. Terry Fielding, or some force borrowing his likeness, came to warn me, just in the nick of time. Whatever happened to me, whatever is going on inside me, it has the power to change the course of my hours, my days, my life. But I didn't pay attention and now I am in deep shit.

'This is gonna be too fuckin' easy,' the smallest one said. 'I almost feel bad for you, know'msayin'?'

The two of them might not be a problem, but the third was a freak. A tall Hispanic with four shoulders and no neck, some kind of bloated-faced goon. The Easton belonged to the short one on the left, bleached hair under a red-and-blue Avalanche cap. *I know why things are the way they are*, Render had told him in the yard. *I know why the others come, preying on you. They are out there right now. They have a nose for weakness, and they will keep coming for you and it will get messier unless you allow me to help you.*

Vince Render, whatever he was, was involved in all of this. Everything that had happened since that day on the lake, it had to do with the people next door.

'Only three?' Mick said. 'I guess the other Mousketeers had a curfew.'

They didn't laugh. The bat changed hands once it all went in motion, and it went in motion quickly.

43

After hugging Amy goodbye, Melanie Smith had closed the front door softly behind her and stepped out onto the curving sidewalk. She walked head down, her heart broken for Amy. Rita Larson was the kind of mother who pretended to be above the stress of parenting, but it was a charade. Melanie knew that the Larsons had been financially reeling since Rita's husband, Don, lost his position as a project manager at Ball Aerospace, after NASA shelved its latest project and withdrew the firm's funding. Rita's back was against a wall here, and if she no longer had health insurance to pay for the injury (which was probably minor but had looked bad enough to scare any parent into shark-infested litigation), she was going to come at Amy and Mick, as Melanie's mother used to say, with both barrels loaded, tits on fire.

Melanie had been trying to remember the name of that ex-boyfriend (well, he was really more of a two- or three-night stand) she'd met a few years ago in Denver, a small claims lawyer and proud ambulance chaser, when a shadow fell over her feet and she almost bumped into the psycho. She jerked in surprise, halted.

A thin woman with black hair was staring at her with beady eyes the color of tin. She was six inches shorter than Melanie and yet her stance was defiant, as if she had no intention of making room for her on the sidewalk.

'Oh, excuse me,' Melanie said. 'The party just ended. Are you here to pick up your child?' But she couldn't be, because all of them were gone.

'No.'

Melanie waited for the woman to elaborate. Finally said, 'Okay. Now's not a good time, so maybe—'

'You should leave now,' the woman said. Her voice was soft and she was not smiling. 'You don't belong here.'

For a moment Melanie was too stunned to respond. Who was this woman? A friend of Rita's, one who had already heard about the accident and come back to rip into Amy? But it had just happened, no way the news had spread unless Rita was tweeting about the party on her way to Urgent Care. During this lull she noticed that the woman wore the same blouse as Amy. And the same skirt. And sandals. And her hair was flat, shining as if recently oiled.

Melanie laughed. 'I'm sorry, what? Is this a joke?'

The woman did not answer but her eyes seemed to darken, the tin deepening to charcoal beneath brows plucked down to broken black toothpicks.

Melanie tried again. 'You're a friend of Amy's? Have we met?'

'Cassandra Render.' The woman's chin jutted forth. 'I am her best friend.'

'Somehow I doubt – hey, wait, you're the ones in the new house? Amy told me about you.' For the first time, a ripple of uncertainty passed over Cassandra's mask of intimidation. 'See, that's funny, because I checked with the title office and that's not your house. The builder disappeared almost a year ago and the bank is about to take it over. You don't belong there. I don't know who you think—'

'Watch yourself, dyke,' Cassandra Render said.

'Excuse me?' Did she just say what I think . . .

The crazy little woman took a step toward Melanie. 'It's mothers like you who create the pressure and expectations that lead to problems like this. But Amy will no longer be judged by inept creatures like you. Go on, Melanie. Get back in your car and go back to your sad house and eat a bucket of ice cream. Call your daughter and make sure she's still safe.'

Hearing her name, her daughter's safety put into question, Melanie's temper went volcanic. 'Oh hell no, bitch, I know you *did not* just threaten me. Don't you dare talk about my daughter, who do you think you are—'

But that was all she got out before Cassandra Render seized Melanie by the ear, yanking her head down with savage force. Melanie cried out, certain the woman was going to bite her ear off, but instead she whispered, 'Go home now and forget you ever saw me unless you want to relive that lonesome October night you spent at the Kappa Sigma house, and this time it will be an alley and all five of them will wear masks.'

Melanie was shoved aside, gut-punched by the airing of a memory so heinous she had never told anyone about it, not even her mother or her best friend, Kana McMullen. She was still reeling in shock as Cassandra continued up the walk as if she had just stepped over a piece of garbage.

'You're gonna pay for that,' Melanie shrieked, rubbing her ear, bet your sweet ass hoping to find blood. 'Do you hear me? And what do you think you're doing? Get away from that door right now.'

She was stomping toward the porch when Cassandra turned slowly and pointed a finger at her, waving it in a circle as a deranged smile drew her mouth into a slit. Her eyes rolled back with pleasure and came to rest on Melanie.

'I put them,' the woman said in a sing-song voice, 'on you.'

Melanie stopped, some deep part of her cavewoman brain warning her not to take another step. Every inch of her skin crawled in repulsion and pants-wetting fear. The only sensation she had to compare it to was the time she had nearly jogged into a nest of recently birthed rattlesnakes out on Eagle Trail, the first dozen already breaching their clear gelatinous sacs, and then backed into the grass and nearly stepped on the depleted and hungry mother, a long, rough diamondback whose pink wet mouth and glass-needle fangs had leapt up at her in such ferocious silence, Melanie had nightmares about it for weeks.

If you take another step, the voice of survival inside her warned, *you will suffer things worse than death, and Rayell will never come home from college again.*

Cassandra Render wasn't mentally ill, and she wasn't merely dangerous. She was flat-out evil. She continued to stare at Melanie, her lips moving soundlessly, until Melanie backed away and ran to her car, slammed the door and locked it, fumbling her keys around the ignition. When she looked up again, Cassandra was pushing the front door open and slipping inside.

Melanie picked up her cell phone to warn Amy, but found herself dialing her daughter's number instead. Rayell was a junior at Montana State up in Bozeman, far away from this madness. And yet Melanie could not help but feel that it – whatever this woman had set in motion – had already come for her.

Five rings, six. On the seventh, Rayell's voicemail answered. Melanie hung up and dialed again. The phone was still ringing when Melanie turned onto Jay Road and headed toward home, pressing the gas pedal to the floor.

44

Mick committed early, the keys welcome weight in his fist. He swung on the bald Asian kid, but it was a glancing blow and only popped the runt into another gear.

The proprietor took the Easton upside his left ear and the big guy drove two palms the size of pie plates into his chest. Mick was dropped to his back, looking up between his elbows, shifting wildly to cover his head. Having traded the bat, the bleach-blond was already crouching on him and pummeling down, right-left, right-left. The big guy was kicking from the side, boots like anvils, the Asian kid running around and squealing as he swung the bat like a golf club.

Mick's thigh took a tee shot that would have snapped his femur if he hadn't rolled with it. White fists battered his cheeks and brow and neck. His ear had turned hot and wet and he was numb with adrenaline, thrashing and dodging until the Easton clanged off his ankle. That felt like a teacup shattering inside, but he didn't have the luxury of dwelling on it. He figured he was going to wind up in the hospital's critical condition wing again ... or not wake up at all.

Alarming to think that moments ago he had been too curious about his premonition to be afraid, but now could hear himself screaming.

'Help, help! Fire!' he bawled, knowing the odds of drawing in a bystander at this hour, in this dead shopping center, were extremely poor.

Someone said, 'His keys, get the keys!' And his friend countered, in a high shrieking voice, 'Fuck him up, fuck him up!' And they danced about him, raining fists and boots, but it was a hyper attack, only a third of the blows connecting as well as they should, and soon would.

Mick scrambled back on his elbows, rolling side to side, looking for a pair of legs to sweep, but there was no escape and he was losing all coordination. They closed around him, fighting over him like a piece of meat. His lips swelled. His nose cracked. His right hook wasn't working the way he wanted it to.

He glimpsed the blond one crawling at him with the bat raised above his Avalanche cap, a dirty little Samurai coming with the mortal chop. Mick kicked out, felt no impact. His blood screamed through his veins and a black curtain of rage fell around him. Glands seldom used were sent into battle. Before the kid could set his knees, the hat floated up and the blond head beneath it bungee-jerked back, his eyes going *what the fuck*-round. The kid screamed as he was thrown aside with brutal force, and his Asian buddy stumbled over him, face-planting as if a wrecking ball had swept through the melee.

The bat fell to the ground and rolled away. *Clingcling-cling* ...

The blows stopped ... or at least paused for some kind of intermission.

Mick flopped onto his stomach, coughing blood through his pulped nose. Behind him, the big bastard was shouting in Spanish – surprise at first, then argument, then a plea of terror. Someone grunted deeply, like a Russian power-cleaning a Volkswagen. The big boy screamed. There was a great smacking sound on the pavement, and the Easton was rolling back to him.

Mick used the bat as a cane to push himself to his feet. His vision was blurred and he might have been walking in outer space.

A head of bleached hair was fleeing around the back of his truck and the proprietor lurched after him. The torn warm-up jacket flapped as the kid ran a few steps in confusion, then stopped and tried to make a stand. Mick brought the Easton around and knocked the boy's jaw about in half. Shithead went rigid for a second, chin raised to the moon, then dropped like a wet towel.

Mick did not slow to consider what had set him free. All he knew was that the tide had shifted and, oh sweet motherfuck, the pleasure of this power reclaimed was nearly sexual. He turned, bellowing. These pieces of shit had been after his livelihood, probably the keys to the restaurant and safe, and they had become the root of it all now, every problem in his world honed down to this moment. There was finally a face to the faceless *them*. Sapphire, Render, the IRS, his shitty customer base, the intolerant suppliers jacking up costs. None of them mattered now because he had these clowns. He was concussed and giddy and he wanted it to last all night.

The big bastard was on his feet again, swaying, distracted by something in the darkness. His back was turned and he never heard it coming. Mick choked up on the rubber grip and the aluminum whistled. Guy's spine caved in with a cracking thud and he collapsed, breath gusting like his lungs had balloon popped.

The bald one was crawling away when Mick brought the bat in low, up into his ribs, so hard the grip sprang free. His momentum carried him pitching over the bodies, spinning as he fell, and he banged the back of his head on the parking lot for at least the second time. He tried to sit up but he hadn't been so depleted since his first junior varsity wrestling meet, when he had swallowed his mouthpiece and passed out cold in the Boulder High gym.

The Easton played its rolling music across the asphalt. Heavy footsteps pounded closer, then faded. Someone's hysterical screaming cut off wetly.

Everything went quiet. He half expected Coach Wisneski to lean over him snapping a smelling salt, but he was alone now, consciousness lost.

45

'I knew you had it in you.'

A slow baritone, laced with a kind of perversion. The voice one hears through the wall of a motel room at four in the morning.

'The first time I saw you. I knew you were a killer.'

It was like a dream, a bad dream, a recurring nightmare. He had been here before, in this presence. His mind whirled in shattered darkness.

'It's not safe here,' the deep voice said. 'We have a lot of work ahead of us. I will clean it up. I've cleaned up worse. But so you know, I saved your life again. And this time I'm not going to let you forget. This time we are bound.'

Mick opened his eyes.

Stars. Sky. Cooling air and the warm gritty hardness under him. He sat forward, aching all over, dizzy. He rolled sideways and caught himself with his scraped knuckles. The parking lot, he was in the parking lot. His head felt like a bowling ball but he forced himself to look up.

His truck was right there. The door was open, the

cab's dome light on. He crawled to it. Raised himself up and leaned over the seat, waiting for the worst of the vertigo to pass. His keys were in the ignition. Thought he was going to throw up but he was too frightened to linger. He didn't remember what had happened, but it had been horrible and something unknowably evil had been right there with him. It could be behind him right now ...

Mick grabbed the wheel and dragged, squirming to get his ass under him. He turned the key and the Silverado's big V-8 grumbled to life. He closed the door and stared at the windshield. His body felt smashed and his shirt was wet, sticking to his chest. The headlights cut a swath up to the grocery store.

No other cars, no bystanders. No people of any kind.

What the hell happened? How long was I out?

Hands shaking, his grip clumsy on the wheel. He closed his eyes, controlling the panic, and a flash of the violence came back to him, the attackers screaming, the baseball bat in his hands as he lost control. The rage limitless, intoxicating. The voice had been correct. He needed to go home *now*.

Mick pulled the shifter into drive and lifted his foot off the brake. The truck idled forward, the wheel playing itself straight. He was searching for the exit lane when the beams landed on the others. He braked, clenching sore teeth.

Three broken bodies on the ground, their clothes torn and soaked. Even from this distance he could make out the bleach blond hair opened over the skull, the exposed white patches of scalp and bone. The big guy was sprawled face down, the other two draped over his legs like he was the felled trunk and they were the pruned branches. The ground was pooled with blood.

Someone was moving. A fourth was crouched beside them, patting and searching as if rummaging through their pockets, or checking vitals. But he didn't look like a medic. Boyish blond hair. Shoulders rolling under a chambray work shirt.

Render. Render had intervened again. The man was a moth to Mick's light, an avenging angel who needed a friend. Mick closed his eyes, swaying.

They're dead. All three of those kids are fucking dead and my neighbor killed them, oh, Jesus Christ, he tried to save me and went berserk and killed those kids. I'm in so deep now. That crazy sick fuck is going to take me down with him. Amy will lose the house, my son will lose all respect for me, Briela will see her daddy behind bars …

When he opened his eyes Render was gone. The bodies were still lying there in a pile. Twenty or so feet to the left of the bodies was a military truck. What the hell was the military doing – no, not military. It was an olive green Range Rover with tinted windows, stripped of its badging. The cargo door was open. There was a white bumper sticker with red lettering which read:

Sometimes I feel like a vampire
Ted Bundy

Render hopped out of the back, hitting the ground in

a smooth stride. He walked to the pile and took one off the top, dragging the bald kid by the feet. When he got within a body length of the green beast's bumper, he bent, clutched what would have been the kid's belt buckle if he was wearing one, lifted and heaved. The body flew into the cargo bay. The SUV's rear struts bounced once and were still. Render performed this chore as if he were loading a bundle of newspapers.

Then he did it again, in the same way, with the second boy.

Dragging, hefting, lobbing.

Except this time he came up a tad short and the head of blood-pasted blond hair bounced against the rear bumper, then hung down around the ball hitch on a neck gone limp as a sock. He doubled back, annoyed, and took the head in both hands, flipping the body forward like he was granny-shooting a basketball. This time the body stayed in.

Mick's labeling mechanisms were temporarily out of service. He watched in numb fascination and slow-burning horror.

Okay, tough guy, that was pretty impressive. Now let's see you lift the big one. The first two were punks not much bigger than my son, but that third one there weighs two-fifty at least. Maybe two-sixty-five, and there's not a chance in hell—

Render stretched his arms. Unbuttoned his shirt cuffs, rolled them back once. He stared at the huge body – which looked like an overturned rowboat covered in ripped canvas – for what was probably only half a minute but felt like ten.

God almighty, what the fuck was this?

The body began to stir. It was just the leg, but it clearly moved, the knee bending up a few inches, the heavy black boot swaying like a metronome.

'Oh, Jesus,' Mick croaked. The kid was still *alive*.

A mangled and trembling brown hand reached up, holding a black gun. The barrel wagged. The gun went *pop* and Render's shoulder jerked back perhaps an inch. The gun fell from the hand. Render touched his shoulder, looked at his hand. Wiped his palm across his jeans.

He took one step forward, raised his right foot, and stomped.

Mick looked away, but not before catching the image of the kid's head bobbing up on the lever of the breaking neck. There was no sound, not from this distance, but when Mick chanced another peek, Render was still stomping. Mechanically, forcefully. Not with anger, but merely as if he were tasked with putting some pitiful creature out of its misery.

Mick leaned over the bench seat and vomited onto the floor mat. All that came out was blood-streaked spittle and the last dregs of the whiskey sours Jamie had made him, but it felt like it was his throat the guy was stomping. *Oh Jesus, this is so fucked up. What in the name of God have I gotten into?* Wiping his mouth on his sleeve, he got himself under control and sat up.

The big Latino was gone and Render was reaching up, then slamming the rear hatch. The noise made Mick jump in his seat.

Render turned and looked right at Mick, staring into

312

the headlight beams. The work shirt had red spots across the chest, but it might not have even been his own. He took a few steps and stopped, bending to pluck something from the ground. It was a baseball cap. Or hockey, to be precise. The red-and-blue Colorado Avalanche lid one of them had been wearing before the real fuckstorm went into high gear. The cap was now more red than blue, and it seemed to hold some significance for Mick's neighbor. He studied it like he'd never seen one before, then put it on and snugged the bill down low.

He continued walking directly at the truck.

Mick's foot landed hard on the gas pedal. The hat thing was about one shot of crazy too many and Mick lost his composure. The truck surged and Render kept walking at him and his face was untroubled, white as the halogen glare reflecting off it. For a nauseating moment, Render seemed to be rushing at his windshield and Mick was sure he was going to dive at him, snarling and maniacal, but he was merely walking calmly, unafraid.

I could kill him now. Blow him out of his shoes with Blue Thunder and leave no witnesses. They would find him later, and blame him for the entire mess. Another restaurant mugging gone awry . . .

But he knew that if he ran Render down now, Amy and the kids would pay for it. They were in trouble, all of them teetering on the brink of ruin, and taking Render out would only accelerate his family's own private End of Days.

Mick yanked the wheel and the tires screamed. Veering right, he glanced through the driver's side window and saw Render come to a stop. His mouth fell open as if wanting to explain, genuine disappointment in his expression. Mick's neck twisted and it might have gone on twisting, captivated by the lunacy as he was, but a horrendous crashing sound – and the ensuing impact upon the truck's front bumper – snapped him out of his trance.

'What the fuck!'

He swerved wildly. The shattered shopping cart became a fusillade of wheels and caging that tumbled over the hood and cracked the windshield as the Silverado shot across the lot, bounced over a parking median with enough force to knock his head against the roof liner, and finally straightened onto the exit lane.

Mick blew the stop sign at the parking lot's entrance and skidded into the far lane on 30th. He floored it past the Bank of Boulder, then blew the red light as he hooked onto the Diagonal. There were a few cars leaving Boulder at this hour, but Mick didn't notice them as he passed them at roughly twice the legal limit. He did not take his eyes off the road until he saw his mailbox. He slowed and turned and made it down the long driveway beside the house.

He shut off the engine and stared across his back acres, over the hundreds of acres of greenbelt beyond, to the other house. For a shimmering moment it was the house of his nightmare journey with Roger, a swaying, hallucinatory shadow reaching across the night for him, pulling at him, welcoming him inside.

Mick looked away and stumbled from his truck,

streaked with blood, sticky and crusted with it, but he didn't feel nearly as awful as he should. The lights inside his house were off and he hoped Amy had not heard him come home.

A heavy engine groaned on Jay Road, a yellow blinker flared and dimmed, and then the olive drab Rover was coasting behind the trees separating the two properties. It reached the end of his parcel and the palazzo's iron gates opened silently, admitting the Rover. The gates closed before he could see Render exit the truck.

Render had instigated this, Mick realized. He didn't just appear tonight. Random crime or not, he'd arranged it or arranged to be there, possibly as retaliation for Mick's refusal of his previous offer. And what exactly had he been offering? What did he want?

This was a conspiracy. A hallucination. It simply could not be happening.

The trees stirred. As before, Render emerged from the border, onto the expanse of Mick's lawn. He was holding a small leather duffle in his left hand, calm as a man on a platform, waiting for the train.

'Are you hurt?'

It was a simple question, but Mick could not put words together.

'Whatever you are feeling,' Render said, 'it's not as bad as it seems. Take a hot shower to warm up, then let it run cold. It will revive you and act as a natural analgesic. Then you need to eat something hearty before you go to bed. By tomorrow morning, it will be like this never happened.'

Mick twitched. 'You killed those kids. I saw you.'

Render craned his neck and smiled slyly. 'Did I? Pretty sure I did not act alone tonight, Mick. Whose fingerprints do you think the police will find on the bat? Besides, it was self-defense. You were angry, as you had every right to be.'

'You knew,' Mick said. 'You planned to be there.'

'I stopped by the restaurant tonight to return this to you.' Render moved a few steps closer and held out the bag. 'I told you we were destined to work together, and I'm here to show you I've been holding up my end of the bargain. You are reluctant to accept my offer, but that doesn't mean you can't have what is rightfully yours.'

Render set the duffle on the grass. When it was clear Mick had no intention of accepting it, Render kneeled and unzipped the bag. It was full of cash. Packets banded together and more loose bills. Hundreds. A big green Benjamin salad.

'No,' Mick said. But he was dizzy with the knowledge of what it represented, what it could do for him.

'Eugene Sapphire kept very detailed records of his shenanigans. That's all yours, to the penny, with a fair market savings rate of five per cent annual interest. Should be enough to save your restaurant, but I'll leave you to decide what to do with it.'

'What did you do to him?' Mick said.

'What did *I* do?' Render smiled. 'I'm just a courier on this one. He made his bed long ago.'

'And now he's lying in it,' Mick said. 'Dead as those boys.'

Render shrugged. 'Go visit him tomorrow, see for yourself. All I did was restore a little decency, right another wrong. That's all I'm about here, Mick. Helping you right the wrongs so we can both get back to our rightful place in this wrong life.'

Mick felt as though he might float away at any moment. 'I won't be a part of it. I won't let you—'

Render shifted with unnerving speed and in a blink his face was inches from Mick's. 'Don't push it, Mr Nash. If you call attention to our business, those who would investigate such claims will never find me, only you. There are no other suspects because no one else was involved. Not on the lake, not at Sapphire's house, and not tonight. It will all come back to you, because as far as the rest of the world is concerned, I don't exist.'

Mick's throat filled with bile. 'What in God's name are you?'

Render sighed. 'You still don't know?'

'I saw your bumper sticker,' Mick said. 'Is that supposed to be a hint?'

'The bumper – oh. You think I'm ...' Render broke into laughter. He sighed. 'Ah, Jesus. No. I just like the sentiment. You might say I am learning to relate to it. But you actually thought ...' He laughed some more. 'That's classic.'

'I'm glad you think this is funny.'

Render turned serious. 'Wait, do you believe in creatures with special powers?'

Mick glanced at Render's shoulder, saw no blood. 'He shot you.'

'There are no real monsters, Mick. You know that. We are sensible men in a world where nothing is more dangerous. You understand there are no superheroes or stock villains, only the wide spectrum of humanity in all its glory. Average men like you and me, vying for our piece of the dream.'

'What is it, then?' Mick said, fed up. 'What is this? What is the point of you?'

'Come on, Mick. Stop pretending. You know I know.'

'I don't know anything.'

Render looked at the stars. He was quiet for a moment, then began slowly reciting names as if identifying constellations. 'Robertson. Percy. Chavez. Greenwald. Weaver. Render.' He lowered his gaze. 'And Nash. What do these surnames have in common?'

Mick saw no point in humoring this sociopath.

'Well, it's a sorrowful turn,' Render said. 'All of these families were strangers to one another, until three years ago. They were brought together by chance, or maybe it was the need to escape the ordinary they shared. Regardless, they found one another and, like good neighbors, they became friendly if not quite friends. It was a magical week. Some were in love, some were fighting, but all had the time of their lives. And then ... well, of course something bad happened. Something abominable and unprecedented. It wasn't anyone's fault, but these families, good families all, were never the same again. They went their separate ways and forgot about what happened that night. They forgot about what they stumbled onto, what they unleashed. And now, it pains

318

me to say, four of those families have disappeared. They ride on the wings of the night. But there are two families left, Mick. And one of them needs your help. I need your help. You owe me your help. You may not care to remember what happened, but I will never forget. I don't have that luxury.'

At any other time Mick would have laughed, but the situation had moved beyond control into outright lunacy. If it was a kind of blackmail, and it had to be, then all of it was building toward some unimaginable demand.

'Listen to me, you fucking psychopath,' he said. 'Everything coming out of your mouth is either a delusion or a lie. I don't know those people and I've never met you. You have the wrong family. I don't know what it is you want from me, and I have nothing to give. Whatever it is, I can't help you. I won't help you.'

Render stared at him for a long time. 'Okay, Mick. It's late. Your wife is irate and she needs you now.' Render turned and went a few paces, then paused and looked back. 'Amy and the kids are coming to the barbecue. A week from today, two o'clock. I hope, for your sake, you will join us. Good night.'

Mick stood in the quiet summer night for a while, staring at the money. His mind raced in a panic of questions with no answers and then slowed to a crawl. There was no decision, only movement. The immediate next steps were all he could focus on. His life had gone from one day at a time to one minute at a time.

He stripped off his bloody jeans and shirt and threw them in the trash bin beside the garage. He carried the duffle bag into the basement and set it behind the crawl-space door, then used the guest suite shower to rinse away the blood. He set the water to cold, letting it numb him until he was shivering. He toweled off, feeling little or no pain. His nose was no longer leaking and it did not appear to be broken, though he was certain it had been. He inspected the rest of his body in the mirror. At least two or three ribs had felt fractured in the truck, but he could breathe much easier. His ankle, which had felt shattered, throbbed dully.

On his way out of the bathroom, something furry brushed against his ankles, yipping, and he almost screamed before realizing it was Thom. The Yorkshire hustled by and a few seconds later Mick heard him bumping up the stairs.

Hard plastic bit into his bare foot, then he slipped on paper smeared with cold mush. He went a few more steps through the wreckage before finding a light switch. The room came into focus. Party hats, cake on his feet. Amy's cold silence all week as he ignored her reminders. While Mick had been covering shifts and waging a battle in the parking lot, their daughter had turned nine. *Some father you are, champ.*

Ten minutes later he was wrapped in a towel, standing over the kitchen island, forking a pile of leftover pasta with heavy cream sauce and spicy sausage into his gob as fast as possible short of choking. He had almost laughed when Render said he needed to eat something, but the man knew what he was talking about. He felt like he hadn't eaten in a month. He dumped more shredded

320

asiago over the steaming mess, shoveling it up between chugs of milk from the jug. He tore a hunk of bread from a stale French loaf and swabbed his plate.

Kyle's skeleton shambled into the kitchen and opened the fridge. His son wasn't wearing a shirt or shorts, just boxers and his sneakers, the cold freezer light slanting across his frail torso and sad, boy nipple hairs. He hadn't noticed his father standing there in the dark and Mick felt no urge to disturb him.

Kyle hauled the carton of Breyer's mint chocolate chip out, foraged a spoon from the drawer, and began to cram a flotilla of it into his mouth. He looked up, saw his father, and tensed. His eyes were red and puffy and Mick wondered if he had been crying or was stoned.

Mick waved for the tub. Kyle handed it over, his eyes widening as he inspected his father's battered frame. Mick dug in with his fork and the cold against his teeth and upper palate was divine. He thought if he wasn't careful he might just eat this entire bucket. Kyle was shaking, on the verge of tears, scared, probably had done something bad tonight, or maybe gotten more than he bargained for. Mick watched him, waiting for it. Kyle opened his mouth, but before he could speak he saw something over the island, and both of them turned to the great room.

Briela was standing in her pajamas, rubbing her eyes. She smiled her gigantic smile and ran to her father. She hugged his leg as if she hadn't seen him in months. As if she wanted to make sure he was real.

'Daddy's home, Daddy's home . . . '

'Shush, honey,' he said softly. 'You'll wake Mommy.'

'I'm awake.' Amy was standing by the hearth, arms crossed, fury drawing her face into a mask Mick barely recognized. 'Well?'

Mick looked down at his daughter. 'I'm sorry I missed your birthday, B. There's no excuse. I was a jerk. I promise to make it up to you.'

Briela smiled, his presence more than enough.

Amy said, 'Have you lost your fucking mind?'

'Amy. Not tonight.'

'Yes, Mick. Tonight. We're all here for a change. Tell your daughter what was so important you couldn't be here for her birthday. Tell your family why you haven't taken a meal with us for the past two years. What was it this time? Did you get in a bar fight? Are you drunk again? Why are you even home? *What is it?*'

Mick looked at Kyle, who was piecing something crucial together and curious to see what was coming. He looked down at Briela, thinking of the years he had left to provide for all of them. He looked at his wife and knew she was at the edge of her own abyss. And altogether, as awful as it seemed, this place they were heading, he felt something like tremendous relief blow over him. There was no going back. They had crossed a barrier and everything was going to change now.

Everything.

He wiped his lips and licked one finger, enjoying the last of the sweet cream until every drop had been absorbed into his tongue.

'I lost the restaurant.'

PART THREE

The People Next Door

If you're going through hell, keep going.

WINSTON CHURCHILL

46

After spending the next thirty-six hours holed up in her bedroom with the doors locked and the TV turned down as low as it could go while still allowing her to hear scenes of hushed dialogue from the *Witches Lane* marathon she had recorded, Melanie Smith awoke before sunrise on Monday morning, hot and itching, her insides begging for something she couldn't have.

Rayell had called her back last night and apologized; she claimed to have been locked in an all-night study session with her phone off, and though her voice was croaky, she promised her mother everything was fine. No, no one had threatened her or been following her. Yes, she still had her mace keychain, stop worrying so much, Mom, you're being paranoid again. Melanie thought her daughter had been up all night smoking cigarettes and drinking keg beer, but she was so relieved to hear Rayell's voice, and her grades from last semester were holding up her 3.6 average, Melanie didn't pry. The girl had better sense than her mother ever had at that age and Melanie didn't want to worry her further, so she agreed: she probably *was* being paranoid.

She kept replaying the incident after Briela's birthday party in her mind, seeing that unstable (*Go ahead, call her a psycho cunt, if there ever was one, she was it*) Render woman's rolled-back eyes and crooked finger, and every instinct inside her confirmed she had not been imagining it – the woman was evil. She had not, of course, put a spell on Melanie or Rayell. That was ludicrous, the stuff of cable soap opera (case in point: Melanie had probably been watching too many episodes of *Witches Lane* than was healthy). But evil came in human forms too.

Amy had not returned her calls. Melanie had tossed and turned all Thursday night, spent most of Friday with the phone in one hand, debating calling the police but resisting out of fear of retribution, until she finally fell asleep around lunchtime and slept for almost seventeen hours.

Now it was a little after four in the morning, and after a snack of yogurt and granola and a glass of pineapple juice, Melanie was going stir crazy. She hadn't been confined indoors this long since her Ben & Jerry's days. Her body needed to flex and surge, to feel the bounce of the road. Was it possible she had overreacted, just a little? Maybe. Maybe not.

But she couldn't spend the rest of her life, or even another day, living with this fear, hiding like a refugee. She would tuck her cell phone in her fanny pack in case of an emergency, or even anything suspicious, and that settled it.

She used the bathroom, drank two glasses of water. She sat nude on the trunk where she had draped her running pants and sports bra, her clean ankle socks and new favorite pair of Asics Gel running shoes. Sleeved herself in Lycra. Tied the shoes, nice and snug. Clipped the pack around her washboard and turned it until it sat on the firm shelf of her ass. Her hair was short for summer, but she tied it back anyway, creating a bristly brown spike. She knew it would be cool for the first mile, but after that the temperature would not matter, so she left her long-sleeved jersey behind.

She didn't bother with stretching. A recent article in *Runner's World* had cleverly pointed out that stretching was responsible for as many injuries as actual training or competing. And anyway she was up to fifty-five miles per week; running eight or ten miles no longer made her sore. She would warm her way into a high-viscosity burn. Her muscles shivered in anticipation, blood racing on the tide of her brave decision, her mind as alert as if she had consumed a venti latte from Starbucks.

She stepped out, the land still dark under a sky turning whale blue. She bounded over the lawn, up toward the elbow turn on Independence Road. No cars, the asphalt worn and cool, the pre-dawn greeting her like an old friend. Welcome, it said. Come and run with me, while the rest of the lazy world sleeps.

She ran toward the Foothills, Boulder Municipal Airport's small landing strip and parked Cessnas and sail planes off to her left. To her right was a great field of undeveloped land, the giant willow trees by the stream, a few houses, including that Eyesore blocking the Nash place. Where the crazy c-word woman and her family were squatting. After her run, she would try Amy one more time, make sure everything was okay, and then together they could decide whether to call the police. Or maybe Melanie would simply stop at a pay phone, place an anonymous call. But only after her run. Right now belonged to her and the road.

Melanie's breath flowed silently, her legs full of burgeoning power. The break in her training had been good for her body, if not her mind. She felt as if she could run to Lyons today. When she reached 47th, she would take the overpass north to Jay, run eastbound to the fire station, then out to Reservoir Road where she hoped to reach the beach by sunrise. Her running shoes made pleasant wicking sounds on the asphalt. She grooved.

For as long as she could remember, Melanie's life had been a series of cravings. As a child she coveted toys and other children's playthings with a ferocity that drove her mother to tears for all that she could not provide, and got Melanie sent to the principal's office dozens of times. By ten it was clothes, the advertisements torn out of *Seventeen* and *Vogue*, glued to her bedroom walls. She learned to shoplift at malls by age twelve, and lost friends in junior high for refusing to give back a Polo sweater, a pair of Benetton jeans, those Guess overalls her mother could not afford.

At fourteen she met alcohol, and she proceeded to loot liquor cabinets around the neighborhood, her nose keen to the scent of parents away for the weekend. Sixteen was pot, and the things she did for high school and college boys – the boys being another craving in their own right – who knew how to get the good stuff.

328

Then acid. Coke. Heroin twice. Crack for a winter. And on it went, into her twenties and early motherhood, two marriages, her life a series of seemingly bottomless longings.

At twenty-eight, after crashing her Mustang into a dry cleaner's storefront, sobriety came easily, immediately replaced by food addictions. She liked to order twenty-four cheese-and-bacon-loaded potato skins from Bennigan's and eat them in the car on the way home. A dozen glazed donuts for breakfast. In the middle of the night, an entire bag of Ruffles, a tub of cottage cheese for the dip. Bacon cheeseburgers and Pizza Hut Meat Lover's pan pizzas in pairs, the stupor of greasy food her antidote to the straight life. On her thirtieth birthday she weighed two hundred and eighty-seven pounds.

She tried everything to combat her hungers, but in the end realized she should consider herself blessed that she had the willpower to switch the object of her desire, if not quench the desire itself. It was – she realized by age thirty-six, having declared bankruptcy for the second time – a matter of choosing healthier targets. So drugs, alcohol, food, and expensive clothes became fresh fruit, gym memberships, yoga attire and videos, supplements and smoothies, infomercial meal plans, bicycles, high colonics and a battalion of running shoes.

Running seemed to be the final solution. It was the only physical activity Melanie had found – short of sex with Keith Darden, who died in a drunk-driving accident four years ago, may God rest his eight-inch wonder dick – with the power to cleanse all negative thought and physical need. She had been running regularly for a little more than seven years – the same period of time required, it is said, for the human body to replace every cell, becoming entirely new. She was no longer the poisoned glutton of her past but literally a whole new being. Healthy, happy, self-forgiven.

Of course she knew that running was her new drug, and that there was always a risk of over-exertion. But she also knew that running was the reason she had lost one hundred and forty pounds, quit smoking, and developed toned muscles and new curves where there used to be sagging corners and flat cliffs. Running was responsible for shearing the wild peaks and valleys off her moods, leveling her mental state into something that was lucid and energized but calm. She was doing better at the office, where it was rumored she would soon be up for a promotion to field sales rep with profit sharing (Preferred Paper sold shipping supplies, boxes and foam peanuts, and she had been an office manager for seven years). Even her relationship with Rayell had improved, mother–daughter competition giving way to mutual respect and support of each other's unique traits, quirks, and life adventures.

She was cresting the big hill on Reservoir Road when the first cramp began to bare its teeth in her right side. She had only gone four miles or so, and was planning on an easy ten, so this minor stitch was troubling. She slowed, the flat plane below her rib cage clenching with a dull, twisting ache. Funny how it was never your legs or feet, the parts that were taking the brunt of the abuse.

330

It had to be something inside, a layer of muscle that felt like some kind of rarely utilized organ you never knew you had. She had taken her potassium last night and she was not dehydrated. There was no reason for this dang nuisance (except maybe for that psycho rhymes-with-punt who had forced her to spend the weekend like a shut-in). She beat the cramp back with willpower and plowed on, the reservoir's white entrance gates coming into view, then retreating as she continued on 51st, where it turned to dirt and curved around the lake's west bank.

But whatever it was, the pain spiked again, bringing her down to a fast walk. Melanie hated fast-walking. She was only forty-three. She could fast-walk when she was sixty-three, not now. She would give it five minutes.

The entrance to Eagle Trail off of 51st appeared and she was glad to see there were no cars parked in the turn-around. She would have the lollipop route to herself, looping around the wide field before turning back to the lake for a six a.m. dip. She walked through the cramp, remembering her tomboy years, the summer she spent catching sunfish with Danny and Luke, then using the sunfish to trap a giant snapping turtle. Good times, kissing boys and playing with fish, learning how to hook a worm while teaching them how to unhook a JC Penny D-cup. The cramp had vanished and Melanie was back to her normal cruising speed.

Farmland opened on all sides. Fresh planes of light diluted the indigo sky, but the land was still dark, the weeds waist-high around the gravel path, the occasional grasshopper springing out of her way, armor clicking. She was a little less than a mile along the lollipop when she heard the nubby gravel crunching sounds behind her. The buzzing approach came out of nowhere, moving fast, and she veered to the right edge of the path. Her ankle twisted on the loose shoulder, but her tendons there were strung by good muscle, and she righted herself with no problem. She glanced left and saw a thin bicycle wheel, a flash of handlebars with small pale hands on the taped grips, and then something jabbed her in the hip bone, knocking her off stride.

Her cell phone popped out of her fanny pack into the dirt and Melanie cried out, more in surprise than pain, as she stumbled into the weeds. She threw her hands out for balance as the bicycle flashed ahead, the short figure hunched and pedaling as if in a sprint for the ribbon.

'What the hell ...' Melanie came to a halt in the weeds, just shy of a nearly invisible irrigation ditch. 'Jesus, watch it!'

The road bike – silver, tall, a man's – was a ways ahead of her, the thin wheels wobbling. The person sitting atop the saddle had short hair, the head as pale as the thin white legs jutting from a bunched-up dress or some kind of skirt – not the attire of a serious cyclist. The bare feet barely reached the pedals. The bike had no lights or reflectors on it. Hadn't the woman seen her? Was this an accident or some kind of harassment?

Melanie's anger walked her back onto the path. The woman on the bike was slowing, swerving wildly, probably drunk.

'An apology would be nice!' Melanie hollered, dipping into the pack for her phone. It wasn't there. 'Idiot.'

The woman disappeared around the bend. Weed buds twisted in the dark, the head sliding out of view. She turned the pack around to her front and dug into it, but the phone was gone. She scanned the ground, during which time it occurred to her that this might not be a random idiot at all, but Cassandra Render.

No, it couldn't be. A confrontation at a neighborhood birthday party was one thing. Following a stranger you had exchanged harsh words with out into the country at four-thirty in the morning was something else. Rich bitches like Cassandra Render didn't ride bicycles and take out their grudges this way. They manipulated your friends, shunned you from dinner parties, spread gossip about your finances.

Another minute passed and her phone was not on the path. She could hear Rayell again. *You're being paranoid, Mom. Chill.*

Melanie heard the bike returning before she saw it, and then it was hewing to the outside edge of the lane on its way back. The wheel, the loose dress, the lowered pale head. It was coming for her.

She halted and spread her feet at shoulder width, wondering what the possible outcomes were here. An apology she'd asked for, but now she hoped the drunken twat would ride off and leave her alone. And if it was Cassandra Render, well, maybe it was time the woman learned what happened when you messed with a member of your own gender who had you by six inches and fifty pounds.

The bike was a hundred feet off and closing, its rider leaning over the bars as if studying the ground, afraid of dumping it at any moment. The tires pinched pebbles that sprang with *doink* and *pling* sounds. My God, Melanie thought, this derelict doesn't even know how to ride a bike. She has to be wasted.

She was still debating whether to run toward the bike and get ahead of it or turn back for the road when the woman rose off the seat and began to pedal furiously. The bike found balance with the speed, and as it closed the distance Melanie realized this was not Cassandra Render – it wasn't even a woman.

It was a child, barely a teenager, and maybe as young as ten. She shouldn't be out here biking alone, and what the hell is she doing on her dad's bike?

Melanie backed into the weeds to give the muppet a wide berth.

That's not a dress. It's a jacket tied around her waist.

And the hair's not short. It's bald.

The bike came whizzing down the center of the path, but at the last second swerved at her. The little person's face came up and Melanie almost got off a scream as it launched itself over the handle bars, baring teeth fenced with plated metal braces. The small body slammed into her chest and the two of them were falling back into crackling weeds. The bike tumbled with them, tangling in their limbs, gears and spokes catching Melanie's fingers, scraping her bare back.

334

The child was growling. Grunting, hissing, throwing some kind of fit. Melanie felt something cut into her rib, screamed and rolled, hurling the bony frame. The attacker rolled in the grass and hopped to her feet, swaying like a tiny gladiator. Melanie blinked, registering details, the lack of certain features, the carnival presence of others.

That's no little girl. It's a boy in a rubber swimming cap.
The eyes are solid black and leaking blood.
Those aren't braces. The mouth is full of blades.

The instinct to stand her ground was extinguished. The deep blooming terror inside Melanie matched and then eclipsed the Cassandra incident. That had been chilling. This was reality-melting, bad-acid-trip fear, the kind of raw alarm that electrifies the limbs. She bolted over the path and deeper into the field, toward the nearest subdivision some quarter of a mile away.

The small footsteps tore at the ground behind her and she watched for prairie dog holes as the weeds whipped at her sides. She saw the three-line barbed-wire fence a second before she would have slammed into it and hurdled off her right foot, certain her shoe or one Lycra-skinned shin would snag. But her training paid off and she sailed over it, her Asics plowing into soft-tilled rows of soil. She put a palm down, pushed off, and sprinted across the rows of low green vegetation.

Her skin came alive with sour sweat. Clods of dirt dragged at her shoes. Her right knee was strained in some way, the cramp had come back with a vengeance, the pain worsening with every step, and she could not keep an even stride. She made out a flatter field of mown grass beyond the soil rows and, higher up on the hill, the first house – a McMansion with a caged trampoline standing in the sweeping backyard. The lights were off, but that did not matter. She would scream, break the door down, find a place to hide, snatch up a weapon, call for help. Maybe once the thing saw the house, it would give up.

She chanced a look back. It had not given up. It was still there some fifty feet back. Running clumsily but, yes, she was certain, it was also learning, somehow improving its stride with each step.

Goddamn it, you're a runner. She had to be faster than this thing. Whatever it was, it was just a kid. Her breathing grew ragged.

The house was less than a city block away now.

Melanie was on solid ground and moving at full speed when she ran into the second barbed-wire fence. Her right leg passed through the gap between the top and middle wires, her waist slammed the top, and her left leg hitched into all three flatly, the spikes of steel puncturing and ripping into her abdomen and thighs, stringing her upside down as she folded over. She cried out, scissoring her legs, hands pulling at the bottom two wires to free herself. Barbed knots gouged her arms and left breast, ripping the strap of her sports bra before she finally tore free and flopped onto her back, her torso and every limb striped in agony.

She was rolling onto her hands and knees to push herself up when the thing landed on her spine and cut her ear off with a swipe. The pain in her back was shocking, blinding. She was smashed to the ground, her mouth and nostrils filling with dirt. Something cold slashed the back of her neck deeply and one of her arms went numb. She struggled, rolled onto her back, and it was above her, thrashing, mouth open. She stabbed out at the face with her thumb, jabbing and screaming frantically. The first poke missed but the fifth or seventh went into the thing's eye and her thumb came away wet as the child-thing wailed and fell off her.

Pain ran in molten streams up and down her back and legs as she got to her feet and hobbled away, almost hyperventilating now, staggering with dirt in her mouth and eyes. She found her stride and in her pure panic the house seemed to meet her halfway. A flower garden, the patio. She pulled on the sliding glass door and fumbled her way inside, slamming and locking it behind her.

'Help! Somebody help me!' Great cramps tugged at her and she fell against the kitchen counter, driving a basket of fruit and a stack of bills to the floor. She retreated deeper into the kitchen, bleeding on marbled tile, eyes on the glass door. She groped around in the dark for a knife, anything sharp or heavy. She knocked the dish rack into the sink with a crash.

'Oh God, oh God ... help me!'

Upstairs, footsteps and voices. The light fixture shaking above her. Then more footsteps, harder, thudding down the stairs.

A light threw itself into the hall and the adjacent dining room.

Melanie rubbed at her face and when she felt for her ear it wasn't there and she tried to breathe but she couldn't contain her panic. She shrieked, her words garbled.

'Oh, God, please, help me, someone's out there, it tried to kill me, call the police!'

A woman in a sheer yellow bathrobe and silk undergarments appeared in the kitchen, staring at her in wonder, arms crossed over her stomach.

'What did you do? How did you get in here?'

Melanie slid to the floor, pointing. 'Out there. Tried to kill me. Please help me ... please ... call help ... not safe.'

The bandy legs, boxer shorts, and pot belly of a man appeared behind the woman. He was short and squinting, hair standing up in wave of thick black curls. He rubbed his mouth and shook his head.

'The hell is this? What's wrong?'

'... says there's someone trying to get her,' the woman said.

He stepped past the woman and unfolded a pair of reading glasses. His nose bunched and sniffed.

Melanie was crying with mild relief but they weren't doing enough. 'Lock the doors ... you don't understand ... it's not human!'

'Mom? What's wrong?' A boy's voice carried in from behind her but Melanie couldn't see him.

'Stay there, Alex,' the woman said. 'She's hysterical. Dangerous. I don't know what.'

The man said, 'I should call the—'

338

The sliding glass door shattered, raining safety glass into the breakfast area. The little body came after it, bare feet walking slowly over the beads. Melanie screamed and tried to stand but her foot slipped and she fell back to the floor now slick with her blood.

The man and woman stepped back and their faces went slack.

'Oh dear sweet Jesus,' the woman said.

'There, now,' the man said.

The little figure darted into the kitchen and found the magnetic knife rack mounted above the marble back-splash and there was a *zing*. Adroitly he crouched in front of Melanie and ran a nine-inch serrated fillet knife in and out of her stomach with the speed and accuracy of a sewing machine.

Melanie ruptured, saw black and red stars, bayed as if giving birth, and lost her breath as her face locked in a silent-movie scream.

The child pivoted and ran to the now fully awake residents and impaled the father first, plunging the kidneys and carving down in looping oval scoops, then abandoned him for the mother. She slid around the corner and disappeared into the hall, and Melanie understood from the squealing and crashing sounds that filled the entire first floor he had brought her down too.

The thing's footsteps trampled up the stairs and the boy screamed and it might have taken pity on him for he was silenced quickly even though his father was still walking on his knees across the floor at Melanie, one hand reaching for his open back the other groping for her

339

as if she could help him now, as if anything could save them.

Melanie no longer had the strength to scream or get up or think of anything else. Her lap was wet and hot. The one that had pursued her emerged around the counter and looked at her and then the man. It was just a boy, she saw now, a boy not yet ten, with no hair to speak of, no sign of emotion in his dark eyes, and he wasn't even breathing hard. In fact he didn't look to be breathing at all.

He finished the man with a swipe across the throat, pulling the chin from above while straddling the larger body. Crimson fanned across the floor and the man fell into his jet stream, the arm that had been reaching for Melanie slapping the tile at her feet.

The boy-thing dropped the knife. He crouched low and watched her. He began to crawl toward her. Hesitantly at first, testing the air and finding what it smelled to its liking, then hurrying into it as the animal inside rediscovered its earliest capabilities and most basic drive.

Moving on a final surge of adrenaline, her body drawing on every resource to preserve itself, Melanie rolled away as the thing crashed into the refrigerator. She clawed at the slick floor and scrambled onto carpeting into a darker space that looked like a den and maybe a better hiding place but she didn't get past the dining room.

It was there, under the table draped in champagne linen, she swooned. Dawn broke across the Front Range and a cold draft swam inside her leg. There wasn't any pain left, only the boy. He wants all of me, she thought, offering herself with the noble acceptance of the impala kneeling under the cheetah. Her will to resist collapsed under his bite and she thought, I wonder why. But as soon as she asked the question, her ancestral genetic code supplied the answer: In the kingdom they waste nothing, consume all. She wished he hadn't found her, but in the end she understood him as clearly as she understood her own history.

Then he was getting into places she had never known, taking and taking and bathing in her, until Melanie Smith and all of her appetites were no more.

47

Amy had no idea what was so urgent that she had to drive to Whole Foods at nearly nine p.m. on a Tuesday night, and she cringed when she saw the glowing green sign across the Mapleton Center's parking lot. She hated shopping here. Ever since Whole Foods had become Whole Paycheck (ho ho! though not so funny now that it was true) and she had reverted to buying donuts and sugar cereals at the regular grocers, she couldn't help feeling like a traitor amongst the Organic Reich every time she set foot inside the store.

She changed lanes on 30th and worked her way up to the front, amazed to find the parking lot half-empty. The awfully planned plaza was usually a hamster farm of Priuses, the sidewalks clotted with enough pedestrians to make one think the store was giving away free coffee colonics – an added-value service that actually wouldn't surprise her if it were offered in little stalls between the non-dairy case and bulk spices – and the sight of so many vacant spaces seemed an ominous development.

But Cassandra said it was important, so she parked.

She didn't see either of the Rovers, but maybe Cass wasn't here yet.

For the first few minutes she simply browsed the bright space, trudging past the salad bar, sushi bar, burrito bar, coffee bar, deli, massage stations, and sparkling wine sample tables, the fresh faces above the green aprons tracking her movements, ready to thrust a slab of Norwegian salmon or tub of in-house-roasted peanut butter upon her with the zeal of airport pamphleteers. The sheer variety and specificity of so many innovative foods assaulted her with a casino's torrent of sensory overload.

She rounded an aisle lined with gourmet soda and corn chips the color of Christmas ornaments and found herself bellying up to a table displaying a slow cooker full of what appeared to be potted meat but was in fact *Not Quite Chicken!* simmering in a vegetable and white bean bouillabaisse. A gaunt man with a brisk gray beard and skin the color of wax paper handed her a paper cup with a tiny wooden spoon leaning out of it, his bulbous eyes blinking rapidly.

'Taste our three-season amino soup? It's our gluten-free pick of the week.'

'Thank you ... Bruce.' She slid the contents back in a shot and stifled a cough of disgust. She owned socks that tasted better. 'Mmm, that's unique.'

'Isn't it?' Bruce agreed. 'Only four hundred calories *per quart*. Zero sodium or fat, high in fiber. I have customers who make a whole pot and eat it for *days*. It's full of anti-oxidants and really cleanses just superbly.'

Amy smirked. 'And, uhm, how do I make that? Does it come in a package?'

Bruce proceeded to explain which ingredients from which aisle she would need, but the instructions went on for over two minutes and Amy lost track of the entire scheme somewhere between kale flakes and psyllium husk powder.

'Sounds great. Good luck with the ... that.' She walked away quickly.

She was standing in the produce section, smoothing her palm over a crate filled with avocados the size of cro-quet balls, $7.99 each, when a woman spoke behind her.

'I *thought* that was you. Oh, this is perfect.'

Amy brightened as she turned, but it wasn't Cass.

Rita Larson, she of the daughter with the fork-tined face, was barreling at her and digging in her purse as if for a weapon. Her corked clogs halted within kicking dis-tance and a cloud of patchouli roiled over Amy. Rita's newfound martyrdom had added a glowing vibrancy to her usual harried Bohemian frump, or perhaps she was just really pissed off. She removed a folded document from her purse and thrust the papers against Amy's chest with a *whack*.

'This belongs to you. I suggest you pay it, unless you want to see me in court.'

'Rita—' Amy began.

'I have *witnesses*.'

'I'm not disputing the accident, but please, can we sit down for a minute and talk? They're kids. No one wants—'

'Accident? Are you joking? That monster of yours *assaulted* my daughter.'

'I don't think it's quite that clear-cut. Please let me explain—'

'Seventeen thousand dollars,' Rita hissed. Amy glanced down at the bill, unable to read the numbers. 'Not to mention the *trauma*. Tami's entire summer is ruined. She's afraid of her friends. You're lucky she doesn't need plastic surgery. You're lucky she isn't *blind*.'

'I'm sorry,' Amy said softly.

'Goddamn *right* you are.'

There were others in the produce aisle. Amy could feel them watching her. It was the Vo-Tech parking lot again, only worse, for this time she was guilty. Grief over some loss greater than good will between parents broke and spread inside her. It was about Mick, and Kyle, and Briela. The restaurant, her weight, her students. Her life was out of control, edging into ruin, and now she was going to have a breakdown in public.

'What do you have to say for yourself?' Rita said, encouraged by Amy's stunned silence. 'Does your daughter have any idea what she's done? How absolutely wrong she was? How dangerous she has become? What kind of punishment will she receive, Amy, that's what I want to know. Where is the respon*sibility* in that house of yours?'

Amy forced herself to meet Rita's eyes. 'My daughter's not well,' she managed. 'We're dealing with some personal problems, Mick and ... I don't expect ... it's all so ... haven't you ever felt like ... Don't you understand that if I could change it ... this is a very difficult

345

time, is what I'm saying, Rita.' Was any of this getting through?

'Oh, spare me. You're not fooling anybody, Amy. I *know* you. You were a selfish bitch in high school and you're a selfish bitch now. You think you and your husband are hot shit because you own that restaurant, but you're just like everyone else in this town. With your big house and your precious family assistant. Turning your daughter's birthday party into another showcase for your conspicuous consumption. It's grotesque. Your life is grotesque. You're a taker, that's what you are. You take and take and you have no decency.'

'That's not fair,' Amy said. 'If I went too far, it was only because I love my—'

'Save it. Enjoy it while it lasts. Because you're headed for a big fall, sweetheart. Don met with the district attorney and he *knows things*. He plays golf with your accountant and he knows plenty. Your husband is in deep shit and you're going to get what's coming to you. And guess what – I don't care. All I care about is that you pay that medical bill before you file for bankruptcy and stick the rest of us with your bad decisions, do you understand me? I want that bill paid and I want a letter of apology and I want your daughter to—'

'Excuse me. What the hell is going on here?' another woman piped up behind Amy, her voice calm and firm. Amy was too poleaxed to recognize it, but when she turned and saw Cassandra Render standing there with a bag of lemons in one hand, dressed as if she had just stepped out of a singles bar, a wave of gratitude broke over her with such force she could have kneeled. Cass winked at Amy and then pushed herself between the two parties. 'Are you harassing my friend?'

Rita's head reared back. 'What business is it of yours? Who are you?'

On the other side of the potatoes and onions pyramids, a male couple in matching art-school glasses and Under Armour shirts paused to enjoy the show. A stock girl pushing a dolly loaded with Japanese melons moved past the women, double-taking off the confrontational vibe that had just gone from heated to ice cold with a slight chance of violence.

Cass took another step toward Rita and her eyes narrowed. 'Honey, you don't want to know who I am. But what you better know, before you speak another word, is that Amy's business is my business. So why don't you start by lowering your voice, *Rita.*'

Rita gasped, and Amy saw the first twinge of fear in her eyes.

Rita said, 'Fine. Your *friend* is responsible for nearly blinding my daughter.'

Cass barked with laughter. The gay couple joined in, then averted their eyes when Rita shot them her disapproval.

'You think that's funny?' Rita said to Cass. 'You think a little girl spending the night in the emergency room is funny?'

'I do, actually,' Cass said, and her voice remained as smooth and sweet as June Cleaver's. 'Because I happen to know it was hardly more than a scratch, and that Tami had it coming. That's right, Rita. Your little butterball is a bully, and now we all see where she gets it. And if there's one thing I hate more than bullies, it's parents who turn a blind eye when their children prey on others.'

'You tell her, sista.' This from one of the guys in his gym clothes.

'What the hell are you talking about?' Rita snapped. 'Briela attacked Tami out of the blue. Everyone saw it. You weren't even there, so please, just don't.'

'Well, jeez, that's not what Theo Havas's father says,' Cass said. 'Larry Havas saw Tami threaten Briela in the bathroom five minutes before she was forced to defend herself with a plastic fork. He overheard your little porker tell Briela that she was going to cut off all her hair if she didn't give Tami half her birthday money, and he's willing to give a statement to that effect.' Cass produced a cell phone, wiggled it between two fingers. 'Want me to call him? He said anytime. He was rather disgusted and – as a local business owner with republican allies in the state legislature – he's fed up with frivolous lawsuits, especially at the hands of the *uninsured*.'

Rita's mouth fell open. 'How dare – this is outrageous. You're lying. Lying through your teeth! And even if that were true, which it is not, that's no excuse for violence.'

'Violence?' Cass said. 'You want to talk about violence? Why don't you share with Amy the little event that transpired in the coat room of Mrs Tally's second-grade class last March? Something involving a pair of scissors, your daughter, and a boy named Douglas Erickson?'

Scarlet blotches crawled up Rita's neck.

'Well?' Cass said.

Rita's body trembled, her eyes watered, and she seemed poised to explode. But it passed, she sagged with exhaustion, as if forfeiting the entire complaint ... then sprang forward grasping for Amy's throat. A split second before she was to be strangled, Amy felt Cass take her arm and pull, a mother yanking her child out of traffic.

Rita grasped at air. Something on the floor squeaked. A single felt clog flung backward and Rita slammed face-first onto the tile floor with the sound of a coconut struck with a claw-hammer.

The produce girl eeeked.

One of the Under Armour gentlemen said, 'Oh my God, that was so Naomi.'

But they couldn't see how bad it was, none of them could. At first.

Rita began to moan again, in a way that was more disturbing than at the party. A brisk managerial young man with a name tag reading *Cal* rushed in warning everyone not to move her, but Rita was already worming herself sideways, then rolling over. Her nose had ruptured and two streams had spread down her chin. Her lips were peeled back and her entire mouth looked like a broken bowl of grape jelly.

'What happened here?' Cal demanded. 'Someone call 9-1-1.'

'She tried to attack us,' Cass said, with what sounded like real remorse.

'I saw it,' the produce girl said. 'She totally lost it and slipped.'

Amy covered her mouth and ran away. She could no longer bear standing there, looking at Rita's teeth, one lying in a pool of the blood, two others embedded and standing upright in the tile, snapped off at the roots. She was crying from the realization that she had enjoyed seeing Rita fall, had been wishing violence upon the woman from the moment she had appeared. She was sickened by the coldness settling into her heart. She couldn't help feeling as though everything she touched or came near these days inspired physical harm to others. It was as if she had become a radioactive being whose mere presence tainted all other living things.

Cass joined her in the parking lot a few minutes later. They leaned against the Passat's hood, smoking a couple of Cass's Benson & Hedges Golds as the paramedics loaded Rita into the back of the ambulance. Tami's mother had walked out with her head up, a giant wad of white towels held to her face, but the paramedics were steering her as Cal followed at their heels, handing them each a business card. The ambulance lights flashed a few times for show but the siren stayed mute.

'That poor woman,' Cass said when the ambulance was gone.

Amy felt detached, worn out. 'How did you know she would be here?'

Cass issued a stream of blue smoke at the sky. 'She always does her shopping at this time.'

'You've been following her?'

Cass flicked ash, took another drag.

'Cassandra?' Amy said. 'Did you plan this? How did

350

you know those things about her daughter? Who have you been talking to?'

Cass rolled her eyes. 'I knew she had it in for you and I thought it would be better if we dealt with her sooner than later. So I did a little homework. But I didn't plan anything, Amy. How could I? The woman slipped. You saw her. Gawd, I don't take any shit, but I'm not obsessed. You should be relieved she didn't succeed in trying to strangle you.'

'She's going to sue me.'

'No, she won't. This took the wind out of her sails.'

'How do you know that? You don't know that.'

'I'll never let anything happen to you,' Cass said. 'You're too important to me.'

Amy tossed her cigarette. 'Why is that?'

'What?'

'Why am I so important to you?'

'We're friends,' Cass said. 'You've welcomed me into your home.'

'No, really. Tell me the truth. Why are you and Vince so interested in our problems? The night we first met, then the birthday party, tonight. And I don't even know what Mick and Vince got into the other night at the restaurant, but it wasn't good. You two keep showing up at the strangest moments.'

Cass's smile had been shrinking during this turn in the conversation. She looked unprepared, hurt.

'I'm sorry,' Cass said, sniffing. 'I thought we were friends, but perhaps I've assumed too much.'

'And I appreciate that,' Amy said. 'I really do. But I

just ... there's so much I don't understand about you. You never talk about yourself. It's always me, my problems, Mick and me. I'm not used to this kind of attention.'

Cass was staring off across the parking lot. 'What do you want to know?'

'See, now I feel like I'm prying,' Amy said. 'That's not my—'

'Wake up.' Cass's eyes had gone cold, glossy and dark.

'I don't—'

'Stop living your life in a dream and face the truth.'

'Okay. I'm not sure I understand that.'

'Deal with your husband,' Cass said. 'Get him in line. Bring him and the kids to the barbecue Saturday. Vince will explain everything. And stop being such a baby, Amy. You *know*. Deep down, you know what's coming. This will help you. Our ... my husband is going to change your life. The least you can do is show some gratitude.'

Amy stared at her friend, their eyes locked in a kind of symbiotic feeding. Amy had the strangest feeling that Cass was thriving on her, literally drawing energy from her like a dead car battery connected with jumper cables. Since her first timid appearance on the patio, the woman had gained strength, blossomed, taken on a ... power. Amy could think of nothing to compare it to, but she didn't think the woman was entirely real in the most basic human way that word implied. Or rather, she was real, but also something else. She was feeding on Amy, driving her toward bad things, in the manner of what

Amy's mother might have called, in her Sunday school fervor, a demon.

Cass said, 'You understand what is at stake now.'

Amy looked away, unable to meet the woman's eyes another second.

'Some day our house, our fortune, everything that is keeping us secure will be yours. But it doesn't come free. Vince and I will help, but you have to do your part, Amy. Starting with Mick and the children.'

Amy was scared now. She did not know what she was agreeing to, but something deep inside her wanted to agree, wanted to find out what was coming, where it would lead them. She felt like crying again, then realized she was crying.

'I have to go home and talk to Mick,' she said.

'Yes,' Cass said. 'He needs to know you're committed to your future. He needs to be reminded what's at stake. If you come to us, there will be no more nightmares. Briela's tantrums will cease. Kyle will no longer be ostracized. Mick will be strong again and your family will be at peace for all your remaining days.'

'I know.'

Cass took her by the chin. 'Do you?'

'Yes.' And she did not know how or why or in what, but in that moment, Amy believed.

Cass released her and walked to her black Range Rover. Amy drove home feeling that something inside of her had changed, that a portion of her soul had just been cut away and bartered. She didn't know what for, only that it was bigger than all of them.

48

At the same time that Amy was leaving Whole Foods, Mick was sitting in his truck two blocks from his accountant's house, waiting – hoping against all logic – for the thief to come home. But after spending three hours staking out his quarry in its native habitat, there had been no sign of Sapphire's powder blue Lexus. Neither Eugene's nor his wife Virginia's car (a white Mercedes wagon, as of their annual Christmas party two years ago) were in the driveway. This road was the only way out of the neighborhood. Which meant that the couple were out of town or the cars were in the garage and they were in the house.

Every instinct told him that his intuition – the vision he had experienced when Sapphire clapped him on the shoulder – was correct. The accountant was Mick's embezzler. Render had confirmed as much and the evidence was sitting in Mick's crawl space. The question now was, what had Render done to get the money back? And if Sapphire had not given it back without a fight, if Render had done something to Sapphire similar to what he had done to the hooligans Saturday night, what was Mick prepared to do about it?

He could go to the police, call Terry Fielding and report that his new neighbor was blackmailing him, dragging him into some violent scheme for God knows what purpose. But he would only be opening himself to more questions, bringing to light his role in the parking lot assault-turned-massacre. It was self-defense, at least on Mick's part, but as Render had pointed out, Mick's fingerprints were on the bat. And where was the bat, anyway? Did that warning mean Render was keeping it in case Mick turned on him? The man had not seemed worried enough about Mick running to the police to even bother with such measures.

More importantly, if something had happened to the accountant, Mick needed to know what it was before he went to the authorities. After all, the motive – some three hundred thousand dollars in stolen funds – pointed directly to Mick Nash, struggling business owner.

Finally, not knowing was worse than knowing. Mick started the engine and drove around the block slowly, whistling to himself. He turned onto Pine Knoll Lane, then into the driveway and parked in the roundabout, beside a berm of Virginia's annuals. They were wilting, the flower bed bone dry and cracked in geometric shapes like salt flats. It had rained a few nights ago, but the Colorado sun was relentless. Maybe they hadn't been home for a while, or weren't feeling well enough to do their watering chores. Maybe, but probably not. He exited the truck.

The Sapphire residence looked like a brick castle that had been stepped on, pushing the wings out in a wide single-story chain of rooms and long hallways that was absurdly spacious for a couple nearing retirement. The lights were off. He walked calmly up the six concrete porch steps, glancing around at the neighboring homes. The lots were an acre or more, with good privacy, and it was dark. He doubted anyone was watching him or could see anything beyond the general shape of his truck. No children on their bicycles passed, no couples were out pushing a stroller or walking the dog. Even though he had damn good cause to be here, Mick felt like a burglar casing the house. He reminded himself that, whatever they had done, these people were old. They were either guilty or not guilty, but it wasn't going to turn into a shoot-out. Stealth was not a priority.

Mick pounded oak with the underside of his fist. He repeated the knocking in hard cycles, growing impatient. He rang the bell again and again. He walked around the side of the house and peered through the garage windows. Sapphire's Lexus and Ginny's white Benz were sitting there in the dark. They had to be here. He felt it in the pit of his stomach.

Virginia had been going a little batty the past few years and Mick knew that her husband feared she was sliding into early senility. The accountant had a nose for details, saved (and stole) and invested wisely. He was the kind of man who never forgets his keys but wants to be sure there's a spare handy, especially if his wife had a habit of locking herself out of the house.

Mick searched under the doormat, in the milk box, checked for loose bricks along the window sill. No key.

He looked for any carefully placed flat rocks in the garden area, kicked over a clay toad. He was about to give up when his eyes landed on the drainpipe running from one of the eaves, elbowing onto the lawn. Mick's own father had used a magnetic box to hide his spare key under the bumper of his Scout, and the drainpipe was the perfect location for the same rig. He ran his palm along the underside of the pipe and stubbed his thumb on something that slid but did not fall off. He pried the small box off, popped the plastic lid, and a brass Kwikset KW-1 fell into his palm.

The key fit both the knob and the deadbolt, and the door opened. He found it hard to believe Sapphire, or anyone with a house like this, would not have an alarm – but none sounded. He searched the foyer wall anyway and found a flat black box with a green LCD readout of today's date and time, but no other blinking lights. He did not think the alarm was activated and he guessed it didn't much matter now.

'Hello? Sapphire? Hello? Virginia? Anybody home?'

No one answered. Mick shut the door and flicked on a few of the deeper interior lights. A hall, the kitchen. He made a quick circuit of the central rooms, including an atrium at the center of the house with a glass roof and sunken hot tub surrounded by ferns and ceramic lizards and parrots, then headed down the east hall, poking his head into two guest rooms, a small reading room, Sapphire's office, two bathrooms, and the garage again. The center and east wing of the house were empty.

In the western wing, he flipped on the hall light and

searched two more bedrooms, a sewing and crafts work-space Virginia had set up, a large guest bathroom, another small computer room, and three closets. All were empty.

All that remained was the master suite at the far end. Mick remembered touring it during one of the holiday parties, the knotted pine four-poster bed and other cabin-style furniture, the jacuzzi tub and dual shower, Virginia's exercise bike and the flatscreen mounted above the gas fireplace. But he couldn't see any of that now because the door was closed.

He stopped just outside the door and listened. The air conditioning was not on and it had to be over eighty-five degrees inside, the house pregnant with the day's heat, and yet Mick was chilled by the silence.

Well, they were either not here, sleeping, or dead. He had come this far and he had to know. Mick rubbed an arm over his face, shook his fingers loose, took the knob in hand, and stepped inside.

Orange curtains spread free of their matching sashes tinted the room with muted flames of streetlight. The scents of lilac and chemically cleaned carpet enveloped him. His eyes went immediately to the bed, which had been made, with the sheets turned back over the duvet.

Eugene and Virginia were lying on their backs, hold-ing hands on top of the covers, staring up at the ceiling. Dressed in everyday weekend wear, shorts and oxford shirts with the cuffs rolled up, feet bare. Even in the dim room he could see that the bedding was clean, free of blood. He walked to the accountant's side, turned on the bedside lamp, and looked down into the open eyes. Both Eugene and Virginia's were filmed over with a whiteness that seemed closer to dry cotton than fluid. Their death faces offered no expression, only that of peaceful rest. Eugene's mouth was closed, but Virginia's lips were parted, enough for Mick to see the small pink tip of her tongue pressed against her yellowing front teeth. He stared at the bosom. He stared at Eugene's rib cage beneath the shirt, their nostrils, but nothing moved.

There were no bruises around the neck, no staved-in skulls. Neither body was locked in a state of heart-clutching anguish, the paralyzed frenzy of stroke. It was if they had lain down together, hand in hand, knowing it was coming for them and had accepted their fate, perhaps even welcomed it together. The punch had been drunk, the pill swallowed, but in the name of what cult? What cause? There wasn't an explanation that made any kind of sense.

Mick turned away from the bed and walked into the attached master bath, bumping his left shoulder on the toilet alcove partition. He fell to his knees, lifting the lid just in time. He hadn't eaten today and nothing came up, but his mind didn't know that and it was in full revulsion, forcing his body to go through old habits. The heaves racked him to tears and cramped the muscles of his abdomen, burning his throat, bursting the capillaries around his eyes. Trembling, he wiped his mouth with a swatch of toilet paper and, out of habit, flushed. He walked slowly to the basin sink of Mexican tile and ran cold water over his hands, his face, washed his mouth.

He reached for a towel and froze. Hanging on faux-bamboo rings to his right was a pair of cream monogrammed towels. E and V, embroidered with looping script. In the coming days, someone – most likely Gene's daughter, Anna, who lived in Wheat Ridge with her husband Peter, also an accountant – was going to have to come and pack those towels up in a box. Mick wiped his hands on his shirt and closed his eyes.

This isn't happening. It cannot be happening.

Somebody had put them down like dogs, in what appeared to be an almost humane way. Render's knowing look when he scoffed at the idea of Mick calling the police pushed the sense of guilt back to the surface. The man was fearless, killed wantonly. He'd done it last night with those boys and, by some mysterious means (poison, a lethal injection, suffocation with a pillow), he'd done it recently to these sad, crooked old people. The work had been all Render's, but the motive still belonged to Mick. The psychotic fuck had saved Mick's life on the lake, recouped his missing funds, saved his ass in the parking lot. What else had he done? And for the love of God, why?

I didn't do this. I didn't ask for this and I am not responsible for this. I won't take the blame. I won't have any of it.

What about joint suicide? Maybe Render merely confronted them, they gave up the money, but couldn't live with what they had done.

Invigorated by this unlikely possibility, Mick walked back to the bed, on Virginia's side, avoiding peering down at them, and searched her nightstand for a note, a

360

calling card, anything that could have been planted. He checked the other side, but both tables and the drawers were clean.

He moved to the bay window, where a thick orange pad that matched the curtains topped the reading bench. There was nothing here, nor on the fireplace mantle, except for photos of the children and grandkids. Mick parted one of the curtains. A shaft of streetlight caught him in the chest and face and he squinted, examining the view. One house perhaps a hundred feet to the west, another slightly north. With lights on in both. Normal people inside. Suddenly he regretted very much his decision to come here, that his truck was parked in the driveway. Anyone could have driven by now, noticed the truck. He would be questioned, evidence would be gathered.

But what did it matter? It would all come out eventually. He wasn't about to cover up anything here. Two people had died, or been killed. It was time to talk to the police, call an ambulance. There was a cordless phone on one of the nightstands. All he had to do was turn around and dial. His conscience said, Yes, do it, it is the only thing to do. But the voice of self-preservation was stronger. He didn't understand all the angles. If he made the wrong move, he could wind up in prison. He needed to talk with a lawyer. His old high-school buddy, Cy Ferris, was a hotshot defense attorney in Denver. He would know what to do. But when was the last time Mick had talked to Cyrus? Could he trust an old high-school acquaintance?

Between the sashes, where the bedside lamp was reflected dimly in the window glare, a blade of darkness shifted. Mick dropped the curtain and turned to see Eugene Sapphire sitting up. The old man was upright, facing the fireplace directly beyond the foot of the bed.

'Oh, Jesus!' Mick staggered back and the reading bench buckled his knees, forcing him to sit. He clamped a hand over his mouth, a physical necessity to prevent him from screaming. For a moment the old man did not move, only sat rigid, as lifeless as he had been lying down, only now he had risen. It was an intolerable thing to witness, but Mick could not move or look away. The scream locked inside his mouth leaked out in a whimper.

Eugene Sapphire's head turned slowly toward him and it was not the same face Mick had peered down at only minutes ago. It belonged to the same man, but this face was opening as he began to move his mouth, razored lines in the cheeks appearing as if the man were somehow *un*healing. As the accountant lifted his chin, stretching his sagging neck wattles, a clean gash appeared from ear to ear and a wide skirt of thick slow blood began to saturate the oxford shirt. The accountant's right hand raised itself from the bed until his arm was extended in a salute and his first two fingers pointed crookedly. The gray, filmed-over eyes found him and the arm began to shake while a dry, ugly moan of distress began to fill the room.

The moaning was coming from Virginia. She started to writhe and mewl beside her husband, the two of them groping at air as Mick leapt up from the bay window seat and backed away, toward the door. The bedding around her waist and shoulders was turning red. Lacerations split her face as her eyes searched blindly for the source of the disturbance.

Mick bounced off the door frame and turned. The hallway was a shaking blur. The foyer seemed to retreat from him, the house elongating. He imagined the two corpses falling out of bed and then dragging one another to their feet as they followed his scent, shambling down the hall with increasing speed as their excitement drove them to new levels of coordination.

He slipped on the area rug and slammed into the front door, but caught the knob just in time to keep from falling. He threw it open with a quivering bang as it rebounded off the spring doorstop, and then he was leaping over all six stairs, flying from porch to lawn. He landed in the grass and his left ankle (the same one he had twisted falling into the Render's yard) failed him again. He collapsed and rolled away from the house, swatting at the air, making bizarre sounds and thrashing as if on fire. He sprang to his feet and glanced back at the open front door.

Eugene and Virginia Sapphire were not in the foyer.

'Sir, I'm going to ask you to stop right there, right now!' a man said.

Mick yelled again and turned to see a tall and whip-thin young man in blue work pants, a white button-down shirt with a gold tag, and blue baseball cap, holding a Maglite the size of a baseball bat over one ear. Behind him was a small white car with a blue badge magnet on the door, a little orange toy siren on the top, not yet flashing. Neighborhood security, some private outfit. The kid was probably not old enough to buy alcohol and he was definitely scared. Mick put his hands up and glanced from the kid to the front door and back.

'I didn't do anything,' Mick said, his words jumbled, coming too fast. 'I know them, they're sick, it's awful, something horrible happened, you have to—'

'Sir! Calm down, sir, and stay right where you are!' The kid did not lower the Maglite. If he had a gun, Mick knew, it would be aimed at his chest. With his free hand, the kid reached for a microphone clipped to his epaulet.

'D Unit six, this is Troy,' the kid said. 'I am at 22 Pine Knoll with possible intruder. Confirming ident, please stand by.'

The shoulder mic squawked. 'Ten-four, Troy. You need back-up?'

'I said stand by, Dallas.'

'Okay, tough guy,' Dallas said.

'Intruder?' Mick had a vision involving real police cars and policemen with real guns arriving to lock him up. 'No. I know them. I am, I was a friend of the Sapphires. He works for me, but listen, something awful happened. They're supposed to be—'

Troy the security guard regarded Mick perhaps one per cent less suspicion. 'What is your business here tonight, sir? Did you get permission to enter this residence?'

'Permission?'

With his free hand, Troy removed a small canister

364

from a Velcro pouch at his waistline, probably mace. 'Our office was not made aware of any visitors and I am responding to an alarm.'

'I'm telling you, I know them, but those people—'

'What is your relationship to the occupants?'

'He's my accountant. One of my father's best friends.'

'Does Mr Sapphire know you were stopping by?'

'He didn't, but he wouldn't mind—'

'Why were you running?' Troy interrupted.

Mick blinked dumbly at Troy. 'You don't understand.'

'What don't I understand, sir?'

'They . . . I saw . . . they're in there.'

'Who? Sir, are you telling me someone's in the house now? Why didn't they come out? Is someone hurt?'

Mick had become untethered. Reality was a balloon on a string and it was floating away. He was struck with the realization that he could not possibly have seen what he had just seen. The Sapphires had been transformed by something . . .

'Sir? Who did you see, sir? Is there someone in this house?'

Mick turned to the door. 'Check the house.'

'Excuse me?'

'Check the house. I saw someone in the bedroom, at the end of the hall.'

Troy reached for his shoulder mic, thumbed the switch, then released it. He stared at Mick with a new kind of unease and stepped back a few paces, as if he were afraid of catching whatever this intruder was carrying.

'What was it you saw, exactly?'

Mick knew what he had seen, but saying it out loud was impossible.

'H-hey, how did you get inside, anyway? We make sure the doors are locked.'

'I used a hide-a-key,' Mick said.

'And how'd you know where to find that?'

'I've been here before.'

'Uh-huh. And what did you say your name was again?'

'Render. Vince Render.' It came to him without thought.

'Okay, Mr Render. You want to tell me exactly what happened?'

Mick almost laughed, but it wasn't funny. 'I'm not sure I can do that, Troy.'

'See, I have to call this in one way or another.'

'Are you going to look inside?' Mick said.

'That is standard procedure. Should I expect something or someone inside?'

'I . . . I don't know.'

'Sir, if you don't mind my saying, you don't look well. Would you like me to radio for an ambulance?'

'No.'

'Well, I have to file a report,' Troy said. 'I need you to stay here while I inspect the house. If you flee, I will be forced to call the police. Probably have to call them anyway, but you won't be doing yourself any favors.'

'Just check the bedroom. I'll come with you.'

'Afraid I can't allow that.'

Mick rubbed his eyes. 'Fine, fine. I'll wait.'

'Do you have any weapons on your person?'

'What? No.'

Troy spoke into his shoulder mic, apprising his co-workers of the situation. 'The intrude— uhm, the visitor is cooperating. Give me a minute here, Dallas.'

He gave Mick a final look of warning.

'I'm not going to make trouble for you,' Mick said. 'Just be careful.'

Troy the security guard swung his flashlight around and entered the Sapphire residence. Mick stood on the lawn and counted to one hundred before joining him.

Island Living

I bolted awake but could not bring myself to move as the screams split the night like lightning. There were breaks in between, some as brief as twenty seconds, others as long as six minutes. A scream, then silence. A scream, then silence. Four or five in a row … and then nothing for ten or fifteen minutes.

I lay there sweating on the bed, watching the blades of the ceiling fan turning above us, listening for more. Maybe it was the roosters, I lied to myself. Traces of a nightmare I had been having. I couldn't be sure of what I'd heard between the crash and hiss of the waves down below and the lightning and thunder. I tell myself now that if I had heard the screams just one more time, I would have gotten up. I might have gotten there in time to prevent something, save someone. But they didn't come.

Eventually the storm lulled me back to sleep.

I was under for scarcely more than a few minutes when something strong and cold took hold of my leg at the ankle, shaking it. I sat up violently to find Bob Percy standing at the end of the bed. He was an enormous shadow, just standing there watching us.

How I refrained from screaming at the sight of Bob Percy watching my wife and me sleep, I am not sure, but I did. My wife did not stir when Bob said in a low, even voice, 'Come on, you have to see this,' and then turned and walked out of the bedroom.

I put on my sneakers, pants and the thin jacket from earlier, and found Bob waiting for me in the living room. He was holding a flashlight. He pointed it at his arm and then lit himself from under the chin. 'It's gone,' he said. He was right about that. There was no sign of the silver iridescence I had seen earlier on or in his skin. He looked the same as he had yesterday, pink from too much sun.

I was relieved but sensed this news was not the reason he had woken me. Reluctantly I followed him out into the night. He would not answer my questions as we walked, only repeated the phrase, 'You'll see, you'll see.' The rain had subsided but the ground was wet all around us and we tracked through the mud of the dirt road, leaving footprints on the main driveway that forked to the other villas. I was sure something had gone wrong with Lynn and the kids, but Bob did not lead me to his place. Instead he veered to the opposite end, to the last villa in his row of six. He went up the sidewalk and opened the front door without knocking.

'Wait a minute,' I said, halting on the porch. 'Tell me what it is first.'

Bob only shook his head, his expression far colder than any I had seen in the previous days. You won't believe me, his eyes seemed to say. You have to see it for yourself.

My curiosity had the better of me. I followed him inside. The villa was similar to ours, with two suites upstairs and two smaller bedrooms at the back of the first floor, a kitchen and bathroom in the center, and a living space near the front where we entered. He showed me the lower bathroom first. The pink tile floor and scalloped stucco walls had been transformed into an abattoir. The bathtub was clogged with something that looked like a lot of black human hair and it was filled nearly to the rim with blood. The walls were streaked with red handprints, and something had managed to spray the ceiling. The basin sink, the mirror, the floor. Even in my shocked state, I understood this could not have come from one person. What we were seeing was the product of several people. There was gallons of it.

'Where are they?' I croaked.

Bob did not answer but led me through the rest of the house. Each time we entered another room, I prepared myself (as if such a thing were possible) for the sight of exploded bodies, leaking orifices, something out of a cholera or ebola epidemic. But all of the remaining rooms were empty and clean. The people who had rented this villa, the Greenwald family of Nevada, were nowhere to be found.

We searched the second villa in the row. There were four bedrooms – two master suites, a double, and one with bunk beds for the kids, for a total of five beds. All five beds were soaked through to the mattresses with blood. The bedding was streaked with pieces of what was unquestionably human flesh and what I could only assume were traces of organ lining. Trails of blood had been dripped across the floors, down the stairway, splashing the walls, and I had no doubt that the Robertson family, who had checked in five days ago from Charlotte, North Carolina, were dead. Dead and more than likely *drained*.

'Did you call the police? A hospital?' I asked Bob Percy, and it was a wonder I still had the capacity for speech by then, because I was in shock and terrified beyond the ability to think rationally.

'The lines are down,' he said, nodding at the ceiling as if the phone lines were in there.

'What about cell phones?'

'Mine doesn't work down here. Does yours?'

I patted my pocket before realizing I'd left it plugged into the wall back in our bedroom. But I had used it on the island a few times and the service was fine in most locations.

'Mine works,' I told Bob, and began to walk away, but he stopped me, once again grabbing my arm.

'Don't leave me alone with this,' Bob said. 'We need to see about the others first. Tracking down the police at this hour is going to take a while. If you go now it might be too late.'

Bob was calm. I guess you could say he was in charge at that moment. 'It won't take long,' he said. 'We do this first, then you go make sure your family is safe.'

That sounded so reasonable at the time.

The third villa was the same as the other two, except this time all the carnage was confined to the kitchen and dining area. The Chavezes, a wealthy family who split time between Miami and San Juan but took long week-ends every couple of months on Vieques, had been enjoying a locally prepared dinner of whole chicken in a *sofrito* and fried plantains when it – whatever *it* was – came for them.

'I don't understand,' I said to Bob. 'Who did this?'

'Not who,' he said. 'What.'

I stared at him in the darkened Chavez villa, waiting for an explanation.

Bob led me to the fourth villa. I did not want to go inside.

'I'll take your word for it,' I told Bob, waiting on the porch.

'They were all in the bathroom,' he said. 'Trying to get rid of it. The whole family ran in there and it just accelerated, took them down like a goddamn blood hurricane.'

Four. Four dead families.

'The Weavers caught it too,' he said, gesturing at the fifth villa. Five dead families. 'They all did.'

'But where are the bodies?' I asked him. 'Did you move them?'

I won't say Bob Percy smiled, but his mouth twitched slightly, one side curling. 'You'll see,' he said. 'This is where it gets interesting.'

'Bob, no, I don't want to see. We need to call the police now, no more.'

I think I was yelling at him at this point, I'm not sure, but at any rate he slapped me. Hard across the mouth.

'Get a hold of yourself. We can't call anybody until you *understand*.'

I was angry, frightened to the point of shaking, but I followed him. He led me to the last villa, his own. We entered the larger of the two master suites, both of which were clean. We walked past the bed, out onto the balcony. They had a spectacular ocean view, and the balcony was large enough to seat half a dozen people. There were four chairs and a small table with candles that had been snuffed by rain. The ocean before us was roiling black under the black and gray clouds.

'We were having drinks, watching the storm,' Bob said. 'We don't even remember it coming on. We just came around knowing it had happened.'

Only then did I look down and see that we were standing on a floor of blood. In the dark it was black and I had mistaken the wetness for rain. There was a grated drain in the center, which was even at that moment funneling the rainwater and some of the blood down a drainpipe, onto the lawn. I was very glad to be wearing sneakers and I noted that Bob was still standing in his flip-flops and that his toes and ankles were speckled with more black dots and splashes.

I backed away from him, reaching for the sliding door to keep from tripping as I turned, but Bob took hold of my arm again and refused to let me go. He shoved me to the terrace's wall and pointed down.

Thirty feet below us, in the swimming pool, were the people.

49

Her husband had spent the past three days skulking around the house, beaten and bruised. He'd come home late last night looking like shit again. Maybe he had been with Vince. Maybe he was out carousing, drowning his sorrows as a failed businessman. Either way, she had indulged his wound-licking too long. When he finished mowing the lawn, Amy would sit him down for the most important State of the Union address the Nash administration had ever faced.

She was watching him now, through the kitchen window. Bouncing around the yard on his John Deere, a can of beer hanging in the nifty cup-holder he had mounted to the mower's dash. Trundling around out there in his Forrest Gump state of rectangular idiocy, punishing himself, she couldn't help thinking of desert beetles, mining slaves, some kind of life form feeding the soil of its own miserable existence.

Finally he buzzed the last strip and steered the mower back to the garage. His eyes under the brim of his baseball cap were small and black, like a skink's. He disappeared into the garage and the mower's engine sputtered off. She took her seat at the breakfast table. Five minutes later he came through the laundry room and paused at the second fridge. A bottle cap tinkled on the floor. He entered the kitchen, stopped, stared at her. He used his T-shirt to wipe his armpits, then lobbed it back into the laundry room. He sat across from her, holding his beer with both hands.

'Okay,' he said, and waited for her to begin.

The contents of Amy's speech appeared like a PowerPoint presentation in her mind. In all the squares were their finances, expenses, savings, everything down to the water bill. She had mental flow charts designed to help him see the big picture. She had the web addresses of several job sites printed for him. She had an outline of their options, pros and cons. She had her closing arguments rehearsed. And watching him stare at her dumbly, with one eye still blackened, his hands smelling of gasoline and grass and the swine sweat of two days without a shower – all of this carefully prepared material dissolved as if it had been written in disappearing ink.

'I want you to move out,' Amy said.

Mick did not respond. She positioned Tami Larson's medical bill so that he could read the sum ($17,566.22) at the bottom. He blinked at the figure but said nothing.

'To the pool house,' she said. 'You can use that as an apartment until the end of the summer. When the kids go back to school. You'll need to come up with the money to pay for Tami Larson's emergency room visit – no, the homeowner's policy doesn't cover it, because you let it lapse, just like you did with the health insurance.

I'll take care of the regular bills and worry about handling the kids. In the meantime, I suggest you take this opportunity to come up with a new plan. I don't really care what it is. But I'm not giving up this house or this land.'

He opened his mouth in protest.

Amy cut him off. 'Trust me, it's better this way.'

Mick looked past her, out the window facing the pool, to the Render house. He closed his eyes and a small smile appeared at the corner of his mouth. He was in his own dreamland again and she wondered if he might fall from his chair.

'You have no idea,' he said softly. 'You are in the worst form of denial about what's happened to us. I saw this coming years ago. I knew we could never sustain it, but you, you act like nothing's changed. You understand nothing about who we have become.'

'I understand you closed the restaurant without consulting me. You need to decide what role you would like to play in this family, and I need some space. You're hiding things and I can't live with this anger. Or do you want to tell me what happened the other night? Want to tell me about Myra Blaylock?'

This got to him. His eyes widened, but he said nothing.

'Right,' she said. 'I don't care where you eat or spend the days, but I can't sleep with you creeping in and out of the bedroom at all hours. I hope you understand, you did this to yourself, Mick. For the first time in our lives, you quit. I married a lot of things when I married you, but a quitter wasn't one of them.' She could see that this wounded him, and she almost regretted saying it.

He went to the sink, filled a glass with water, but instead of drinking it he poured it down the drain.

He said, 'Ten years I brought home an average annual income of two hundred thousand dollars while you hid in the sweet little fairytale world of your classroom. What's your paycheck going to be this year, Amy? Thirty-two-five? Forty with the knuckleheads at Vo-Tech?'

'You're the reason I had to take the Vo-Tech job, Mick. The restaurant hasn't turned a profit in almost three years. We're surviving on fumes.'

'You have a bad day when Scooter doesn't return a playground ball at the end of recess. When your budget can't cover nine months' worth of chalk. Do you want to hear about my bad days, Amy? Do you want to know what I face every day?'

'I've heard it all before.'

'In the past five years I've been sued, robbed at gunpoint, embezzled by my accountant. I've got five national chain dining concepts within a quarter mile, in a town with over a hundred bars. I've got a negative equity building in the deadest shopping plaza in Boulder because you were afraid to invest in that space on the mall.'

'I didn't want you to lose more money,' she said. 'The bank said you didn't have the brand profile to make it downtown.'

'My weekly budget is more than your entire annual salary. I am a human resources manager, a bartender, waiter, janitor, marketing chief, cook and CEO. I'm on my feet sixteen hours a day. I put in eighty-hour weeks to your thirty-five. You think I work nights because I don't want to be home for dinner? I work nights so you don't have to find a real job. You could be a professor at CU but you don't want that because reading *Make Way for Ducklings* just drives you to the brink.'

For a moment, Amy could not see. The world was black with her rage. 'That is beyond unfair, you shit. You wanted me at the same school as our daughter—'

'Yes, and you wanted me to work days, nights, and everything else so that we can send Kyle to any college in the country, so you can shop for a whole new wardrobe every time you gain or lose ten pounds, and keep your Boulder Country Club membership, even though you haven't set foot on a golf course or tennis court in six years and have no friends to play with. But that's all irrelevant now, because we've had a couple bad years and I'm the dead weight. The economy goes into the shitter and I'm no longer a good provider. I hope you understand how disgusting you're being right now.'

'You're a bastard,' Amy said. She was crying and she hated him for making her cry. 'You blew it. You squandered a fortune.'

He was no longer speaking quietly. 'I squandered it on you! Now, I'm sorry I didn't share the decision to close the Straw. But did it ever occur to you I've been trying to protect you?'

'From what? I don't need protecting. I need a husband!'

'What do you think this is?' he said, smiling in a way that frightened her. 'A setback? A rough week, a bad month? This is a death match. The country is fucking crumbling into dust and all those people out there – all those poor fuckers on the news? That's *us*. We're *them* now. We are the idiots who refinanced our home up to our tits so you could have a kitchen out of a magazine. We are the idiots who didn't save a year's pay. We're the idiots that had to have more more more. You want me to make everything better, but you won't cut back a god-damn thing. You want me to get out of your way and not come back until I solve all our problems. Fine, you got it, lady. But while I'm out there in the doghouse, you might want to look into what's making you so bitter and fat. It's not your weight. That's a symptom. I don't give a shit about your weight. You've given me two beautiful chil-dren and I love you and I don't care how big your ass is. I *like* big asses. I love you and I want to be your husband. I tried to give you a decent life, but you're not content with that. You want that' – he pointed to the Render house. 'You want to be perfect, in that top one per cent. Well, guess what? It's never going to happen. This is it. We're in the shit now and all we have is each other. *Had* each other. What will you do when I'm gone? Have you thought of that yet? What will you do with all your hate when I'm gone?'

He was right. She hated him. With every cell in her body.

'Move out,' he said, laughing. 'Yeah, we'll see what happens at the end of the summer. We'll talk to a judge about how much of my parents' money you've flushed down the toilet and he'll have a good laugh, and then I'll fucking sell this place right out from under you and you'll never see a red cent. "Move out." That's the funniest fuckin' thing I've heard all week.'

He strutted across the kitchen. Amy stood, picked up his beer bottle, and threw it as hard as she could. It spun and shattered against the back of his skull. She saw blood there immediately and she thought maybe now he would come over and hit her. But he only turned and stared at her, murderous amusement in his eyes.

'That's assault,' he said. 'And if you really want to take me out, you're going to have to do better than that.' He walked out.

Amy went to the bedroom and gathered his clothes and shoes from the walk-in closet and began throwing them onto the back lawn. It crossed her mind – as she was hurling his cigar box of watches and pocket knives onto the flagstone patio – that maybe she shouldn't have taken Cassandra Render's advice so literally.

But this was a fleeting thought, one Amy banished as quickly as it appeared. Because even though she was crying and screaming hysterically and wished her husband dead, fucking dead in the ground with ants in his eyes, *this felt good*. It felt really good to let it all out. It was an almost sexual release of raw anger, and about that part of it at least, Cass had been one hundred per cent correct.

50

Why couldn't she see that he was trying to protect her? Preserve what was left of their lives? Keep her safe from this dirty man's business? There was a time when she trusted him, could tell by glancing at him it was better not to push. But they had strayed too far from one another. The bond was breaking, or broken. She couldn't know how much trouble he was in, and so she hated him for 'allowing' their security to fall to pieces. Maybe he would have to tell her the truth eventually but, for now, let her hate him. Let the kids wonder if Mom and Dad were getting a divorce. It was a horrible thing to stand by and watch, but it was better than involving them in what was quickly becoming a game of murder by proxy.

Thus exiled, Mick regressed. He embraced the guest house the way a student embraces his first off-campus apartment. He opened the windows and kicked out the rusted screens. The cardboard boxes seemed to have been waiting for him, dislodging his Boulder High yearbook (Odaroloc 1987), a Bon Jovi T-shirt, a ratty pair of black Chuck Taylors, a case of Penzoil. The tiny closet revealed his old Technics hi-fi system, a silver battleship with huge knobs and an orange needle that moved as if through sludge. He heaved it onto a pair of cinder blocks and turned up the classic rock station loud enough to blow dust from the cones of the coffin-size speakers.

He got a window fan going but the heat was merciless. He stank of sour sweat and dried blood, a funk that would not wash off no matter how he tried, and he was beginning to like it. Felt more natural. Went with his shredded Levi's and the greasy white T-shirt he had been affecting for the past three days. He moved everything out on the lawn and threw a twelve pack of Coors in the mini-fridge. He swept, but didn't mop the floors or scrub the tiny toilet. Upstairs was a loft, the roof slanting low over the lumpy spring-loaded cot folded up in the corner. It came apart like a giant gray clam and smelled about as fresh.

By dusk Springsteen was singing and there was a Rockies game on the snowy TV and he was feeling a little fucking crazy in here, in what his life had become. He opened another beer and sifted through the boxes. In the closet he found his weed dragon blow-torch and six quarts of propane, as well as the backpack he'd fashioned so he could wear the gas like a 'Nam grunt with a flamethrower while he burned up the lawn. There was a wooden crate of returnable bottles from the Pop Shoppe, a dried-up Winmau dartboard and his set of tungsten darts with the KISS flights from college, his dad's .12 gauge pump action, a leather roll of his father's chef knives, the set he had won for graduating first in his class from the culinary institute in Denver. A half-full bottle of Yukon Jack, the complete 1991 *Penthouse* his ex-girlfriend Myra had given him for his birthday. Oh, Myra, what happened to us? You've got breast cancer and I'm losing my shit. Maybe they deserved each other, he and Myra. The dying and the dead on his feet. Maybe he'd give her a call. But probably not.

He didn't long for sex or new-old romance. He longed for another target. Someone to absorb more of the blows. He re-hyped on the violence, the feel of the bat in his hands, the power. He stewed, thinking about Render.

What had Render done with the bodies? The guy loads them into his Range Rover like luggage, and then comes home minutes later? No way did he have time to dump them somewhere. Had he gone back out that night? The next day? Where would you take three bodies? What would you do with them?

Mick had been following the *Daily Camera*, the *Denver Post*, and even the *Times Call* out of Longmont. He ran Google searches for assaults, disappearances, missing persons, any reports of three boys or young men who might fit the event in any way. There was nothing. The police did not have anything about it either, or the mess at Sapphire's house. If they did, they were keeping it private for now.

The guest house was hot with evening sun, and yet Mick felt cold inside. He was cornered. Render had him. There was nowhere to run to. Maybe it was time to give up. Find out what the man wanted, and give it to him.

See you at the barbecue. Saturday, two o'clock.

Tomorrow, then. One way or another, it would all come out tomorrow.

The second floor was still musty and the heat was no longer amusing. He went to the last window he had not opened. It was a tiny square in a wooden frame, with an old spring-loaded latch, baked shut. He used a screwdriver to pop it free and stuck his head out to have a look around.

The view over the property was exceptional. The house was dark except for the bedroom, but Amy was probably in there crying on the phone to her mother, or Melanie Smith. The lawn looked good mowed low, but he'd missed a few spots with the string trimmer, the weeds around the flagstone. Tomorrow he would bust out the weed dragon, burn baby burn.

There was a naked woman in his swimming pool.

51

Three of the four underwater lights were burned out, and in the twilight he hadn't noticed her until the delicate splashing sounds cut through the drone and fade of traffic on Jay Road. She was performing a series of lazy laps, her lithe figure slipping like a pale otter, twirling and pushing off with her feet when she reached the end. She had the body of a nymphet, with small hips and buoyant buttocks, the long squid of her black hair bunching and trailing with each stroke. He watched her make three end-to-end turns without raising her head, and on the fourth he realized she still hadn't drawn a breath.

He sat up straighter in the window, sure he was mistaken. But she continued through five more laps – her pace steady if not exactly qualifying for the Olympics – without drawing a breath, and he knew she hadn't for the entire nine or ten, because he had been trying to get a look at her face all along. The pool was only thirty feet long, but this seemed rather unbelievable. She either had a massive set of lungs in that small body or . . .

At last she coasted, rolling onto her back, eyes turned

to the dusk's first stars. He was staring at her small breasts, trying to come to terms with the absolute lack of areolae and the smooth, featureless delta between her thighs, when she rotated her chin and looked up at him in the window.

He did not hide or look away. For a moment she only floated, arms wide, her expression neutral. Eventually she kicked herself to the shallow end and climbed the steps, dripping on the slate border. There were no towels or clothes waiting for her. She twisted her black hair in a rope over one shoulder and water pelted the lawn. With her hair aside, he noticed a thick vertical line running the length of her spine, stark white against the rest of her already pale skin, the scar of a major back surgery.

Cassandra Render, was his guess. Amy must have told her to help herself to the pool, but didn't they have one of their own? And would Amy really approve of this sort of baiting? Then again, he was a dog to her now. Maybe she had even put the neighbor up to it, yank his chain a bit. No, Amy wasn't the type to play kinky games. If anyone was tempting him, it was Vince.

She turned and walked toward the pool house, watching him until she disappeared beneath him. He assumed she was going home, but a few seconds later the guest house's french doors opened with a sweep of rubber insulation against the tile floor. As softly as possible, he set his beer down on the window sill, hoping she would go away. Seconds ticked by. Water dripped.

He headed toward the stairs and stopped short, unable to descend. The stairway ended at a ninety-

386

degree turn, with only the small square landing serving as the final step into the main room, and it was here, a few seconds later, that her arm appeared, then one leg, then her full profile, turning on the landing. She was a wet shadow and looked very small down there, naked. He could not read her face, only the contours of her pale form.

'May I come up?' Her tone was more polite than seductive.

Mick swallowed. 'What for?'

'I want to help you.'

'With what?'

'Vincent said you were injured.'

So, she knew they knew each other, and probably something about what he and Vince had been through together. Vince had put her up to this.

'No. That's not necessary.'

She smiled, her teeth white in the dark space. She began to climb, one hand on the rail.

'This is . . .' But he didn't know what this was.

'Turn around,' she said.

Feeling ridiculous and not a little frightened, he did.

She took more stairs. 'Lie down.'

'On the floor?'

She didn't respond, so he went to the cot and sat. She reached the top of the stairs and plucked a concert T-shirt from one of the boxes. She worked her arms and head through, but not before he caught another glimpse of her frontal anatomy. To his relief, there were actual nipples, though too pale and smooth to register as more than drawings. His eyes moved down, to the place all heterosexual men's eyes must fall when chance allows, but the shirt fell to her thighs before he could determine its character or any new details, and that was just as well. He looked away, ashamed.

'Are you all right?'

Mick laughed.

'I can help,' she said.

'The injuries were minor. I feel fine.'

'No. Inside of you.' This wasn't shaping up to be the seduction he had imagined. She had a nurse's clinical but human aura of duty and it filled the room, changing the air, loosening something in him that the beer hadn't been able to reach. 'I can't fix it unless you tell me first.'

He leaned back against the wall and laughed softly. 'I'm numb. I can't feel anything and I can't stop watching my family fall to pieces.'

'Lie on your stomach.' Her voice was firm and he found himself obeying, the cot protesting beneath his weight. 'Tell me what you want,' she said. 'Don't think. Just tell me what you really want.'

His chin hung over the edge of the cot. 'I want my life back. I want to kill your husband.'

'Sometimes I do too.'

He didn't hear her feet come closer but soon her hands were on him, soft and pleasingly cool. First gliding around his lower back, barely grazing, then under his shirt. He remembered he was filthy and decided it did not matter. He closed his eyes. Pressure was applied. His lower back cracked and popped several times, to great relief. She worked the tissue upward, on the sides of his vertebrae. Her palms seemed to press into his kidneys. No other part of her body touched him.

'Why did you come here?' he said. 'What do you want from us?'

Her voice quieted, the conversation taking on a new kind of intimacy. 'Life.'

'Why do you think we can give it to you?'

'Because of the things that happened. I know about terrible things,' she said. 'Things people don't talk about. You are not alone.'

Her hands continued working their magic on him. Smooth cloth sliding against his skin. She pressed and throttled the neck, ground into his shoulders, thumbed under his arms. He realized his shirt had come off, though he did not remember lifting to remove it. She moved down, thumbs grinding into his ass cheeks and the back of his pelvis, which also popped, and down his bare legs. His jeans were gone too, as if dissolved. For some reason this did not disturb him. A great warmth had flooded his body, despite her cold hands. She massaged knots from his calves, pushed the pain up out of the arches of his feet. He felt soft everywhere, the blots of pain he had been ignoring blazing and fading like dying stars.

'The truth scares you,' she said. 'You're afraid to be yourself.'

'I don't know who that is any more.'

'You are not in touch with your body's changes. You

cannot ignore its needs. The mind is powerful enough to fool itself.'

'I'm sorry,' he said, but he didn't know for what, to whom.

There was an intake of breath, his or hers, and she leapt, landing somewhere above and behind him, balancing in such a way that the cot did not tip or buckle or even make a sound. Her hands continued to walk the paths of his body, out along his arms, and the air moved between them, suddenly warmer, hot as the summer night and heavy, and then she was pressed to him from foot to breast, aligned, her weight sinking into him, compressing him, her skin bare all along his back, the surface they shared pliable.

All energy in him drained out, his body relaxed utterly, and he was not so much aroused as happily melted. He could no longer determine where her body began and his ended, there was just this weight and its energy moving through him. It was better than any drug and his mind allowed it in, pooling with the absence of thought, until he was in a place far away, resting on a beach of moist packed sand, the sun radiating through him while the sound of waves lapping in a perfect rhythm caressed and pulled him deeper within himself, beyond himself, to a state of pure and innocent sensuality he had never known.

We were in an accident.

He lay there in this foreign land, wrapped in warm penetrating sun and the hiss of water reaching up the shore, for a long time, hours or days, it did not matter, he was only healing in her light. He was comfortably lost – and then awoken by a pang of worry that he could not afford to be lost, other people depended on him, his family needed him. He opened his eyes and sat up, blinking into the sun.

He was on a beach. Before him stretched a plate of sea so bright blue and sparkling it hurt his eyes. The cove of black rock and white sand and rubbery-leafed plants arced to either side and no one shared this beach with him. To his left, some fifty yards away, tucked under a leaning palm, were three lounge chairs of blue-and-white striped canvas. A battered red cooler, towels hanging from a branch. Something bit his leg and he swatted his skin, wiping red ants away.

Where did they all go?

He stood and walked toward the chairs, then followed the footprints up the white-sand tide line, into the vegetation which quickly turned into a low, dense kind of jungle. There were three sets of footprints, one small and two medium-sized – his wife and children's. Where had they wandered off to? His son was probably chasing iguanas again.

The iguana.

He remembered how they had seen the lizards sunning outside the villa this morning, and later on the side of the road, on the way to the beach, and the boy had gone wild in the backseat of the rented Jeep. It was an underdeveloped island, a place where wild horses walked the beach and goats loitered in the road. There had been little traffic on the single lane leading to the

391

beach, but the few cars they passed going the other way had been driving recklessly, too fast and down the middle, so that whenever they crested a hill, he had to ease far onto the shoulder while his stomach knotted and he prayed no one came over the rise.

His son had been leaning between the front seats, watching through the windshield, counting peacocks and lizards. They rode in the heat, windows down, smiling and laughing, until he spotted the iguana up ahead. It was staggering in jerking circles, damaged, all equilibrium lost. He knew immediately the animal was injured, had been swiped by another car very recently. One of its hind legs had torn loose and dragged uselessly, its tail twisted at a cruel angle, and yet it veered from one side of the road to the other in manic confusion, unable to decide in which direction cover lay.

He told his wife to put the boy back in his seat, but it was too late. The boy was already crying. And then their daughter saw it and she made a miserable sound. Do something, his wife commanded, but they were moving at almost forty miles per hour and it wasn't safe to stop here. The road ran in a straight shallow dip for a few hundred meters but jungle crept right up to it on both sides. The humane thing to do would be to run the iguana down, put it out of its misery, but he couldn't do that with them in the car. He began to slow anyway, telling them, yelling at them not to look. But of course his son had to look and was scrambling around in his seat.

The iguana was a magnificent adult, easily five or six

feet from nose to tail, thick as a house cat, the dorsal spines a bright shade of tangerine with black bands around the whipping bent tail. It was a small dinosaur, and dying.

The battered Suzuki Samurai came rising over the next hill at nearly double their speed. He veered onto the shoulder that did not exist, branches and thick banana leaves slapping the hood and windshield. He braked and the vehicle stalled. His wife screamed and his son was thrown against the door. His side mirror missed the Suzuki by a hand's width, and then he was watching in the small oval, a sickness in his belly as the beautiful lizard tumbled under the Samurai's chassis like a rolling log, skin flapping. Oh my God, his daughter wailed, and then the three of them were crying and he barked at them to calm down, he would fucking deal with it.

He got out and slammed the door, heading back to the roadkill, a simple trip to the beach ruined, everything sweaty and itchy, the tiny black gnats flitting at his eyes as if they wanted the moisture inside. Fucking family vacations. They should have stayed home, saved the ten grand. Everything was a headache now, and he needed a beer to quell the tequila hangover from last night. Late night on the villa's terrace, the couple in the next villa, Bob and Jenny or maybe Bill and Sarah, he couldn't remember, but nice people, and fucking alcoholics at that. Smokers from Ohio. The wife had looked good though, hard with big brown eyes, her sunburned and sun-spotted chest sweating in that little halter thing she had been wearing, and had she been looking at him? Laughing at his jokes and shooting him glances when her husband got up to use the can every fifteen minutes because his prostate was already turning into a walnut? Maybe, you never knew. The tropics did things to people, even the conservative ones from the mid-west.

He looked both ways before leaving the relative safety of the shoulder. There were no cars now. The Samurai hadn't even slowed, probably a local, the people down here used to mowing down lizards like long-haul truckers pasting bugs and skunks. Well, he'd drag this one off the road just so the kids didn't have to see it again. He could tell his son he'd done something for it, even though the thing was finish—

The lizard was still alive. It was lying on its side, two-thirds of the tail severed and twitching over in the sand shoulder, the coarse pebbled scales of the rib cage flexing rapidly. Left front appendage shredded, lesions along the plated head and leathery back and nearly white stomach, the blood thin, dripping quick like iodine. The black pupil inside the golden ring oscillating, watching him like a dog on the vet's table.

Help me, the damn thing was telling him. Eat me, release me from this, whatever this is. Just get it over with.

He glanced back at the SUV. His wife was looking over the seats, talking to the kids. He waved, signaling for her to make sure they weren't watching, but he had no idea if she understood. He looked up and down the

394

road as he kneeled, one hand already reaching out. One twist, he was thinking. Break the neck quickly and then carry it into the jungle and put some leaves over it.

Something clamped down on the outside edge of his hand, nubby and firm, then let go just as quickly. He jerked away. Fucking thing was up on its three remaining feet, stub tail twitching a phantom whip. The pink tongue on display as it hissed at him silently, accusing. He stepped back, more in surprise than fear. Hadn't even broken the skin on his hand, just left a sort of half-oval depression. The teeth like a wood file, dry. The iguana watched him and he it. It wasn't breathing so hard now. The bleeding had stopped dripping, was congealing in thick beads along the flapped open hide. Jesus, this was some animal. Tough as a fiberglass hammer. Maybe he could save it after all. He took one step and the iguana pivoted, darting away. It ran in a straight line into the sand, the trees, vanishing. He'd never seen anything like it and he didn't know whether to laugh or cry.

When he got back to the rental, his wife and daughter were okay but his son was still crying. Hey, hey, it's all right, kiddo. It lived, it ran away. Didn't you see it? I promise. He was tough. The car didn't hit him, just the wind passing over him. Someone was watching out for him. Couple of scrapes, like you when you crashed your bike last winter. That old green monster trampled off into the jungle, back home to his family. What? No, I couldn't catch him. He'd been through too much already, better to let him go. We'll find you another one. Later, down by the beach maybe. We'll take a swim, have some lunch, and then go looking for a couple of his buddies. Can you bring one home? Ah, hell, I don't know. Maybe a small one in your suitcase. Why not?

Crisis averted, the boy smiling again, everyone relieved and ready to press on. It was a gorgeous day. They had a cooler full of sandwiches, bottles of Sol and that orange soda the kids loved. His wife said it was the cane sugar and while they were down here they could have as much as they wanted.

That had been what, two or three hours ago? Six? Sometime this morning. He must have dozed off while they were swimming. They couldn't have gone far, his wife would have woken him up.

He tromped through the jungle, catching strands of black seaweed or some kind of dry moss on his sandals. Itching bites on his ankles, probably sand fleas or bed bugs from the villa. He began to sweat. Their tracks were still clear, and the road they came in on was right around the corner. They couldn't have gone far. This park was too small to get lost in. Hell, the island was too small to get lost on. The beach area was tiny, the forested jungle behind it protected. A nature preserve, though the locals claimed entire acres were still contaminated from the years the United States Navy had used it as a bombing range. Weapons testing, until a bunch of hippies went out to sea in their inner tubes and the protests achieved international media coverage. Too small to get lost on, and the trees, these bushes, all this growth, it was too thick. He couldn't fathom his wife and daughter agreeing to brave this mess. Maybe the girls had to tinkle and didn't want to leave the boy on the beach while Dad was sleeping.

He looked up, but the sun wasn't above him any more. It was lower, far on the horizon. Hell, he must have had too many beers. Headache setting in, a little hungover. Skin dry and stinging a little, tight along the arms. Sunburned but not too bad.

He opened his mouth to call their names and halted.

A white void flashed in his brain.

wife – son – daughter

He laughed to himself, standing there in the jungle. Sweating. Are you kidding me? This was absurd. He tried again.

— — —

Mouth hanging open. He couldn't remember their names.

'Oh, come on,' he said, just to hear himself, to hear a voice. 'Are you serious?'

Something was wrong. He wasn't drunk. He could not summon the names of his wife and children.

Or their faces.

He looked around in a mild panic, the jungle – shit, it wasn't even a jungle, more like a low-growth woods of twisted trees, tiny leaves, thick bushes of yellow and lime green, sand burrs, the same white sand everywhere with the black moss, dirty from it, like the sand you used to see in ashtrays outside of office buildings before the whole world banned smoking – the vegetation and sweltering heat seemed to close in around him, and now he was dizzy, nauseated, thinking seriously about the term *sunstroke*.

Why can't I remember? What happened here? Where did my family go?

The fear burst through him in a fountain and he began to run, sandals digging in the soft floor, but it was like a nightmare that way. No matter how hard he concentrated, he couldn't run and the sand seemed to be swallowing him even as he began to cry out *Help, somebody, please help me.*

He ran until he came into the clearing, where the limestone well opened like a door to hell, and the water two hundred feet below was mercury silver, and he knew he was about to find them again. This was the day that had changed them and altered their lives forever.

Mick woke with a start, body trembling. He was staring at the floor, head hanging over the cot. He twisted over and sat up, rubbing his face, blinking to bring the room back into focus. Tears in his eyes, a fading scream sinking back into his throat. The sun was rising outside the attic-room window. The guest house, he was in the guest house. Home. His family was close, in the house.

Amy. Kyle. Briela.

He remembered their names now, but he could not remember ever having – *suffering* – a nightmare of such intensity and lucidity. It wasn't all clips and fragments and nonsensical pieces like most dreams were. It had been continuous, with the heat and the ant bites, an experience in full immersion. Running through the jungle, he had never felt such impending doom, or so helpless to stop it.

The realization that Cassandra had been here and now was gone was of secondary interest. He could not shake the reality of the other place, the certainty that he had just walked in another man's shoes, during the final hours leading up to the pivotal moment of his entire life.

52

Amy was in the kitchen fussing over the proper wine when he let himself in through the sliding glass door, cracking the shell of aloof cheer she had constructed this morning. He looked better than he had yesterday, but this in itself was unsettling. His hair had been combed and his eyes were low-lidded, serene. He had shaved and dressed in a clean red polo over a pair of age-washed khakis that were cuffed over a pair of black Converse she hadn't seen since 1992, and he wore a boyish grin to go with the healthy luster in his cheeks.

Until he went to the second fridge in the mud room and opened a beer and stood leaning against the washing machine, staring at her almost lasciviously, she didn't realize how much she was hoping to abscond with the children to the Render barbecue without him.

'Do you need something?' she said, restocking the pinot in favor of a chablis.

'Are the kids coming?'

She bobbed out of the fridge, lips pursed.

'Fan it,' he said. 'I was invited.'

Amy cleared her throat. 'By whom?'

'Vince. We're friends like that.'

Well, if Vince had invited him, there was probably a good reason.

'I mean, how could I miss it, Amy? The Renders are going to take care of everything. Isn't that right?'

'I don't know what you're talking about,' she said.

'Sure you do.'

She went to the sink and began washing her hands for the fourth time in an hour.

'It's what you want,' he said. 'And for once, I agree. It's time we dealt with the true depth of our predicament. We will go and give them what they want, and in return they will shine a golden light on us. Our financial woes will be solved and you will let me back in.' He crossed the kitchen and rested his hands on her shoulders. Their roughness made her flinch. 'You will believe in me again, and love me like you once did.'

He kissed her neck and she wanted to scream.

'Stop it,' she whispered.

'It's too late for that,' he whispered back. 'We are beyond playing nice. They've cornered us.'

She turned to argue, but he had already left the kitchen. Her hands were shaking. She went to the fridge and gulped from an open bottle of wine without noticing the color. She coughed, almost regurgitated it, and put the wine back. Somewhere Cass was laughing, she was sure of it.

Kyle schlepped into the kitchen. 'They gonna have food? Freakin' starvin up in this piece.'

'It's a barbecue.' She composed herself and handed

him a fruit and cheese plate she had cut up. Burnt crostini, green apples, black cherries, roquefort. 'I'm sure they'll feed you. Is your sister coming?'

'Ready!' Briela's feet pattered down the hall. She had put on the white denim jumper Amy got for her at Crew Cuts, her adorable white-with-orange-polka-dot flats, and an orange headband.

'What about Dad?' Kyle said.

'I think so.' Amy tried to mask her dismay.

'What about Ingrid?' Briela said.

'She's helping Cassandra set up.'

'Does she work for them too now?' Kyle said.

'We're sharing her. Be polite, both of you. And no horsing around.'

Kyle tsssed.

Briela put her hands on her hips and thrust her chin at her brother. 'That means say please and thank you, dumbhead.'

Kyle pulled her headband off and threw it across the room.

Briela shrieked, 'He's ruining my hair!'

Amy said, 'Enough.'

They went out. Mick was standing in the garage, finishing his beer. He lobbed the bottle into a steel trash can where it shattered explosively.

'Here comes trouble,' he said. Briela hugged him. Mick clapped Kyle on the back, hard. 'We're s'posed to be grounded for staying out too late, sport model. But the warden says we get a day pass, so what say we go show these monkeys how it's done?'

402

Kyle grinned. Briela took her father's hand. The Nash family walked four-astride up the drive and the gates opened, welcoming them onto Render property. Amy shifted the wine in its foil snuggie and thought, Please don't fuck this up.

53

'Hello, welcome to our home,' Cassandra Render said with a strength and confidence that did not match the timid woman Amy had described, or the clinically efficient water sprite he had met last night. 'Please come in.'

'Cass! You look amazing,' Amy squealed and they air-kissed.

'I love your hair.' Cass fingered Amy's new deep brown tresses and amber highlights. 'Is that off the shelf?'

'Is it that obvious?' Amy said, and they laughed.

The hostess turned to him. 'You must be Mick. So glad we could pry you away from your work. I've been looking forward to meeting you.'

So it was going to be like that. No winks. We've never met. Fine.

He smiled. 'I wouldn't miss it. Nice to meet you … Cassandra, is it?'

'Call me Cass.'

'Sure, but I need your number first.' Cass laughed and pulled him in by the forearm. Mick did not know a woman could make a striped Williams Sonoma apron look so good. He thought about the scar on her back and repressed a shudder. Cass took the platter from Amy as they entered and stood dumbstruck, like tourists.

Well, it was what Mick had expected. Foyer with the sweeping staircase, plaster dome ceiling, oil paintings in burled gold frames. A mini-Bellagio of polished marble and exquisite rugs, very Mediterranean and bright, decadent air conditioning.

Behind them Cass cupped B's chin in her right palm, caressing her cheek. 'You are the angel, aren't you? A real angel among us.'

Briela looked dazed.

Amy said, 'This is our son Kyle.'

'Hey,' Kyle said.

'So handsome,' Cass said, winking. 'June's out back. In fact, why don't you all step out on the patio and grab a drink. I'm just finishing up with the ... the uhm ... pre-meal foods. Mick, you can help Vince light the grill? I don't think he knows how to operate that thing.'

'Can do.' Mick nudged Amy. 'Pre-meal foods?'

'Don't be a shit,' Amy hissed. 'I think she was raised in a foreign country.'

They walked a long dining hall, passing a den with a large oak desk, a red billiard table in a game room with a sideboard, skirted the kitchen, and then moved into a great room (or was it a gallery?) with motorized windows that retracted behind the taller panes above them, creating an open-air bridge onto the backyard patio. Long drapes of gauze had been strung, the light breeze billowing them between the plaster pillars like dusters.

Mick stepped out onto the wide and very white stone patio, shooting his son a devious grin.

'Pretty little house, huh? Relax. She's just a girl.'

Kyle snickered nervously, stopped. Mick followed his son's gaze over the lawn, down to the pool area. June was mowing the grass with an ancient push cutter. She wore track pants and a dirty T-shirt, her hair in a ponytail under a greasy mesh trucker's cap. Mick spoke into his son's ear. 'What I just said? I don't know what the fuck I'm talking about. You're in deep.'

She waved, munching up the last strip, then parked the mower against the shed and bounded up the hill.

'Sorry, I'm running late. I'll just clean up. Help yourself to the cooler!'

Kyle said, 'Right on.'

'Soak for ten minutes. What's this nonsense? I want fire now!' came a voice from the corner of the patio where a large black Weber kettle stood. The Render patriarch wore black jeans and a black polo, the blades of his tortoise sunglasses sinking into waves of greased blond hair. Cologne steamed from his pores and stung Mick's nose from eight feet away. An unopened bag of charcoal was standing upright in the basin and he was reading a plastic bottle of lighter fluid. 'How many briquettes does it take to cook eight buffalo burgers?'

'Just douse the whole bag,' Mick said, thinking, My grill's bigger than yours, slick. 'Set it on fire and wait half an hour.'

'Hey, hey, there he is – King of the neighborhood!' Vince turned and offered his hand. I'll play your game for another ten minutes, Mick thought, then I'm calling your bluff, you psychotic fiend. Mick shook Vince Render's hand. 'How's work, boss?'

'Early retirement's sounding better every day,' Mick said.

Render leaned in close. 'We'll be polite for a few minutes and then get down to business. Don't you try to run on me, champ, because we're all out of time.'

He released Mick with a hearty laugh. Mick glanced around to see if Amy was watching them, but she was helping arrange the food on a glass picnic table with a Cinzano umbrella while Cass poured her an aquarium of red wine.

Vince popped the top from a Stella Artois. 'Is this all right, Mick?'

Euro piss, but it would do. 'Good beer, thanks.'

Vince struck three matches together and set the bag of charcoal on fire. Burnt paper and orange sparks began to rise from the kettle in a hot cyclone that made the mountains shimmer.

Render gestured at the grill. 'Haven't used one of these things in ages, but I can't get on board with those propane jobs. I know they're quicker, but somehow the meat never quite tastes the same.'

'Soon as the pile turns white, you're in business.' Mick wished he could read his host's eyes behind the Ray-Bans. He didn't think they would match the jocular tone. He thought they would be jaundice yellow, lined with blood.

Amy moved beside him, whispered, 'Can you believe

this? She's got a day spa in the south wing and something called a restoration chamber.'

'Awesome.' Mick sniffed. 'Hey, where's Ingrid? I thought she was filling in today.'

Amy looked around, surprised by her assistant's absence. 'We can't afford her. I never trusted her anyway.'

'Maybe they haven't let her out of the trunk yet,' Mick said.

Amy didn't laugh.

On the other side of the pool, a mature Russian olive tree rustled and something resembling a large raccoon leapt out onto the lawn in a shower of gray-green leaves.

'Addie, be careful,' Cass called out. 'Good heavens.'

The raccoon tumbled in the grass and stood, shedding twigs. The bushy-topped boy in the brown T-shirt and camouflage army pants was Briela's size and he walked toward them with the pugnacious stance of the family runt.

'Adolph,' Vince said. 'Be a gentleman and say hello to our new neighbors, the Nash family.'

Adolph waved, his beady brown eyes studying them. Everyone said hello to Adolph Render. The boy went to the cooler, eyeing Briela with haughty interest as he snatched an Orange Crush and jammed it into his cargo pocket. Briela looked away, scowling.

'You be nice,' Amy said to B.

For a moment Mick thought his daughter was on the verge of tears, but trying so hard to be a good girl. Mick felt a pang of remorse. He hadn't been here for her much the past three years, and now she wasn't really here herself. She was retreating into fantasy to avoid the disintegration of her family.

Maybe they all were.

For a moment, standing here in the blinding Colorado sun, he did not know who he was or where he had been or what had led him to this moment.

'Mr Render?' the kid was saying. 'Is everything all right? You're not supposed to be in here, sir. I asked you to wait outside.'

They were in the long dark hall, in the west wing of Sapphire's house. Troy the security guard was standing at the end, one hand reaching for the closed door. His Maglite was like a star, giving him a royal beast of a headache.

'Mr Render?'

'I don't think you should open that door, Troy,' Mr Render said.

But he wasn't Mr Render. This was all a lie. His entire life was a lie.

'Why not?' Troy said, voice cracking.

'I don't think you're going to like what you find on the other side.'

He began to walk into the light.

'Feeling all right there, Mick?' the blond man said. Behind him the bag of charcoal was shriveling, turning black.

'Nothing another one of these won't fix.'

Mick sipped his beer, thinking it such a shame that his family had agreed to participate in this charade. Amy, who wanted so badly to please them. Kyle, who wanted so badly to be normal, fit in with them. Briela, who was too young to understand the magnitude of her family's problems. And here we are, even now, everyone pretending this is a normal Saturday afternoon between neighbors. It's like we wandered into a swingers party, he thought. Except that instead of getting naked, any minute now one of them is going to rip open my son's throat and drink his blood. Take us all hostage and announce their plans for the second coming, a new master race. Resistance is futile, now drink your punch.

Behind them, Amy laughed.

54

When June came out, Kyle almost choked on his cola. Her hair was slicked back and glistening, and she had changed into yellow terrycloth shorts and a gray hooded top sheer enough for him to see her yellow bikini top beneath. She chatted with her mom as she set the patio table, but she smiled at him twice.

He kept trying to look mellow, idling by the pool, but inside he was twisted up about what they had done. He kept seeing that security guard lying on the ground, the event replaying, infecting his wide-awake dreams. In some he was torn apart, cut up in a hundred places like someone had gone at him with a lawn-mower blade. In other dreams, like the one last night, the man's limbs were severed at the joints, as if he had been drawn and quartered there on the parking lot. Each time the event replayed itself, Kyle and June were stuck to him, unable to run away, slipping and sliding in a pool of the man's gooey blood like flies on a sheet of yellow flypaper.

He told himself he was just scared. His mind was fucked up. He'd been going stir crazy while grounded and June had not answered any of his texts. The rest of

411

that exchange had been amazing, but most of all it had seemed far more intimate than this – the sight of her tromping around in daylight. Now she was a person, not a disembodied series of digital words, and he had no idea how to talk to her.

'I am so sorry,' she said, coming up behind him, rolling her eyes. She pulled two lounge chairs over by the side of the pool. 'Have a seat.'

Kyle ass-hopped back into the lounge chair. He fished for clever lines, got nothing.

'Looks like our parents are hitting it off,' she said.

'Yeah.' *Think of something, idiot.* But he didn't know how to look into her eyes.

'Are you doing okay?' she said.

'I guess so. Are you?'

She took his hand. 'It's going to be all right,' she said. 'It will all be over soon.'

'If you say so.'

She squeezed, her eyes watery. 'It won't be easy, but no one will ever be able to hurt us again. Like that man down by the creek. The way he hit you.'

'You saw that?'

'You handled it very well.'

'I got my ass kicked.'

'No, you were a man. You didn't resort to unnecessary violence. You're good inside. You give me hope that all of this is going to be all right.'

Kyle looked at her. 'Is it? Going to be all right?'

'I don't know. But no matter how strange it seems, we can still do things.'

Things.

What was she offering? Couldn't be what he was thinking ...

She took his other hand. 'All kinds of things. Whatever you want.'

Kyle's hands trembled in hers, but she would not release him, and he imagined taking her body now, here on the patio chair, his hands around her ribs, easing her back, touching her skin under the shirt, sliding her yellow bikini top up, over, the underwire pushing her nipples before his mouth was on her. He wanted to feel inside her. He wanted to use his fingers and press his mouth to her, lick the heat from her to stop him from shivering, to erase the horrible dreams and replace them with a world that revolved around her.

She leaned her forehead against his and her lips parted.

'June, Kyle!' Cassandra called from the patio. 'Come get some food.'

June pulled away, her eyes filled with tears. 'Stay with me,' she said. 'Just a little longer now and then we'll have eternity.'

She stood and led him to the table. Everyone was milling around plates of spicy corn on the cob, spinach dip in a bread bowl, and other tapas Kyle didn't recognize. He wasn't hungry, not for food. He couldn't stop staring at her. He didn't notice until minutes later that none of them were eating. Mrs and Mr Render were too busy talking with his parents, but they weren't even holding plates. June said she was on a diet and only sucked on her crostini. The boy, Adolph, was just staring at his plate, and maybe the rest of them, in disgust. Something was wrong with him. The greenish hue in the cheeks, the pinpoint brown eyes and patchy homemade buzz cut. The kid gave Kyle the creeps. They all did.

Except for June.

55

At first she was afraid of Adolph, but soon Briela realized he wasn't so different from all the other boys at school, and he was kind of cute. He pretended to be tough, but he was just shy, even though he couldn't stop looking at her. They argued about which kinds of pop were best. He said Orange Crush but she liked Cherry Coke. He showed her his hiding place behind the trees, where he'd built a little wooden fort that looked like a rabbit cage, and no, she did not want to get in it.

Now they were running in the yard, pretending they were hunting (and being hunted by) the alien creatures he made up, hiding behind trees and the house's little coves and overhangs, in the garages, then racing around the pool. Briela thought it was dumb at first, since she knew the aliens were make believe. But Adolph kept adding details in between attacks. The aliens were only two feet tall. They had sharp green eyes and bald heads and long skinny tails, pink and pointy. The mouths were small, hardly large enough to fit around a carrot stick, but inside, Adolph said, were seven rows of teeth, clear as glass and sharp enough to bite through wood.

Around that time, even though it was daylight and she wasn't really afraid, Briela could feel the little creatures watching her, hiding behind the bushes and the big trees that threw deep shade across the backyard. She could hear their quick alien footsteps in the grass, the scuffing of their scales against the tree bark as they came for her. She ran behind Addie, always trying to catch up, but he was too fast. He kept laughing and tricking her, turning this way and that, taunting her even as the creatures got closer.

Every time she looked in Addie's eyes, he was so excited, she could see that he was pleased, that he liked her, because in playing his made-up game she made it real for him. He whispered in her ear, his lips cool at her neck.

There's two of them right behind you. See? Back there, behind the gazebo. He keeps poking his head out, waiting for the right time to pounce.

We have to run now or else they'll get you and eat you. They like to eat the feet first. They'll dive at your heels and drag you down. They'll eat your toes and make a cake out of your brains.

We have to go now, hurry! The one with the yellow eyes is the meanest one, the leader, and he's on his way to get you right now!

And not long after that Briela lost control. She ran wild, shrieking, her panic thrilling and pure, the vividness of the things he described as real as the chairs on the patio, as her brother and June sitting around the table. She ran blindly, her chest aching, her tummy knotted tight, and still she fell behind Adolph. She came to a stop and slumped down in the grass, unable to go on. He was laughing and making his fighting sounds. He took his shirt off and whirled it above his head. He was a devil, a wolf-boy. And she was frightened for him as he kept looking back, watching her, watching her watching him, showing off for her.

Something was wrong with them, she knew now. Not just Adolph, but the whole family. She should have tried harder. She should have told her family to stay away and never set foot in their home, because now they were friends and soon it would be too late to stop the monsters that were coming for them all.

56

'I'm still not used to this Colorado sun,' Render said, removing his sunglasses. 'I feel exposed under this big sky, like someone took the lid off the world.'

In the kitchen, Render removed another Stella from the side-by-side and handed it to Mick. He wasn't drinking, Mick noticed. But he did not have the air of a teetotaler. If Render had the air of anything at all, it was that of a playboy or a prince, an entitled man-child with a streak of sadness beneath the cool veneer. He moved with a slow, casual grace, but there were fine lines around his eyes, as well as a certain weariness in the eyes themselves, a fried, battle-tested numbness only men of tragedy, heavy drug use, or middle age acquire. Something inside Render was not well, not well at all.

'Can't imagine it any other way,' Mick said.

'And those mountains? All that forest? No thanks. Might as well put your family in a rubber raft out in the middle of the Pacific.'

Mick laughed.

'I'm serious,' Render said. 'What do you have here?

Cougars, rattlesnakes, bears. You ever take the family camping, Mick? Spend a few nights roughing it?'

'Years ago.'

'It's like that thing on the news. Those two teen boys went up the canyon with some beers and a gun, hoping to have a little harmless fun.'

Render looked at him for some acknowledgement.

'I must have missed that one,' Mick said.

'Less than ten miles from town, they just disappeared.' Render wiped his hands theatrically. 'Rangers found a few scraps of clothing and a bunch of blood in the dirt. The boys were never seen again. Makes you wonder, doesn't it?'

'Wonder what?' Mick said.

'What got 'em.'

Mick shrugged and followed Render to a wrought-iron spiral staircase cut into the corner of the den. 'Where are you from, anyway?'

'The Midwest originally,' Render said. 'But I've moved a lot. Can't say I'm a native of any place, not like you.'

'How'd you know I was a native?'

'I know all about you, Mick. Remember?'

Mick felt his insides clench.

'Watch your step here.' Render descended the narrow steps in a nimble, almost sideways canter. 'This one's a little tight.'

They reached the basement, a single long and unfinished space. Wood framing had been erected here and there about the concrete floor, a drain at its center, and

419

some drywall lay stacked in a corner. A row of huge cardboard boxes lined one foundation wall, like they had ordered ten refrigerators, but there were no labels.

'I have only the one room for now,' Render said, walking to the south end. A bundle of sewage-gauge PVC piping lay across the floor, and an industrial-sized sink of the type Mick had in the Straw. Three basins, wide flares to stack dishes. 'Center of operations is under construction.'

In the far left corner stood a brick oven, something he had considered putting in the Straw back in the days when he was mulling an Italian makeover. Wood-fired pizzas, rotisserie chickens, a hearth that warmed the entire dining room. He thought it strange Render had installed one in his basement.

They approached an unpainted door set in a wall so wide Mick had mistaken it for the end of the house. Render opened the door and stood to one side.

I asked you to wait outside, Mr Render. You're not supposed to be in here.

Go ahead then, Troy. Open the door.

Mick entered, and Render flipped on a light as he closed the door behind them.

It was not an office of the kind Mick had ever seen. The room was at least sixteen by twenty, and the change in decor was disorienting. The carpet was bright aqua blue. Two black leather sofas faced each other, a tinted yellow glass table between them. At the back of the room was a twelve-foot swath of desk space built into the wall, with three black computer monitors lined up, the blade server machines humming beneath. On the wall was a map of the United States with clusters of red pins around half a dozen metro areas. Five cell phones were arrayed on a pad of black felt. Surreal canvases of modern art were mounted on the walls, desert motifs featuring black saguaros, skinny coyotes, blood-red suns. Others with no real scene, only mesmerizing saturation. Gaudy maroons and blacks, wilted flowers of orange and pink. Another wall featured a series of paintings with purple skies and black amusement park rides, carousels, a pointy ferris wheel, forests lit by gas lamps, futuristic bicycles, small leashed dragons, faeries, swirling Van Gogh stars, paths of emerald grass, and strange men with handlebar mustaches courting buxom women twirling parasols.

On the end tables, black crystal balls were perched on chrome vases. A screen of red silk, like an Indian sari, was mummy-wrapped around a white plastic mannequin with no arms or legs, her busty trunk impaled on a black iron rod mounted to the ceiling. What Mick knew about art would fit into a matchbook, but if forced he would have called it Alice in Wonderland by way of New Age crap with a death miasma. It was unpleasant to look at, all of it cruel in some way.

'I collect strange art,' Render said. 'Things that do not reflect the world out there, things which remind me of nothing. It helps me unplug, prepare for the other side.'

'It's ... something.'

'Have a seat.'

Mick sat on one of the leather couches, Render collapsed across from him. Here they were, all done flirting,

421

and Mick had the strongest urge to run now, just grab his wife and kids and get the hell out of here while he still could. But he didn't. Because he was no longer afraid. Maybe, in that moment, their shattered lives weren't worth worrying about and there was nothing left for Render to do that had not already been done. The two of them stared at each other for a minute, taking in the silence and each other's flat expressions.

'So,' Mick said. 'How did you get to be this way?'

Render raised an eyebrow.

'Obscene wealth,' Mick said.

'Ah.' Render nodded. 'Does your dog have a chip?'

'A what?'

Render patted the back of his neck. 'A microchip. An implant for identification purposes.'

'Amy adopted Thom from the humane society. I have no idea.'

'Funny name for a dog, by the way,' Render said.

'Amy used to be a Radiohead fan.'

'I don't get it.'

'He's a Yorkshire. Thom. Yor— Never mind. Not important.'

Render nodded. 'Well, they chip most of them these days. If he does, there's about a seventy per cent chance I made it. Or, my former company. I still hold the patents. Little pill about the size of a grain of rice. Made hundreds of millions on the dumb things, sold my stock in the early nineties.'

'But it's not enough to save you,' Mick said. 'You're still dying.'

Render nodded. 'How far did you get last night?'

'With what?'

'When she came to you.'

'Hey, I didn't touch—'

'Relax, Mick. I'm talking about the dream. If she did what I asked her to do, you should have stumbled onto something.'

Mick puckered his mouth, said, 'Nope.'

Render tried to stare him down. Mick offered him nothing.

'All right,' Render said. 'For a long time I assumed you had to know, because the alternative seemed impossible. But I have to admit, the way you've stonewalled me, I'm still not sure. So I'm going to ask you one more time. Do you know what this is all about? Or are you just trying to drive up the negotiation?'

'Who said we're negotiating?'

'I already offered you the house,' Render said.

'I have a house. It's our home and we intend to stay in it.'

'I recouped your embezzled funds.'

'That was your money,' Mick said. 'For show. Clever, but you didn't fool me. Someone else already got to Sapphire.'

'You know who?' Render said.

'I have a pretty good idea.'

Render stood and went to the desk built into the wall. From underneath he removed a silver suitcase of the sort drug smugglers prefer. He carried it to the yellow glass table and set it down. He worked the combination locks, popped the latches, and spun the open mouth of it toward Mick. It was filled with cash.

'Unmarked, of course,' Render said.

'How much?'

'Three point five.'

'Is that all you got?'

'How much more do you need?'

'I don't need any of it.'

'I can put it in an overseas account. I have everything arranged. Think about what kind of security that will afford your family.'

'I haven't done anything to earn it.'

'Oh, but you have, Mick. You've done so much. And now it is time to trust each other. I'm going to lay my cards on the table. We're going to finish our business today, because the world is changing quickly and you really do need to prepare yourself for what's coming.'

Island Living

When Bob Percy forced me to look down over the balcony, everything I thought I knew about life and death and the borders in between vented from me in a single, childish gasp of disbelief. Of course, by then disbelieving was no longer an option.

All of the families, including Bob's wife and children, were standing in the swimming pool – which was mercifully not lit. I could see that some were naked, others were clothed. They weren't doing anything except standing in the water, facing the ocean like mannequins. Sculptures in a fountain. It was not a large pool but there were more than twenty of them crammed into it like sardines, standing shoulder to shoulder. Husbands and wives, the teens and younger children, some as young as five or six in the shallow end. At least two were elderly, perhaps grandma and grandpa had been invited on the trip. The rain continued to plop and sprinkle around them, but they didn't mind the dark or the weather or anything else. I don't know what their minds were on, or if at that point they even possessed minds.

I stared at them for I don't know how long. I was

beyond shock now. I was completely unmoored. They were so still and collective in their demeanor, I felt as though I were witnessing a ritual, that these people were waiting on a divine revelation, or for their cult leader to appear.

'Do you see it?' Bob whispered beside me.

Of course I saw it.

'No, not them,' Bob suggested.

What else was there to see?

But then I did see it. The water. The surface of the pool was as he had described the water inside the cenote his son had fallen into. It was silver, twinkling and flashing like his arm had been. No light shone down on it – the moon that night was obscured by clouds – but the water reflected something, glowed like a thousand tiny dulled diamonds, scales on the back of a giant snake, writhing and shimmering, alive.

They had taken to the pool, and taken it with them.

'It's beautiful,' Bob said. 'You can't imagine what it feels like.'

'You've been in with them?' I whispered in disgust.

'I don't feel refreshed,' Bob said. '*I feel reborn*.'

The wind was still blowing and the waves were swishing and sighing not a hundred feet away. We were speaking softly. They couldn't have heard us.

Nevertheless, at that moment they began turning in unison, like they were all experiencing the same premonition or the queer sensation of being watched. They turned and looked up at us on the balcony. At first their faces were nothing more than expressionless dark spots

426

in the darker night. But soon I could see faint spots of white, their eyes and teeth, and then more white, in the same places, and I realized they were grinning. They began to murmur and mumble unintelligibly and it did not make sense but they were clearly ... aroused ... by our presence.

That is when I turned and ran away from them. I ran down the stairs of the Percy villa, out the front door, into the night. I ran blindly up the road and I don't remember looking back, but I *do* remember them chasing me, walking after me, all twenty or thirty of them half naked and drained and maybe that was my imagination working on a boost of adrenaline as I had never experienced, but then again maybe it wasn't.

I crashed into our villa and woke my wife and our children. I told them to leave everything, throw on some clothes and get in the car. We had rented a Dodge Durango with four bald tires and a weak battery but it started. The tires slipped and squeaked on the wet road but we got out of there. I drove us to the tiny airport just a couple of miles away, but of course there were no planes available, not at a little after three in the morning. I was all but hysterical. The first ferry left at six but that was too slow and what if some of them decided to take the ferry with us? We purchased tickets for a puddle jumper leaving Vieques at 5:45 a.m. Whatever I had seen, whatever Bob had seen me run away from, I could not shake the feeling that he and the others would be displeased. That they wanted me to participate. That they would come looking for us.

We needed a place to hide for the next two hours.

I drove in circles, up and down the narrow streets of Isabel Segunda until I found the police station – and even then I debated stopping. Every minute that we lingered was another minute we were at risk of the infection, or another encounter with the infected. But I could not in good conscience just leave them to their own devices, possibly spreading it. I was certain it had changed them in some terrible way.

I knocked on the door but the police station or small annex we found was deserted. We crossed the island and found another in Esperanza, also deserted. We searched these two small towns for a patrol car or officer on horseback but the island was asleep. No one walked the wet streets. I had left my phone at the villa and we had no other options. We went back to the airport. We would deal with matters from the big island, after completing what was only a twenty-minute flight.

By sunset we were safely among the masses of travelers at San Juan International. I checked us into a chain hotel across the street. I told my wife the truth, of the infection from the well, sparing her the worst details but mentioning dozens of 'victims'. We inspected ourselves and the kids, but, perhaps incredibly for me (for he had touched me at least five times), none of us displayed the symptoms that Bob had. We showered and scrubbed anyway, and dressed in new clothes purchased from the lobby gift shop.

I called the police department and two officers met me in the lobby of the hotel. I forced myself to speak calmly in as plain a language as possible. I told the truth inasmuch as I could without making them think I was insane while also scaring them enough to ensure they sent manpower back to the island. I gave them the name of our villas and the address and said there was what I believed to be an infection or outbreak of some kind among the people renting units next door. I used the term buckets of blood, said six families had been sickened, some were possibly dead. In an effort to 'cleanse themselves' they had taken to the pool in the middle of the night, but many were not 'coherent'. The ones I had seen were catatonic but upright, I explained.

To my surprise, a detective on Vieques called me less than two hours later, just before we were to board our American Airlines flight at 12:45. We were in a food court in the terminal, seated at a crowded cafeteria-style restaurant. The kids were tired and sullen, but my wife and I were still filled with anxiety. The detective introduced himself as Javier Arguelles and he sounded every bit a professional officer who had taken my report seriously, not some Third World lackey who promised to look into things *mañana*.

He confirmed my name and the address of the villa we had stayed in. He stated that he and a fellow officer of the Vieques *policia* had visited our abandoned villa as well as the six neighboring villas. He and his partner introduced themselves to the tenants (he would not confirm their names to me, though I had given the ones I remembered to him) and were granted permission to perform a search of all six villas. The families were not injured and did not appear to be ill, and all were friendly but expressed dismay at the inquiry. They claimed to have no idea who I was.

No rooms with blood. No traces of any violence or of a cover-up. Just five families cooperating with what was sounding more and more like a crank call. Detective Arguelles asked me to repeat my story, and I did so before asking him to confirm that he had the right address and complex of villas. He did, but by now I was beginning to annoy him. I lost my temper and eventually the call was disconnected. I am not sure if Detective Arguelles hung up on me or if it was simply a dropped call.

Perhaps they got to him.

The airline announced that our flight was boarding and I saw no reason to stay. Whatever further inquires I decided to pursue, I could do so from home. We left Puerto Rico and our lives resumed, but I did not forget about that night or any of the things I had seen. The image of those people in the pool haunted me for many days and nights, and I lost a lot of sleep wondering what had become of the families. Had they gotten off the island, like we had? Had it changed them permanently, or was it a passing sickness? If they had survived, were they functional enough to return to their normal lives?

The answer to those questions came nine days after we returned home to Colorado. My wife caught it first. Then my son, and very soon after, our daughter. I was the last to go, so I was the one who watched them bleed and writhe in agony. Twenty-six minutes was all it took to bring all four of us down. It happened too fast for any of us to call 9-1-1. By the time I thought of reaching for the phone, my wife was dead. By the time I realized my attempts to revive her had failed, the kids were gone. By the time I surfaced from the rapture of grief long enough to feel the fever spiking, my wife was rising from the bathtub.

She cleaned up the children and locked them in the basement. She could not bear to look at them alone. She waited for me to come back, and then we began the discussion about how to deal with our new condition. We decided not to tell the children. Perhaps one day they would be ready for it, but not then, not that first night, or during that first endless week when we all stayed in the house together, showering and showering and pretending we were 'only sick with a terrible flu'. We did not leave the house for six days, but on the seventh night we were forced to leave.

We were very hungry and the food we had in the pantry had done nothing to slake our appetites.

Of course my wife and I fooled ourselves in more ways than one. The children knew how they were different, how we had all changed. But as we took our first meal together, as our eyes met over the first body we took there in the field off of Niwot Road, a high-school boy walking home late because he was too drunk to drive, we each understood that we now shared a tremendous secret. We each understood that this was a thing outside of the rest of our lives. We each understood that

431

we would have to be very careful until we found a cure, or a way out.

It occurs to me now, we never really left the island. We came home, but we have been stranded ever since. We understood a great many things about what it meant for all of us, but we did not talk about it. We never have. How could we?

Sometimes it doesn't seem real enough to bother.

57

'Tell me how you found us,' Mick said.

'We were there, of course. In the fourth villa.' Render stood and began to pace the room, studying his art. 'After it all went down, I did not know the first names of the other families, but I had their surnames and, more importantly, I knew Bob Percy owned a car dealership in Mt Horeb, Wisconsin.

'Using a Yellow Pages Internet search, I phoned Bob at his dealership. It was a Friday morning, five days after we had returned. A receptionist transferred me and Bob answered in less than a minute. I recognized his voice instantly. He did not recognize mine, nor did he remember me when I introduced myself by name, nor through the recollection of what had happened.

'"Buddy," Bob Percy laughed, and it was the same laugh I had heard less than a week ago, "you sound like a nice guy, but I don't have the foggiest dang clue what you're talking about."

'"Vieques," I insisted, clutching the phone. "Last week. I was in the villa next door. The well. The storm. Your neighbors . . . ?"

'"Via-what?" Bob said. "Where is that again?"

'"In Puerto Rico," I shouted. "Why are you bullshitting me?"

'"You must be confused, sir." And he was so genial. He was either an amazing actor or truly believing the words coming out of his mouth. He said, "I've never heard of Vieques, though I wish I had. My family and I have never vacationed outside of the fifty states. I wouldn't mind taking a trip like that right about now. Hardly November here and already colder than frozen snot."

'"Your health problems," I said. "I know all about them. You need a new hip, you have diabetes, and more than likely a heart condition."

'Bob said, "Ahhhh, okay, now we're getting somewhere. See, now I know you got the wrong guy. I don't have any problems like that and I have never felt better in my life."

'I argued. I pleaded and raged and calmed down again and Bob Percy, give him this, he was patient and polite, but he did not give in. I realized there was nothing more to accomplish over the phone. I was furious. How many Bob Percys are there in the world who live in Mt Horeb and own a car dealership?

'I was in the process of purchasing a plane ticket to Madison six days later when my wife showed me the news item on MSNBC: *Mt Horeb, Wisconsin family found dead in home.* The media called it a heinous murder-suicide. People who knew the couple claimed they were such decent folks but yes, matter of fact, they had been

434

having serious financial problems. That was the story, but I didn't believe it.

'The reason I did not believe it was because the Percy children, Tanya and Timothy, as well as Bob's wife, Lynn, had been beheaded before someone moved Bob to the garage, doused him in gasoline, and set him aflame. Where the investigators saw a mentally unstable man under financial duress, I saw local townfolk, neighbors, someone who *knew* what an abomination they had become, coming for the Percys in the night, like villagers waving torches and pitchforks outside of Frankenstein's last stand.

'Two weeks later another item broke in the same area, this one concerning two high-school students – a sixteen-year-old boy and his fifteen-year-old girlfriend – from Dodgeville, Wisconsin. That's a small town less than twenty miles from Mt Horeb. They had been missing and their parents thought they had run away together fifteen days earlier – they had disappeared just one day before the Percy massacre.

'The girl's Chevy Caprice was found in the woods near Yellowstone Lake, less than twenty miles from her home, covered with tree branches. A hunter stumbled upon it and though he was seventy-eight years old and hardened by farming life and two wars, he required medical attention from the shock of the discovery. The bodies inside had been stripped to the bone, devoured by something the likes of which this hunter had never seen.

'I tracked down the other families through the rental

agent who owned the villas. She was based in Seattle and knew nothing useful. From there it was not difficult to locate them. I bought a large map of the States and a box of red pins. I followed the local, state, and national news. The map began to grow clusters of the sort police use to triangulate a serial killer. The clusters matched the metro areas of each of the families. Disappearances, missing women and children who went for a walk or a hike and never came back. Two of my investigators connected the Greenwalds of Las Vegas to three beheadings in the Nevada desert thought to be the work of organized crime, the bodies desecrated by coyotes. A spike in disappearances from the casino hotels. It went on and on. The faces on the milk cartons changed.

'For the next two years I became obsessed. I traveled, I surveilled, and eventually I introduced myself. I got close to and met with three of the families. The Robertsons of Charlotte, North Carolina, and the Weavers of Boise, Idaho. Both claimed never to have been to the island of Vieques and pretended to not remember me. All of the family members were in exceptional health. The Chavez family were back in Miami, but were increasing their travels to New York City to visit relatives there, where they had a greater population to blend into and poach from. I rescued them from a warehouse in Hoboken where they been living like animals, stockpiling victims. Even after I confronted them with the evidence of their nighttime adventures, they did not remember what had happened, and they did not know what they had become. Except, in a way, they did.

You could see it deep down inside of them, buried like a history of incest.

'Whatever it did to them, it not only has the power to heal, like it only temporarily healed Bob Percy, it created a dark other inside them that allowed each of them to carry on separate lives. Dahmer, Gacy, the Zodiac and Green River killers. All of the great hunters operated with separate personas. It's how they got through their sloppy days.

'I helped them get it under control. I established safe houses for the families, fortified compounds where they could keep a low profile until everything was organized. And I knew there had to be others. What if this thing could be harnessed at the source? Imagine the power of containment, the value of patenting, the government contracts, the number of lives this could save in combat theater, controlled manufacturing in the pharmaceutical industry, a cure for heart disease, alzheimer's, cancer . . .

'I went back to Vieques, of course, making three trips in the eight months that followed that first trip. I searched every square inch of that island for the cenote, but I never found it. A small team of archeology students I paid to scour the jungle happened upon a blast site full of sand and rock near a beach that was being graded for new construction, but there was no well. Maybe the Navy caught on and filled it in. Maybe the local authorities covered up one of the last great mysteries. But all that is history. Dying history. The world is changing and we have a lot of work to do.

'What I am curious about is why you are so quiet. I

437

find it strange you have not asked me the most important question, because there is a gaping hole in my account of what happened on that island. What do you think, Mick? Did you see it? Do you see the black bottomless well in your world?'

Mick did not respond for a long time. He was trying to see a way through this and the only available path was dark.

'I don't know,' he said. 'I don't know what you want from me.'

'Yes, you do.' Render leaned forward. 'The villas, Mick. A row of six. Six villas, six families. But I only mentioned five. The Greenwalds, Gomezes, Robertsons, Weavers and Percys . . . '

'And the Renders,' Mick finished. 'You're infected like the others.'

'Such an ugly word, infected. We prefer evolved.' Render smiled. 'So that's only six. You're forgetting, Cass and I were hiding in the sixth unit, the one you never entered during your inspections with Bob Percy. There is still the matter of the seventh family, the one in the stand-alone unit. What happened to them? Who are they? What have they become?'

Troy the security guard turned away and opened the master bedroom door. He stepped in, shining his light around. Into the bathroom, around the fireplace and bench seating area, across the neatly made bed.

There's nobody in here, Mr Render. What did you say you saw?

I don't remember, Troy. I get so confused these days. The

438

timing of these things. It's hard to keep track of the nights when you live like this.

Why did you shut the door, Mr Render? Sir? I'm going to ask you to back away now and please exit the house.

One of us was here already. Check the walk-in closet, Troy. I know they're in here somewhere.

'It makes you wonder,' Render continued, standing, pacing the room. 'When the living see the dead, we call them ghosts. But when the dead see their own kind, when the dead see their victims, what do we call them? What do you call yours, Mick?'

The light in the room seemed to dim. Mick felt funny inside, and then he felt nothing at all, as if his physical sensations were only memories.

'It's over,' Mick said softly.

'It's only beginning,' Render said. 'Eugene and Virginia Sapphire are not over. You saw them. Were they behaving like the good little dead senior citizens they're supposed to be? Or were they ... something else?'

The closet door opened then, and Troy turned, raising his Maglite. But it was too late for him. Eugene and Virginia came forth, healing and bleeding and hungry, and it was too late for all of them. Oh, Amy, I'm so sorry I left you alone. I should have taken them out myself.

'Which one of you was it, Mick? Can you even keep track of your family any more?'

Mick felt trapped inside a box. He couldn't breathe. He felt as though he were having a heart attack. He placed a hand over his chest and felt nothing but a deep ache spreading into his limbs. His heart did not beat. His lungs did not fill. His body was so heavy. He was so very tired. He was always tired now, except when he was fighting to preserve –

Render stopped pacing and hovered above him, eyes alight. 'We breathe as if by habit. We sleep with open eyes. We can barely stomach ordinary food and we are always hungry. We bleed without purpose and our hearts beat only in memory.'

'No,' Mick said. 'You're sick, a parasite.'

'And you're running out of time!' Render yelled. 'I can't keep cleaning up after you. It's time to work together and increase our numbers or we are headed for extinction!'

'You don't know us. You have no right . . . '

Render said, 'How long do you think you can continue to operate in this town before someone sees you the way I have seen you? Eric Pritchard and Jason Wells, cut down like trees in the forest. Who was there to hear them scream?'

We walked into the woods together, all dressed in black. We'd followed the Honda in Amy's Passat, then parked up the road from the turn-off, covering the car with pine branches. The children did not ask questions, only followed their parents, their instincts awakening as they trekked deeper into the hills. The silence between us as what we were about to do stirred our hunger. I pointed up the hill and separated from them as I took the road and they flanked the boys in the gully. I looked back one last time at my son's face and saw a kind of frightened wonderment and, beneath that, predatory intensity.

'Officer Terrance Fielding of the Boulder Police

Department,' Render said. 'What was happening in your restaurant after hours, Mick?'

I crouched before the bar's refrigeration unit while Terry droned on and on about the missing dentist. I saw white, and I changed. I turned and rose, finding the baseball bat under the bar and bringing it up and around so fast Fielding never had time to pull his gun. The blow staving in the temple as the cop spun sideways and flopped to the floor. I rushed around the bar to finish it, thud thud thud, the wood striking the skull. Dragging Fielding into the kitchen to find Carlos my chef and Jamie my best server watching me, the blood draining from their faces. Carlos going for the door as Jamie screamed, but they didn't get past the hanging rack of skillets before I caught them. Quick bites along the necks. The long night of sitting with them, waiting for them to resurrect.

'Dr Roger Lertz and his mistress, Bonnie Abrahams, whose bodies were never found. Why did Amy take the boat back out after I had already pulled you out of the water? When did you get to them? Before or after lunch? Did you take them alone or with your entire family? What was it, envy? Did he provoke you?'

Kyle was excited by the sight of blood. All of us were excited by the prospect of blood. We turned back to fetch the ski, then trolled in the afternoon sun, coasting up on Roger's vessel before the dentist even knew we were there. I boarded first, opening the cabin door, seeing Bonnie in there with her broken nose.

'It was an accident,' Roger said. 'She slipped, Mick. Tell him, Bonnie.'

Bonnie was crying. 'You bastard. Don't touch me! Get him away from me!'

Roger lunged, calling her a lying bitch, and I stepped in to separate them, Roger fighting back, fighting back and losing. Amy and the kids boarded to join me, breaking a bottle over Roger's head and then jagging him across the throat while Bonnie screamed at us, a free for all until the berth was packed with bodies thrashing against one another.

The swimming after, to wash away the blood. To cleanse. To forget.

I dropped my family off on the dock. Silent, mutual under-standing between me and Amy: You have to go back and clean it up, clean it all up, Mick. *She waited and waited for me to erase all evidence, throwing the bodies overboard, and then I slipped, knocking my head against the gunwale, falling into the lake.*

How many hours was Roger underwater before he revived? How did he spend his hours waiting for dark to fall, until it was safe to come back and warn me about our new neighbors?

'And why do you keep returning to the lake?' Render continued. 'The swimming. The others couldn't stay away from the water, either, as if that well was still call-ing them, trying to bring you all home. Myra Blaylock. You must remember her.'

Myra's bronze minivan exiting the lot, Amy's wagon emerg-ing from the shadows with its headlights off to follow her. I turned away, lying to myself, even after I returned home that night to find her Passat missing, the guest room empty.

'She was your lover before any of this started. She vis-ited your restaurant and was never seen again. The boys in the parking lot. I watched them be destroyed myself, and I have a good bit of it on video. Would you care to

442

see the footage? If you watch closely, you can actually see the moment of change. The rage comes over you and you turn, rising from the ground with the strength of five men.'

I was blind with rage, seeing spots, my blood roaring, glands seldom utilized sent into battle. Despite what should have been a broken femur, a shattered ankle, a paralyzing black-out concussion, I got back up, throwing them off as I sprang to my feet and the pain-obliterating rage cut through my fog and sent me into an ecstatic fury.

'No? Then how about this?' Render went to the table, opened a box, and removed a rubber swim cap. White, with a blue Speedo logo, smeared with dried blood. He flapped it in front of Mick's face and dropped it in Mick's lap. 'Do you recognize that? Your daughter likes to swim, yes? It protects her hair and disguises her rather nicely. I found it at that house off of Eagle Trail, where Melanie Smith took her morning runs. Melanie was last seen at your daughter's birthday party, but I cleaned her up. Melanie and a family of three. Hunted down by a nasty little blonde monster. There are more, people close to you. What is happening to them, Mick? Why does everyone who crosses you and your family wind up in pieces? How much longer can your family survive without protection? Where does the evil go? The Percys lost control early, but the other families worked with me and learned how to integrate their Gift. I'm offering you fortress and fortune to join us for the coming change, but you have to do your part. *You have to do your part!*'

Mick shoved Render away and stood. His fury was

back, as all-consuming as it had been in the parking lot the night he was attacked. He was going to kill his neighbor, put an end to it all right here once and for all so they could go back to the way things were. He opened his mouth to tear into Render and someone upstairs started screaming hysterically.

58

Amy was studying Cassandra's beautiful face, the fine blue veins beneath her cheeks that touched the corners of her mouth, when the hostess's eyes shifted abruptly behind her sunglasses, registering trouble.

Kyle shouted, 'Briela, no!'

Amy turned and spilled her wine, the red falling in nearly suspended blobs as the afternoon slowed with the hyper-clarity of impending trauma. In the final split seconds before everything changed, Amy felt the wine splashing on her foot and glanced down to see the red there staining her sandals, dripping from her toes.

The night she first met Cassandra, on the patio, when her strange new friend stepped on the wine glass. Amy bent over with a broom in one hand and a dust pan in the other, kneeling on her flagstone patio, leaning down with a hungry moan, tongue flicking, first on the stone and then tasting the sweet copper of Cassandra's blood. Lapping it up like an animal, every last drop, until the stone was clean. She thought of the orange cinnamon rolls, how she retreated into some darkened corner of her mind where Amy Nash could continue living as she always had while the other one, the hungry beast inside of her, came forth.

The wine splashed around her feet.

Amy looked up.

Life as they knew it ended.

There was a flash of blonde hair, her daughter in motion, running full speed and in the same blur a tremendous banging of metal, the sound of cymbals crashing.

Briela was looking over her shoulder at Adolph when she collided with the Weber kettle. The entire bag of coals were now, to a briquette, at their white-hot cooking prime. Briela tripped over the tripod legs and sprawled between the toppled grill's basin and flipped lid, rolling in dusty clods of red-white charcoal that sank into the skin of her chest, neck, right cheek and arm. Her beautiful blonde hair singed and flamed to life, her blouse cratered and smoked. The flesh over her ribs and shoulder blackened, rippling and curling, and great blisters of pink swelled and opened around her collar, up the side of her face.

And in the midst of her own private inferno, Briela did not scream or cry out, only blinked, her mouth working at sounds that refused to come, her beautiful blue eyes large and sky bright. She was frightened, Amy saw, but not of what had happened. She was terrified of what it meant for them, what would happen now.

She knew, Amy thought. *She's not crying because she's known all along and she's been trying so hard to be a good girl, to conceal it the way we all have.*

For a moment, time elasticized beyond all reason, no one moved. Amy was rooted by the broad daylight reality of it. Cass stood by, her expression dull, eyes unreadable behind her glasses, while before them Briela rolled in the fire, thumping side to side like a small mammal caught in a trap. She used her good arm to prop herself up and patted the small flames at the bib of her new overalls.

'It doesn't hurt,' she reassured them, a child afraid of being spanked. 'I didn't mean to, Mommy. It was an accident.'

'For the love of God,' Ingrid screeched behind them, running from the house with a towel, breaking the spell. They used her to watch us, Amy realized. Convinced her to help and now Ingrid was with them, part of this day. The day of our intervention.

And then there was only her love for her daughter, Amy's undying love for Briela. It did not matter what they had become or what happened next. Her daughter needed her. Her daughter, who would never be an adult, would always need her.

Amy sprang forward at last, but Ingrid got to Briela first, clobbering the girl with the towel. Amy's feet, shod with designer strappy heels, slid on the patio and she fell and rolled among the coals but felt no pain. She crawled and reached for Briela but Ingrid was already pulling the thrashing girl away.

The towel covered the face and most of the body, but Briela's right arm was flung to one side, stirring dumbly on the stone like a lizard's amputated tail. For a moment Amy was sure it was no longer attached, but when Ingrid lifted Briela the arm came up with the rest of the bundle

447

and folded against their sitter's body, leaving a streak of black and red across the white stone patio.

'Call an ambulance!' Kyle shouted, in denial. 'Call 9-1-1!'

'It's all right, Kyle,' Cass said with cool authority. 'There's no need.'

'Give me my daughter!' Amy screamed.

Ingrid turned, cooing into the girl's ear as she backed away from Amy. The small body writhed against her breast and the small feet twitched at Ingrid's thighs. Psychological reflexes for dumb limbs.

'Ingrid, give her to me,' Cass said.

'What are you going to do with her?' Ingrid said as Cass walked toward her. 'Stay away. All of you, keep away from her. You're sick. She needs help!'

Amy screamed again. Briela's head lolled over Ingrid's shoulder.

'Mom!' Kyle was wailing, fumbling Egg. 'Where's Dad? What's going on? Where's Dad?'

June moved alongside Kyle and took the device away, mumbling to him urgently. Kyle stared at his girlfriend with pleading panic but the look in her eyes stopped him and he settled into a numb daze.

Ingrid continued backing away from Amy and Cassandra.

'Give her to me, Ingrid!' Cass said. 'You don't have any idea what's happening.'

Amy wailed at both of them. 'What did you do with my husband? Give me my daughter!'

'Stay back!' Ingrid backed off the patio, into the grass.

448

'Hold still, Briela, hold still, baby, it's not so bad. I'll take care of you, I promise.'

Amy screamed a third time.

Briela squirmed in Ingrid's arms, and Ingrid wrestled her under control. She turned her face into her nanny's neck.

'Be careful, Ingrid,' Cassandra warned. 'Calm down, Amy. I told you this was coming. Everything's going to be fine but first we need—'

Ingrid gasped and let go of Briela but the girl clung to her, biting into her throat. The first bellowing scream was cut off and there was a sucking-tearing sound as Ingrid fell backward in the grass. Briela thrashed on top of her, shaking her head like a dog with a pheasant. Blood fountained up onto the back of Briela's burned hair and sprayed the lawn.

'Briela, stop! Stop, stop, stop!' Amy screamed, running in and taking the girl by the waist, pulling but unable to separate her from Ingrid's neck.

Beneath them Ingrid's eyes rolled back and her mouth overflowed with blood that bubbled at her teeth.

Behind them June started screaming. Kyle fell into a lawn chair, stunned.

Amy pulled with one arm and slapped Briela's back and head with the other, until the girl released the dying sitter and turned on her mother, teeth gnashing. Amy caught one of her daughter's arms and the girl snapped mindlessly, cutting into her forearm twice before Amy was able to fall on her, pinning her to the grass, her nostrils filling with the scent of burning pork ribs, her mind

449

recoiling in disgust even as her stomach growled in hunger.

Vince emerged from the house at a fast walk, glancing around with alarm but not panic – until he saw Ingrid on the lawn. Ingrid twitching, the life pouring from her. She coughed and her throat leaked a while and then she was still. Render turned away, looking at his children, his wife, and their guests.

Sobbing, Amy clutched her daughter and pushed herself up, the two of them stuck together in blood and melted flesh. Adolph watched Briela as Amy carried her away from them. He seemed torn between sympathy and excitement, wanting to see more.

Mick followed close behind Vince. Amy would never forget the look on his face as he noted the fallen grill and the mess of Ingrid on the lawn and his daughter in his wife's arms. It was not surprise or fear. It was a soldier's hardened gaze, the look of a father who has already buried three sons, the cold determination of a man who beholds ultimate horror and finds himself *quite up to the task*.

'Take her home,' he said. 'Now, Amy. Go home.'

'I have medical equipment,' Vince said in a hoarse whisper, not looking at any of them but reciting lines he had been rehearsing. He cleared his throat. 'Ingrid's going to be okay. We can treat her here. She looked to both our families as her own, and now we will treat her as our own for the rest of her days.'

'Stay away from my family,' Mick said to Vince. 'Amy, go home now. We're all going home.'

'Amy, stay,' Cassandra said. 'You don't know what's at stake.'

'You don't know how bad it's going to be,' Vince said to Mick and Amy. 'You don't have to be afraid any more. We are connected to the other families and our time has come. You won't make it on your own. This is the only way.'

'Kyle!' Mick barked, shaking Kyle from his catatonia. 'Do as I say, son. Go with your mother.'

Warily, the boy went to his mother. Amy squeezed Briela to her breast as her husband and son closed around her.

'We're leaving,' Mick said to Vince. 'If you follow us it will be the end of all of you. The very end.'

The Nash family turned and headed toward home.

'It's not over,' Vince said as Cassandra and their children came to stand with him. 'I won't let you jeopardize everything I've worked for, Mick. The others are waiting. You have until midnight and then we're coming to finish it. We're all coming for you.'

Behind the Render family, the grass at Ingrid's feet began to stir.

59

After having her bath, where her father had rubbed away the flesh that could not be saved and bandaged the seeping patches around her arm and cheek, Briela was as close to sleeping as was possible. The worst of the burns were already puckering, tightening in delicate pink strands and regenerating in smooth patches, the infection healing her as it had healed them all three years ago.

Mick unclogged the drain while Kyle made a circuit of the house, locking every door and window, then ordered Kyle to stay in Briela's room, guarding her until Mick and Amy had decided what to do.

Amy did not emerge from the master bathroom until the sun was down. Mick had heard her in there, sometimes crying, sometimes making the sickness sounds. She stayed in the shower far longer than was necessary to wash away the blood. It reminded him of the showers they had all taken the first night, when the change came over them and turned them inside out, not speaking or even able to look each other in the eyes as they struggled to come to terms with the changes in their bodies. The showers they all took at odd hours to wash away the evidence of their feedings. The showers that had become a private ritual between the glimpses of what they were and the lives they were forced to carry on. He knew tonight would be worse for her, now that everything had been exposed and the spotlight of shame was fresh upon them. He had to keep them all together now. Together they would survive. Without each other, without his wife and children, he would be condemned for eternity.

Amy exited the bathroom quietly and sat on the bed, facing the large picture window with its view of the Flatirons and the long Front Range tapering off into the night. She wore only a thick robe with her hair pulled back and she was very still. He sat on the other side of the bed, watching her back.

'Don't shut me out,' he said. 'I can't live without you and the kids.'

She answered a minute later. 'You call this living?'

'We're still here. I don't care about the rest. Only you and Kyle and Briela. Nothing else matters to me.'

Amy stood and walked to her dresser in the corner of the room. She opened the smallest drawer, the top center where she kept her jewelry. She took something from within and walked back, standing above him. He looked up her. Her eyes were inflamed with a decade of sorrow. He wondered what they would look like in another fifty years. A hundred.

'Here.' She held the earring out for him and it fell into his palm. A pearl set within a silver spiral, Myra Blay-lock's. 'I took it from her,' Amy said. 'I don't remember where or when. But I remember the way her hair came out in my fists. I remember the sound of her lips when I bit them off. I remember the taste of her heart. Can you live with that?'

He hesitated only briefly. 'Yes.'

'The Sapphires too,' she said.

'I know. I should have confronted him sooner, but I can live with all of it.'

'I don't think I can. Not any more. Ingrid ...' She moved away from him and he rose to catch her as she fell to the floor. She curled against the wall, shaking with grief, beyond tears. He leaned over her, tried to hold her still. She recoiled but he wouldn't let her go. He lifted from under her legs and back, carrying her to the bed as she beat at him with her fists, raked at his cheeks. He set her on the bed and she backed away from him, pressing herself to the headboard.

'Yes, you can,' he said. 'You have and we will. Nothing's changed.'

'Everything's changed! Ingrid's dead!'

'They manipulated her. Convinced her to take our daughter. I will handle them.'

'I want to die,' she said. 'I want to burn until there is nothing left but ashes.'

'Think about the kids.'

'I am. We don't deserve them. None of us deserve to go on.'

'How do you know that? Who gets to decide that? Why were we allowed to survive if we were not meant to?'

'We're freaks. There is no place in the world for us. How can there be?'

'We can do better. We can change. If we work together, we can control it, learn to use it. You don't know—'

'I know we haven't been able to control anything,' she said. 'We don't even know what we're capable of. It's like living as two people, leading separate lives.'

Mick crawled toward her, took her wrist. She kicked at him but he pushed her legs down and sat on top of her. 'We were hiding from the truth,' he said. 'We lied to ourselves and to each other. It was destroying us because we pretended it wasn't there, Amy. If we embrace it, if we work together ...'

'I wasn't pretending! I lost my mind!'

'Now's your chance to get it back,' he said. 'We have a right to life.'

'Whose lives? What gives us the right to take from them?'

'The others deserved what they got. They hurt us. They stole from us, threatened to harm you and the others at school, they came after our family and we didn't let them. It happens every day in this world. There are predators and victims, the strong and the weak.'

'There are laws, morals. There's no room for ... this.'

'I say there is. There has to be. We are proof.'

'Who are you? What gives you the right to decide?'

'I am as my maker made me. We paid for this life with our own. We survived. How do you know there isn't a reason for that? How do you know we weren't meant to come back and change everything?'

'You've lost your mind. I don't know you. I don't know who I am any more.'

455

'I am your husband and I love you.'

'If we have any soul left, we will destroy ourselves.'

He looked back to the hallway, toward the kids' rooms. 'What will you tell our children? That they don't deserve to live? That they are a disease? How will you do it, Amy? Because I won't help you. I won't let you. You will have to kill me first and then do it alone. What is the humane way to end the only life they know? Will you burn them? Inject them? Bury them in the backyard?'

She screamed at him. She fought him. For a long time he did not have control of her and he thought, only for a moment or two, that maybe she was right. Maybe it would be easier to end it all, end them all tonight. He imagined starting with her, doing it quietly before the kids woke up, but he couldn't imagine what would come after that.

Later, she was lying under him, hands pinned above her head, and she knew that she could fight him until they were both lying in bleeding tatters, but she was tired of fighting. The resistance went out of her and he was staring down at her with eyes that looked black in the darkened bedroom and she wanted to laugh now that she had ever called him a quitter. He wasn't a quitter. Tonight he was a killer, capable of anything.

'How would it be different?' she said softly.

He relaxed his grip on her wrists, leaned back but did not get off her.

'We can go away,' he said. 'Tonight. Never come back. Start over somewhere we don't know anybody.'

'I can't imagine leaving Boulder. What would it change?'

456

'If we stay, we will always be at risk. There are too many connections.'

She thought about that. 'We shouldn't have made it this long.'

'They've been cleaning up after us,' Mick said.

'Not all of them, though,' she said, thinking of the disposals. 'What did you do with yours?'

'I used the restaurant. Late nights, in the kitchen. It's all a blur but I remember ... I remember the tools. Taking out the trash.'

She shifted beneath him, not minding the pressure on her hips. Her eyes were wide, her voice very low. 'Did you like it?'

'I must have. I think ... yes, I did. I felt stronger after.'
'Yes.'

'But there was always a hangover. The come-down.'
'Yes.'

'I couldn't focus on anything. Work was hell.'

'Everything was hell.'

'I kept seeing them,' he said. 'They started following me to work.'

'In the classroom,' she added.

'Roger was here, in the house. I followed him into the yard. He was trying to warn me about the new people. He saw it coming.'

'It was a vision. A warning. You saw it coming,' she said. 'Like Briela's tantrums. She knew. We see things others can't. It's like holding down three jobs. The real job, then finding them and doing it, cleaning up after, re-entering the regular world. And then the burden of pretending, carrying it inside. I don't want to do that any more, Mick. I can't.'

He rolled off her but his leg stayed draped over her thighs. She didn't want him to go away. When he was close like this, she almost felt warm. It had been three years since she'd felt any warmth at all.

'You don't have to,' he said. 'If we stay, we will do it all differently. We'll have more resources.'

'How?'

'Vince has some kind of plan,' he said. 'He said the other families that are like us are working with him.'

'To what end?'

'I don't know, but we must be worth a lot to him. He offered us the house and everything else.'

'Money?'

'Millions.'

'Do you believe him?' she said. Her right hand rested on his thigh.

'He helped me. That night, after Briela's party. I was attacked by three junkies trying to rob the restaurant. I handled the first two but the third took me down and Vince finished him. I saw him do it. He's serious.'

'I'm scared,' she said, pulling him closer.

He held her tighter, kissed her neck, her ear, pressed his nose into her hair, trying to remember the way she used to smell. The bigger question occurred to her then, and perhaps to both of them as they lay in silence for a few minutes.

'There will be others,' she said. 'If we don't end it ourselves, it will spread.'

'Maybe that's how it's supposed to be.'

'Unless there's a cure,' she said.

'There won't be unless one of us is caught. Imprisoned, studied, cut into pieces.'

'Whether we stay or go, someone will find out and we'll be hunted down, Mick. They'll take the kids away.'

'I will never let that happen.'

'Promise?'

He crawled back on top of her.

'Hold my arms again,' she said.

'Like this?'

'Above my head.'

He raised them up and pushed against her. Held her wrists with one hand and opened her robe with the other. He looked into her eyes. She did not look away. They had never been this close.

'There's nothing left to hide behind,' she said.

'No. You know the worst things about me. You know everything.'

'No one else knows me the way you do,' she said. 'They don't know what we have.'

'It's ours.'

She arched under him and he kissed her neck, her breasts, her belly.

'Is it disgusting?' she whispered.

'This is all I want. You are all I want.'

'Don't ever turn away from me again,' she said.

'Keep me warm, Amy.'

Their bodies could not generate heat on their own, but the things they shared replaced all the cold inside and closed the distance that had grown between them.

After, when his mind was empty and the house was silent and she was stretched across him and licking the blood from the cuts she had made in his chest, he slid his fingers into her hair and cradled the back of her head. He massaged the base of her neck and she became still, more content than he had known her to be in years.

'What happens if we say no?' she said.

'I don't know. He might try something, but it wouldn't involve the police.'

'He planned this for a long time,' Amy said. 'He must have a plan to deal with us if we refuse.'

'On the other hand, what is the downside to agreeing? How would it be any different than our lives now?'

'That house.'

'The security.'

'It's like a compound,' she said. 'With a view.'

'We already have a view.'

'We need to find out everything.'

'He said midnight,' Mick said. 'He's not going to wait. I need to go back soon. You can stay with the kids.'

'I love you, Mick.'

'I love you, Ames. I'm sorry it got to be this way.'

'It's not your fault.'

'At least we're not alone.'

'Never again.'

60

Kyle lost track of how long he had been standing outside her window when he heard the latch open and the window began to slide, opening for him. He could not see her inside the black rectangle. She did not speak. He had nothing left to lose.

He climbed through, his feet sinking onto a soft surface. Her bed. He crouched low, one hand steady against the window sill.

'June?'

A form sat up in the dark and a warm hand took hold, pulling him down. He fell on top of her, the heat coming off her in waves as she pushed the bedding back and his cold body pressed against her warm skin. The softness of her thighs and breasts, the heat of her breath against his ear. She was shaking, writhing against him.

'Hurry,' she whispered. 'Before they come back to check on me.'

'Are you sure this is what you want?'

'Do you promise to wait for me? Will you take care of me after?'

'Yes.'

'No matter what comes next? You won't leave me alone?'

'Never. I promise.'

'Do you love me?'

'I loved you the first time I saw you.'

'Make me feel good first, Kyle. Make me feel good and do it quickly.'

His kissed her face, her nose, felt her wet tongue in his mouth, the plump pressure of her lips. She pulled his shirt over his head and he felt his bones against her softness. He traced his fingers around her smooth edges, his touch delicate. She breathed harder, pulled his hair, pushed him down. He licked her neck, her chest, pulled one nipple in his teeth. June moaned and pushed her hips up. The rough surface of her pubic hair was warm against his hip, her leg wrapped around him and squeezing. He moved lower, tasting her skin, the warm salt taste and smooth soft hairs around her navel, taking her hips in both his hands. He pushed his tongue into her, tasting, tasting, filling with her heat and when she began to cry and tighten against his mouth he turned and bit into the soft inside of her thigh, tearing her open in a clean, deep pull and held to her while her blood surged into his mouth. He sucked and swallowed, sucked and swallowed.

June screamed and thrashed and he reached up and clamped a hand over her mouth. She fought free and he let go of her leg to keep her body still. He held her down and ate more of her, taking from the neck and breast and rolling her in the sheets, sinking his teeth into her hind flanks, soaking the bed and drinking from her until they were sliding wetly as fish. She shuddered in his arms and fought him. He held on, amazed at the force of her resistance, her body clinging to the life her mind had forsaken. He kissed her again, fighting with her to get past it, until *she went still. He rose above her, her blood dripping from his lips onto her chest. He looked into her wide eyes, the glass of them shiny in the dark. She seemed to be glaring at him for the longest time, but finally the lids lowered and she wilted beneath him.*

I've killed her. I've killed my flower girl.

Kyle pressed his face between her breasts until he could no longer feel the heartbeat and they were at peace together. He sobbed. He buried his mouth in her bedding and sobbed for what he had done. He felt the warm blood soaking under his mouth. He turned and began to clean her then, lapping at her wounds and bathing her, drawing his mouth along her calves and thighs, around her hips and under her arms, tasting every part of her and securing her warmth in his memory, savoring that which he would never have again, cleaning and loving her while he waited for her to wake up.

Wake up wake up wake up . . . !

Kyle shook violently on the floor and stared up at the blinds, not remembering where he was. Then he saw his sister's bed and remembered. He wiped tears from the corners of his eyes. The sky outside B's window was still black. He hadn't gone yet. June was still alive . . .

But she wasn't warm. She was cold, like him. She wasn't a real girl, he wasn't a real boy. He understood her attraction to him now. It wasn't because of who he was. It was because of *what* he was. She was using him for some purpose. Recruiting him, following her father's orders. His whole family was being adopted into some cause, one that Kyle did not understand and cared nothing about.

Except, maybe there was more to it than this. Maybe she did care about him. She had tried to warn him, hadn't she? Talked about running away? She said they weren't her real parents, they were monsters. She wasn't comfortable in her new life, in this condition they had in common. Maybe there was still time to save her, save her from them. Maybe they could be together, in their own way. If she loved him the way he loved her, she would leave with him. But it had to be soon, tonight.

His parents had not come out yet. He'd heard them fighting a while ago, but now they were quiet. In there together, determining the fate of the family. He couldn't wait for them to say no, to refuse, to pack the car and flee. If he waited until his parents came to the wrong decision, he wouldn't have a choice. He would never see her again.

Kyle stood and waited at the door, to see if Briela would stir or open her eyes. As softly as his feet would carry him, he went down the hall, into the living room and kitchen area. He let himself out the back door, over the growing summer grass, toward the only thing that mattered in his cold world.

I have to be with her. We have to be together, otherwise there is no point to living this way, none at all.

61

When they came in to check on Briela, Kyle was gone. He wasn't in his room either.

'Where did he go?' Amy said.

Mick rubbed his face. 'Where do you think? You saw the look in his eyes. He loves her.'

'But what's he going to do with her?'

'Whatever they want him to do,' Mick said. 'I have to go get him. Now.' He turned to leave but Amy stopped him.

Briela was stirring before them, moaning as she opened her eyes.

'Hey, baby,' Amy said. 'We're here. Everything's all right. The monsters can't hurt you any more.'

Briela's eyes widened. Her mouth opened as if she were attempting to scream and her body began to shiver.

'Briela? What's wrong?' Amy said. 'Mick? Do something.'

They kneeled at her bedside, hands on her chest and legs, smoothing her hair.

'Briela,' Mick said. 'Talk to me. I'm here. What is it, honey?'

Slowly she stopped shivering and her mouth began to close. Her eyes focused on them.

'Is it your arm?' Amy said.

'She saw something,' Mick said. 'What is it, honey? Is it Kyle?'

Briela shook her head, no. She looked terrified.

'No matter what it is, you have to tell us,' Amy said.

'He's lying,' Briela said softly. 'He's hiding it.'

'Who?' Amy said. 'Who's she talking about?'

Mick sat back. 'Render. Is it Vince? Vince is lying?'

Briela nodded once.

'About what? What's he hiding?' Amy asked her.

Briela began to cry. 'The future. We can't stay.'

Mick got to his feet. 'I'm going over. Stay here with her.'

'You can't go alone,' Amy said.

'I'm not putting both of you at risk too.'

Briela sat up. 'You need us. There's gonna be too many of them.'

62

Kyle stood in the Renders' backyard, looking at his Egg, reading June's text from the other night.

come out and see for yourself. keep me company. house behind yours. my room = corner window 1st floor.

But the house had four corners, so which one was it? Probably not at the front of the house, which left two possible corners in the back. He remembered seeing a den or some kind of study and billiard room on the northwest corner during his tour yesterday before the barbecue. That left the southwest corner. He walked around the back, sticking close to the house. All the lights were off. He could not see inside any of the windows. He passed the row of tall convertible windows that opened onto the veranda and turned the corner.

There was a set of three smaller windows. One large at the center of the frame with a smaller window on either side. He pressed his cheek to the frame and tried to make out the room behind the glass. He couldn't see

467

anything, it was too dark inside. He was about to try removing one of the screens when he remembered the Egg. Maybe she had her phone with her. It was worth a try. He typed:

Are you there? I came back for you. I'm outside your window. Need to see you. I'm sorry and I love you. Please let me in. Kyle.

Minutes later the Egg vibrated in his pocket. He removed the device and looked down at the screen.

parents trying to kill them all. Adolph and i are trapped in the3 basement, plese help og god kyle make them stop i don't want to be a part of it

63

Mick led them to the guest house, upstairs, to the boxes he had taken from storage yesterday afternoon.

He donned the backpack with the one-gallon propane tank connected to ten feet of hosing and the wand of the weed dragon torch. He opened the tank's valve, thumbed the dial shut on the handle, and slipped the sparker into his left front pocket. He unstrapped the leather roll of Ittosai-Kotetsu chef knives, the blades ranging from four to nine inches. He removed the longest of the set and used his belt as a scabbard. He handed the shortest, a paring knife with a four-inch blade, to Briela.

'Keep the tip pointed away from you at all times,' he told her. 'Hold it at your side and if anyone gets too close to you, you poke them with it. Understand?'

Briela nodded.

Mick loaded his father's Browning 12 gauge with three shells and handed it to Amy.

'I don't know what to do with this,' she said.

'Don't bother unless we get close. Then you brace it against your shoulder, aim it, and pull the trigger.'

Amy frowned as he set the safety for her. 'Maybe it won't come to that,' he said.

'What are we doing, Mick?' she said.

'Getting our son back.'

'And then what? Are you going to kill their entire family?'

'That depends on what he wants, and whether or not we can trust them.'

They went over the fence behind the pool, Mick boosting Amy, Amy pulling him up, the two of them swinging Briela between them in a chain that landed them in the grass as softly as cats. The backyard was empty. The tall windows of the veranda were closed and would be impenetrable.

They backed in close to the house and filed around to the driveway. Amy and Briela flanked to either side as Mick prepared to take the front door at a run, but the front door was already open.

Mick put a hand up to warn them to stay behind him as he crept up to the door. The foyer was empty, none of the lights were on. He waved Amy and Briela forward and they slipped inside and moved left.

'You and I will go in and try to find him,' he told Amy. 'B, you stay here and watch the door. If anyone comes, cars or people on foot, you scream for us and go out the back and run home. All the way home, okay, honey?'

Briela nodded, stepping behind the curtain at the front window, the short knife held against her right hip.

Mick and Amy waded into the house, splitting around the stairway, Mick breaking right, into the living rooms;

Amy branching left into the laundry, running at a crouch through pantry and dining room until they met up again in kitchen. The front rooms were empty.

'They could be in the basement,' Mick said, glancing at the spiral stairway at the end of the great room. 'He had equipment down there. He's building something.'

'Or upstairs,' Amy said, holding the shotgun across her chest.

'I don't think he's hiding. Let's start downstairs and work our way up.'

They were halfway to the stairway when Mick caught a movement to his left. He stopped, putting his right hand up, the dragon's wand at his left.

'What?' Amy whispered.

'Shadows,' Mick said. 'In there.'

They rounded the corner to the sealed interior of the veranda. The vast room was dark until they reached the arched entrance. A humming noise filled the first floor, the retractable windows opening, letting the warm summer night in.

Then the lights came on and they saw all the people gathered to greet them.

64

Briela was standing between the front window and its thick velvet curtain when she heard the humming sound. She had been watching the driveway and front grounds but now turned toward the source of the humming on the other side of the first floor. The humming lasted until she had counted to eight and then the house was silent. She could feel it about to happen, the moment before everything went out of control, and she braced herself, holding perfectly still. The air on the other side of the curtain stirred and she glanced down.

In front of the black toes of her boots were a pair of dirty white feet.

Briela opened her mouth to scream, but the curtain was yanked aside and a cold hand fell over her mouth before she could make a sound. A loop of black rope fell around her neck and cinched tight. She was swept up, off her feet and rising, until she was staring into the grinning red mouth and lifeless gray eyes of Ingrid Gustafson.

65

Vince Render was standing at the center of the court, his wife Cassandra at his left, the two of them surrounded by the others. In his left hand he held a large silver pistol with an infrared sight, the light skidding across the floor and then disappearing for a moment before finding its home between Mick's eyes.

Kyle and June were standing to his right, their mouths sealed with tape, their wrists bound with plastic zip-ties. Kyle looked ashamed and frightened. June was flushed and crying. Beside her, guarding them, was little Adolph. He appeared to be feeling proud of himself, loyal to his father, ready to pounce.

The others here, all forty or fifty of them, shared the death complexions of gray-white and some of the wounds and slashes were still visible but healing, even now healing. They had combed their hair and done their best to make themselves presentable to one another. They were here, upright, waiting. They were the Nash's people, regarding Mick and Amy and Briela with cold black eyes and expectant smiles.

Roger and Bonnie were near the front, holding hands

still crusted with dried blood from feedings they had pursued on their own. Behind them Sergeant Terrance Fielding, who held a glass of iced tea he could not taste. Myra Blaylock, her chest flat and sexless, her hair long and straight. Amy's students, Eric and Jason, as well as three others she recognized from school, were huddled together at the back, near the fluttering curtains. There were others from the restaurant Mick did not remember infecting, or who might have been taken by Render. Jamie and Brett, his chef Carlos and a Hispanic woman who must have been Carlos's wife. Kyle's friends, Ben and Will and the Persian boy, Shaheen, who wore no shirt, his once smoke-dark skin now a deep, almost lavender gray. Melanie Smith, who stood hunched over a gaping absence of flesh at her middle, and the entire Larson family, Rita and her daughter Tami, the husband Don. The three thugs from the parking lot in new warm-ups of black, the blond boy with a scalp mending itself in puzzle pieces. A heavy-set security guard with the familiar neck wounds. Eugene and Virginia Sapphire, no longer looking old and feeble but restored, the wrinkled planes of their faces smoothed and pale. Dennis Wisneski, scowling as usual, his eyes fogged with the cataracts that marked his transition back toward the human camouflage. And more, others Mick did not recognize, the ones the Renders had taken since coming to town, or who had become victims of the other Nash victims. Somehow they had been drawn here tonight, organized by Vince, all of them standing in near-perfect stillness, not speaking, but waiting for someone to tell them what to do.

474

'I'm glad you came back before I was forced to come for you,' Vince Render said, watching Mick. 'Things have changed.'

'Kyle!' Amy cried, surging forward, but Mick took her arm and held her back.

'Why did you take so many?' Mick said.

'I don't leave witnesses, Mick. I convert them. These aren't just your neighbors now. They're family. And that has always been the meaning behind the larger enterprise. Family. Cass and I were never able to bear our own children, but thanks to the change, we were able to rescue June from a life of small-town drudgery and Adolph from a foster family who did not deserve to live. Our family is growing, expanding every day.'

'Touching,' Mick said. 'But my son is not your family. Untie him now.'

Cassandra smiled at Amy. 'What do you expect, Amy? He's in love. He chose us.'

'Romeo and Juliet got it into their heads to run away,' Render said. 'But they'll come around. This is not a world where our kind can hope to survive on their own. You know this, Mick. Why do you keep pretending it can be any other way?'

Mick hooked his finger through the ring at the end of the sparker, but kept it in his pocket. 'What do you want, Vince? What is the point of all this?'

'The Percys lost control,' Render said. 'But not before creating their own survivors. I told you the other four families have come on board. They are doing their part, and doing it well. It's moving around the country now.

It's gone exponential. Nothing can control it. The only course now is to be a part of it, to work together, to hold on until the tide turns.'

'You want to infect everybody,' Amy said. 'You want to change everything. Are you insane?'

'Vince knows what he's doing, Amy,' Cass said. 'He's building another company and this time it will be an empire.'

'I found other cases,' Vince said. 'I found evidence of outbreaks in Nigeria, Borneo, the Congo, and one very promising, truly isolated case in Peru, but none of them were as functional as the ones carrying the Vieques strain. Former members of my engineering team have run the algorithms. Cass and I and a small handful of interested parties ... some in the government, others you might call investors with substantially deep pockets and a healthy interest in their own immortality ... we've run the projections. Once we came to grips with what was coming, once we understood which side would come out on top, well, we admitted this was no longer an infection. It's become a quantum leap in evolution.'

Amy was unable to take her eyes off her son, who, she understood now, was being held hostage by a madman. And what about her daughter? Was Briela still hiding?

Vince read something in the change in her expression. He smiled, said, 'Ingrid? Did you find her?'

Behind the crowd, moving in from the terrace, was Ingrid. Her hair was a red crusted mess, her eyes were dull black, and her neck was wrapped in thick layers of gauze. Only a month into summer and she seemed almost bored of dragging and half-carrying Briela, who had been hog-tied.

Amy lurched forward again, and Mick pulled her back again. 'Amy, no.'

'That's right, Mick,' Vince said. 'It's important to keep our heads. We have business to conclude.'

'Let her go!' Amy cried. 'You don't need us!'

Behind Render, Eric and Jason produced muffled sounds of amusement.

Cassandra took Briela by the arm and yanked her away from Ingrid. The sitter held on and stumbled a few steps before Cassandra backhanded her into place.

Mick opened the dial-valve on the weed dragon's wand, removed the sparker, and squeezed the tongs before the cylindrical nozzle. A ten-inch flame the width of a beer can wavered faint orange and blue as Mick raised the torch overhead.

All forty or so of the infected people present stared up at the torch with numb curiosity.

'Let my children go,' Mick said, nudging Amy in the back with his elbow. 'Let your daughter choose if she wants to be a part of this. You have thirty seconds before I burn us all out.'

Render laughed. 'I've seen one of those before, Mick. It's a garden tool, not a flame thrower.'

'Are you sure about that?' Mick said.

'Listen to me,' Render said, planting the laser sight between Mick's eyes. 'I'm trying to help you. I am trying to be your friend. I need your help and I want you to be on the right side of the change that is coming. This thing is strongest at the source, and we – the five surviving families, including yours – are the source. The rest of them, the third and fourth generations, they're dumbing down from the mutations. They're not much more than animals. They're not interested in moderation and continuing civilian life. It's going to get ugly out there. There are two sides now, but there won't be for long. Do you want to live like a king or die like a mutant? Those are the only two choices.'

Mick blinked as the red light flicked over his eyes.

'I never wanted to be a king,' he said, raising the torch higher, opening the valve all the way, the flame burning with the sound of a tiny jet engine now. Amy was fixed on Cassandra while Briela's eyes stared back them, pleading. 'I just wanted a better life for my family.'

'What a waste of my time,' Render said, thumbing the hammer.

'Now,' Mick said.

Three things then happened simultaneously: Amy leveled the shotgun at Cassandra, June dodged sideways and kicked back *hard*, knocking her father off balance, and Mick withdrew the chef's knife from his belt.

Render's aim faltered and a shot rang out overhead, echoing off the high ceilings. Mick dropped the torch, raised the blade and threw. The knife tumbled through the air and found a soft landing in Render's stomach. Cassandra panicked at the sight of her husband with a blade in his belly and Briela slipped free as she reached for him. Kyle turned, took his sister by the waist with both tied hands, and dragged her out of the melee. June

478

ducked and ran after Kyle, first toward Mick, then veering into the shifting mass of bodies.

As soon as Briela was out of the way, Amy squeezed the trigger and blew Cassandra's midsection open, peppering half a dozen others standing close to her.

Mick began walking at Render.

Render raised the gun and fired into Mick's left shoulder.

Mick advanced, bending to scoop up the weed dragon's hose, swinging it around like a whip, the flame passing before a blur of pale faces that recoiled and snarled.

Render fired two more shots, taking Mick in the shoulder and side of the neck.

Mick flinched and continued walking. Behind him, Adolph leaped on Amy's back, knocking her down and sending the shotgun twirling across the slate floor.

Cassandra fell and three of the infected fell on her, clawing into her buckshot stomach. She howled and thrashed as two others took her by the arms and began to drag her out onto the patio.

Render staggered as he fired again and the fourth bullet tore into Mick's thigh.

Mick continued walking. 'Get the girls out!' he said to Kyle.

Kyle found the paring knife in Briela's back pocket, cut the rope at her feet, and the two of them crawled from under the swarm of trampling legs. June stopped to subdue Adolph, tearing him away from Amy.

The boy fought her until June screamed, 'They're not

your parents! Your parents are dead!' Adolph screamed again but allowed June to lead him away. They followed Kyle and Briela to the front door, out into the yard.

Render reset his stance and fired into Mick's face, blowing six teeth and a good portion of his cheek into a powdery wet mist.

Mick shook his head once, spitting blood, and continued walking.

Render's hand was shaking as he squeezed off shot number six.

Mick did not feel the passage of hot steel through his splintering ribs.

Render was clutching his stomach and preparing to let off the seventh shot when Mick caught the wrist holding the gun with his left hand and with his right removed the nine-inch Ittosai from Render's stomach and drew it sideways through the throat. Moving in the fountain, Mick released the arm and took a fistful of Render's hair, snapping the neck back as he spun, pulling the blade around in a full circle, severing the spinal cord. He broke Render's back with his knee driving the body to the floor. With a fist of Render's blond hair in his left hand, Mick sawed in a circle, pulling the neck with all his strength until the vertebrae snapped and the last of the flesh came free. He stood and raised the head for the others to see. The twenty or more who had not gone after Cassandra stopped in their tracks and regarded Mick with blank confusion.

A howl of fury came from the darker patio area, and Cassandra followed. She came running in pursued by the others intent upon devouring her. One of her arms had been torn from the socket, her clothes and large chunks of her hair were torn, and one of her eyes was a bleeding socket.

Mick charged at her holding Vince Render's head like a warning light. When they were less than fifteen feet apart, he stopped, kicked the shotgun back, and threw the head at the shrieking widow. He dropped to the floor and rolled away.

Amy clawed her way forward, took up the shotgun, and set the stock against her shoulder. Cassandra ran full speed into Amy and was falling on her when the barrel flashed, obliterating Cassandra Render from the jaw up. The body swayed and fell back, following what was left of her brains to the floor.

The others began to surge forward in bloodlust, but halted when Mick pulled the hose around his waist and caught the weed dragon's nozzle in his right hand. He waved the flame at them, drawing it back and forth as he backed away.

Amy came forward to stand beside him, the shotgun raised with one shell left.

The crowd of more than thirty faces stared back at them, waiting.

Amy and Mick glanced at each other one last time. In their eyes was a reflection of the promises they had made in bed only hours ago, and of the bond that had survived for fifteen years. Mick nodded and Amy covered him, shifting the barrel from one to another as he walked calmly to the wooden door frame and set fire to the house.

The others watched the flames catch hold and enlarge, until a serpent of orange crawled up the wall and expanded across the ceiling, splitting, then feeding on plaster and the oxygen blowing in from the yard on a sweet summer breeze.

When the house became too hot to inhabit any longer, they turned away and one by one shuffled off into the darkness, some crawling over the fence to disappear into the fields of open space, others finding the roads that would lead them to another town, into the trucks and cars and homes of welcoming strangers, making friends of neighbors, turning enemies into lovers, uniting lost souls in new congregations, forging new connections with expanding populations, hoards of citizens rejoicing in their newfound gifts, until what once was a secret among the living had become a routine way of life among the dead.

Mountain Living

Set against a log-cabin wall, powered by a cable running into the floor and under the exterior ground, up into a waterproof shed constructed on a concrete foundation and housing a solar- and gas-powered generator, pulling a scratchy signal from an ancient aerial antenna, there stands a small plasma television. The sound is muted.

On the screen:

Live continuous footage of mass looting and burning furniture and four-story heaps of garbage in a darkened city, a city without a name, a city the viewers do not recognize and do not care to recognize. Fighter jets streak overhead, strafing coffee emporiums. Office buildings collapse in molten columns. Cars lift from the rear on rolling balls of flame. A city bus rocks from side to side while its passengers slide from the windows, pulled down into the street by faceless forms of all colors. Bed sheets draped from a window have been painted with scripture. Small bodies and old bodies dangle from street lamps and stray dogs sniff their feet. Hairless, malnourished women indistinguishable from the skeletal men march with picket signs in support of Mother Nature. A young man in welder's goggles and wielding a samurai sword screams in silence before impaling a burning effigy of the President and seconds later is run down by a yellow cab stained red. Children crouch in the gutters, feeding.

Below the live feed, news headlines scroll within a bright yellow tape.

... Los Angeles New York Miami Philadelphia Newark Cincinnati Chicago Milwaukee Denver St Louis confirming outbreaks ...

... Caribbean territories and Central America teeming with persons infected with unknown biological agents ...

... CDC evacuated, unnamed spokesperson claims 'epidemic now far beyond our scope and ability to manage. There is no cure but the True Death' ...

... White House and Congress unanimously sign sweeping legislation instituting martial law ...

... local governments and 39 state governors declare sundown curfews, recommend sealing homes with any and all available reinforcements ...

... Senator Elias Orringer (D-VT) proposes deportation and execution camps for the infected ...

... Mumbai Singapore Kuala Lumpur London Paris Rome Buenos Aires Santiago Beijing Tokyo Moscow Helsinki reporting massive civilian demonstrations, catastrophic violence, tens of thousands of casualties ...

... Pakistan loses control of nuclear armory as Muslim leaders blame West ...

... Central Intelligence and FBI calling outbreaks 'a coordinated uprising with hundreds and possibly thousands of

*co-conspirators', denies knowledge of scope and timing of out-
break . . .*

*. . . World Health Organization identifies at least seven
strains, viruses believed to be mutating rapidly . . .*

*. . . Pope Peter Laudisio tweets from underground Vatican
bunker 'The Second Coming is upon us, pray for His forgive-
ness' . . .*

On the screen, three men and one small boy, all wearing red plaid hunting jackets, bullet-proof vests, and
night-vision goggles, move forward in a coordinated clus-
ter, AK-47s shouldered, firing in timed bursts.

Some move slowly, others are inhumanly fast, but all
are fair targets now.

A motorcycle piloted by a body cloaked in leather,
faceless behind the black-screened helmet, speeds
through the carnage and the camera turns as it passes,
following its trajectory to its inevitable conclusion, a col-
lision with a phalanx of armored tanks which crush bones
while above low-flying unmanned drones emit streams
of tracer fire upon humanity's last stand.

The images collapse in a shrinking ball of white light
and the television screen goes dark.

'That's enough of that for one morning,' Mick Nash
says, dropping the remote and turning to his son. 'Didn't
I ask you to help your mother?'

Kyle sits forward on the couch. 'Don't you want to
know how it all turns out?'

'We'll know soon enough, but not today. Come on,
let's go outside, champ.'

Kyle follows his father out onto the front porch.

Before them stretches a rolling meadow beside a placid lake which itself reflects the snow-capped peaks on three sides. Amy, who has lost thirty-seven pounds and whose blonde hair has grown out to be cut and replaced by new, naturally brown strands the color of buckwheat, is chopping wood. Seeing Kyle and Mick come out from the cabin, she plants the ax in the stump and glances back at the shrinking pile.

'You can finish this cord,' she says to Kyle.

Under the tall pines behind her, sitting on a blanket, are Adolph and June, who now goes by her given name, Keelie. The only 'Render' survivors, like each of the Nashes, carry firearms holstered at their ribs at all times, and all have spent hundreds of hours training at various distances with paper targets. All are prepared to fire at their own kind and on clean humans, without hesitation, should any hostility or bloodshed arise.

Adolph is reading *When the Legends Die* and seems to be engrossed in the story, though he glances up at Briela, who is collecting berries at the edge of the forest, from time to time. He does so with a look that is equal parts cold respect, childish resentment, and a sibling's duty to protect at all costs.

Keelie is writing in a leather-bound diary. She has been recording their days since they arrived here in August and the diary is almost full. She does not pause in her scribbling to look up at Kyle. She knows he is there, watching her, and though she loves him deeply and in profound ways, she knows that she can never touch him, nor allow him to touch her. Perhaps someday, when they have learned to control their urges and separate young lust from animal appetite, but not now. She does not believe he will ever attempt to hurt her, and she has no desire to do him harm, but sometimes, at night when his family is sleeping, she catches him staring at her and her heart pounds with longing and raw fear.

Kyle begins to lose himself in the labor that is necessary to sustain them for the coming winter, and Mick watches his son with approval. Amy joins him on the porch, pinching his waist.

'You're too thin,' she says, resting her head against his chest.

'You're one to talk,' he replies.

'How many days has it been since we've eaten?'

'You asked me that yesterday.'

Amy nods. 'I'm going to ask you again tomorrow.'

'Tomorrow might be different.' Mick closes his eyes, feeling the sun on his face. Its light, but not its warmth. Never its warmth.

Amy lifts her head to look at him. 'How?'

'We might have a visitor.'

'You think there are others all the way up here?'

Mick considers this for a moment. 'Like us or like we used to be?'

'Either kind.'

'There must be. Mass exodus from the urban centers. It's only a matter of time.'

'Will we be able to stop ourselves this time?'

'Tomorrow, yes.'

'But?' she prods him. 'What about when winter comes? What happens when we are skin and bones?'

Mick opens his eyes and looks down at her. 'We could always go back down the hill for that waitress who was rude to us at that last truck stop. Can't imagine anybody would miss her if we turned her into a little Christmas Eve goose with all the trimmings.'

Amy slaps his arm.

'Side of mashed potatoes, some cornbread stuffing,' Mick says. 'That's all I'm saying.'

'I'm serious,' she says, her perfect fair skin pulling with a sadness that only he can touch. 'What will we do?'

Mick doesn't need to search long for the answer. 'We'll find a way to survive.'

Neither speaks for a few minutes as the sound of birds and the chopping of wood fills the clean air. Mick takes his wife's face in his hands and kisses her nose.

'We always do.'